DESTINY BAY

DESTINY BAY

BY DONN BYRNE

Fredonia Books
Amsterdam, The Netherlands

Destiny Bay

by
Donn Byrne

ISBN: 1-4101-0311-0

Copyright © 2003 by Fredonia Books

Reprinted from the 1928 edition

Fredonia Books
Amsterdam, The Netherlands
http://www.fredoniabooks.com

FOR

HEDDA, ST. JOHN, JANE OLIVE
AND BRIAN OGE

" Look unto the rock whence ye are hewn, and to the hole of the pit whence ye are digged. . . . For the Lord shall comfort Zion; he will comfort all her waste places; and he will make her wilderness like Eden, and her desert like the garden of the Lord . . . "

The Author of DESTINY BAY *has requested his publishers to announce that in using the word "Ulster" throughout the book, it is merely because his childhood was spent among the mountains and lakes of Ulster and on the cliffs of Ulster. To him the old province of Meath and the kingdom of Kerry are the same as the Ulster of which he writes, and he firmly believes that a countryman out of the Rosses and a fisherman off the cliffs of Moher have the same Irishry in common. If any phrases in this book of* DESTINY BAY *show a predilection toward one or the other way of politics, the Author prays that they may not be taken as serious. He has never yet seen a government that brought heavier apples to the trees or heavier salmon in the rivers or a more purple heather and for this reason politics mean nothing to him.*

CONTENTS

CONTENTS

ONE

TALE OF MY COUSIN JENICO AT
SPANISH MEN'S REST

ONE

Tale of my cousin Jenico at Spanish Men's Rest

I

My aunt Jenepher, who is so beautiful, and is blind, was sitting on a marble bench in the herb garden, whistling, and I was standing by her. I would have you know that my aunt Jenepher is the best whistler in the world: it is one of the many gifts vouchsafed her for the loss of her eyes. She was imitating the clear liquid trill of a blackbird, and the blackbird himself, a fat rascal who had been gorging on the cherry trees, was hopping about in front of her on his inadequate yellow feet, his glossy head nearly as glossy as my aunt Jenepher's, now cocked on one side now on the other, puzzled and a little angry that a mortal lady had stolen his dance music, while in the hawthorn bushes his consort gave loud squawks of dismay.

"Now who the devil —" said I, for I had been looking down the drive, and had seen my uncle Valentine — "now who the devil has he with him now?"

My aunt Jenepher turned around and faced the drive. Her beautiful pale hands lay quietly in her lap and she was as though dreaming. "I think I can tell you, Kerry," she said. My aunt Jenepher had the faculty of seeing people without her eyes. I always felt that she left her body, she stood outside it, and in some mystical way saw people soul to soul. An expensive Dublin physician, with side whiskers, once told me that this was rot, that the human organism has eyes everywhere, in the back of the head, as the saying is, and in the finger tips. They only need developing, and in my aunt Jenepher's case they are developed. I have given a lot of thought to this, and I have decided that the expensive Dublin physician, and his side whiskers, can go to —— But need I be explicit? My aunt Jenepher saw people soul to soul.

"It is a very old man," said my aunt Jenepher, "and a very feeble one. A very great nobleman, Kerry, and a very poor one. And —"

"And the boy, Aunt Jenepher?"

"The what, Kerry?"

"The boy in the clothes that are much too big for him."

"Is very noble," said my aunt Jenepher, "and good and very poor."

They were upon us now. My uncle Valentine is one of the most striking figures in Ireland, and, by natural corollary, in the habitable world. A six-foot-four giant is my uncle Valentine, with an immense red beard to his waist, that is more like a burnished breastplate than a beard. All he needs is one of those Norwegian helmets with wings and a great axe to be a chief of Goths who sacked Rome. But he wears Irish tweeds and glossy Irish linen in the daytime, and always has the appearance, with his immaculate dress, his red beard, and his red setter dogs, of a king of the solid type on his country estate. Certainly no king, not even our Sovereign Lord, has a greater courtesy than my uncle Valentine's.

In his youth, and that must have been sixty years before, the old gentleman with my uncle Valentine must have possessed a giant's figure and bearing. Even now he was nearly as tall as my uncle. He had great wide shoulders, very bowed; and though nearing the century, his hair was perfect, but so short, so white that it seemed a cap of some new fashion. His brown face was a maze of wrinkles, and under white eyebrows grey granite eyes probed you to the depths of your being. He had an immense hook nose, like our Duke of Wellington's, and he held his hands behind his back as a very old man will do. His hat was a grey felt, such as was worn that moment in London, but his coat was of a cut that London had never seen or even dreamed. It was something like an overcoat, its tails coming near the heels, and it was also something like a morning coat, cutting away sharply from the waist. It was neither one nor the other, though. It was of a sort of grey whipcord, with grey metallic buttons. The vest was double-breasted after the old manner, and a pair of tubelike pepper-and-salt trousers dropped like a curtain to ridiculously small, spatted, black shoes. It was immensely grotesque, and yet there was dignity to it.

The boy with him wore a suit of tweeds that a woman might have made for a man, and that a woman probably did make for him. But barring that you noticed that they were too big for him and horribly cut, you noticed little beyond his face. It was a girl's face, brown, soft, unmarred by beard of any kind. And on the face was an expression of fear and haughtiness it would be impossible to analyse. Brown eyes lighter than the brown of the face looked at you challengingly, telling you to stay where you were. I don't think the rudest person in the world would have laughed at his clothes with that deadly look in his eye. He would have been, without seeing his teeth, sixteen or seventeen years old.

"This," said my uncle Valentine, "is my sister Jenepher, who is blind." The old gentleman kissed my aunt Jenepher's hand with that grave, that terrible politeness that dies with our elders. The boy made a motion as to curtsey and came forward to kiss it too. "And this," said my uncle Valentine, "is Kerry MacFarlane, my dead brother's son, and heir of Destiny Bay. He is known in the Erse jargon as *Kerry na Kopple*, or Kerry of the Horses, and as Long Kerry."

"A good name," said the old gentleman, "Kerry of the Horses."

"How do you do, sir?" and I shook his hand. "And how are you?" I shook hands with the boy.

"And this," said my uncle Valentine, pointing out the big figure coming over the grass, "is my valet and my friend, James Carabine."

"Your Lordship's Honour!" bowed Carabine. "And your young Lordship's, too."

"This, Sister Jenepher and Kerry," said my uncle Valentine, "is Don Diego de Leyva, Duke of la Mentera and Marquis of Monreal del Campo, in the Kingdom of Spain, a Knight of the Holy Ghost, which is the first order of chivalry in Christendom. And this is his grandchild, Don Anthony."

"A very poor nobleman, Miss Jenepher," said the old Spaniard.

"In Ireland, sir," said my aunt Jenepher, "it is, if not a vice, a mistake to be rich."

And then, because she knew the lad was afraid, and growing inimical from strangeness, my aunt Jenepher did something she had never done even to me. She put her arm around the boy's shoulder.

II

It was Sergeant Aloysius MacSweeney, said my uncle Valentine — it was Sergeant Aloysius MacSweeney who drew his attention to the foreigners in our midst. Though it is fourteen miles from any railroad station and twenty miles from Derry Walls, yet in the district of Destiny Bay we are not unaccustomed to strangers. Here the European gypsies stop for a while, when visiting Ireland, coming from Glasgow to Londonderry, for at Destiny Bay the mountains have the finest, strongest heather in Ireland, and out of this the gypsies make their brooms; and in the brown bogs are acres of sallytrees, which the un-Irish call osiers, and from these are made the baskets and lobster pots which you can always buy from a gypsy caravan. Here, too, gather the northern tinkers, who are the Irish gypsies, and are not quite true gypsies, but a sort of wandering pagan tribe, and do not speak Romany but a jargon called Shelta — here they gather around Hallow E'en to exchange wisdom and wives. Here too we have the Raghery and Tory fishermen, great hulking giants with children's feet and immense hands, with homespun trousers and white flannel jackets, and broad-brimmed Italianate hats, and these folk can sit for six hours on end without saying a word or moving any muscle except those needed for smoking their short clay pipes. Here too pass the mountainy men of Donegal, brown, sly-eyed men, with no English at them —— as they say, walking barefoot on the roads to save their boots, which they will put on only when they go into a town.

There are in all, I should say, thirty square miles of the district called Destiny Bay, but so far from everywhere is it, so little is there of trade there, that except for the gypsies, it is the most unfrequented spot in all Ireland. And yet no place in Ireland is so beautiful, no place in Ireland so strange. Northward of us roars the Atlantic to the Pole, now gentle as a lake, as a blue lake at noon, as a violet lake when the evening star comes out, now ruthless and fierce as the Ancient of Days, grey and horrible as the Baphomet of Templar tradition, and as merciless. And south of us is the brown belt of bogland, white in summer with the lonely *canavan*, the white bogflowers, and the gentle sally-trees, from which harps are made; brown bog and black water. And here lie the last of the great Irish elk, and the Irish wolf, and the Irish bear, beneath the short stiff bog grass; the snipe, and the red-billed moor hen and the bittern of the ghostly call are now its denizens. About us are high mountains, gold and purple in summer with sun and heather, and in winter wearing caps of snow that are suitable to their ancientness. Here is our place, Destiny Bay, that low big granite house, whose foundations date back to when Irish history was but tradition and guesswork. Great Shane O'Neill burned it on us, and him we forgave, for a roystering boisterous bird was the Big Earl. *Ree Shamus*, King James of the Cowardice, burned it on us, too, from sheer spite when he retired baffled from Derry Walls, but we closed that account at the Boyne Water . . .

There it is, the low vast granite house, with the ivied walls, with the slated roofs golden with stonewort, the happy, peaceful house. Here is the old-world garden, the paradise of bees. Here is the formal fancy of my great grandfather, the lawn with the fishpond, with the yew trees carved into grotesque shapes, a phoenix, a galleon, a knight on horseback, which the men in the fields will insist is Great King Billy. Here roam the peacocks, the peacocks of gaudy colours and the white peacocks, while in the rear of the house among the stables, gentlemen, are birds that will interest you more, the finest breed of gamecocks that ever fought a main while the police were sleeping off their liquor, and no bird of which would this Irelander swap for the legendary Coq d'Or. There it is, the gentle house, with the gentle ghost, the solid house where the wise bees have elected to keep their home.

Beneath us is Ballyfale, the small village of ten houses, of which seven are licensed to sell beer and spirits, for the road between Derry and the Highlands of Donegal is a long road, and a droughty one. Also there are politics, which must not be forgotten, and that makes for many public houses, for what sturdy Nationalist could drink with equanimity in The Orange Delight, or what Ancient of the Royal Black Preceptory trust the beer of The Poor Croppy Boy. There are also the Glasgow Arms, and the Romany Van, for the gypsies, and Kate MacShane's, for the tinkers.

There is the Whaler's Home, for the sailors, where nothing but Gaelic is spoken, and there is the village hotel or caravanserai, called the Widow McGinty's. Here provisions are also sold: China tea and bacon; coarse calico for dresses; men's shoes with brass tips; soap; pig's twist — which is a manner of tobacco, and other rural commodities. The three remaining houses are the bakery, the post-office, and the police barrack. There is no butcher's. The butcher comes twice a year from Derry, on the Saturday before Easter and on Christmas Eve. Such is Destiny Bay.

Welshman, Turcoman or heathen Chinee might come to Destiny Bay and be welcomed. But from neither Orangeman nor Nationalist was there a kind word for Sergeant Aloysius MacSweeney and his three fine policemen from the County of Clare. In the days when there was a Royal Irish Constabulary it was the policy of a government with the serpent's wisdom to send potato-mouthed peelers from the South into Northern districts, and stout Orange fellows into Cork. These armed exiles had no friends, no political ties in the district. They dug their little potato patch, they patrolled the roads, they read the works of Mr. Charles Garvice, the eminent English author, they took census returns, they spent an hour a day greasing their hair. But everything in the country was known to them. Three-card tricksters had the fear of judgment before them, and delirium tremens became a strange exotic disease. In those days, chroniclers of a thousand years hence will write, in those days there was peace in Ireland.

But admirable as these men were and kind to their aged parents, yet we one and all, from Irish peer to Irish pauper, had an extraordinary aversion to them, as deep-rooted and inexplicable as the Hindu's aversion to the succulent beefsteak. My uncle Valentine was no exception to this phenomenon. Indeed my uncle Valentine had once defined a policeman as one with no liking for honest work and not enough courage for crime. So that when Sergeant Aloysius MacSweeney saluted him smartly in Ballyfale and would fain have speech with him, my uncle Valentine regarded him with no gracious eyes.

"Begad, Sergeant," he said, "but you're the fine juvenile figure of a man. It must have been for dirty work you got the stripes so young."

"I would like a word with your Honour," said the Sergeant.

"I'm sure you would," said my uncle Valentine, and was passing on.

"'Tis in the interests of the Realm and on His Majesty's Service," said the Sergeant.

"Out with it then," said my uncle Valentine.

"On the thirteenth instant, or vulgarly this day week," said the Sergeant, "two foreigners came and took up residence in the hostelry owned and conducted by Mrs. Marion McGinty of this town. They gave their names as Don Diego and Don Anthony de Leyva, and the elder or older claimed to be the Duke of la Mentera."

"Is it against the law to be a duke or to lodge with the widow McGinty?"

"'Tis not, your Honour, but when them foreigners keep dodging around the strand by moonlight, especially around the property of your nephew Mister Jenico Hamilton, Spanish Men's Rest, 'tis suspicious."

"And what are you suspicious of?" asked my uncle Valentine.

"Designs," said the Sergeant darkly, "designs against our Sovereign Lord the King, His Crown and Dignity."

"You've been reading a book, Sergeant," said my uncle Valentine. "Now, don't deny it. I can see it in your eye. Now, haven't you, Sergeant? You big, thick-footed, herring-fed Southern gom!" he ended abruptly, and left him.

He went across to the Widow McGinty's hotel and entered, amid curtsies and bobs from the staff. The widow was a plump-cheeked rounded woman of forty, with a roguish eye. Indeed it was hinted that she was neither widow, nor had she been wife. But her beer, wines and spirits to be consumed on or off the premises were beyond reproach. Too much virtue cannot be expected in one small house.

"Well, Widow," said my uncle Valentine, "I hear you've gone up in the world."

"God bless your Honour's Worship," said the widow and curtsied; "Sir Valentine, sure I never knew I was down."

"It's dukes you've now, Widow?"

"Ah, sure, Sir Valentine, your Honour, is it the ould one above and the lad with him? A nice kindly spoken gentleman if ever there was one. But a bit touched in the head, for Sir Valentine, your Honour, and begging your Honour's pardon for using so objectionable an expression, especially in front of the nobility and gentry," and she curtsied again, "but jook me elbow!" said Mrs. McGinty.

"And why not, Widow?"

"Did your Honour's Worship ever hear of a jook with four shirts?"

"In troth I did," said my uncle Valentine. "I know one who has only two."

"Ah, yes, Sir Valentine," agreed the Widow McGinty, "but this one pays his way."

"I'll walk, trot and canter him," said my uncle Valentine.

"Maelmorra MacGilla Espick," the Widow McGinty shrilled to the ancient boots, "ye deaf ould cod, will you be after showing Sir Valentine where the foreigners do be."

It was the village schoolmaster, Manus MacManus, who hit off my uncle Valentine's character to a nicety, in describing him, "like Caesar's wife, all things to all men."

You might see him, loud, explosive, around the grounds and coverts of Destiny Bay — I doubt if you could imagine the icy courtesy of him the morning he killed the Italian at Knocke in Belgium for making free with the name of a very noble, very pretty, very indiscreet Irish lady. "There lies a bloody ruffian!" said my uncle Valentine, and that was the Roman Marchese's only epitaph. Can you see in the Master of Fox Hounds, whose reputation for cursing hound tramplers is nation wide, the buck of Monte Carlo, the friend of princes, and not the adorer but the adored of the pretty ladies of Paris in the days when Paris was naughty but not vulgar? Can you see in the brigadier general of the war against the Boers the kindly figure who gave up the possibility of the marshal's baton to take care of his blind sister and dead brother's son in Destiny Bay? You can't. Then you don't know Ireland.

How he did it — how my uncle Valentine does his impossibilities — is a mystery, but within twenty minutes of his first meeting them, my uncle Valentine had tucked the Spanish duke and his grandson under his wing and had insisted on their staying at Destiny Bay. "For not only would it be a reflection on myself, dear sir," said my uncle Valentine, "but an insult to the Irish nation if you were to refuse our hospitality. Were I, an Irish gentleman, in your manorial grounds in Spain, would you suffer me to stay in a pothouse?"

"Manorial grounds," said the Spanish gentleman, "I am afraid our family has no more, and my own house is no better than a peasant's, yet I could not suffer a person of quality to remain there."

"How much less could I, then," said my uncle Valentine, "who, by the hazard of circumstance, am wealthy."

But the grandson was against leaving. The boy, Don Anthony, had hair, that if it were a girl's would be called chestnut and very beautiful, and topaz eyes. Evidently feeling how girlish he seemed to our Northern robustness, his voice had been cultivated into a husky fierceness, and his eyes were inimical. They were too poor, he said, for a wealthy gentleman's house; they were here on business, also: their stay would be too long to take advantage of hospitality; and this reason and that one. My uncle Valentine heard him with patience and gravity.

"If you've finished, my little red fellow," said my uncle Valentine, "you can take your hat and come on."

If my uncle Valentine was a sort of beneficent red god in Destiny Bay, then James Carabine, his valet and our butler, the broken-nosed, broken-handed, London prize-ring fighter, and a fine soldier, was his Angel of Judgment. My uncle Valentine might jest and be cajoled, but Carabine's word was scripture and irrevocable. Carabine had gone down to the Widow McGinty's to collect the baggage and edit the reckoning.

"So you've the ould one up wit' ye, Mister Carabine!"

"What ould one?"

"Th' ould one who says he's a jook."

"And isn't he?"

"Hell to your sowl, Mister Carabine," and the Widow McGinty flopped like a burst football; "do you mean it's true?"

"'Tis," said Carabine.

There was this about the Widow McGinty, you might knock her down for a minute, but she was up like a shot. That night, with immense labour and much smudging of ink, she indited a letter to Derry, and a week afterwards her hotel blazed forth under a new sign as "The Royal Arms." "By Special Appointment" — the widow's geography was vague but her business sense unimpeachable — "By Special Appointment to the Duke of Portugal."

Which sign is there till this day.

III

At dinner that night it was rather pathetic to see the two Spaniards, the elder one in formal clothes that must have dated back to the fifties, the younger one in a dinner jacket that the village sempstress might have put together. The ancient duke had the manners of one who in his twenties had mixed with kings, the boy had a rare formal courtesy, which could only have been taught him by the old man. There we were, my uncle Valentine, magnificent as only a great Irish gentleman can be, my aunt Jenepher, dark and beautiful with her warm friendly silence; the old duke, with his immense hooked nose, his white hair, his greyish, and, now I saw, stricken face; the boy with the chestnut hair and light brown eyes — the wild inimical look was passing from them. Little by little we got their story. The old man and the boy were the last of their race. The old man had soldiered in Africa in his youth, and retiring to his country vineyards had lived far away from court and city until his name was all but forgotten. The duchess had been dead these thirty years, and his only son, who had married an Austrian lady of no fortune, was dead in Cuba at San Juan Hill. He was a wild lad, the old duke hinted, and baccarat, our old friend *Neuf à la banque*, had him in thrall. The inheritance coming to him at his father's death he had signed away. Though there was no legal hold on him, the old duke had felt it incumbent to meet his son's debts. Beneath this calmly told story there was a great deal of tragedy, I am thinking. However, there they were now, the old duke and the soon-to-be-duke, and hardly a *peseta*, if that is the coin of their country, between them.

"My forefather was the great Alonzo de Leyva," said old Don Diego.

'S Truth! I had it. I knew now why the two poor devils had come to Destiny Bay! I looked across toward my uncle Valentine but he was listening in his courtly way to the old gentleman, and that bronzed face of his, which could be like the sphinx's when need arose, showed no evidence that the name was known to him. I glanced toward my aunt Jenepher and I could feel a quick understanding coming from her. The boy must somehow have felt it, for he flushed to his chestnut hair.

Don Alonzo de Leyva! The name carried me back to a June day of three and a quarter centuries before, when the great Armada set out on the Enterprise of England, as they called it. A hundred and thirty ships there were, great galleasses of over one thousand tons; galleasses rowed by three hundred slaves, the best appointed vessels of Spain and Portugal and Italy. The Captain General of the Ocean their commander was called, and Alonzo de Leyva was second in command. There they set out, the great floating cities, the great floating forts, the *Capitana*, the *San Martin*, the *Santa Aña*, the *Señora de la Rosa*, the *Raba Coronada*, the *San Juan*, the *San Pedro*, their vast galleasses, their light despatch boats, their fleet corsairs. There they set out, the men who had conquered Mexico and the West Indies and Peru, their heavy guns, their boarding axes, and their gear of war. The royal standard of Philip floated on the *Capitana: Exsurge Deus et vindica causam tuam,* it bore: Arise, O Lord, and avenge thy cause! And in each ship six little boys sang " Buenas Dias " in the morning and " Ave Maria " at the close of day.

Of how they fared every man knoweth — of how Drake and his Devon men came out of Plymouth Sound, and harried them to Calais; and of how at Calais he was joined by Sir John Hawkins and Admiral Frobisher, those devils of the sea; of the week's fighting in the Downs; of the great gallantry of the Spanish men, who died where they stood, striking never a flag; of the retreat northward. Northward toward the Pole the Spaniards drove, starving and shat-

tered, and feeling they were being driven into the freezing
circle of Dante's hell, so different were the lowering fogs
from the golden waters of Spain; and turning and fleeing
home by the west coast of Ireland, there arose an enemy
greater than Frobisher or Hawkins or Drake. He did blow
with His wind, the sea covered them, and they sank as lead
into the mighty waters. The men who had laughed in the
beard of the outrageous Horn on their way to harass Peru,
were mangled by the unimaginable Irish sea, the teeth of
the Irish coast.

It is one of the blots on our Irish annals, on which there
are blots not a few, that these wrecked men who had fought
so gallantly against Drake were butchered ruthlessly on the
shore by the aborigines. Their chains, their rings, their
gold-inlaid swords were looted. In England, we know, they
would have received succour and help, as a beaten enemy
always deserves. But the chiefs of the clans with dog-
whips and swords could not drive the loot-maddened countrymen away. In Lord Edward's rebellion the pikes were
the Armada pikes, and many a golden piece of a peasant's
dowry is a Spanish ducat, and here and there in Ireland you
will see rings and chains of antiquity whose history it were
better not to ask. So that we Irish gentry are embarrassed
in the presence of Spaniards, and there is nothing we will
not do to help or honour a Spanish man or woman, unless it
be a matter of treason.

Of all the gallant captains and gentlemen adventurers
who perished on the dreadful Irish coast, none put up such
a great fight as the Vice Admiral de Leyva. Off the Nore,
his ship, the *Raba Coronada*, had fought until she was
scupper deep in the water, and until he had only thirty
cartridges left, but by some miracle of seamanship he navi-
gated her homeward until the great wind struck him off
Killybegs, and there she perished. But the Vice Admiral
saved his crew, his arms, and treasure; and fitting out his

galleass, he started to row home, setting out a course by the Orkneys and Shetlands, but off Destiny Bay a vast wave came, and the cruel, the ever cruel and merciless sea, hurled the intrepid company against the cliffs, destroying men and treasure. They were picked up by our own clansmen, thank God, and buried in a great field on the westward horn of Destiny Bay. Though we were of the Church by law established, yet we found a minister of their own faith to say their service. There they sleep, and none of us begrudge them their few acres, the Vice Admiral and his captains and gunners, the gentlemen adventurers, the common soldiers, and the little boys who trilled "Buenos Dias" in the morning, and sang "Ave Maria" at the close of day, and that field and townland is known as Spanish Men's Rest.

The strakes of the galleass have been used as beams in cottage and farmhouse, and the doubloons and chains of gold and rings set with Peruvian gems have passed over the counters of wineshops and thence God knows whither, but of the great treasure chest there is no word, written or oral. And not many of us in Destiny Bay care much, for we are superstitious enough, or wise enough, to believe that wherever is treasure trove, there are devils, and wherever the treasure goes, go the devils with it.

IV

"I suppose then," said my uncle Valentine, "that you have hopes of finding your great forefather's treasure box."

"I had thought," said the old gentleman, "that it would be no less impossible to find that treasure than to find money any other way."

My uncle Valentine had looked at me, I think involuntarily, because I know the coast, the currents, and also knew much of the peasant lore of the neighbourhood. I knew myself that there was not the remotest chance of finding anything on that coast. A strong box would be ground to nothing in the underground gardens of the Black Man and the Devil's Delight. Also this, the coast line had changed a great deal since the days of Elizabeth. Every year the furious sea exacts tithe of anise and cumin from the land.

"You seem to think it impossible, Don Kerry," said the old man.

"If anything is ever impossible, sir—"

"For myself," said the old man, "I care nothing. I am very tired and very old, and less and less does me as the days go by, but for this child—" he nodded to the boy— "he must soon embark on a world which even so tough an old soldier as myself has found difficult. In older days the name would have been an asset, but now—" the old man smiled a little bitterly—"there are so many broken noblemen that they have become a nuisance. Without money one can achieve a philosophy, but without money one cannot practice chivalry."

I am afraid that the necessity for money of a boy of eighteen did not impress me overmuch. Too many of our countrymen, gentle and simple, have gone out in the world with no more wealth than a ready smile and a hard fist, not wishful for wealth but for dreamed cities and unkissed mouths. Many an Irish nobleman thinks back with joy of his mining days in Arizona or of punching cattle in the Argentine, or of tending bar in Australia. The boy before me, with his reddish hair and girlish look, didn't seem the type to enjoy the world as we rougher Irish would, making of poverty a game, a club in which to meet all conditions of folk.

"However," said the old gentleman, "treasure or none, I am going to tell you something that Don Valentine will understand, though you, Don Kerry, are too young to have felt it yet, and Doña Jenepher will never know, for because of something the feeling never comes to women. When one is a grown man one comes to many crossroads of life, and though one way may be stretching patent before you, yet an overwhelming feeling of right brings you down the small lane. And what you thought at the time was a foolish whim, you see later to have been the irresistible hand of Destiny . . . I have come; that is all."

"You have come among friends, sir," said my uncle Valentine.

V

I had persuaded the young Dago to come for a gallop with me, while exercising Pelican III, the old clever hunter, and a new moke, a bit of a rogue, that I had been stuck with at Derry. Don Anthony made quite a fuss about going. He had no riding things, so that a new pair of cord breeches was impounded for him by my aunt Jenepher, with boots I had grown out of. He would have been no ornament to a respectable hunt, that lad, with his coat and waistcoat by the village sempstress, and his soft shirt that was more like a girl's than a boy's. Myself, I think a good horse needs dressing up too. My aunt Jenepher had given him a new tweed cap of mine. I remember thinking that hospitality had distinctly its limits.

James Carabine brought out brown Pelican, and the rogue horse. The rogue was a good three-quarter bred, with a fine turn of speed and a nasty eye. It had also an uncomfortable habit of waltzing around on its hind feet. Even a three-in-one bit couldn't cure it. It began the "Waltz me around again, Willy" in the stable yard.

"Which'll you have?" I grinned.

Young Anthony looked at me with something like hate in his eyes.

"You'd better throw a leg up on Pelican," I said.

"You think me afraid. You think me afraid to ride that horse. You think a Spaniard is an afraid man."

I saw there were tears in his eyes.

I said, "What the hell's wrong with you?"

"I show you am I afraid? You smug Englishman, you corpse-plundering Irish robber!" And before either Carabine or myself could stop him, he was on the rogue and through the gate.

"That," said James Carabine, "is a hard saying, Mister Kerry."

"I hope he breaks his blasted neck."

"Devil a break!" said James Carabine.

I swung up on Pelican and astounded that staid fencer with a couple of resounding larrups on the ribs so that we went through the drive and the village of Ballyfale in the style of a two-year-old coming up the five-furlong stretch at Leopardstown. A mile out, on the Derry road, I came on my young Spaniard sitting disconsolately on the rogue horse.

"Don Kerry," he said, and his voice was trembling, "can you forgive me? Will you forgive me?"

He looked so contrite, so heartbroken, that I laughed.

"I must seem so ungrateful to you and Don Valentine and Doña Jenepher —"

"Is it for putting you up?" said I. "Sure what is there in it, and why shouldn't we? The travelling tinkers of the road eat more —"

"That's it, Don Kerry," he answered. "We are nothing more than travelling tinkers of the road. Our duchy and marquisate are ridiculous things, like beggars wearing a king's mantle. Don Kerry, you have no idea how poor we are. I suppose I should not be ashamed of it, but I haven't the philosophy of my grandfather, nor the great gentleman-liness of you and your uncle Valentine. So I am worried, Don Kerry."

"About what?" I asked.

"My grandfather is so old," he said. "In the very old

the fire burns down until it is grey ash, and then suddenly a great spurt comes and for a moment it is blazing, and then an instant later it is cold, and out. I am afraid this coming to Ireland is the last spurt, Don Kerry, and if my grandfather dies here, what shall I do?"

"If he dies here, young Anthony, he dies among friends and there is the same hospitality for him dead as alive, for he has more need of it. At ninety a man has the right to die, to rest, and to go to his friends. And as to you, you stay where you are until you want to go elsewhere. Hell!" I said "You're not in a city now, where the folk can't see any farther than the end of the street, or the bank at the end of the street. What you need, my boy, is to lie on your belly on the top of Slievemore Mountain, in the heather of it, and look northward over the Atlantic towards the Pole. A week of that— Well, what the blazes are you crying about now?"

"Can't I cry if I want to?"

"Not when you're out with me, my son, if you ever expect to come out again. For God's sake, sit back in your saddle and keep your heels down. Stop bearing on that curb. I've a mind to give your own jaw a good squeeze just to let you know what it feels like."

He was a funny lad, that Dago! We had something going on under cover at Destiny Bay that half the United Kingdom would have given their eyes to see. My uncle Valentine had brought over from Edinburgh, where he had been golfing, as fine a middleweight as ever resined his shoes in a ring, but utterly unknown as he had just come from New Zealand. We were grooming him for a novices' competition at the National Sporting Club, and had our money down at a hundred to one. Under the eye of James Carabine, who has forgotten more about boxing than our moderns ever knew, we trained the lad. We had a brother of Ike Weir, the old Belfast Spider, to help us, and I made

up his speed, for I am rather an overrated amateur heavy.
I have been lucky in tournaments. However, I made Scott
step to keep out of the way of my right hand. We had the
Spaniard in once, but at the sound of the gloves' thumping,
and at the sight of a dribble of blood from a cut on the eye-
brow, he got white as Death and left, nor could we get him
in any more. Nor could I entice him to cockfighting mains.
But when he came to the races at Dundalk and Baldoyle,
he was beside himself with joy. My aunt Jenepher, who
liked him so much, persuaded him to take a loan, and he
cleaned up, as our saying is. There was a weight-for-age
race for gentlemen riders at Baldoyle, and I was up on my
cousin Jenico's Communist, a horse we were for hurdling
next year. Communist was second favourite and I told
young Anthony I thought I had a chance. As it happened
I straggled in fifth, but I saw him cashing in after the race.

"You didn't bet on me?" I asked.

"No, Kerry. You didn't have a tinker's chance in hell."

Oh, he was learning Irish all right!

"And how did you find out the winner?"

"Oh, I picked him in the paddock," said he. I was beginning to have a respect for that boy.

But foreigners are a funny crowd, deep, past understanding. That summer around Destiny Bay, they were poking
great fun at my expense over Sir John Brannagan's wife,
Pretty Molly Brannagan, as she was known in the countryside. I liked Molly; as a matter of fact I felt awfully sorry
for the girl. Being cooped up in London, and all that. As
a matter of fact, Brannagan was a bit of a brute, though
he seemed decent, as she as much as told me. I'd have
liked Jack Brannagan but for that. Didn't understand her
the least bit, if you know what I mean; no sense of her soul,
and what not. She hated the London season, and Deauville
and all that stuff. Told me she'd rather live in a cottage
with a purling stream, and a beehive, and so forth. Hated

going to court, and being photographed in Hyde Park all the time. It's jolly hard on a girl with rustic tastes and an inner life, if you understand, to be imprisoned, as it were. She was like a wild bird in a cage, she told me. Awfully hard luck; I thought a great deal about it. I had a photograph of her she had given me, a photograph in court dress. As it happened she had no rustic snapshots. Young Anthony saw it in my sitting room.

"Who's the old girl?" he asked.

"She's not an old girl," I said severely. "She's a very nice and beautiful woman. Very misunderstood."

"I suppose she told you that," he said.

"How did you know?" But he didn't answer.

"She's forty, if a day."

"She's twenty-nine."

"I suppose she told you that too," he laughed. "Look at the chest on her. She's like Rule Britannia."

"I wish you wouldn't be foul."

"She's got bandy legs!"

"I say, look here—"

"She's got bandy legs. I know."

"How do you know? You've never seen 'em."

"No, but I've seen hundreds of others, just like her."

"You're a filthy little blackguard!"

"Why shouldn't I know about legs?" he asked brazenly.

"Now, look here, Tony," I said; "I know you're foreign and all that, and have a broad outlook and all that, but let me catch you mucking around with any of our maids, or the country girls, and let there be one word of trouble, you know what I mean—"

"Don Kerry," he flushed until his face was redder than his hair, "Don Kerry, how dare you? How can you forget yourself so far as to mention such things to me? Is this your gentility?" And he rushed out of the room.

By the personal piper of Moses!

VI

It might have been the strong liquor of the ocean air that lulled the old man into sleepiness, the air of the Atlantic Drift that has flown from Bimini and the Bermudas to our Destiny Bay, and has something of the peace and drowsiness of those islands when it reaches us. All of our home has peace. The fields of sea drift, the whitethorn bushes, and the glory of the heather. The scent of the heather, the purple of the heather, the soft tinkle of it, there is great peace in that. And the bees put a sleep on you. And at night when the moon comes out, there is the soft flight of the bats, or the flapping of the owl's wings, and him after the sleek field mice. The soft chiming of the waves and the shoheen-shoho of the wind in the ancient trees. It is the grand place to rest in, our Destiny Bay.

Now and again he would pull himself together, the old Spaniard, and say that to-morrow or the next day he must go to the beach near Spanish Men's Rest, and sit there, " and maybe God would send him a message." Which I wager is as good a way of finding buried treasure as with maps and divers. But each day he put it off until another, and with his grandson, or with my aunt Jenepher, he would sit in the orchard in the sun, and tell us stories of his father who had met Napoleon face to face, and had fought against Sir John Moore, that most gallant of gallant soldiers, at Corunna, and against our great countryman, the Iron Duke. Also his father had known Cagliostro, that vast impostor or that great magician, whichever you prefer, and had danced the country dance with Marie Antoinette. At times the old man's mind would wander, and he would mistake his grandson for his son, and talk to him of domestic things of fifty years before, and he would ask my aunt Jenepher, did she remember Eugénie, Empress of the French, and her wedding, and Marshal MacMahon. But my aunt Jenepher, with that gift of hers, would take him by the hand out of that world of shadows and lead him back.

"He will never go to Spanish Men's Rest, sir," I told my uncle Valentine.

"Indeed he will, Kerry," my uncle Valentine said to me.

The young Spaniard came up to my uncle Valentine.

"Sir," he said, "my grandfather's going to die."

"And why shouldn't he," said my uncle Valentine. "When you're as old as he is, and as tired, you'll not like that any one will begrudge you your rest."

"But if he dies here, far from his country—"

"Have you any friends in your country?"

"None, sir." The boy's voice faltered. "I was too young and too much at school to have made friends, and my grandfather has outlived all his."

"Well, he's better here than anywhere," said my uncle Valentine.

"But the trouble, sir, but the putting of your house about—"

"Now you're talking to me as if I were some damned hotel keeper." And my uncle Valentine frowned.

"Sir," said the boy, "what brought us to Destiny Bay, and what brought you to our lodging, is a great mystery to me. But I think, sir," and his voice became nearly a whisper, "that it could have been nothing else but the Finger of God."

"And sure what else could it have been?" said my uncle Valentine.

But the old man didn't die. He still drowsed in the sun, treated my aunt Jenepher with the immense courtesy of an older day, and I began to think that my uncle Valentine was right—that he would go to Spanish Men's Rest. I had gone down to the Curragh to see the Irish Derby run, a trip that cost me a hundred times the fare, for a Scottish entry, a horse with the neck of a goat and the head of a camel, and a jockey with the evil face of a magician's familiar had nipped home in the last furlong. A sad day for Ireland! But the night of my return, going into the village, I met Shiela Broon.

In the countryside they gave Shiela Broon a hundred and fifty years of age, but myself I wouldn't put her a day over a hundred. She was a strange old woman who lived upon the mountain side, and had no English. But she cultivated a herbal garden, and was the doctor of the peasantry. Government sends doctors to the public dispensaries, charming fellows with splendid athletic records, fine followers to hounds. They are grand lads to play cards with, to hunt with, but if there's anything wrong with you in our Irish village, send for the *ban fassa*, the skilful woman.

She had a winsome face, had Shiela Broon, and a fish in the water was not cleaner. She was sent for when any one died, or when a little one was about to enter the world. Also she had knowledge of many mysteries beside the use of herbs, but these are not spoken of. I knew it was not a child coming into the world, for there was no hurry on her.

"Who has gone home, Shiela Broon?"

"No one as yet, hinny. No one as yet. But there's one in your house, long darling, that's packing his bag."

"Is it the foreign man, white mother?"

"'Tis, hinny. 'Tis himself. I'm going to sit down on the ditch, hinny, for the road is hard from the mountain to here."

We sat down in the moonlight, the very old woman with the brown face and the small pipe, and myself tall, with my cigarette.

"'Tis a funny thing, a hard thing, white mother, to have come from the soft land of Spain to the hard land of Ireland, and to be within a dog's bark of what you've come for, and not to see it."

"If 'tis the Admiral's chest you mean, Kerry of the

Horses, 'tis not there. Though how I know, I know not myself. But for him and his, is there not the friendship of Clan Farlane, of yourself, strong lad, and of Valentine Aling, Valentine the Magnificent, and of dark Jenepher. Long Kerry of the heart, the wise of the head say different, but a friend is better than gold."

"Aye, but to be baffled is a hard thing, Shiela Broon."

"Maybe 'tis not baffled he is at all, at all, Kerry of the Horses. Maybe he's finished his mission. Maybe he was sent for."

"And sure, who'd send for him, Shiela Broon?"

"The lonely dead folk of Spanish Men's Rest."

It is a queer thing to be putting down on paper and a queerer thing for folks to be reading in town houses, and in flats maybe, where if thoughts cold and clear as stars come at all, people are afraid to look at them, but we sat there, Shiela Broon and I, in the silver moonlight, with the mountains rising purple about us, and the chime of the sea in our ears, and talk about dead folk is no more strange than the talk in cities about the weather, or about buying and selling. The winds from the mountain clear your head of dross, and many is the queer byroad your mind will wander in, and sometimes in depression you'll think that this earth is hell, and that you're suffering it for a sin you've forgotten in a life you can't remember — and then you see the blue of the kingfisher along the river, or in the morning you'll come across a badger by chance that's mistaken his track, and he'll look at you as much as to say: "This is the devil and all, and are you gentleman enough to let me pass?" or a girl of the countryside puts a twist on the opening notes of "The Red-Haired Man's Wife", and you know that it's only been a cloud that's come over you, and which the wind has already started to blow away.

We are not afraid of the dead or of God in Destiny Bay. The one we have a friendship and respect for, and the

Other, well the Other is the Master of the Brethren and a very great gentleman indeed. I don't think we're exactly Christians in that country, but I don't think we're any the worse for that.

"What would the dead folk want him for, Shiela Broon?"

"They're a queer folk, the dead folk, Kerry Oge. They're human in a lot of ways. Were you yourself, Kerry of the heart, in the dark of Africa or in Cream Tartary for forty years, and you not able to go home, there would come a great drought on you for news of Ulster, of the sight of a man of Ulster. So that in the end you'd send for a relative of yours to be coming and having a crack with you, if he could be spared, you'd be that sick for the ways of Ulster and the speech of Ulster, and the little air of Ulster."

"But sure, I thought the dead knew everything, could go everywhere, Shiela Broon."

"There's a power of nonsense talked about the dead, Kerry of my pulse. They do be talking of them even in churches in the most ignorant way. Myself, young love, who see more of the dead than the living on the mountain side, myself that doesn't know how old I am, and have seen them come into the world and go out of it, in divisions of armies you might say, myself still knows little about them. But 'tis the way, lad Kerry, we here are like childer on the floor, and the dead are grown up. And the way the big people are to us, and we small, are the way the shadowy folk are to us now. Magnificent and strong and past understanding. I do be thinking, Kerry of the Horses, that dying is like a boy's voice breaking and his putting on trews, or like a young girl and she letting down the hem of her skirt and putting up her soft hair. I'll be hitting the road. At the house, if they want me, they know where I am."

"Kerry, young hero," she said, "let you not this year ride a horse with four white stockings."

"And why not, old mother?"

" If you promise me, I 'll tell you. 'Tis how I saw in the tub of water, a great jumping horse with his legs broken, and near him a rider twisted and broken too, but what face was on him I could n't see. You 'll mind a horse with four white stockings ! "

" I will, Shiela."

" God go with you, Kerry boy ! "

I met Carabine on the drive.

" How 's the old gentleman, Carabine ? "

" Bad he is, Mister Kerry. All of a sudden the life is rushing out of him, like the turn of a spring tide. He won't last the night, I 'm thinking."

He did n't.

VII

So the old gentleman came at last to Spanish Men's Rest, as my uncle Valentine had said he would. Thither, in the summer afternoon with the bees droning, and Slievemore putting on its purple cloak, now that the sun was westering, there came the first dweller and sojourner for three and a quarter centuries. There were my uncle Valentine, and my aunt Jenepher, and my cousin Jenico who had just come from London, and myself. And there, standing proudly, but with a face drenched with weeping, stood the new duke. There were James Carabine and a host of others. There was our red-faced hunting parson, but it was not he who read the service, but Father Malachi, the little Roman priest of the village. Myself, as true blue an Orangeman as ever sat in a lodge, have nothing but liking for the Father, for if there was ever a saint it was he. He was n't one of your saints who did things but a saint who was. A gentleman, a knower of Horace, a lover of dogs, and no more kindly person in the world. He would n't share his last crust with a beggar ; he 'd give it all to him and go fasting himself.

" 'Lamb of God, Who takest away the sins of the world!' "
went on the Latin service.

My uncle Valentine stepped forward and looked at my
cousin Jenico and myself, and at the bereaved boy.

"Gentlemen," he said, "but lately you saw this venerable
man, who is sleeping, and because two of you are my
nephews and one of you my guest, I could wish no better
for you when you come to his age than that you should be
like him. He had great dignity, and honour, and no fear,
and that simplicity which when kings lose it, they lose their
crowns, and what is the reality behind the symbol of government, the hearts of their people.

"Gentlemen, that all men are born equal is a doctrine
tenable only by the ignorant. Scripture is against it; history also, and the experience of travelled men. Why there
should be noble and lowly, as even were among animals
when Noe brought them two by two into the Ark, is a
mystery known in its fulness only to the immense wisdom
of God.

"You who are born noble," said my uncle Valentine,
"have a harder destiny than have the people. It is your
duty at all times to act and think chivalrously. It is you
who will be first in battle to vindicate your country's honour or defend her boundaries. You must be generous, for
the bitter constraint of poverty has not galled your arms
and narrowed your gestures. Live honourably so as to give
example in life and when you die a lifting to men's hearts.
The name of the Bourbons, who were bad kings, has no
sweet chime in our ears, but the name of Plantagenet is a
ringing trumpet sound.

"Young gentlemen, this ancient man lived honourably
and chivalrously. In the end poverty had no terrors for
him. He had been so true to his order of chivalry, gentlemen, that he could go anywhere in the world, as well to
Russia or to China as to Destiny Bay, and accept hos-

pitality nobly, knowing that chivalry is everywhere and shall not die, as each master of the secret knows that Hirman Abiff is but sleeping and shall rise again.

"As to what shall happen to this gentleman now he is dead, that is beyond knowing. He arrived at his harvest of years intact in his simplicity and his fearlessness, his kindliness and courtesy, thereby showing, young gentlemen, a signal victory against the Prince of the powers of Darkness, who is no myth but a reality, and is ever holding a line of battle against us, as Scripture states and history sheweth, and is known by experience to all travelled men. I am persuaded that the greatest and noblest of all Kings shall not forget or be ungenerous toward one of his knightly commanders.

"Father Malachi," said my uncle Valentine, "you may go ahead with your service now, for I am done."

VIII

At one end of Destiny Bay, the east horn, is our own house, and surely I am telling no lie when I say there is no happier, sunnier place in wide Ireland, no place that is more beloved of bees, and bees have no liking for a sad house. They are a selfish sort of folk, the bees, but great company and very peaceful, so that I wouldn't like to be saying a word against them. At the west horn of Destiny Bay, the America side, as the country folk say, is Spanish Men's Rest, my cousin Jenico's place. I wouldn't call it an unhappy place, or even a sad place, but there is a cold dignity about it that is depressing. The house is squat and grey, good Newry granite, and roofed with that beautiful greenish slate you find in Donegal. Within the house of Spanish Men's Rest, there is a darkness as if the blinds were drawn, but the blinds never are. Neither are there great walls about it, nor ancient trees, as at Destiny Bay, but still it is dark as though there were. There is more fine lawn than flowers about the house, and the trees on the drive are great poplars, not like our own yew and hawthorn trees, constrained by the Atlantic breezes to the shape of wings. Proud and dignified the poplars stand. Even the Night of the Big Wind did not conquer them. They are like the banners of some dour fighting company, some reserve of battle.

Between the house and the trees lies the field from which the townland takes its name, Spanish Men's Rest. It is an acre, more or less, bounded by a wall of stone cemented with mosses, and covered with gorse, but a gorse that has no gaiety. Within the grass grows high, and the red and white heads of the clover, but there are no bees, nor do the meadow larks nest there, rising perpendicularly from the surly field to let loose their cataract of melody. Under the waving grasses, mound by mound you can distinguish the ancient resting places of the Spanish Men. In most of God's little havens there is peace and quietude, but here is a surliness, a sort of bitter feeling in the air. For one, I am not satisfied that the Spanish Men rest.

I cannot blame them. They had stood up bravely against the guns of Drake, and when a greater Adversary attacked them, when He blew with His winds, they were scattered, they had seamanship and courage enough to weather the storm. They had braved the knives of the treacherous Irish aborigines. Surely none deserved better than they to come home to their own country, but the merciless unsatisfied sea has no chivalry, so here they are.

You will pass out of the townland of Ballyfale, singing a song, some rollicking road chanty like the Palatine's Daughter, or you will be thinking of the beauty of some woman, or better still the beauty of a horse. Your head will be like some apple garden at sunset, with the birds singing the small melodies that come to them at the close of the

day, but once you step over the little stream that separates
Ballyfale from the homestead of the missing men, there will
come on you a sense of loneliness, a sense of being baffled.
And you will try to shake it off, saying, "What the devil is
wrong with me anyhow?" And you will look about you.
Westward you will see our own house, peaceful in the sunshine as some drowsing hunting dog. There are the caravans of the gypsies near Ballyfale. There is Ballyfale itself, sturdy, with the white road winding toward Donegal.
There, westward, is the Irish Village, its whitewashed and
thatched houses cheerful as heaven. But here, in Spanish
Men's Rest, there is a cold transparent veil between you and
the sun. And "there'll be no fun or excitement on this
road," say you, and rightfully you turn back.

They will tell you there are ghosts at Spanish Men's Rest,
and perhaps in Glasgow or in New York, or some place
where he is out of the uncanny hearing of the dead, some
man of the place will tell you he has seen them. But I
should put no belief in that, if I were you. No man around
Destiny Bay has seen them. Myself passing in the darkness have felt my dogs come closer to me, and heard their
little uneasy whines, and riding on horseback, have known
the mare to shy and sweat, but no man's eye, as far as I
know, has seen them. But then, the sheeted kitchen ghost
is a vulgarity past believing, and as for forms of horror,
the Agony of Christ is between us and them. We come
home to the bright fire and the steady lamp and laugh with
the others at the mention of wraiths and apparitions, but
alone in our sleeping rooms we forget or pass lightly over
that canon of the church which forbids prayers for the dead,
and we say, "God give them rest and caring, poor souls!"

How Spanish Men's Rest came into our family and how
eventually it came to my cousin Jenico was thus: Our grandfather, Sir Alastair MacFarlane, had for first wife an
O'Donnell of Donegal, who brought to him the townland

and house of Spanish Men's Rest as dowry together with
other things; a row of houses in Kentish Town in London,
and a very excellent brewery in Louth. The O'Donnells
are not a strong or a long-lived family, so the poor lady
died, after having given birth to a daughter Catherine, to
whom all the dowry was willed by my grandfather, when
he married his second wife, my grandmother.

My aunt Kate, as she insisted on being known, "Plain
Kate MacFarlane", had a great deal of my grandfather's
peremptory ways. She insisted on living by herself in
Spanish Men's Rest, though it had not been inhabited for
centuries. Tin baths, and all the horrors of the early Vic-
torian age were her portion, but it was hers, and she was
going to live in it. You would have thought my aunt Kate
to be something of a suffragist but she had more contempt
for women than she had for men, which was not little. My
aunt Kate had nearly a masculine face, but she was a very
handsome woman. She drank like a dragoon, which I can
understand now that I know Spanish Men's Rest, but she
carried her liquor like a gentleman, and had a fine supple
vocabulary. When my grandfather died, who abhorred
long sermons, she took it on herself to keep the incumbent
of Saint Columba's-in-Paganry within bounds. When he
had arrived at "sixthly", my aunt Kate would drop her
prayer book, drop her hymn book, drop her parasol or umbrella, as the season was, and if this did not answer, would
utter a loud "hum" which brought the parson to heel as
by a keeper's whistle. She was very firm, was my aunt
Kate.

My aunt Kate had the family failing for horses, and kept
a half dozen in training, but she never won a big race until
she was thirty-nine years old. She had a good average of
the small ones, but the classics eluded her. In the end she
lifted the Royal Hunt Cup with Stotius, that close-coupled
beautiful jumper, Captain Sylvester Grant up. I don't

think Grant knew what happened to him until he married her. He was a nice chap, twenty-four years old.

"It's a damned shame!" said my uncle Valentine.

"What?" said my aunt Kate.

"He's only twenty-four and you're thirty-nine, Kate."

"He's the best gentleman rider in England, and I'll win at Aintree with him up."

"Then it's a worse shame than I thought—"

"Look here, Valentine," said my aunt Kate, "if that's the only way you can talk to a lady, get to hell out of here."

They were very happy for a year, I know. Grant often said no man knew a horse as my aunt did. At the end of the year my aunt Kate was brought to bed of a son. This was my cousin Jenico.

"Is it a colt or a filly?" asked my aunt Kate.

"'Tis a grand wee bouncing fellow, Miss Kate," she was told.

"Good!" said my aunt Kate, and she died. I must say I like my aunt Kate's way of doing things.

My uncle Grant was killed six months after in a steeple-chase in France. He had sweated down so much to make weight that when his horse fell, he had not strength to crawl out of the way of the field, and the flying irons finished him. He was an intrepid fair rider, and everybody loved him. So Jenico made his home with us in Destiny Bay.

Being half foreigner, as it were, Jenico went to Eton and Oxford; myself, following the Ulster tradition, went to Portora and Trinity. So that from twelve years on, Jenico and I drifted apart physically. We were more than relations, we were firm friends. My cousin Jenico flirted a little with politics, but he found out that what the politicians saw of value in him were the street of houses in Kentish Town and the excellent brewery in the County of Louth. My cousin Jenico is no man's fool. He quit. With all his money, and more money seemed to come to him always, he might have done anything, lived anywhere. But my cousin Jenico insisted on living at Spanish Men's Rest.

"After all, it is my mother's house, sir," he told my uncle Valentine, who remonstrated with him because of the shadow that was on it, "the house where I was born. Not a lost dog or a deserted woman is as pathetic as an old house with nobody in it, the windows unlighted, dead leaves upon the gravel path. Somebody built it with love and hope and put a bit of their heart and mind into it. I would not desert any house, much less my mother's."

"How would it be," said my uncle Valentine, and he plunged his hand up to the wrist in his great red beard, "if I were to go up to Dublin, and invite tenders for a handsome merry-spoken girl would marry you and cheer up the house?"

"I think, sir," said my cousin Jenico, "that's a job of work I'll attend to myself when the time comes."

"Aye, and you'll make a mess of it," roared my uncle Valentine, "because you won't listen to one," he said aggrievedly, "that's spent my life studying them for the benefit of Kerry and yourself. Wait until you see the fine-hocked, sweet-cantering filly I'll choose for him." And he looked at me.

"I'm damned if you will, sir," I answered most ungratefully.

So Jenico made his home in Spanish Men's Rest. A quiet, dignified and comfortable house it was. But it always seemed to me that Jenico was more of a garrison holding it than an owner enjoying it. My uncle Valentine and my aunt Jenepher were worried for him, knowing that it is in solitude and gloom that our national pitfall awaits us. I could tell stories of lonely gentlefolk in Ireland drinking themselves to death seriously and secretly that would bring tears to your eyes. But Jenico didn't. Suddenly he would start up and leave the place for a while, and go shooting lions in Africa, or bear in the Caucasus, or chamois in the Alps, and when he would return he would write a solemn book about it, full of fine plates. They must have cost him a power of money, but they passed the time pleasantly in Spanish Men's Rest. I have a great admiration for those books, they are so solid and beautifully bound, and some day I shall read them.

Here is a clumsy description of my cousin Jenico at the time of the old duke's death. He was not a very tall man, about five feet eight inches, but sturdily built, and as hard as nails. He had brown eyes and brown hair, but his face is so tanned that the hair seems light. He has a handsome face, smallish nose and a cleft in his chin, and at first sight he looks like a subaltern in the brigade of Guards. He is always beautifully turned out and I have never seen the parting in his hair disturbed. But on his face, for all his twenty-five years, there was a sombre look. You had an impression there was a terrific power in reserve somewhere. My cousin Jenico was not the sort of person you would pick a fight with, and he was the sort of person you'd be glad to have with you in one.

He spoke very little, making one word do the work of three (that's what makes those books of travel of his so damned heavy, if those who read them are to be believed!). He has one physical peculiarity, a slight limp in his right leg, where Derry Belle rapped him with her iron when she had a touch of laminitis and he wanted to have a look at it, but for all that he can move fast as a dancer. He has a beautiful easy seat in the saddle, but his hands are a trifle heavy on a horse's mouth. His eyes are half closed. Where my uncle Valentine must roar, and I must curse to get the Irish servants to do anything quickly, my cousin Jenico just directs in his low speaking voice, and it's no sooner ordered than done. "'Tisn't that we're afraid of him, God bless your Honour, Mister Kerry, 'tis that we're just impressed."

IX

The young Spaniard stayed on with us. Neither my uncle Valentine nor my aunt Jenepher would hear of his going. "Let you wait until the estate is settled up," said my uncle Valentine, "then you can be off wherever you like. But let you keep away from the lawyers while they're settling it. Lawyers," said my uncle Valentine, "are the devil and all." The young Spaniard asked one favour, that all should continue calling him Don Anthony, and not by the name of his duchy.

"May I still be Don Anthony, Sir Valentine?"

"You can be Judas Iscariot, if you want to," said my uncle Valentine.

For all his queer ways and girlish looks you couldn't but be fond of that boy. He had a knack of being silent and thinking deeply, and then saying what was in his heart in an unabashed way that captured your good feeling and friendship. "If it hadn't been for you and Don Valentine and Miss Jenepher, Don Kerry," he said, "I should have been miserable over grandfather's death, but you take it as so natural and as so much his right to die, that I think it would be selfish to grieve. In Spain, Don Kerry, death is dreadful. There is hideous ceremonial, the black horses and the censers of incense and the intoning of the Dies Irae, and in the gloom of the church, Don Kerry, you can imagine the red flames of hell. And you think your poor friend has little chance of Paradise. Here I see it different. I don't think, Don Kerry, that God likes us to crawl on our bellies—"

"Stomachs, young 'un, stomachs. Bellies is low."

"Well, stomachs. I think God must be very like your uncle Valentine, but with a white beard instead of a red one, and less abrupt," said he, "because God is older."

My uncle Valentine looked him up and down.

"How is it," said my uncle, "that I find you wearing a blue tie, and your grandad hardly cold in his grave."

"I have no other, Sir Valentine."

"Then it's Dublin for you," said my uncle Valentine.

I offered myself to go with him, but in the end it was decided my aunt Jenepher should go with him, and James Carabine should accompany them. When my aunt Jenepher went to Dublin it was always a great function. Rooms were engaged in Morrison's Hotel ("and bright in history's pages be the name of Morrison!"). With her went her Islay maid, Morag, tall and gaunt as a grenadier, strong as a man, who had only one warm spot in her heart and that was for my aunt Jenepher. With her went Carabine with his broken hands and broken nose of a prize fighter and looking so respectable that one would easily take him for a dissenting parson. My aunt Jenepher looked like some princess out of a tale by Grimm with the ogreish maid and the tall, wide fighter. And this time, with the young Spaniard, it looked as if they had added to the party a page disguised in modern clothes, but a page from the time of Bourbon kings.

"Go to Farley," I told the youngster, "he makes the best trousers in Dublin. Tell him I sent you."

The boy seemed to blush, as if trousers were anything to blush about.

"And if I do be meeting Pretty Molly Brannagan," he jeered, in his imitation of our Irish speech, "what will I be after telling her from you, please your Honour."

"Hark 'ee, my lad, some of these days you'll come foul of a clip on the lug."

"Leave the boy be," said my uncle Valentine, "and now, Kerry, for a week of the grandest cockfighting and card-playing the North of Ireland has ever seen."

It was a good week. One of our guests, the eighty-year-old Earl of Belturbet, said that though the card-playing was gorgeous the cockfighting was thruly magnificent. It was after this week that Sergeant MacGinty left the Royal Irish Constabulary and became a lay brother in a monastery. He averred that the upper classes in Ireland were going the way of Sodom and Gomorrah, and only continual prayer could stave off fire and brimstone. Myself I think the sergeant was always a religious lad and only needed an excuse to go monk.

My aunt Jenepher and young Anthony arrived home on Monday. He had new suits of Irish tweed and new shirts, but they were as capacious as the ones he arrived in.

"The Irish tailor who made you them, my lad," I told him, "had the delirium tremens. Why the devil didn't you go where I told you."

"They're Spanish style," he said.

"They're not Spanish style," I told him. "Haven't I seen pictures of Spanish bullfighters and the clothes on them as tight to the skin as bedamned."

"I wish you wouldn't be coarse, Don Kerry," he said.

"Come here," I said, "come here 'til I be after looking at the name on that suit." But he backed into a corner. James Carabine stood by, uneasy.

"Come here." I reached out for his collar, and at that moment I received as vicious a kick on the shin as ever I got. Automatically I started a punch jawwards, but James Carabine caught my wrist.

"Sure, he's only a delicate child, Mister Kerry."

"He's got the kick of a mule," I growled.

Young Anthony was standing before me, white, very white.

"I am sorry, Don Kerry," he said, "sorry for kicking you, for, first, it isn't a thing an Irishman does. Secondly, because it hurt you, for it must have hurt you, because I kick hard. But I can't stand anybody touching the back of my neck, it tickles so. I am sorry I hurt you, Don Kerry."

As he stood there, the tears began to jet out of his eyes. It was so funny I could n't help laughing. I roared.

" Now, I 'm not sorry at all," he snapped. " Damn you! " And he walked past me out of the room.

" He 's a queer one, that! " I said.

" Ah, queerer nor your Honour thinks," said James Carabine.

X

From the first day young Anthony saw my cousin Jenico, he conceived for him that hero worship of a boy which is more devoted, or seems more devoted, than the love of women. When Jenico was in a room in Destiny Bay, and young Anthony there too, the Spaniard's grey eyes never left him. My cousin Jenico could talk a lot of nonsense, as wanting university extension lectures for artisans, or teaching sanitation in Connemara. If there 's anything an artisan wants after a hard day's work, it 's a game of spoil five and a pot of porter, and in Connemara they 'd prefer a dose of strychnine to an open window, it kills more quickly. But then Jenico was a great reader of books — But young Anthony would listen to all this blether as though it were Holy Writ.

He was full of questions about Jenico. Had n't I known Jenico from childhood? and was n't it queer that he had never fallen in love? or had he?

" Well, to tell you the truth," I informed him, " Jenico 's a queer bird. If he were walking with the Queen of Sheba on a moonlight night, if you can imagine that, and not a human being, or a policeman itself, within an ass's bawl of them, it would never occur to Jenico to kick the feet from under her and give her a roll in the heather. No, bedad! " I laughed, " he 'd talk to her about the amelioration of living conditions for the lower classes."

" Don Kerry," he looked at me, " you 're a horrible fellow." He wrinkled his nose. "Still, in the society of old selling-platers like your Pretty Molly Brannagan, you're not encouraged to be formal."

"Do you see James Carabine there?" I said. "Do you see his left ear?"

Carabine bore the stigmata of the ring in the shape of a left ear whose cartilage had been battered to the shape known to the "fancy" as "tin."

"Well," I said, "I'm going to give you a present of one of those."

"Don Kerry, you wouldn't," he said, frightened.

"Wouldn't he? And hasn't he?" laughed James Carabine. "'Tis himself has the gift, from six inches away and twisting the knuckle as he hits, pretty as drawing a duck's neck."

It was a long time before he mentioned Molly Brannagan to me again.

After dinner when Jenico was with us, Anthony had a habit of taking out one of Jenico's books and reading it, lifting his head at every paragraph to look at Jenico. It made Jenico quite uncomfortable, you could see that from the way Jenico squirmed and got red.

"'These two consummate Armenian scoundrels,'" young Anthony read aloud, "'both the elder and the younger, having conceived the nefarious project of annihilating me in hope of pecuniary gain—'"

"'In hope of pecuniary gain,'" I repeated. "Go on. God's Truth! Anthony, 'tis elegant."

"'—chose the fourth of March to bring their scheme to fruition. Observing the former advancing on me in the shadows with a raised hatchet, I had, to my infinite regret, no option but to pistol him, whereupon the latter, reaching for a rifle, forced me to do likewise. This occurrence left me, for an appreciable period, in great perturbation of mind.' I don't quite understand, Don Jenico."

"This is what he means in English," I translated. "There were two bloody ruffians, an old one and a young one, who tried to do Jenico in, but he got there first."

"What I can't understand," said my uncle Valentine, "is the perturbation of mind."

"Brother Valentine," said my aunt Jenepher, "even people as far away as Armenia are men and women."

"Hut, woman!" said my uncle Valentine; "what damned nonsense! Male and female, yes. But men and women," said my uncle Valentine, "are confined to the Anglo-Saxon race, the Scots-Irish and the Norman-Irish. Some Scottish I will admit, but the Welsh people I cannot in all conscience give the name of men and women to. Derivatives of these ancient races, such as are domiciled in America, in Australia and New Zealand, are also entitled to this noble appellation."

My uncle Valentine laid down his fine Manila cheroot and attacked the subject seriously.

"The people of such countries as have fought valorously against us at various times, such as Spain," and he bowed to Don Anthony, and Don Anthony bowed to him, "are denoted as inhabitants, as the inhabitants of France and the inhabitants of Spain. Other countries in Europe have merely natives. It is correct to say: the natives of Portugal and the natives of Italy.

"Outside of Europe the wide term of aborigine suffices, as the aborigines of Persia, the aborigines of Africa. With one exception — we speak of the inhabitants of China, because of that country's advancement in art, science and letters.

"It is also to be noted," said my uncle Valentine, "that one country has a special term for itself. We speak of the denizens of Russia. So that —" my uncle Valentine counted them on his fingers — "the population of the globe is divided into five classes — men and women, inhabitants, natives, aborigines, and denizens."

"And where," asked James Carabine, "and where would your Honour place the gypsies?"

My uncle Valentine resumed his cheroot and thought for nearly a minute by the clock. "The gypsy race," he decided pontifically, "the gypsy race, James Carabine, is a growth!"

I have never known a man so various as my uncle Valentine, a man who so nearly approached Confucius' ideal of the Superior Man. The least bit inaccurate at times, but when you cover so wide a range —

It was extraordinary how quietly and how fully the young Spaniard lad had slipped into a place in our Irish life. He had, of course we knew, been brought up in some vague preparatory school in the South of England, but the South of England is not the North of Ireland by a long shot. However, it gave him a grip of the English tongue. It was extraordinary also how quickly he had captured the affection of the household, for we like our men and boys in Ireland to be markedly masculine, and that was just what young Anthony was not. For a boy there was an immense beauty in his face; with his longish hair and honey-brown eyes and girl's mouth he was like a singing boy in cathedral — it only needed surplice and cassock to complete the illusion. But he liked horses, and he was game to the core. I've noticed him time and again white with fatigue when Jenico and I were tramping the mountain streams after trout or along the river for a salmon. But he wouldn't give in. In the end we'd have to commandeer a horse and saddle from a farmhouse and send him off. He'd get up quick enough when we threatened to lift him. None could put a finger on him but my aunt Jenepher or my uncle Valentine. He'd plead to be let stay.

"But I'm not tired, Kerry."

"Go on home," and I'd catch the horse a clout on the croup with the butt end of the fishing rod.

"Damn you, Kerry MacFarlane!"

"Go on home t' hell out of that!"

At home in the drawing-room of Destiny Bay, when the lamps were lit and the peat fire gave out its crimson and gold, then that sort of calm happiness that is like a dream would come over him. And he would talk while my uncle Valentine would listen with his vast kindly courtesy, and my aunt Jenepher would sit at her great piano playing very softly some melody that had come to her, out of an old song and the singing of the birds. And I would be thinking of the winter coming and the great runs we'd have after the fox, picking out a line for myself across country, and flying the jumps like a bird. Ah, the quiet of Destiny Bay!

"Dear Sir Valentine," young Anthony said, "when this little estate of mine is settled, do you think I could buy a small place near here, and fish in the summer and hunt in the winter, and be near you and aunt Jenepher and Don Jenico, and even Kerry, and not forgetting James Carabine," he smiled, for James Carabine had just brought the coffee in for us.

"God bless your young Honour!" said James Carabine, with the bow of a Spanish grandee.

"Most of my early days were spent in England, and in Spain I have few friends, and you know, sir, how hard it would be for me to live there—"

"How would it be hard?" I asked.

"It's a secret, Kerry," said my aunt Jenepher, "that you'll know soon."

"I think it could be managed," said my uncle Valentine.

"I doubt it," said I. For I knew there wasn't an acre of land to be bought for love or money around Destiny Bay.

"Did you ever see a thing I couldn't manage?" said my uncle Valentine.

Many's the one, but I knew better than to say it. If anything my uncle Valentine undertakes falls through, he just tells us it's the Will of God. He is just simply stopped in the affair but retains full honours as though successful. Anything I undertake and fail in is due to my own damned stupidity. Thus my uncle Valentine.

We were going to have a little trouble on this account, I could foresee. I know when a thing is just an idea in a person's mind, and when his heart is set on it. And young Anthony was becoming rapidly Irished, which is a deadly disease for foreigners. He had got to the point of singing "Believe me, if all these endearing young charms", and when a stranger gets that far in Ireland, his fellow country-men can take a long sad farewell of him, for the land of his birth will know him no more.

He had a niceish voice, like a contralto's, and he would sing it while my aunt Jenepher played it on the piano.

> "Oh, the heart that has truly loved never forgets,
> But as truly loves on to the close,
> As the sunflower turns to her God when he sets,
> The same look that she gave when he rose."

"Any nation that sings that song is a true-hearted beautiful nation."

"But that song's all my eye and Betty Martin," I told him. "Every Irishman knows that. The man that wrote it knew it. If there's one thing the Irish nation is noted for, it's inconstancy. Still and all," I observed, "that song does the trick. If any poor Irishman wants a rich English wife to take care of him, that song and a romantic look, which is the result of two days' starvation, will act like a charm."

"Don Kerry," said the young 'un, "you become more and more a horrible fellow. Also, I don't believe you."

It was about this time that a strange thing happened, and that was repeated every time the young 'un went to Jenico's house. We three had gone in for lunch, and it suddenly occurred to me that the house seemed gallant and gay for

the first time I had known it. The shadow of the surly
Spanish Men had lifted, and I remembered that the old
name that was on the place, in Irish, before it got its name
of Spanish Men's Rest, was *Greenawn Anaraga,* " the sunny
place by the sea." We went out into the garden, and I
heard birds singing, and the droning of bees.

" Jenico," I said, " do you hear that?"

" It 's not possible," he said. " I hear it, but it seems
impossible."

" But it 's only birds singing and the humming of bees,"
said the Spanish boy.

" Yes, only that," said Jenico.

XI

My cousin Jenico was always a solitary sort of bird.
Men deferred to him, because of his wealth, because of his
travels, because of the shadow on his face. Women were
a little afraid of him, very flattered by his notice, but that
elaborate courtesy of his, which was colder and more formal
than my uncle Valentine's, was like a walled city about him.
He hunted well, he went to race meets and betted shrewdly,
he kept a nice small stable of his own. But whether he did
these things because he liked them, or because they were
the proper thing to do in Ireland, I could n't quite make out.
Something of each, I think.

My cousin Jenico was this sort of bird: I shall illustrate.
The most important week in Ireland is the week of the
Dublin Horse Show. The best hunters, the best draught
horses, and the nippiest harness ponies in the world are on
show. At Leopardstown there is the best flat-racing of the
season. Grafton Street becomes a garden of girls. There
are more marriages made in Dublin that week than in the
rest of the country all the year round. If you were to mix
the height of the season in London with the gaiety of Paris

and the smartness of Vienna you might come to an idea a little short of Dublin in Horse Show Week. In fine, I doubt if Venice in all its glory came up to the Dublin Horse Show.

To Dublin for that week, the English send their best theatrical companies over to be properly appreciated. And parties were made up to go there. My cousin Jenico would go to the races, go to the grounds at Ballsbridge. But when it came to the evening, and you told him, "Now we'll have dinner at Jammet's, and will take the Brabazon girls, and Lady Brannagan, and go to the Gaiety—" he'd say no; he thought he'd drop around to the Kildare Street Club, which is a quiet sub-branch of the British Museum, and have a chop, and a rubber of bridge. A chop, and a rubber of bridge, when he could be dining in the company of Pretty Molly Brannagan, with all her beauty and wit! But there was my cousin Jenico for you. As a matter of fact, to bring him into a gay gathering would be like walking up behind a man dancing a jig and landing him a tremendous and most vulgar kick. Not that my cousin Jenico was a hermit. After the theatre or ball you could go to his rooms and have a drink and sit there until three in the morning while he talked about the Near East and drew startling analogies between the Druses of Lebanon and the Ancient Order of Hibernians, tracing each backward through masonic channels to a common parentage in the Old Man of the Mountains and his assassins of Crusade times. He'd have you nearly convinced until you went out into the fresh air, and told yourself, "Be damned to that for a story! Sure them things just grow."

It was very strange how quickly Jenico took to the Spanish lad. The Spanish lad could be very serious when he wanted to be, and at other times he could be merry as a cricket. Mercurial, you might say. You wouldn't think Jenico would take to a boy of eighteen at all. But one day he surprised me.

"I'm thinking of cutting out," he said, "and digging off for the Atlas Mountains for a while. Good hunting and what not. You'd better trot along," he told young Anthony; "get your mind off things and what not. See the world. Lawyers can settle up things while you're away. Share my tent. What?"

"Go alone with you and share your tent!" said young Anthony, and he gave Jenico a look as if Jenico had suggested their breaking open a child's bank. But Jenico wasn't looking.

"Why not?" said Jenico. "You won't be in the way."

Young Anthony gave that silvery laugh of his, like a girl's. "I couldn't, Don Jenico," he said. "I'd like to, but I couldn't."

"Why couldn't you?" I asked. "Are you afraid?"

"I am not afraid," and he gave me his dirty Spanish look. "Don Kerry, you are a most horrible fellow. At any rate, I should not be afraid of anything with Don Jenico there."

"Why don't you go?"

"There are reasons, Kerry. Don Jenico, do you mind if I don't go. I think it's a great compliment from you to ask me, and I should like nothing better than to go with you, but I can't."

"I don't see what reasons keep you from a good hunting trip," I said.

"Suit yourself, nipper," said Jenico; "if you change your mind come and tell me."

A few days later, we were going up to Anaglass, "the Grey River" in English, on something to do with the carrying away of the weir, or part of it. It was a golden late summer day, and young Anthony had turned up to come with us.

"Can you swim?" I asked him.

"Like a fish," he told me.

"My sound man!"

When I speak of Grey River, I would not have you bring to your mind anything like the grey, scrofulous, crapulous look of Anna Liffey from Guinness' porter house to the sea. " Glas ", in the Erse language, means both grey and green, and Grey River has that wonderful colour of grey, deep, transparent, that the grey eye of a woman has. The deep blue of the sea and the wonderful transparency of mountain streams mingle to give it that shade of colour, and beneath all are the golden sands. It starts on Slievemore and comes down gently to us, pausing at the Old Bridge to turn Jonathan Armstrong's mill where the countryside has its oats converted into meal, and at the Irish Village to give Jimsy Johnson a chance to scutch the flax. For the mile downward from the last weir, it is a dream of beauty. On one side is a heathery brae, purple but for the white scuts of the rabbits as they play around their burrows. On the other is a stretch of wood, hazel, heavy with leaf and nut, and small sturdy oaks. In spring the bank is a long cloud of primroses and in the woods the blue foam of harebells. At low water there is a ford for carts across the river and everywhere are pools where, on the going out of the tide, slow crabs and small fishes are caught, and once in a pool there I have seen a little octopus brought hither by some vagary of the West Atlantic Drift. The tide will be out, and suddenly you will hear a humming at the bar and the green water will begin to rush in as in a mill race. When high water is there you can see the small head of the sleek brown seal in the water, and from a boat you can see the ponderous eels back from their parliament in the Sargasso Sea, and the dart of the large sea trout.

There is no mile of water in the world so sweet as Grey River and the tide in. The unbelievable purple of the heather on one side, on the other the green woods where the finches are ever singing, and the grey water, grey of a girl's eye, cut into tiny ripples and furrows by the currents, the sand soft as feathers. There is a legend that here once was a city where the men of Erin mated with the daughters of the sea, and that Mananan MacLear, the Celtic Neptune, fearing that his kingdom was in danger, flung the vast sea bed over the city one night of titanic storm. We don't quite believe that but we don't actually disbelieve it. Certainly there is an air of sweet melancholy about the place that speaks of some splendid thing prostrated. A professorman with a goat's beard and steel spectacles once came to Destiny Bay, to persuade my uncle Valentine to let him dig for kitchen middens, trying to persuade us that our ancestors were a hairy sort of animal who went in for three-day dinners of shellfish on the strand, when we know them to have been accomplished cultured gentlemen, with a civilisation surpassing the Egyptian. My uncle Valentine had the man certified as a common lunatic by the local doctors and shut up in Omagh Asylum. His thin acidulous daughter and his university had the devil and all of a time to get him discharged. He may still be uttering his foul propaganda, but not in Destiny Bay.

My cousin Jenico had gone ahead of the young one and myself over the heather brae, for I was having a bit of an argument with the nipper, trying to wean him from the "Wearing of the Green" and "Believe me, if all — " by teaching him that noble anthem, the "Boyne Water." One of all my uncle Valentine's red setters, magnificent and red as his own beard, came up and stuck his muzzle into my palm, so that I knew my uncle was in the offing, as the sailors say.

"Come on, now. You know the tune. Out with the words.

'So praise God, all true Protestants, and I will say no further,
But had the Irish gained the day there would have been open
    murder.
Although King James and many more — '"

"But I am not a Protestant, Kerry. I am a Spanish. There are no Protestants in Spain."

"So that's what's wrong with it, eh?"

"Don Kerry, you are a most horrible fellow, and I will not sing that song." We went down toward the water. "Who gave Father Malachi twenty guineas for the starving families of Inishowen?"

"Who told you that?"

"I know."

"Well, I gave it so that they might eat themselves to death, if you want to know."

I saw Jenico's clothes in a heap farther down the brae and in midstream noticed his head, sleek as a seal's. I pulled off my shooting jacket, and began to unbutton my shirt.

"Off with your duds, my lad. We'll see what sort of a swimmer you are."

"Don Kerry, you are surely not going to undress."

I pulled my shirt over my head. "So are you," I said.

"Oh, Don Kerry, please don't take your clothes off."

"What the hell do you think I am going to do? Go in with them on?"

"Come on, Kerry," shouted Jenico. "What's keeping you?"

"It's the nipper," I said, "making the usual row."

"Pull his blasted trousers off," shouted Jenico, "and chuck him in."

"Righto!"

I walked toward the boy, and he looked very white. And suddenly he had a large knife in his hand.

"Look," he said, "if you touch me, I stick that, I stick that in your belly."

I said, "I don't mind your crying. I don't mind the kick in the shins. But when you start Dago tricks with a knife, then you're going to be punished. I'm going to take your clothes off, and then hold you by neck and heels under water until you 're half choked." I went for him.

"Mother of God!" he gave tongue like a hound, and slipped past me through the heather.

And as I turned to go after him, there stood my uncle Valentine. He put his arm around the boy. The boy nestled into his red beard.

"What is it, my dotey lamb?" crooned my uncle Valentine. "What were the dirty Irish ruffians up to?"

"They were trying to pull my clothes off."

"Gentlemen," said my uncle Valentine to me, and to Jenico who was treading water, "there was a time when a lady could be trusted among Irishmen without fear of insult. Even in the most perilous epoch of our history, a woman could travel alone from Galway to Dublin. 'Rich and rare,' writes Thomas Moore, 'were the gems she wore' — "

I looked around for Jenico, but Jenico was sprinting seaward, his heels churning the water like the propeller of a boat.

"Cinders of hell!" roared my uncle Valentine, "if you and Jenico want this foul mixed bathing, why don't you go to Margate, where you can poke barmaids in the ribs. Look at yourself, Kerry MacFarlane! Look at yourself."

And he went off up the brae with the nipper along with him, while I stood there stripped to the waist, holding my shirt by its tails. A rabbit that had poked its head over the heather — even the rabbit made gestures of repulsion with its nose.

XII

The long twilight of the lateish summer was in it, not the crisp steel-like atmosphere of autumn, but a haze, a mellowness. Though far off, one could think of October, the reddening apple, the browning nut. It was like a magic in

Destiny Bay, as though here were the resting place of the Earth Spirit, breathing easily in its sleep. Behind the trees, the apple trees, the elms, the horse chestnuts, and the flaming copper beeches, the smoke rose from the chimneys of our house in slender blue columns. The linnets were twittering their evensong, and the shrill exclaiming swallows in groups of five or six darted through the orchard. Over the ancient turf through the ancient trees walked a slim whiteness, a slim vital whiteness unknown to me, and that for a minute I took to be possibly some phantasm of the dead, some lady of the MacFarlanes come in the twilight to revisit the antique house of happiness, and lest something should be lacking to my kinswoman, I went forward, my heart going so fast that I knew I was afraid, and cursed myself for it, for there is nothing so discourteous toward the dead as fear. But it was no phantasm, it was most vital. There in a frock of white muslin decorated with gold embroidery in the Lyons fashion was the one we were accustomed to call Don Anthony.

I must have gaped, for with the change of clothes had come a change of face and spirit that was extraordinary. You would have thought that one who had seemed effeminate in a boy's garments would have looked boyish in a girl's. But no! There was a slim vitality like a birch tree's. That was all. Her hair, which I could see now was not red but copper-coloured like the copper beech, was a frame for her sweet grave face, her calm virginal hazel eyes. One would not notice it was short, unless you saw the back of the slim strong neck. It might have been some cunning way of doing it. There was something proud and lovely about her, like a fine two-year in the saddling enclosure waiting to go to the tapes.

"My God!" I said. "Amn't I the fool of the world?"

"Yes, Kerry," she smiled.

"And who might you be?" I asked.

"I might be the Queen of Sheba, or Queen Victoria herself, but it happens that I'm Antonia Dorotea Sophia Eugenia Maria del Lamen de Leyva, Duchess of la Mentera, and Countess of Monreal del Compo," she said, "if it please your Honour!" And she curtsied.

"That's a lot, isn't it?"

"I'm usually called Ann-Dolly. I'd like you to call me that too, Kerry — Ann-Dolly."

"Look here," I said. "I don't get the hang of this at all. Are you sure you're a female woman?"

"Of course," she said. "I don't come up to the shape of your friend Pretty Molly Brannagan, the barmaid's bust, and —"

"That'll do," said I. "Listen, when you were a boy, you told me you learned English at school in England. Now where are you?"

"I learned English at a convent, Roehampton to be exact. Kerry, I do believe you think I'm some sort of adventuress. You think I'm lying."

"Well," I said, "I don't think you're an adventuress, but as to lying, didn't you come here in a boy's clothes, and live here in a boy's clothes. If that's not lying," said I, "I don't know what is."

"Kerry dear," she said patiently, "when my grandfather, the old duke, took to wandering in his head and wandering in his feet, I had to come along with him, and when I tell you we were poor you don't understand, for a poor person to you is a barefoot person with a shawl. But, Kerry, a shabby young woman can go as a young man with a day suit and a dinner coat, and stay at small hotels, and not have a lot of fuss and expense."

"I never thought of that."

"And perhaps that's not exactly the real reason, Kerry. But a lad in the world, defenceless and poor, can get through, but a girl is another matter. Also, if you are a penniless princess, you have more trouble than if you were a girl of the people, for every cheap wealthy man bothers you, and even your own people, your own caste, if you are pretty, have less mercy than on a midinette. Kerry, if I were in Spain or France, alone, and had changed from boy's into girl's clothes, and some one had come into the garden, as you have come, do you think they'd have asked me who I was, and called me a liar?"

"Why not?"

"Dear Kerry, you are wrong. They'd have called me beautiful and kissed my hand, and tried boldly to hold it, and overwhelmed me with sickly oversweet compliments. When you have a father and brothers, or money in the bank, it's very different."

"Well," said I, "you won't be overwhelmed with compliments here, though I suppose in your way, now that I come to look at you, you're quite good-looking—"

"Quite good-looking! I'm the most lovely person you've ever seen."

"My girl," I told her, "if you're going to change your clothes, you'd better change your attitude. It doesn't strike me as being particularly ladylike."

My uncle Valentine came down the garden. "Well, Ann-Dolly?"

"I was just going to tell Kerry, sir—"

"Tell him nothing," broke in my uncle Valentine. "Tell him to go to hell!"

"That was what I was going to tell him, sir," said Ann-Dolly.

To me she was just a new lovely phenomenon like some April evening, the downy breast of spring. She was like a river singing among willows, where kingfishers skim. She was there, and you thanked God she was, as you thanked God for a fine day, and then went on your way, taking it for granted. The queer thing to me was this: that it seemed as if she had been always in Destiny Bay, like the great copper beech trees, and the hierarchy of bees. Also it seemed as if she were n't to leave Destiny Bay, for my uncle Valentine tossed me a bundle of papers from our solicitors, and I could see it dealt with the ducal estate.

"It comes to about a hundred pounds a year," I worked it out.

"There or thereabouts," said my uncle Valentine.

"Sure she can't live on that," I said.

"No," said my uncle Valentine. "Well, what are you going to do?"

"She 'd better stay here."

"But how?" said my uncle Valentine. "Can't you see, you poor mick, that it is n't fair to give her charity, and that she 's too proud to take it. You 'll have to regularise it, Kerry."

"We 'll give her a job of work."

"Grooming the horses, maybe," sneered my uncle Valentine.

"No," said I, "grooming my aunt Jenepher, not grooming, training; what the devil is the word? Companion. Companion to my aunt Jenepher."

My uncle Valentine rose, as was his custom when profoundly moved. He shook hands silently with me. He slapped me on the back — something like being hit with a sledge hammer.

"My sweet fellow, Kerry! By damn! But my sound man!"

So Ann-Dolly was made happy in Destiny Bay. She felt she had a standing in the house, and worried no more about money. The sweet gravity of my aunt Jenepher was set off by her merriment. To see her in the garden fighting with Duncan for flowers was a sight. Also you might come on her standing in the stableyard, her hands in the pockets of a shooting jacket, discussing the form of horses with

James Carabine. At evening, though, she became once more the young princess out of Grimm's tales, soft auburn head and eyes of wonder. I couldn't find much fault with her now for singing "Believe me, if all — " It isn't a song for a man, that, but it's a grand song for a woman, women being so optimistic.

I had wondered what Jenico would make of the metamorphosis, how he would act, what he would say. It's a funny thing, but I could always trust cousin Jenico to be more gentlemanly than myself. When it comes to the stud book, I can give Jenico a stone and beat him by five lengths in as many furlongs, for I am MacFarlane of Destiny Bay through and through. My mother was a De Vesci, and her mother a Beauford of Athy, whereas Jenico is a Grant, nice Scottish gentry to be sure, but that's all. His mother was a MacFarlane out of O'Donnell, aboriginal Irish. I'm better bred, if there's anything in that, but Jenico, on occasions of ceremony, makes me look like the village gawk. Jenico is never rude, as I am. He is courteously aloof. Of course Jenico is never genteel, but then he takes no pains to show he isn't, such as making a healthy racket in the feeding trough. We both do the right thing, I hope, but Jenico does it nicely.

So I was keen to see the finished courtesy, the man-of-the-worldliness Jenico would exhibit when introduced to Ann-Dolly. After all to meet formally for the first time the young duchess, from whom, a few days before, you were urging to have the trousers removed, is a sporting event. I settled down in a good ring-side seat.

He greeted her with a nice formality, said it must be a relief to assume her wonted attire — "wonted attire" I felt to be a good horse! And then he asked her if she thought the weather would hold.

She seemed just as awkward in meeting him as he in meeting her. A funny thing, but they looked at each other in a strained sort of way, and looked away from each other. And then Ann-Dolly, nearly white in the face, said she thought the weather would hold, and Jenico said he hoped so. And there the conversation languished.

All through the evening when she was not looking at him, he was looking at her, and when he was not looking at her, she was looking at him. There was a dog beginning to be fashionable then, a dog called the Belgian Police Hound, that was neither Belgian nor police nor hound, but the German sheep dog, which is neither a good sheep dog, compared to ours, or a good companion, and I was speaking of him. Jenico hung on my words. I might have been the Sibyl at Cumae, from the attention he gave me. At last he went. In the hall I found Ann-Dolly, her eyes bright with rage.

"Kerry," she said, "your cousin Jenico's a damned fool."

"He's the world's greatest idiot, Ann-Dolly. Sure, the whole countryside knows that. Sure, you ought to have known that before. Didn't you read his books?"

"Kerry," she said, "when I called Jenico a fool—"

"A damned fool you called him."

"Well, a damned fool, then—I meant I was a bit sick of him, just that—"

"At times, Ann-Dolly, he nauseates me too."

"Kerry, you're a filthy brute. Good night."

XIII

My uncle Valentine, spick and span as a bridegroom, leaned across the breakfast table with concern upon his tanned brow. He held an imposing looking banker's draft in his hand, a huge green cheque with black embossed lettering. But for what amount it was drawn I couldn't tell. Those things are deceptive. It might have been for twopence.

"I wonder," said I to myself, with memories of the barn-stormers in my mind, "if it's a thing that the old homestead's gone."

"The English," said my uncle Valentine, "the English, Kerry, I regret to find, are an inconceivably drunken nation."

"I hadn't noticed, sir. I thought they were never particularly intemperate. Rather a sound crowd."

"That's the worst of it, Kerry. They are secret drinkers. A nation of secret drinkers. I have before me," said my uncle Valentine, "a dividend cheque from Jenico's brewery. The profits on this investment are so large as to be immoral. The amount of beer that company brews and disposes of is incredible." My uncle Valentine shook his head. "It's the end of the Empire," said my uncle Valentine.

"But why should it be drunk in England?" I asked.

"Where else is there to drink it? The Frenchman consumes wine. A Frenchman drinking beer in public would be hanged by a patriotic crowd to the nearest lamp-post as a British spy. Germans drink a sweet beverage which they call beer, but it is of exclusively German manufacture. Russians I grant to be never sober, but they are drunk on vodka. Italians consume quantities of rough wine. As to Spain— Do they drink beer in Spain, Ann-Dolly?"

"I don't know," said Ann-Dolly. "What is beer?"

Behind me I could hear James Carabine stop in his buttling, and draw in his breath hissingly, as a man does when hit in a vital spot. For myself I just let my head fall on my chest, and I groaned.

"The very name of beer," said my uncle Valentine, "is unknown to Spain, and probably to Portugal too. In America the wine of the country is rye whiskey. Swedes, Danes, Finns are addicted to schnapps, whereas the adipose Hollanders' only beverage is gin. The Mohammedans are teetotallers, whence the various tribal troubles in Afghanistan and Egypt — "

" But in Ireland, sir? "

" In Ireland whiskey is drunk. When whiskey is not drunk, porter is. Stout and whiskey. Baptists drink water."

" But I 've seen beer drunk in Ireland, sir."

" Oh, yes, Kerry," granted my uncle Valentine, " you have seen beer drunk as a phenomenon, but you have never seen beer drunk as a drink."

Well, damn it! You can't argue with a man like that!

The truth of the matter was that my cousin Jenico was becoming most putridly rich, though riches were ascribed to him that were n't his at all. A week before I had been down to Strabane, and an old lawyer, Alec Cornish, had mentioned to me a legacy of fifty thousand pounds that was coming to Jenico.

" Begor, Mr. Kerry, but some people have the luck of the world! "

" Where is the money coming from? I 've heard nothing of it."

" 'Tis from a cousin of his father's, a Grant that went to America, and from whom nothing was ever heard. He died with his money, and your cousin Jenico is next of kin."

" Thanks for telling me, Cornish. I 'm going to get it out of him."

There are queer spots in Ireland, queer, dark, unhealthy spots, and I don't mean unhealthy in a physical sense, but in a mental, or spiritual one — I don't know exactly how to describe it. But one of these places is a large island called Tonamora, " great waves " in the English language. Tonamora is about ten miles square, very fertile. People say that the Tonamora men are Spaniards, descendants of the survivors of the great Armada, but that to my mind, and I know Ireland as well as any man, is sheer rot. They are tall, spare, leather-faced men, with a taciturn temperament, and cold slate-green eyes. The rare fishery inspector or policeman who lands there is told by them that they speak no English. That is a lie. Whence they came God only knows. They are as much at home on the sea as an ordinary farmer on dry land. A Tonamora man can always find a billet as boatswain or quartermaster on no matter how big a ship. They see the world. They come back to Tonamora.

The race — Egyptian, Barbary Corsair, Sidonian, God knows what — has a diabolical vitality. When new blood is wanted girls are stolen from the mainland. After a week, when they are discovered, they don't wish to go back. The Tonamora man will marry them. He'll stand with a sneer in his eyes while Father Malachi marries them.

Father Malachi goes to Tonamora once a month in a curragh to celebrate his liturgy there. Father Malachi is a saint, and a gentleman. But for days after his monthly visit, he is white and shaken. They listen to him with an aloof courtesy and that dreadful sneer in their eyes while he tells them about Calvary and One who took on Himself the sins of the world. And when Father Malachi has gone, they take from its hiding place the " Neevogg ", the Sacred One, and put it in its niche in the living rock, on the ocean side of the island, and to it they sacrifice a goat. And they may sacrifice worse than a goat to it, for within a dozen years a dozen children have been missing from the mainland. A revenue officer who had landed in secrecy and lay in hiding says it is the figurehead of an ancient ship, a black man, with a crown on his head. Myself, from a sloop, with glasses, have seen the Tonamora folk dance in a ring on the strand, naked, around something on Midsummer Eve.

Well, if any man wishes to deny God, it's his own business, so long as he doesn't kick up a fuss about it. But putting up an image and sacrificing to it is another thing. There are too many demons going about the world looking for homes. There's many a one will deny a God, but there's no man, who has seen anything of the world, will deny a Devil.

I want to see Tonamora bought into the family from the English landlord, who knows nothing about it, wouldn't believe it if he were told, and probably doesn't even know where the place is. I want to see us bring our private clergyman there; whether he is a priest of the Coptic rite, or a Seventh Day Adventist, it doesn't matter. I want to see the Neevogg burned. I want every death, every marriage accounted for. I want two policemen, even though private policemen of our own, there. I'm not so sure that I don't want a triangle and a cat too. There's a good deal to be said for feudalism. Modern law supposes that the power of darkness has been wiped out of material strongholds these hundreds of years. They haven't.

I tackled Jenico immediately.

"What's this I hear about fifty thousand pounds?"

"Hey?" said Jenico, startled.

"I hear you've been left fifty thousand by a relative of your dad's. Listen, Jenico. I want you to buy Tonamora."

"Tonamora!"

"Yes, Tonamora. Neither the landlord nor the Government will do anything about it. I think we ought to handle it ourselves. We can beat civilisation and decency into those wild skulls. What do you think, Jenico?"

"I think it would be splendid."

"Well, buy it."

He hummed and hawed a bit; walked around; looked uncomfortable.

"The truth is, Kerry —" he began.

"What?"

"Haven't got a legacy."

"Haven't —?"

"No. It's a mistake."

"Damn! Well, if you haven't, you can't." But I decided the next time I met John Cornish there'd be a row. I hate to have my hopes raised and then dashed to the ground again. Also I could see Jenico was disappointed. He seemed so put about.

He kept on visiting us every night at Destiny Bay, though what pleasure it was to him I cannot understand. There he sat, dumb as a fish, looking at Ann-Dolly as though she were some weird exhibit. There was Ann-Dolly looking at him when he wasn't looking at her. There was a constraint between them. One night I saw him on his way home "past the gander", as we say, a bit of the lane. He asked what Carrickore meant, the big rock with a cave in it near Spanish Men's Rest.

"It means Golden Rock."

"Would it have anything to do with the Armada treasure, Kerry?"

"Nothing," I said. "It comes from the look of the rock when the sun shines on it, the quartz in it and the sands about it. When the sun is setting from certain angles it looks like a mass of gold."

"That seems to me very fanciful, Kerry," he argued, for he would argue — that was the Scottish in him. "What with the legend of gold and the cavern and what not —"

"Listen, Jenico. If gold had been found there, they'd call it the Gold Rock. They wouldn't call it Golden Rock if treasure were to be found there. It's a question of experience."

"I see your point," conceded Jenico. "Still and all —"

The next night, when he was over, I mentioned it.

"Jenico thinks," I said, "that treasure might possibly be found at Carrickore."

"Hut," said my uncle Valentine, "the man's daft."

"Oh, no," I thought that was going too far; "just soft like."

"What I meant was," Jenico reddened, "it would be a pleasant idea. If money were there, it would be, of course, a jolly nice surprise for, ah, Ann-Dolly—"

Ann-Dolly worked herself up suddenly into a temper most beautiful to see.

"Ah, Ann-Dolly," she mimicked, "doesn't want any Spanish treasure. Ah, Ann-Dolly is quite content as she is. If Sir Valentine and Aunt Jenepher will let her stay with them forever, ah, Ann-Dolly will be quite happy, for outside them, ah, Ann-Dolly doesn't give a tinker's damn for any one. Except Kerry, whom I like a little, and James Carabine, whom I like very much, the rest," said Ann-Dolly, "can go to hell!" And she swept out of the room like some slim young Amazon.

We laughed. My uncle Valentine gave that great roar of his, that is like a Bull of Bashan's, and I contributed my own full belling note. Even my aunt Jenepher, who is ever smiling, but laughs rarely, gave her precious silver trill. But Jenico was silent, distressed, as though he didn't understand it at all. But then Jenico could be a glum blighter when the mood was on him.

"Now who the devil," said my uncle Valentine, wiping his eyes, "has been teaching that young woman the Irish language?"

XIV

Autumn had come to us like some grave tanned traveller. A hush: the flutter of a leaf: the purple departing from the heather. The Michaelmas daisies showed up gallantly, and the geese were wondering why every one was paying so much attention to them and increasing their rations. The full moon of October rose in the Irish sky, so vast, so near, that you could shut your eyes and think: a few steps, a hell of a jump, and I can catch the rim of it, and swing through it into that country of which Grimm tells tales. There is such magic in the October moon. It glints over the sea and makes a floor of gold there. The cliffs are vaguely blue in it, and the shore becomes a silver street, and what the mountains are dreaming of is past imagining. The trees of Destiny Bay in the moonlight throw a marvellous pattern on the grass: the lacework of the apple and pear trees, the vast mushroom the copper beech makes, the shifting of the shadows of the elm trees as the wind moves them. And there is the mysterious alley of the yews, where as likely as not you will meet our Georgian Gentleman, in knee breeches and tri-cornered hat, under the October moon. You can lean against the bole of our copper beech in that month's moon, and your soul will go out of you when you close your eyes, and learn high courageous things from the mountains, which words are not equal to.

The October moon had wrought its sweet magic on Ann-Dolly, so that she could not remain out of the apple garden. My uncle Valentine had gone to Derry on some business of the Grand Jury, and Jenico had walked over from Spanish Men's Rest, so that she brought him into the garden of the silver trees. Myself, it is a great hardship on me that I have little time for the October moon. At summer's end there is the big activity of harvest, and it is a tradition of ours to look after our farming interests ourselves — if you want kindliness out of the earth you must give it kindliness. There was the skilful stacking of corn to be looked to, the steeping and drying of the flax, the potatoes for next year's seeding to be built carefully into their bins, the cottages of the Irish Village to be examined lest they need thatching against the coming winter. Even the humble mangel-wurzel has intricacies of culture. There were a thousand things and one thing. So this October night I spent at accounts in the gunroom, with the red setters before the red turf fire. When the work was finished I stayed there, thinking of the winter coming when all would be holiday. Fox hunting, the roads like iron, the sally hedges rising out of the mist, and riding home in the evening with a moon like a steel mirror in the sky. The steeple-chasing at Baldoyle and Leopardstown, and Punchestown and Fairyhouse in spring. And coursing for hares, puss cunning as a fox, eluding, fooling the flying greyhounds. Drawing of badgers with the game blue terrier. It is only in cities that winter is dull.

The old clock in the hall had rumbled out eleven when the door of the gunroom opened and Ann-Dolly came in. She helped herself to a cigarette, lit it, and went and sat by the fireplace.

"Where's Jenico?" I asked.

"Gone home," she said.

She seemed to have a serious fit on, sitting there and looking at the fire. She could be a very grave beautiful woman when that mood was on her. I wondered what she was thinking about. Spain? Or the curious chance that had led her to Destiny Bay? She was not thinking of the future. I knew that, for when a person thinks of the future, the soul, which is usually about its private affairs, or is sleeping, comes to the surface in them, and peers, as a lady from a battlement will peer.

She turned from the fire and looked at me — her grave look, her deep grave look.

"If you got the opportunity, Kerry, would you kiss me?"

And I had been thinking of her as ruminating over the heavenly mysteries!

"Is that a request to be courted, Ann-Dolly, or is it an academic question?"

"It's a what-you-say question."

"Well," I considered, "I might and I mightn't. If I had a lot of bookmaker's money in my pocket, and a song at the end of my tongue, and nothing on my mind, it would be a grand way of passing an hour after dinner. It would be like listening to a good man on the pipes or watching a pleasant unimportant horse race. But if I had a high mood on, the way I'd be thinking I understood why the stars were in their courses, and the language of the trees, and knew distinctly that I was immortal and why, then I consider kissing a girl an abominable vulgarity, not to be considered by a person of my spiritual standing. If I were just as I am ordinarily, with my horses and dogs, and a good belief in myself as my own best companion, I wouldn't give you the satisfaction of my knowing you had a mouth on you."

"But if you loved me, Kerry."

"That's different. But again," I said, "I might and I mightn't. If I kept thinking that you had a grand pair of eyes, and long slim legs and a well-shaped head and well-shaped hands, then I'd probably be for kissing you every time I could lay a hand on you. But if I started blithering to myself about you as the drift of white hawthorn, or the swan on the lake, I wouldn't kiss you at all. I'd stand off and admire you."

"Then if you were very much in love with me, you wouldn't offer to kiss me." She sat there, unrolling this ridiculous thesis as gravely as though she were discussing the dangers of Home Rule.

"I wouldn't. I'd be too much in awe of you to try. But, Ann-Dolly, I may as well tell you, it isn't for that reason that I don't kiss you. I like you, but I don't give a tinker's curse for you that way."

"Sure I know that, Kerry," she uttered gravely.

"Then," I said, "what the devil are you asking me for?"

"Because," she said, "I like what-do-you-call-'em questions."

"My girl," I told her, "you're getting morbid. You want some good reading. I'll give you a couple of books —"

"Oh, yes, I know," she said, "the Bible; and Ruff's 'Guide to the Turf'."

"Well," I said, "find me two healthier ones."

XV

I must tell now of the shadow that fell between me and my cousin Jenico.

I had gone down to Strabane, for some reason or other, and for the second time had run into Old John Cornish, the solicitor who had told me about Jenico's windfall. He was as decent an old chap as there was in the province, red-faced, white-haired, dressed in tweeds and a deerstalker wound about with the catgut of fishing flies.

"Just a minute, mister honey!" I hailed him. "Aren't you the damnedest liar from Hell to Haulbowline?"

"Do you mean that, Mister Kerry, or is it just a manner of speech?"

"'Tisn't a lie exactly," I said, "it's a mistake, more or less. Do you remember telling me that Jenico Grant got a fortune."

"I do."

"Well, it isn't true."

"Who says it isn't?" asked John Cornish.

"Jenico himself."

The old man, who had been laughing, flushed at this.

"I'm a pretty old man, Mr. Kerry."

"Sure what's that got to do with it?"

"Just this: when you've lived as long as I have and tried to be straight as long as I have, you'll not relish being called a liar behind your back."

"Who's blaming you? It was a mistake."

"Mister Kerry, I'm not Mister Jenico Grant's lawyer, so that I can say anything I like about him, provided it's true. Now I'm a person of substance in this town, and I'm a

lawyer, and I say this : " — he shook with anger — " between
Mister Jenico Grant and me, one of us is a damned liar, and
it is n't me."

Well, I thought, that's funny. Why did Jenico tell me
that? As between him and John Cornish, I never hesitated
for a minute as to which was telling the truth. Jenico
might be my cousin and my good friend, but John Cornish's
word was Bible. I could no more think of John Cornish
making a mistake, when he was as serious as that, as I could
of the sun forgetting to rise. If John Cornish said Jenico
got a windfall of fifty thousand pounds, well, Jenico got it,
that was all. Now that I come to think of it, he had looked
a bit sheepish when I mentioned it. His replies about Tonamora had not the quick quality of honesty. But why? If
he had n't wanted to buy Tonamora, why had n't he said so
straight out, and told me to go to blazes when I argued, as
any Northern man should have. God knows he had money
enough, with the brewery and what not, to be comfortable
always. He did n't need this windfall.

Also it occurred to me Jenico had been getting a little
queer this while back. In Ireland, when a person becomes
a little queer, it's just as well to have your eye on him.
There is something in the air. Also there is loneliness.
It is a good thing to live among mountains and by sea air,
but it is a good thing, too, to quit that for a month every
now and then, and get into streets full of men and women,
and use an ordinary urban speech. With most of our
friends, when they go queer, we can manage. When the
Resident Magistrate in an outlying district begins to shake
unaccountably, and look in corners of the room, we know
what's coming. A nursing home, and when he emerges,
a conspiracy of teetotalism around him helps. When the
Indian Colonel begins over-quoting the Bible, and mention-
ing the possibility of the Second Coming being a little nearer
than any one believes, then we get and keep him pleasantly

tight for a month. A course of musical comedies adroitly administered works wonders on any one believing that the Lost Tribes of Israel are the Anglo-Saxons, as can be proven by Holy Writ. And when one of us, afflicted by God, becomes a Nationalist, then we just laugh at him and don't argue, until the attack dies through lack of nutrition, and the patient returns sheepishly to the doctrine of the Glorious, Pious and Immortal Memory.

But when a man begins liking money for its own sake, I don't know what can be done with him. There is a meanness at which you laugh, like the chap's who gives a threepenny tip to a cabman after a ten-shilling ride. There is also a closeness about money which can be pathetic, as that of people who have suffered abominable sordidness of poverty at one time, and now that they have money are afraid to part with it, lest grey foul days come on them again. But there is the mad vice of the miser, for whom each gold coin becomes alive, a sort of demon that can be released to do his bidding, his money being his familiar, and who is as secretive about it as a necromancer is about his familiar, if these things exist, which God forbid. I don't think there can be any vice as cold, as hard to understand.

And yet they exist, these strange people, the squire dressed in a threadbare green coat who will not have fires lit in winter, and the millionaire who walks rather than spend money on a tramcar; the student who grudges himself a penny candle. Drink, women, murder we can understand, and drugs a little, a very little. And to all of these folk our charity goes, but none have a good word in their hearts for the miser. It is like black magic, a cold vice. An aloof, a dark vice.

I might be wrong, of course, and I'd be very glad if I were. But even apart from the meanness about money, Jenico had done an unforgivable thing to a clansman and

a friend. He had lied. That circle of us all, my uncle
Valentine, my aunt Jenepher, my cousin Jenico, and the
outside relatives and the outside, all had been like a walled
city in mutual trust. Even Ann-Dolly I would trust with
my life. And Jenico had made a break in the wall. Damn
him! I said to myself, why couldn't he have told me to
mind my own business, or simply go to the devil? That's
what a friend does, but the backdoor of a lie— God!
That's what outlanders call the Irish trick!

When I came home Ann-Dolly met me in the hall.

"Was Jenico in Strabane?" she asked.

"Damn Jenico!"

"What's wrong, Kerry?" She came close, and put her
hand on my shoulder, and her voice was solicitous and kind.
She had so many moods, had Ann-Dolly. She never made
a mistake as to your feelings. She knew. You could always depend on Ann-Dolly to do the right thing.

"It's only my rotten temper, Ann-Dolly. There's nothing
wrong." But I could see she wasn't satisfied, although she
said nothing more.

XVI

I had turned out at five that morning, for I had to ride
down to Forty-Acre. Carabine had rustled breakfast for
me in the kitchen, and I had swung into the saddle and
started cantering along the cliffs. The sun had not quite
arisen, for all the chatter of the birds in the trees, and I
knew by that sense you get by the sea, that it was low tide.
Back of me Green River trickled its crystal depths into the
Atlantic, and as I turned the headland I looked down on
the shore, near Spanish Men's Rest. At Carrickore I saw
a huge cart on the sands, and the figures of men.

"What the blazes can that be?" I said to myself. For
I had never seen a cart on the sands there before. My

cousin Jenico has riparian rights there. None can remove the sand without his permission. But I had never seen any one attempt to. The dulce gatherers, the men who collect seaweed for fertilising the fields, use donkeys and creels. Before sunrise and at low water! I threw my leg over the horse's neck and slid down.

"I'd better look into this," I said, and I picketed the moke.

There's a short cut down the cliff, if you've a clear head and steady feet. Now you've got to touch stones as gently as if you were touching eggs, and then you've got to swing all your weight on the broom shrubs. There's a drop of twelve feet on the end, but it's on sand. It's just a nice warming-up exercise. I alighted sweetly, and strolled around the cliff.

The cart itself was a brewer's lorry, out of Jenico's own brewery in Louth, and the horses attached were shire geldings, powerful, beautifully feathered animals. For a moment it came to me that Jenico was doing business with the smugglers, of whom we've always had a few, running French brandy from Bordeaux in fishing smacks. That has been a small commerce with the local inns, but if Jenico had gone in for it on a big scale — The cart had nothing in it, unless something were concealed by the piece of sacking.

There was the seashore, with the Atlantic breaking on it gently, very gently. There the fish hawks had set out to sea, looking for mackerel, and an old eagle from the Donegal Mountains likely, was waiting a few hundred yards off, for the fish hawk to come in with his catch so he could take it from him. There he stood huddled patiently on the sand. Here was Carrickore, the golden rock, with its opening like a cave into the underworld. Out of the cave came two men. They were vast, heavy, stupid men. They wore the high glazed brewery hat, the padded sleeved brewery waistcoat.

Jenico must have brought them all the way from Louth. Damned secretive! the whole thing!

"What are you doing here?" I asked.

They said nothing. They looked at each other guardedly. They looked at the opening of the cave. They looked at something on the sand near the cave mouth. What they looked at were three bars, like short crowbars, heavy, metallic. But they hadn't got the black of crowbars. They were yellow like the sand.

"Did you hear me speak to you? What are you doing here?"

They shuffled; looked uneasy; said nothing. At the sound of my voice Jenico came out of the cavern opening.

"What hell's business is this, cousin Jenico?" I asked. He became white and red. Alternately red with embarrassment and white with a fear of discovery.

"It's a private business," he answered.

"So private evidently that it's got to be done when few Christian souls are stirring. What are these?" And I walked across to the crowbars.

"Don't touch them," said Jenico sharply.

I paid no attention. I stooped down for one. I am a strong man but I could hardly lift it. As I stood bowed there I got chilled. I straightened up.

"God damn you!" I said quietly to Jenico.

I went toward the cave.

"Keep out!" said Jenico.

"Stand aside!"

He made no movement to do it. "Remember," he said quietly, "this beach is my property."

"There are a few words I want to say to you, Jenico. Send your men and dray off, and tell them to keep away."

"Get off down the beach," Jenico told them, "and don't turn up until I call."

They disappeared around the cliffside and left us alone.
"Well?" said Jenico warily.

"So not contented to be a damned liar," I told him, "you must become a stinking sneak thief. You picked a soft one, too, an unfortunate orphan girl without kith or kin. Well, have you nothing to say?"

"You don't understand," said Jenico.

"I understand well enough," I told him. "There's little MacFarlane in you. Only the cheap Scotch horse coper."

He went white with cold anger and fury

"Are you mad?" he cried.

"I'm not mad."

"Then if you're not mad," he said quietly, "you're going to get the damnedest beating for that it would be possible to receive." And he quietly took off his coat.

"Good enough." And I pitched mine on the sand. "Any time you're ready," I said.

And there on the sands of Destiny Bay, while the sun was rising, and the birds singing, and the old eagle waited for the fish hawk to bring him his breakfast, Jenico Grant and I fought as I never want to fight again.

Given a regulation ring, padded posts, and gloves, I don't think my cousin Jenico could have laid a hand on me, what with such sound principles of boxing as James Carabine had instilled into me. He is a smallish man, Jenico, a good two stone lighter than I, but fast as lightning, compact, hard to catch. If you want to see Jenico at his best, you would see him on a football field, elusive to tackle, hard as nails. Myself, I am loosely built, fair, and in boxing I rather look like, and box like, that paragon of style, Billy Wells. Of course nothing as finished as that, but what I mean: the low guard, the straight left and right cross, school of Sayers. There we stood on the sands, myself as though in a ring, Jenico poised on his toes, hands close to his sides, just looking cold, calm fury.

He was at me like a driven golf ball. Mechanically I hooked right and left to his head as he came in. I discovered that boxing with bare hands and boxing with gloves are two different matters. My knuckles seemed to have been driven back into my palms. Jenico drove three stiff punches into my short ribs. I chopped him viciously on the neck, and shoved him back. Jenico was breathing savagely through his nose. His head was down, his elbows into his sides. I caught him a pretty jab on the right eye, but he was inside me before I could stop him, driving short arm punches that didn't exactly hurt, but through the bruises of which vitality seemed to ooze. Suddenly, with a left swing, he caught me heavily on the thrapple, to use the only word I know for that spot, a punch that shook the inner me in its envelope of flesh and bone. I shook him off, and noticed that in the outrageous white of his face his right eye was beginning to assume a pretty plumlike colour, halfway between red and blue.

It struck me if I were going to win this, I'd better get to work. I steadied down and began to plug at him with long left leads to the head and, when I got close enough, a hefty bang with the right to the body. I worked him close into the rocks to finish him, but he danced lightly away and as I moved around to get him into hitting focus again, he was at me with a rush, and a vicious right-hander opened my face on the cheekbone like a split greengage. I tell you that worried me.

But the next minute I got him. He poised himself for another rush, and as he came, I straightened out the left with everything I had behind it. It caught him smack. Carabine in his heyday could not have timed it better.

"That'll hold you!" I said.

He stood there teetering on his heels, his hands uncertain.

"And this'll finish you!" And I let him have the right on the point. He dropped as if he had been poleaxed.

There he lay, stiff, his hands clenched, his eyes glassy, breathing stertorously through set teeth. It was the perfect hush-a-bye, baby, though I says it myself as done it.

I walked off and into the cave, a bit groggily, and picking up the candle some one had left there, I went in. I lit up, and in the distance I could see a pile of sand. I went up to it, and nearly fell into the hole over a pile of the yellow bars. There was an open iron box down in the sand, with bars in it too.

I suppose I ought to have had a thrill, looking at the old Armada treasure, but I didn't. There was no feeling of it, if you know what I mean. It might just have been a butter firkin. Even an old book, not a century printed, will give you a sense of antiquity, but this didn't. I lowered the lid of the box. It looked old, it looked old as blazes, if you follow me, but it felt new. Great flakes of red rust, and what not, and strong! That box would have held the crown jewels! And the bars of gold might be the proceeds of the looting of Yucatan, but they might be too from the vaults of the Bank of England.

"This isn't hell's business," I said to myself, "but it's a funny business."

I opened the box again and as I ran my fingers along the inside of the lid, I felt a little piece of paper, like a label. I had to get down on my back and put my head into the hole to see it, but when I did, it was worth it. With the candle's light I made out "Wm. Moore & Son, Aston Quay, Dublin. Trunkmakers to His Excellency the Viceroy of Ireland." The laugh I let out of me was intensified by the cave until it sounded as if Destiny Bay itself were giving vent to a vast Gargantuan roar.

I went down the strand to where Jenico was sitting up. The tide had risen and trickled the back of his neck, and brought him to. I helped him to his feet.

"I'm sorry, Jenico, for calling you a liar and a thief. I

should have known better, and as for your father, he was as fine a sportsman as ever wore silk. But it's the mercy of God I came down here this morning."

"How?" said Jenico.

"If word had come out that treasure trove had been found here, don't you know that some damned official would have seized it for the King's Majesty? And then you'd have had to explain, and you'd have been the laughing stock of the Three Kingdoms. A thing like that can never be kept quiet. Aren't you the lucky fellow I came along here this morning?"

"Am I?" said Jenico. "Have you broken my nose?"

"I couldn't tell you for sure," I answered. "As a matter of fact, I can't see anything of your face clearly except your ears. We'll know later."

"Well, if you have itself," said Jenico, and he looked at my split cheek, "you'll carry my mark on you till the day you die."

Which I call damned ungrateful of Jenico.

XVII

I had to get four stitches in my cheek, and my uncle Valentine viewed it as he might view some new phenomenon.

"It's none of my damned business," said my uncle Valentine, "but from sheer admiration of the punch, who handed you that?"

"Jenico did," I said.

"Begob, Kerry," said my uncle Valentine, "I didn't think he had it in him. My opinion of that fellow's gone up I couldn't tell you how far." And at that he left it. No further word passed his lips. A wise man was my uncle Valentine. But James Carabine was furious.

"If you had only kept your left hand straight out, with six inches for play, that would never have happened to you!

Be damned! What's the use of my teaching at all, if at the first bare knuckle bout you forget everything I told you, and walk in to get punched like a draper's assistant?"

But as to who left his mark on me, and what it was all about, James Carabine was incurious. That is a great virtue in northern men. To Ann-Dolly I told a cock-and-bull story about falling from my horse. But my aunt Jenepher was not so easily put off.

"Ann-Dolly told me you had fallen from your horse and have your face cut, Kerry." She put her fingers on my arm, and turned her head toward me. It was incredible that she could not see my face. "Who have you been fighting with?"

"I had an argument with Jenico," I said, "but it's all right. It was a mistake of mine."

"There is no bad blood between you and Jenico?"

"Of course not, Aunt Jenepher. I was just a fool."

It might have passed over like that, and none have known anything about it, but for the village idiot. We are an old-fashioned people in Destiny Bay, very attached to ancient institutions. We keep up the old-fashioned Christmas, the village drunkard and the village idiot. It was the village idiot, Willie John McIlhagga, had seen us from the cliffs and had given his version of it to the town.

"My bould Mister Kerry was taking his morning's trot on his horse, and my bould Mister Jenico was taking his morning's walk on his feet. And when he sees his cousin, my bould Mister Kerry goes down till the strand. 'And how are you, Kerry?' says Mister Jenico. 'I'm bravely,' says Mister Kerry; 'and how's yourself?' 'Och, I'm not too bad,' says Mister Jenico, 'but I'm feeling the want of exercise.' 'Sowl!' says Mister Kerry, 'but I'm feeling it myself. Will we go in and swim in the say?' 'We've nothing till dry ourselves with when we come out,' says Mister Jenico. 'What do you say if we throw the stone?'

'And where would you be finding a stone on the sands?' says Mister Kerry. 'Are you for a bout of boxing, fighting, and bloody murder, and the man that's first knocked unconscious will pay the other a pound?' 'Heth, but I'm your man!' says Mister Jenico. 'My sweet fellow!' says Mister Kerry.

"So they stand up to each other just like the lion and the unicorn. Mister Kerry is leaping like the unicorn and Mister Jenico is growling like the lion. 'Derry, Aughrim, and the Boyne!' screeches Mister Kerry, and he catches Mister Jenico a belt on the gob would kill a bullock. 'No surrender!' says Mister Jenico, and he lifts Mister Kerry from his feet with a clout on the chin.

"Mister Kerry tries Corbett's Favourite and the Cornish Strangle, but Mister Jenico is there with the Glasgow Throttle and the Executioner's Delight. Och, hould your tongue! Great scientific fighters, the pair of them. Bathering and murder. And the yells of them, the grand Protestant cries: 'Derry Walls!' and 'Croppies, lie down!' And then Mister Jenico gives Mister Kerry the Foot and Slap and has him staggering. Sowl! but I thought he was gone. But my sweet Mister Kerry is clever — as clever as an otter, you might say. He makes a dash for Mister Jenico, swinging his foot, letting on to foul him. 'What are you up to?' says Mister Jenico, and he drops his hands. 'I'm up to this,' says Mister Kerry, and he welts him one on the jaw you could hear in Dublin. And Mister Jenico drops on the sand, and his face turns black, and he's done for.

'Mister Kerry goes somewhere and sits down for a while to rest and then comes back and lifts Mister Jenico to his feet. 'You're bet,' says he. 'I'm bet, and you're the better man, and here's your pound note,' says Mister Jenico. 'You're a natural country fighter, Jenico, but strategy won,' says Mr. Kerry. And they went off with their arms around each other, laughing and joking. Och, hould your tongue! The likes of them are n't in England, Ireland, or Asia. Grand men, and roaring, gaming fellows, and great houlders with the ancient customs. Aye, I'm fit for another pint," said Willie John McIlhagga.

XVIII

I came up through the orchard with the dogs behind me in the dusk. I was whistling "As I roved out", and there among the trees was Ann-Dolly in a dark frock, her sweet head on its longish graceful neck like a flower on a stem. I shall always think of Ann-Dolly in the orchard of Destiny Bay. When the blue dusk descends, and I anywhere, there comes to me the picture of Ann-Dolly among the kindly old apple trees, and the blue shadow of the mountains between our old house and the setting sun.

She came toward me and her face had not the sweet gravity I had come to see in it at that hour, but was strained and white and had bistre-coloured shadows under her eyes.

"Kerry," she said, "I want you to tell me something."

"If it's what will win at the Curragh this week, Ann-Dolly, I'm damned if I know. I wish I did," I said, ignorant-like.

"If it were only that!" said Ann-Dolly. Then she looked at me straight. "Kerry, what were you fighting with Jenico about?"

"Who told you we were fighting at all?" I asked.

"Everybody knows it."

"Well," I said, "it's a hard thing if a couple of relatives can't take a belt at each other without people making a song and dance about it. It is n't the first time we've fought and it won't be the last time. My dear Ann-Dolly," I said, "you don't understand us at all. Did n't you ever hear of the

Irishman that was blue-moulded for want of a beating?"
And I was for moving off.

"Please, Kerry!" She stopped me as I was going.
"Kerry, you know I think your uncle Valentine is the greatest gentleman in the world."

"It's a big field, Ann-Dolly," I said, "and a long hard
course, but he starts my favourite."

"And next to him and nearly beside him, Kerry, I put
you."

"Are you daft, woman?"

"No," she said, "I'm not. Kerry, you wouldn't ever
tell a lie, would you?"

"Well, I don't suppose I would," I answered. "I haven't
got brains enough to think up a good one. And besides,
it's a bit of a cowardly thing, isn't it?"

"Then, Kerry," she shot at me, "was my name mentioned the morning you and Jenico fought?"

I suppose I got red. It was the last thing in the world
I was expecting.

"We were talking about a lot of things," I said. "I can't
rightly remember."

"Was it implied?"

"My dear Ann-Dolly," I said, "if you think we were
fighting about you—"

She said nothing. She came over and took my hands.

"Kerry," she said, "I want you to be always, always,
good friends with Jenico."

"Sure, and amn't I?"

"But I want you to promise, Kerry."

"All right, then," I said. "There's no need to. I
promise."

She tiptoed, and kissed me on the cheek.

"God bless you, Kerry," she said. "I'm very fond of
you. You're a good friend, and a brother."

"Away with you, woman!" I said, but she had fled

through the garden. "Girls are queer!" I thought, and I went in and dressed. All that evening Ann-Dolly was gay as a linnet. She went upstairs with my aunt Jenepher.

When I came in for breakfast next morning she was not at table.

"Where's Ann-Dolly?" I asked.

My aunt Jenepher said nothing, and Carabine looked worried. My uncle Valentine handed me a letter.

"Do you know anything about this, Kerry?"

"Let me see, sir."

It was a note from Ann-Dolly, saying a great loneliness for Spain had come on her, and that she had given in to it. She was slipping away at night so as to avoid saying good-bye. Her love to Aunt Jenepher and Uncle Valentine and Kerry, and she would write. She would never forget us. The letter became incoherent and blotted. It looked to me as if she'd been crying.

"I think Ann-Dolly had the idea that Jenico and I had a dispute about her. That is not true — exactly. There was no reason why she should have gone, sir."

"Well, then, Kerry," said my uncle Valentine, "what's to be done?"

When anything like this turns up at Destiny Bay, for some unknown reason I take charge immediately. My uncle Valentine, I'm sure, could do it all better than I could, but then I've got a trick of snapping everybody into action.

"She's put on her old boy's clothes, Kerry," said my aunt Jenepher, "and I'm sure she hasn't a penny of money."

"There's a son of Robbie McGuckin's home from America with one of those new-fangled motor bicycles," I told Carabine. "Have him sent hell-for-leather to the station at Ballyneagh to see if any one like her turned up to take the train. It's fifteen miles there and fifteen back," I said, "tell him he can go back to America if he doesn't do it under the hour. Also he's to keep an eye out on the road,

I 'll ride over to Spanish Men's Rest to see if anything 's
been seen of her there. It 's unlikely she 'd leave without
visiting her grandfather's grave."

"It 's all right, Aunt Jenepher." I stopped to pat her
hand. "I 'll have that girl if I have to comb Ireland."

I saw Jenico standing by the old Spanish graveyard. He
had a great wedge of sticking plaster across his nose. He
looked like some member of a secret society in a mask. A
great chill and forlornness fell on me as I rode up. Never
did I feel the shadow on Spanish Men's Rest so heavy
before.

"Well, Kerry?" said Jenico.

"Do you know," he went on, without giving me a chance
to speak, "I saw a ghost here this morning."

"How do you know it was a ghost?" I asked.

"Well," he answered, "do you know anybody who would
go into Spanish Men's Rest at four in the morning on a
waning moon?"

"What did it look like?"

"It was like a boy or a small man," Jenico answered.
"I was awake and came to the window. There was a cloud
across the moon, but I saw it as distinctly as I see you,
going across to the old duke's grave."

"I wish you 'd gone and spoken to it," I said.

"I did," he laughed. "I went down to the gunroom and
slid two cartridges into a twelve-bore, and banged a couple
of charges of shot across. It roused the house, but I could
get nobody to come with me. When I dressed and went
into the field I could find no one there. There 's no trace of
blood this morning, so it must have been a ghost."

"You damned fool!" I shouted. "You might have
killed her."

"Killed whom?"

"Ann-Dolly."

"Oh, my God!" said Jenico. He became white, and had
to sit down, so shaken was he. "But she 's all right?"

"I don't know."

"How don't you know, Kerry? Isn't she at Destiny Bay?"

"She's not," I told him. "She's run away in the night."

I never saw a man so taken aback. You might have thought that the sun had reversed its course and was returning eastward at noon, to see the stunned look on his face.

"If you're going to have the hysterics, Jenico," I told him, "you're no damned use to me. If you're not, you might have that American pacer of yours hitched to the dogcart, and follow me to Destiny Bay. I need speed." I gathered Pelican's leathers and dug my heels into his ribs. "Hup, you pig!"

At Destiny Bay my uncle Valentine and James Carabine were awaiting me. "She was seen at Spanish Men's Rest at four this morning," was all I told them. "Any word from the station yet?"

"Nothing at the station," said my uncle Valentine.

"If Miss Ann-Dolly wanted to get away, please your Honour," said James Carabine, "it isn't likely she'd take the first station. It's likely she'd take the second or third. And it's not likely she'd take the road; she'd stick to the cliffs and the mountains."

"Even at that," said I, "she'd have to pass Bailin Wigniss."

Bailin Wigniss is a passage through the purple northern hills from Donegal and Destiny Bay to the lowlands of Derry. The Gap of Loneliness is the English translation of the Erse name. Here the last Irish wolf bitch and her litter were killed in the time of the first George, and here stood a gibbet in the troubles. An eery place, Bailin Wigniss, all heather and blue slate crags, and a turbulent muddy stream tearing down from the summit of Slieveroe, the Red Mountain.

"Well, she won't starve," said I. "There's apples and nuts, and there's moss to sleep on, and she has matches,

I 'm sure, and you can always catch a trout with your hands in one of the little pools. She 'll be all right. But if she gets to Derry, we 're done for."

"Sure, she has no money," said my uncle Valentine.

"She 's got rings, sir, and old brooches. She can sell those."

"I 'm afraid she 's lost, our wee Ann-Dolly," said my uncle Valentine. And there was a little catch in his voice that made me sorry.

"Not at all, sir," I told him. "I 'm going down to the post-office to telegraph the police in Derry, Larne, Belfast and Dublin to arrest her when she turns up."

"But sure they can't arrest her!" said my uncle Valentine.

"They can," said I, "for stealing the family spoons."

"I 've just been thinking," I told James Carabine, "that Miss Ann-Dolly was well liked by the gypsies. There was nothing they would n't do for her. She might have persuaded them to hide her and remove her later."

"They might, your Honour," said James Carabine, "but I doubt it. Their loyalty is to this house."

"At any rate, you might as well parade the gypsy king. Have him here by the time I come back from the post-office."

I found the old chief with my uncle Valentine in the orchard when I returned. My uncle Valentine in tweeds and red beard looked very much the lord of the manor, looked like the Viceroy of Ireland, looked like the King of Ireland himself, begob! But this gypsy chief was the wildest, the most free and unfettered thing I have ever laid eyes on. He was taller than my uncle Valentine by a head, but had no vastness. Thin and lean, like some high hardy tree. His copper-coloured face, his long black beard, the great gold rings in his ears, and the rings on his grimy brown hands — he was undoubtedly something out of the East. His breeches and gaiters were as well cut as my own. He wore a blue flannel shirt, and an old shooting coat, with deep poacher's pockets. Out of the right-hand pocket peered the head of a gamecock, with a hard bright eye, a proud deadly eye. Beside him stalked a Scottish deerhound, a lean splendid dog, high as a calf. His coat was filthy and he could have done with a can of flea powder, but for all that he was a magnificent dog. The old chief had the look of an eagle about him, of an old eagle, of an old unbeaten eagle. I admired him, but I did n't like him. I have an academic weakness for Christians.

"The chief," said my uncle Valentine, "says that neither he nor his people have seen anything of Ann-Dolly."

"Oh, he says that, does he? All the same, I think we'll have a little search in the gypsy city."

"I don't think you will, Mister Kerry," said the king. "We are a free people, and though we are treated as sorners and vagabonds, yet we are an honest people."

"By the heels of Christ," I swore, "there'll never be another bunch of heather plucked in Destiny, nor a willow branch cut to make a basket. And you and your honest people can clear out of here by sundown."

"Very good, sir," said the old king. "It's only by the courtesy of your uncle Valentine and yourself we are here, and I thank you for your hospitality up till now. Of course, we shall be out before sundown, as Mister Kerry directs. I am sorry he will not accept my word of honour that the little lady is not with us, but I feel I must uphold the dignity of my people."

"Look here," I said, "I'm fearfully sorry. It was abominable of me. Please stay. You'll make me feel awfully cheap if you don't stay."

"Then we shall stay, Mister Kerry, and if it gives you any pleasure to search the gypsy city, please do so. I came up, Mister Kerry, to ask you if you'd do me the favour of accepting this small bird," and he took the gamecock out of his pocket. "It is a bold cunning bird and will not fail you."

Damn it all! You wouldn't think a wanderer like that could make a country gentleman feel like a battered three-penny bit, but he did.

"I shall go now," he said, "to ask our young men to go out on the search for the little lady." And he bowed and was gone. A great old cock! Don't let me hear anything said against gypsies any more!

Jenico was fuming in the stableyard, standing beside his black pacer.

"Let's go!" and he was for getting into the cart.

"When I've had a few slices of cold beef and pickles, a pint of beer, and a cup of tea."

"Damn it, Kerry, you're not thinking of eating."

"I hunt no woman," I said, "on an empty belly."

"But she may be gone for good. We may never catch her."

"On the other hand," I told him, "she may be in some ditch, dying with a charge of your buckshot in her ribs."

"Oh, my God!" Jenico began running around in circles. "Oh, my God! Oh, my God!"

"If you don't stop keening like the Shan Van Vocht," I said, "you can stay at home."

We got under way at last, Jenico and I on the front seat, Carabine behind. I shook the rein gently, and the black pacer moved as a boat moves under a keen pressing wind. There was something thunderous and free about him. I could see his beautifully held head, and imagine the throwing of his forefeet. Fine action in a harness horse is one of the most moving things in the world. I can understand the contempt of the men who race trotters for the "bang-tails", as they call the flat-racers and chasers. Jenico's American pacer was the best horse I have ever sat behind. There came into my head the text: "He sniffeth the battle from afar, the thunder of the captains and the shouting." He was that sort of horse, if you know what I mean.

"Man, Jenico," I said, "but you're the lucky fellow."

But Jenico only groaned.

I pulled up at the Mountainy House, the pub that is a quarter mile from Bailin Wigniss. Carabine unhitched the pacer and I went into the bar.

"Man of the house," I asked, "have you laid eyes this day on a red-headed young fellow has the air of a girl?"

"Your Honour," he answered, "there hasn't been a Christian here or hereabouts this day. There has only been two policemen."

"I'm leaving a horse in your stalls," I said, and walked out. Jenico came with me. Carabine followed us from the yard.

"I don't know, Kerry," said Jenico, "if you'll think me foolish, but there has come a funny idea into my head. Was there ever an Ann-Dolly at all? Or is this a dream we are all in the middle of? It's a queer country here we dwell in, and you as well as myself know the stories there are, of women who have come out of the sea, and married men, and gone back to the sea, leaving them silent and desolate. I don't know if you ever noticed it," said Jenico, "but I've never seen beauty the like of hers. Such warm beauty, Kerry. Beauty from within. There were shades of her hair that were like new heather, and there was no warm whiteness like the whiteness of her skin — "

We were at the bridge of Bailin Wigniss. I turned to James Carabine. "Either she has passed this way," I decided, "or she hasn't."

"True for your Honour," said James Carabine.

There was a tall ash tree with a long jutting branch over the road, a sad and eerie tree. All was eerie and cold, the tumbling river, the shadowy mountain, the sad tree.

"You know, Kerry," said Jenico, "it seems damned strange to me that the old Spanish duke should come from Spain to be buried in Spanish Men's Rest. I don't think he ever came from Spain, at all," said Jenico.

"Where do you think he came from?" I asked.

"From Spanish Men's Rest," answered Jenico.

I must say a little shiver came into my bones, as though I were stripped on a mountain side, and a grey freezing wind were blowing about me as about a stripped tree.

"But how about the girl?"

"There may have been a girl on the galleon," said Jenico. "Kerry, do you remember Black Trewethy of Ardona, the one that had the Lone Woman's Grave in his garden. A woman with black hair and glowing eyes knocked at the great door one night and Black Trewethy answered it. She said she was going to Enniskillen and had lost her way, and Black Trewethy said he'd put her right. Both his butler and manservant saw her. But once Black Trewethy passed out into the night he was seen no more of."

"And when, ten years later," Carabine said, "the Lone Woman's Grave was opened, there were two skeletons, and one of them had the great frame of Black Trewethy."

"Kerry," said Jenico, "do you remember where I loosed the charge of buckshot. She was going home."

"Be damned to the pair of you, and your winter nights' stories!" I laughed, but I wasn't very easy myself.

A little cart had come up to the bridge drawn by that very small brown donkey we of Ireland call the Jerusalem Ass. The cart was driven by a small rat-faced man in a suit of reach-me-downs and a grey cap. There was a pile of merchandise, covered with a tarpaulin on the cart, and back of that the framework of a Punch and Judy show. The man was of a type that is the pest of our northern country, bringing in cheap tea which is traded for valuable Carrickmacross lace, tenpence worth of tea for two guineas' worth of lace;

cheap jewellery for fine Donegal tweed. They even take the children's coppers with their Punchinello booths.

"Did you see anything of a lad on the road," I asked, "with red hair, and a bit girlish in his walk and ways?"

"I did not," he said, and thumped the donkey.

"You've damned little manners," said I.

"And less time," he answered. "Hip, Jack!"

We are a courteous people in Destiny Bay. We have not the abrupt ways of cities. We resent off-handedness. We resent it all the more when it is from a roaming pedlar to the Younger of Destiny Bay. Carabine caught the donkey's rein.

"Come down out of that," I said, for something had caught my eye.

"I'll have the law on you," he said, but he came down.

"I don't know where you come from, my cheating fellow," I told him. "But now you're in the Black Heart of the Black North. The law here is laid down by my uncle Valentine and by myself. Did you ever hear tell," I asked him, "of Quiet Kerry Mac?"

I think he must have heard a story or two, for he turned white.

"Now tell me," I went on, "you've seen nothing of the lad I mentioned?"

"No, sir," he said.

He was wearing no collar or tie, but a red handkerchief tied around his throat costerwise, or in what we call the Killevy knot, with the ends flaring. I put out my left hand and caught him by it, giving it enough twist to make his eyes bulge. I opened his coat with the right hand, and pulled out of his vest pockets a heavy watch and chain with a bunch of seals.

"Then where did you get this watch and chain?" For I knew it to be the old duke's.

"'Twas left me by my grandfather."

"And this ring?" I twisted his hand around and the

emerald inside glinted dully. "Your grandfather left you this too."

"He did." Though he was white he didn't falter. It's extraordinary how people will stand up against odds for property.

"That's enough," said I. "Jenico, look in the cart for a couple of pieces of rope, or anything that will pinion his arms, and tie his ankles." And we had him trussed in a minute. "Carabine, back the cart under the bough, and let down the tailboard."

I rummaged in his cart until I found a good length of rope. I worked a nice running loop on one end and slung it over the projecting branch of the ash tree. I belayed the loose end with a stout clove hitch.

"Now sling him up on the tailboard of his cart," I told Jenico.

"Damn it, Kerry!" Jenico shouted. "You're going too far."

"In the absence of your uncle, Sir Valentine," I said, "I'm head of this family. If you don't like the way I do things, get out."

"All right," said Jenico. And he lifted the man standing.

"Do you, Carabine," I directed, "give the Neddy a whack on the rump when I tell you." I dropped the noose over the pedlar's neck. "'Twas the mercy of God," I said, "that there was a tree here."

"Are you for hanging me?" said the chapman.

"Just that."

"You'll hang yourselves for it."

"Not at all, my dear man," I told him, "not at all. For when I've drawn your neck into the shape of a corkscrew, I'll cut the pinions from your arms and the spancel from your feet, and it'll be the bonniest suicide seen in the country for years. You'll be a *ne plus ultra* to coming generations."

The man's face was yellow beneath a mask of sweat.

"I met the lad you spoke of," he quavered.

"Sure that's no news to me."

"I met him three miles down the road, and he was for Derry across the mountains."

"And you cut his throat, I suppose, and took the watch and ring from him."

"I did not," he could hardly speak; "but gave him fifty shillings for them, and him near dead with hunger."

"Then why," I asked, "did you lie to me?"

"Sure I was afraid he'd stolen them, and when you asked after him, I thought you'd take them from me and I'd lose both them and my fifty shillings."

"You'll lose your fifty shillings anyway. Here, let him down," I told Jenico. "Now, away west wi' you!"

I went over and sat on the bridge while Jenico and Carabine helped him on to his cart for he could hardly stand. I saw Jenico get the ring, but I saw him, too, hand over fifty shillings. There is a strain of weakness in Jenico.

We weren't much further advanced than before, for the mountain trail to Derry is a vague wide trail, and it is scattered with mountain villages all deserted, where the famine of Forty-eight killed off the people, and cleared the survivors to America. Sheep land most of it; houses with the thatch fallen in; blind windows, all the pathos and dejection of a deserted house. At night in the mountains there is a vast loneliness. Ourselves, the country people, are not at home in those mountains by night. There was nothing, I knew, to harm Ann-Dolly there, but the sense of being alone on the Irish mountains with nothing about one but space,— there is something in it too big for the human spirit.

"Hadn't we better be getting on?" said Jenico.

I looked at him for a minute and turned to Carabine.

"Go down to the Mountainy House, and harness up, and drive to the Ferret McClure's. Tell him I want Heckler's Joy and Sweet Marie, and bring them back with you. I'll walk on down the road to 'The Orange Sash.' You'll find me there. And as for you," I told Jenico, "go back with Carabine to the Mountainy House, and borrow a bicycle. Go back to Destiny, and ask Jenepher for one of Ann-Dolly's shifts—"

"I'll be damned if I will," said Jenico.

"Och, do as you're told, Mr. Jenico," said Carabine wearily.

"Would a handkerchief do, Kerry?" Jenico asked.

"I said shift." And I moved off down the road.

At "The Orange Sash" there was a great welcome for me. There were Johnnie McGloomy and his wife Carsie, and Johnnie's old grandfather—one of the last thousand survivors of the noble six hundred of the Light Brigade. He was supposed to be one hundred and eight years old, but Johnnie had added a few years for the good of the house.

"And what brings you our way, Mister Kerry?"

"I'm hunting a young fellow that's run away on us," I said. "A red-headed fellow has the great look of the girl about him."

"Sowl!" said Johnnie. "But that one was in here two hours gone. He was dead with tiredness and his feet were nearly cut off. Talked with a touch of foreign accent and drank sarsaparilla."

"That's him," said I.

"Well," said Johnnie, "he bought a loaf of bread and a tin of sardines and was off over the mountains. You'll have a queer job finding him."

"I'll find him," said I.

I sat in the bar, eating the meal Johnnie and wife got for me, waiting for Carabine and Jenico, and thinking to myself how everything you do in life comes to profit sooner or later. God knows how many years before it was that I brought home from Belfast a big book called the Memoirs of Casanova, translated from the Italian. A rare scoundrel this fellow was, cheating at cards and fooling women. In effect, a true foreigner. My uncle Valentine picked it up from the table where I laid it.

"Did you read this?" he asked.

"I did."

"And did you like it?"

"I did."

"It's rare reading for a lad of fifteen," said my uncle Valentine. And he thought for a while. "There's a book I'd like you to read," and he went out and brought a copy from the gunroom, "and it's a grand book entirely." He gave me a book called "Uncle Tom's Cabin."

"Now read that," he said. "And so's it'll stick in your mind, you'll copy it in fair script from the title to the last word."

I looked up at him aghast.

"Or there'll be no racing this summer."

I must say it struck me as an overrated book. There were some weird birds in it, an awful bounder called Simon Legree, and a most pious old coloured man, called Uncle Tom. But what struck me particularly was hunting the Negroes with bloodhounds. Of course they couldn't have been real bloodhounds, probably boarhounds or great Danes, for the bloodhound is the most affectionate of all dogs, and the gentlest. Still, if it hadn't been for my memories of "Uncle Tom's Cabin," we'd not have found Ann-Dolly that night. She might have died in the mountains of starvation and exposure. It only shows that things which appear foolish at the time are profitable in the latter end.

XIX

The mountains were imperial and stark. They were purple and aloof. In the twilight they threw shadows that could not be seen but felt, triangular shadows, like magis' caps, and most long. The sickle of the new moon rested on the summit of Slieveroe like some strange symbol, and one felt that when one attained the summit, one would have achieved a pilgrimage of some mystic kind as in medieval legend, and the sea we would sense from the mountain top would not be Mother Atlantic but some vague sea of futurity, of infinity.

The hounds were solemn and most wise. Their huge wrinkled faces, their slow certain movements, gave the eerie sense of superhuman sagacity, the sagacity of ants, the sagacity of birds. Beside me Jenico stood, his face so white as to be luminous nearly, and James Carabine was gaunt and huge in the dusk. He had, with his kindly foresight, picked up a mountain pony and saddled it for Ann-Dolly. He stood there with the reins in his hands.

"Pick it up, boy. Pick it up, sweetheart," I called to the hounds. "Quickly, darlings, quickly." Heckler's Joy stood still a moment, sniffing the air, and then suddenly he gave the bloodhound's deep bell-like note. The bitch looked up a-quiver, and then joined him.

"We're off," I said.

The lights of the inn in the distance began to recede, as the lights of a port recede from the taffrail of a ship. We went over the soft half grass, half heather of the mountain side. The pony's hoofs gave muffled thumps, like the thumps of a muffled drum.

"We're all right if we don't cross a sheep track," I thought. As we went on, the moon dropped into the sea, and there was nothing but starlight, cold, unearthly. The mountains were no longer purple, but steel blue. The grass was crisp beneath our feet, for a frost was coming, and in the morning the bogholes would have their skin of ice on them, that would not melt until the sun was high. Now and again something rustled, a hare or badger, and my heart stopped lest the hounds should lose scent, but they got together, whining gently in communion, and were off. The sharp distant barking of the shepherds' collies answered their belling tongues.

"There are mad shepherds in the mountains, and bad dogs, Mister Kerry," whispered James Carabine to me, though why he should whisper I don't know.

"I know that," said I; "that's why I'm hurrying."

"What's that?" asked Jenico.

"Oh, nothing at all, Mister Jenico," answered James Carabine.

We struck through an abandoned village where from the bare walls of the cottages our footfalls and the pony's trot struck an echo that re-echoed in my heart. Under the starlight it seemed abandoned even by ghosts, which is the most dreadful abandonment of all.

The hounds swung sharply to the left as if they were going straight for the mountain top, instead of skirting the shoulder. Already the pace and climb were beginning to tell on me. "God!" I thought. "What a lionheart she has!" And then it occurred to me: "She will never get over this. If we don't find her soon, she will be dead. After this walk she will have lain down to die. In the weariness that's on her and the black frost that's in it, she will this night die."

We had come up to a part of the mountain where a small lake is. It may be an ancient bog hole. It may be an extinct crater. Who knows? All I know is that it is black and deep. And there the hounds checked.

"Oh, Jesu!" said Jenico.

A small stream runs down the side of the mountain from Lochbeg, the little lake, and a hundred yards off is the ruins of one of Shane O'Neil's towers. I tried cast after cast with the hounds but they came back to the lake's brink.

"I don't suppose for a minute," I said, and I looked at Carabine and Carabine looked at me, "but I may as well make sure." And I threw off my coat and began to loosen my shoes.

But the bitch had waded through the stream and gave tongue on the other side. I may say I was dizzy with relief. Now I knew what had happened. She had stopped there to bathe her feet.

In Shane's Castle we found her, standing flat against the wall, terrified before the deep baying of the dogs. Her feet were bare and she was standing in a clump of nettles, so unconscious was she of everything but the presence of the hounds.

"It's only us, Ann-Dolly!" I called. "Here, Carabine, show a light." And I changed the hounds' baying to shrill yelps with a couple of ungrateful kicks. Carabine tied a piece of oiled flax-tow to a stick and lit it.

"Ah, sure, my poor girl!" I said, when I saw her.

"Ah, Miss Ann-Dolly, but you've wandered far," said Carabine.

But Jenico said nothing.

She gave me a tortured little smile, with a twitch at the corner of her mouth, as if she were about to burst out crying, and she gave Carabine another. But at Jenico she stared whitely, and Jenico stared whitely at her. And neither said a word.

"Come out of them nettles, Ann-Dolly," I told her, "come out of them nettles, and explain to me why you ran away from your comfortable home—"

Carabine was pulling me by the sleeve.

"Mister Kerry," he said, "come on. The Ferret McClure will be wanting his hounds back."

"To hell," said I, "with the Ferret McClure. He'll get his hounds back when it suits me and not before."

"Come on now, Mister Kerry. God knows what they'll be feeding the pacer down at The Orange Sash."

"To hell," said I, "with the pacer. They can feed him

boiled beef and cabbage for all I care. It's not my horse. It's Jenico's."

"Come outside, Mister Kerry, till I tell you something."

"Will you let me alone, Carabine?" I said. "Sure you can tell me nothing I don't know. What are you two gawking at each other for?" I asked Jenico and Ann-Dolly.

James Carabine stuck his torch in the ground and lifting my twelve stone in his hands as easily as though I were a child, he carried me out.

"Mister Kerry, your Honour," he growled, "will you, for God's sake, come on to hell out o' this, and leave your cousin Jenico and Miss Ann-Dolly by their lee lone?"

XX

One of the poets, Shakespeare or Thomas Moore, I don't know or care which, speaks of a "sea change." And a sea change, the turn from the grey dullness of the sea to its jewelled fresh beauty, is the only word to use for the metamorphosis of that house and townland. Sheena Spanya, it had been called of old, before my grandfather in his admiration for what he termed the King's blasted English, had it changed in the county survey to Spanish Men's Rest.

There had hung over it an invisible veil of tragedy. Something lay between that sweet house and the sun. And no birds were there, nor bees. The fruit trees were not barren but ungenerous, and the flowers seemed always to say: What are we doing in this lonely unmusical place? And when the trees rustled it was not crisply, making a gay small music, but heavily, as though they were weary, weary. And that field where the Spanish men lay — you sat on the dyke of it, and there was no sweet peace there, such as smiles in our Church of Saint Columba's-in-Paganry, such as makes you feel that beyond the bronze doors of death is sunshine and singing and old friendships taken up again.

There was no peace there, but a dreariness, a dreariness as of grey rain and blackish yew tree. The field was a surly desolation.

But since Ann-Dolly went there to live in and be mistress of my cousin Jenico's house, the veil has lifted. It seems as if the Spanish men had ceased warring against the estate from beneath the grass. Now that their sister and their duchess reigns there, and after her will reign the little children of her body, it would appear as if a pact had been arranged between the restless men and the enchained land. For now the land is free. Where once the sunshine was heavy as a fog, it now is gay like a child's song. Even the rain is gentle. In the woods about, the bluebells toss their heads, like pert young women. The primrose smiles gently from the banks, and everywhere are birds, fat blackbird and trilling thrush, small linnet, robin redbreast and the bishop wren. As you pass through the garden, where soon small children will be, the apple and pear trees seem to stop you, so vital they are, saying: See, all spring and summer we have laboured to produce the golden and russet fruit. Surely you will not pass us by! And everywhere is the serious bee, and that rejoices one, such a token of good will to a house the golden bees are.

But of all miracles the greatest is the Spanish Field. It, which was so desolate, where the grass was grey, which was dumb of birds, is now gay and smiling, is bathed in sunshine, and at the sleepers' heads the Atlantic is repentant and sings a soft low lullaby and above them the skylark flings out his brave joyous song. Their coverlet is blue in spring, and in summer is gay with daisies and buttercups. They slumber well now, and we do not grudge their sleep or bed to them. Our hearts are in the soil of the realm they rose in arms against. But they were greatly valorous, and it is so long ago. So — God rest you, valiant gentlemen! Give you good night!

TWO

TALE OF MY AUNT JENEPHER'S WOOING

TWO

Tale of my aunt Jenepher's wooing

I

I don't suppose that one family ever held two more out-wardly dissimilar people than my uncle Valentine and my aunt Jenepher. My uncle Valentine is a vast violent man, his shoulders spreading like a sail, and bearded from belly to eyes. That great fan-shaped ruddy beard, very like Samson's, covers — ladies of quality have told me — one of the handsomest faces in the United Kingdom, but ladies of quality have a way of overrating the lovers of their youth. My uncle Valentine's entry into a room illustrates that actuary's phrase, riot and civil commotion. My uncle Valentine never speaks, he bellows. There are three great sounds that have dignity — thunder, the crash of the sea against rocks, and the conversational tones of my uncle Valentine.

My aunt Jenepher, though not a small woman, is tiny be-side that immense red presence. My uncle Valentine is second of the immense family my grandfather had, and of which there are left only he and my uncle Cosimo and my aunt Jenepher. My aunt Jenepher is the youngest, and it would seem that out of a gallant and handsome line (whose beauty has not descended to this generation, more pity!) she was the masterpiece. You would never have taken her for a woman in her middle thirties, so girlish was her figure, so lissom it was, so like a young eager tree. There is no blacker, more silken hair in all Ireland than is on my aunt Jenepher's head. Her brow and nose are noble, but not that cold Phidian nobility of statues. Her mouth is among the prettiest mouths in the world and always smiling, either the open smile of merriment or the soft smile of reflection. Her head is balanced like a flower on its stalk, like a soft dignified flower on its graceful stalk. The lashes of my aunt Jenepher's eyes are like the petals of a flower. It is impossible for unhappiness, black unhappiness, to exist where my aunt Jenepher is. When my aunt Jenepher enters a room, you feel that windows are thrown open in the springtime. When my aunt Jenepher speaks in her sweet contralto, you feel you have never known the full values of human speech before, so soft, so vibrant that deep voice is.

My uncle Valentine has an eye like a hawk, to use the country expression. There is nothing he cannot see, from the look of guilt in your eye to the defect in the horse you are trying to sell him, no matter how cleverly concealed. There will be one shrewd look, and you will be treated to an apocryphal genealogy of your family in no generation of which is the issue legitimate, but always interesting. There is a belief in Ireland that my uncle Valentine can see around a corner, to use another country phrase.

To watch Aunt Jenepher walk about that old house of ours, the gardens and lawns, you would not know she has not two eyes as good as any other person's. When one has walked in the dark since ever so little, one develops a sense of direction and of obstacles. This is a very good explanation. There is also another, quoting Saint Luke: "He shall give His angels charge over thee, to help thee: and in their hands they shall bear thee up, lest at any time thou dash thy foot against a stone." You can take your choice. Myself I prefer the latter one. About Destiny Bay she went without any help, if you except that gold-headed ebony stick she carried that had once been the sainted Bishop Berkeley's. Every flower in the garden she knew: the violets and daffodils of spring, the roses of summer, the great hedges of lupins, with their heavy honey odour; and where the hives of the bees were she was at home. That ancient mysterious commonwealth had a kinship with her.

"There is no honey in Ireland like our honey," the old gardener used to say: "and do you know why, young fellow, your Honour? Because the bees like working for your aunt, Miss Jenepher."

The feathered quality of the ferns and the glossiness of the flowers he ascribed to her presence. "For what do flowers grow on?" he would ask. "'Tis not th' excellence of soil, but the kindliness of the people. For God's sake," he would call out to my aunt, "will your Ladyship leave them dahlias be. You have the heart crossways in me."

"Have you any flowers for luncheon, Duncan?"

"I can spare none," he would say grimly. But he would turn up five minutes later with bunches. "—and let your Ladyship not be bothering me again."

She always says she never misses her sight, does my aunt Jenepher. She pities us, because this sight of ours interrupts our other senses and we cannot get the true value of the lark's song, or of the thrush's or the linnet's or the blackbird's rhapsody, or the song the wind makes among the heather, or the scent of the heather itself, the soft intoxicating Celtic scent.

That may be. But, my God! Not to have eyes for the sweet heads of the two-year-olds in the paddock, for the glossy pack racing up the five-furlong course to the post! Not to see the huge Atlantic break in rosettes, in fountains, in clouds of foam on the cliffs of Destiny Bay! The unnamable beauty of the evening star by the small crescent moon! The mountains with their purple regal coats! The daffodils that sway like young girls dancing! How can one believe in God, if one has not eyes?

"There is only one thing I cannot imagine, Kerry. Flowers and mountains, horses, men and girls, I can imagine. But one thing is a mystery to me."

" What is that, Aunt Jenepher? "

" Clear water."

" Water! " said my uncle Valentine in a voice of horror, for my uncle Valentine is none of your blue ribbon men. " Water be damned! "

II

After a while in electric New York; or in soft unchanging London; or on the golden strands of the Caribbean; or in Venice singing with beauty; or in that Monegasque gambling den, where sooner or later all good Irishmen are to be found, it is good for body and soul to wander back to Destiny Bay. It is an Ulster cranny. Around the thirty square miles or so of the district the mountains spread like a horseshoe, and in front of it are the cliffs and strand facing the Atlantic like an armed man. No railroad comes within ten miles of my people's house, for there is nothing to develop there. Here and there are great fertile fields where grows barley, or flax. Here are great stretches of bogland, where the red-billed moor hen and the snipe, and the invisible whistling otter are sole tenantry. Those of the peasants who speak Erse speak the beautiful tongue of Bishop Bedell's Bible. Those who speak English speak the tongue of Cromwell, the simple powerful phrasing of the solemn oath and covenant. They are all planter folk, barring ourselves. The only other family there of high standing — I speak of those mentioned in " The Nobility and Gentry " — are the Pascoes, Cornish soldiering people who came over and were granted lands. The name Destiny Bay has a peculiar derivation. The Erse name was Port Fale, but my grandfather, Sir Alick MacFarlane, a most dogmatic man, had it changed. Some whirlwind of Irish politics decided him to erase everything Irish from his manor. He had the local schoolmaster come to him.

"What does Port Fale mean?"

"The bay of the cliff, Sir Alick."

"Isn't there a word 'Fale', destiny?" asked my grandfather. "How about Lia Fale, the Stone of Destiny?"

"It isn't the same word, Sir Alick."

My grandfather bristled. I am told that one of the supplementary wonders of the world was to see my grandfather bristling.

"Are you contradicting me?" he asked the poor little man. And so our home and the district about it came to be known as Destiny Bay.

The only place in the United Kingdom where the gypsies ever intermarry with householders is at Destiny Bay. So that between the Scottish, and Irish, and Cornish and gypsy blood we are a violent restless folk. The people of Donegal call us the "Paganachs", or pagans, and the dwellers in Derry speak of us as the mountainy people. But of course that is nothing to what we call these good law-abiding folk. It is certain that the Most Reverend the Lord Primate of all Ireland mentions us specially in his prayers, but this was due to an incident concerning a narrow-minded vicar who objected to having his church used for a main of cockfighting. It isn't very interesting and you can read about it elsewhere. His sister published a pamphlet entitled "The Martyrdom of the Reverend Timothy White."

Always Destiny Bay was a good place to return to. The hawthorn trees heavy with moss, the shrubs near the cliffs, flying like sphinxes landward, because of the weight of the Atlantic storms, the crying of the curlew and the peewit, the vast sailing moon—all these were things not to be duplicated elsewhere. Always there would be my aunt Jenepher with her gracious beautiful presence and her understanding, and my uncle Valentine, who is the easiest man in the world to borrow money from. Always there was something of interest in Destiny: a London Prize Ring fight be-

tween a gypsy and a local man; a horse race for ten pounds
a side; or there would be great news, as of Molly Mac-
Guigan, the barber's daughter, having gone to America with
the Hibernian Players and been hailed as a second Bern-
hardt; or how Johnny Malone had won the accordion
playing championship of the world at Crystal Palace,
London.

I had come back from Denmark, whither I had gone as
honorary secretary to the Head of the Irish Agricultural
Commission, investigating why the melancholy Danes were
cutting us out of the English butter market. Just hard work
on their part.

"I'm glad you're home, Kerry," my uncle Valentine
greeted me. "I'm back from Dublin myself. I'm gey
glad you're home."

"What's wrong, sir?"

"Your aunt Jenepher's dying."

I was terrified, for there was something in the dejection
of that great violent man that was like a battleship of the
line striking her colours. I sped to my aunt Jenepher. I
found her sitting by the fire in the Tower room.

"Is that you, Kerry, long lad?"

"What's amiss, Aunt Jenepher?"

She was thinner, paler than usual, but nothing about her,
it seemed to me, betokened dying. I told my uncle so after
dinner.

"It's just a foolish idea of yours, uncle Valentine."

"I tell you the woman's dying."

"She's not dying."

"The woman's dying."

"But she's not, uncle Valentine!"

"She's dying," insisted my uncle Valentine, "but she'll
die happy," said he.

He told me that she, who had loved the garden so much,
loved the bees, loved the wind from the heather mountains,

would go out no longer, but remained about the great rambling house.

"You know how she loved to walk down the yew lane, even in winter weather."

I said I did. I could never think of the dignity and beauty of our long alley of golden yews without seeing the beauty and dignity of my aunt Jenepher, and her walking between them in the last warmth of the setting sun.

"What's come on her, Uncle Valentine?"

"Somebody has bought the Pascoe house and is doing it up to live there. Who it is I don't know, but an American of some kind, I think, and it's broken your aunt Jenepher's heart."

There was a romance in my aunt Jenepher's life that had to do with the Pascoes. The last of them, Digory, and she had been betrothed. Digory had been terribly wild and had spent the last of the family money, racing unluckily, and it was at my aunt Jenepher's suggestion he had gone East to make a new fortune. I think the six months before he went and while he was engaged to my aunt Jenepher were the worthiest and happiest of his life. He was a tall handsome fellow, with dark passionate eyes. He set sail for the Malay States, to work on a rubber plantation, but at Marseilles he disembarked, waiting over between boats, and went to Monte Carlo on the chance of recouping fortune there instead of in the East.

"While he was there," said my uncle Valentine, "he had the devil's own hard luck, and as often happens he took a dislike to a man playing at the same table who was always winning. You go a little crazy in a gambling place, Kerry my boy; and the thought came to Digory that this man was the cause of his bad luck.

"This man was a fat tubby little fellow, who had made a fortune in groceries, and was now lording it on the Riviera. There was nothing this man wanted to be taken for more

than a great gentleman. Digory, as you've seen from his
picture, looked like a king. He had the manners of a grand
duke, too, had Digory. Only for the cruel strain in the lad
he'd have been a great fellow.

"Digory gets it into his head that if this man could be
induced to leave the tables his luck would turn. So he
bumps into the grocer man. 'You've struck me!' says
Digory. 'I'm sorry,' says the grocer. 'Sorry be damned!'
says Digory. 'My friends will wait on you.'

"So he sends Sir Alastair Baird and Roaring Johnny
McLaughlin around to the poor grocery fellow. There
weren't two finer men in Ireland than Baird and Johnny.
Nobility was oozing from them. They told him Major
Digory Pascoe wanted satisfaction for the insult. And the
grocer fellow, mind you, afraid not to be thought a gentleman, consented. Baird told me the sweat was pouring from
him.

"Digory said: 'So much the better. If I kill this fellow
my luck'll change.' Digory was superstitious. I've never
seen a better shot with a duelling pistol than Digory. 'Twas
he killed Captain Kelly at Boulogne. Begad, Kerry, Digory
was nearly a teetotaller for fear it would spoil his aim.

"So they met the next morning back of Monte. The
grocer's knees were knocking, and he had to tie a handkerchief around the butt of the pistol on account of the wetness
of his hand. Roaring Johnny said it was the funniest thing
he had ever seen in his life. My bold Digory was cool as
be-damned, for it wasn't his first nor his fifth time out,
so —"

"I don't want to hear about it, Uncle Valentine. I think
it's scandalous for a gentleman to kill an inoffensive beggar
for a whim."

My uncle Valentine gave that vast laugh of him, that is
like thunder.

"Begad, no!" he said. "The grocer killed Digory."

III

My uncle Valentine was a bad liar, because he was not practised in the art. This is not to be ascribed to virtue but to arrogance. Where the meaner sort of person had to double like a hare, he stood like the Irish wolf dog. In the matter of the death of Digory he could not tell the truth, so in putting off an explanation of Digory's end through floods by land or sea, the Act of God or the King's enemies, he fell into a worse lie. He kept Digory alive for the present. At Christmas and at Easter we wrote letters from Digory, addressed from the Malay States, or Borneo, or Cochin-China, telling how his health was, his prospects, and of the hard luck from simooms and hurricanes and tornadoes which was retarding his progress. My uncle Valentine would vanish into his study and coming back with an armful of letters tied with ribbons of various shades, from one of them he would select a pleasant sentiment, which even to my inexperienced ears sounded hardly masculine. We posted them in Dublin or Belfast in time to get to Destiny Bay for Christmas morning or the Saturday before Easter.

"My dear Jenepher," my uncle Valentine would read aloud. "This is trusting you are in the excellent health which I enjoy, and for which God be thanked." And then would follow a dissertation on the simoom or on rubber, which we had bodily taken from the excellent encyclopedia of Mr. Britannica's. "To-night when the stars are in full glory in God's heaven, and when I should be revelling in the jewellery of the universe my thoughts are with you and my Ulster home. O Head of dark locks!" We had changed "auburn" to "dark." And concluded: "Yours very sincerely, Digory Pascoe." Damned good! we thought it.

"Thank you, Valentine, and thank you, dear Kerry, for reading it," my aunt Jenepher would say.

"We'll be losing you some of these days, Jenepher. But we won't let you go for a long time yet. Hey, Kerry?"

"Dear Valentine! Dear Kerry!"

But afterwards my uncle Valentine would wipe his forehead and say:

"Begad, boy, we'll have to send Digory home some of these days and drown him on the voyage. That'll make a good elegant end."

But for twelve years, Digory managed to evade his "good, elegant end", until it seemed, according to my uncle Valentine, that my aunt Jenepher was near hers.

"Go down," said my uncle Valentine, "to the Widow McGinty's hotel, and bring up what I left there. 'Tis something I got in Dublin."

"Have you brought something else home?"

"Mind your own business and do what I tell you!"

There was always a sporting element about what my uncle Valentine brought home. Once it was a large brown bear he had purchased from a gypsy. "'Twill keep away burglars," said my uncle Valentine, as though any poor God-forsaken burglar would trust himself to the hellhounds of Destiny Bay. He chained it in a corner of the stables, and fed it with honey and turnips and an occasional bottle of whiskey. One morning the bear escaped and cleaned up the Croppy Boy bar of patrons and attendants, and getting most riotously drunk it made straight for the police barracks, where it clawed the tunic and trousers off a constable and was proceeding to embrace the sergeant when a bullet put an end to its career. It became over-Hibernicised, poor Bruin! And once my uncle Valentine, playing picquet with the Duc de Corey, that peer of the old Holy Roman Empire, brought home the most prized ducal possession. The duke was of an extremely religious disposition as well as having a passion for cards, and so had his coffin made, a beautiful mahogany affair, silver-mounted. He loved picquet to distraction, but he was no match for my uncle Valentine.

"Put this in the drawing-room," my uncle Valentine told the astonished servants. "We'll use it as a cellarette." And only the prospect of tears from my aunt Jenepher restored his last home to the poor old duke.

So that I didn't know what to expect at the Widow McGinty's hotel.

"Did Sir Valentine MacFarlane leave anything here?"

"He left a gentleman, Master Kerry, the nicest-spoken gentleman I ever did see, a poodle dog, and three cases o' German wine. The wine and the dog I'm sending up, and here's the gentleman."

He was a tall swarthy man, with something of the gypsy in his appearance. A fine-looking, brave man. A man you would trust your life to.

"Your uncle Valentine," he told me, "asked me to come up and stay a while here. Your uncle Valentine," he smiled, "is a very cogent man."

"He is," I agreed. "But forgetful. He omitted to tell me your name."

"My name is Patrick Herne," he said. "But your uncle Valentine asked me to go under another name, the name of Digory Pascoe."

"Great God!" I said to myself.

"Your uncle explained he had a sister who is blind and not well, and that there was a boy-and-girl attachment between your aunt and this Pascoe. If this deception can help the unfortunate lady I am only too glad."

"You are very kind," I uttered savagely. And then my heart misgave me, for looking at the man I found he *was* very kind. And looking more closely still I found him intensely like the old picture of Digory my aunt had. Many years older, naturally, but uncannily like Digory.

"You aren't Digory Pascoe? Are you?"

"No," he said. "I'm not. I'm just Patrick Herne."

IV

I told my uncle Valentine that the whole scheme was outrageous. And moreover, my aunt Jenepher would know at once that it wasn't Digory Pascoe.

"My dear Kerry," my uncle Valentine patronised, "when you've seen as much of the world as I have, you'll be surprised how easily women are fooled."

"That may be, but how are you going to explain —"

"Explain?" roared my uncle Valentine. "Didn't I find him? Haven't I done my share? It's up to you to explain him," he said. "Aren't you the world's champion explainer? Didn't I hear you explain successfully to the Colonel of the Welsh Borderers that your twenty-year-old blind hunter was a slip of a colt and would one day win the Grand National for him? You could explain the horns and tail off the devil himself."

There was no need for much explanation, for the man Patrick Herne had better brains than either of us, which is not saying a lot, God knows. Besides, my aunt Jenepher asked for no explanation at all. With his immense kindness there was great dignity to Herne. It was a pleasure to me to sit by him and my aunt Jenepher and hear him talk of the East Indies where he undoubtedly had been. He made you feel the explosive sunshine of the places, the brown Cingalese and men of Java and Borneo, the flowers that had strange dramatic colouring, the yellow priests with shaven heads, the stately elephants, the gongs of the temples. He knew so much about animals that it enchanted us, my uncle Valentine and me, to listen to him. We, who had been bred to dogs and horses and our quarry the fox, knew the authentic note when he spoke of the elephant and tiger and the spotted pard, and the little sun bear of Borneo, that is not bigger than a big dog, and has the pathetic quality of a child.

"I had a bear myself once," said my uncle Valentine,

"that got to taking a drop too much, and one day — " and he would proceed to relate the scandalous episode of the constable's trousers.

It seemed to us that we had known this man all our living days, so much at home with him we were. He came with us to races, he came to fairs. He stepped into the rugged, somehow florid life of Destiny Bay as though he belonged there. A smaller man would have been swamped by it. I have never seen anything in life or on the stage like his grave courtesy. He was as much with my aunt Jenepher as possible, and it was he who enticed her out into the gardens and woods again, saying he had forgotten this and that. I liked to see them together, wandering through the garden or down the alley of yews, he so big, so rugged, so handsome in his way, so gravely courteous; she so lovely, such beauty shining from darling soul through sweet perfect body, and her low laughter coming like music at some story of Herne's, or her face attuned to wonder at some recital of foreign parts. He had a manner of giving his arm that I doubt if even my uncle Valentine, great gentleman though he was, could equal.

My aunt Jenepher had two great talents, though she was very shy about them. She was a wonderful pianist, though of, I suppose, a low order of playing. I mean this: anything she had ever heard she could play through and of course she could not read and so naturally there was an immensity of music unknown to her. My uncle Valentine used, three or four times a year, to get a man from Dublin to come and play new famous compositions, and so wonderful was Aunt Jenepher's memory that she could always remember them. Myself I'd rather hear her play the searching folk music of Ulster, or pipe music such as she could imitate wonderfully, than anything else. I suppose people will laugh at me, just as I myself smile at an unknowledgeable man on a horse. or handling a boat. But there — As though

Patrick Herne were as close to her as myself or my uncle Valentine, my aunt Jenepher went to the great piano and played: I can remember nights when we sat in the drawing-room of Destiny Bay in formal broadcloth and linen, while my aunt Jenepher played. It is a great square room, with heavy furniture and paintings of MacFarlanes, with wax candles and lamps, and through the doorlike windows which my uncle Valentine had put in, the golden August moon rose high over Creetyre Point, and a very faint chiming of the sea seemed to keep time with my aunt Jenepher playing.

It struck me, and I nearly had to laugh aloud, that my uncle Valentine was a very puzzled man. Before he had brought Patrick Herne to the house, he had imagined for himself a picture of my aunt Jenepher dying, wasting away as the ladies in the early part of the reign of good Queen Victoria wasted, of a romantic but quite sanitary disease. They grew frailer every day, while the lover of their youth stood by, a strong silent figure suffering visibly. They drew a last romantic breath, the broken-hearted family bowed in grief, the strong silent figure went into exile, to shoot rhinoceros in Mashonaland, or to visit the Dalai Lama in Tibet. That is what rhinoceros and the Dalai Lama are for.

And here was my aunt Jenepher, in the best of health, playing my uncle Valentine's favourite, in fact his only opera, "The Bohemian Girl", her exquisite white hands flitting like butterflies over the keys. There were lines of wonder in my uncle's red forehead. There was a look of wonder about his immense red beard.

I have said my aunt Jenepher had two talents: the other was a trifle grotesque, and of which she was very much ashamed, but which had a quaint vital beauty. My aunt Jenepher was the best whistler I have ever heard, as I have previously said.

There is supposed to be something unladylike in this performance, and there is a country proverb that directs you to beat the devil out of a woman caught in the act. But I challenge you to find anything but beauty in my aunt Jenepher's whistling. You might be passing by our house and lands and hear the sweet high trill of a country song distilling itself in the clear air, each grace note, each shake, clear and crystal as dewdrops falling from the whitethorn branches, so that if you were a country person you would say: "Is it the fairies are in it, I wonder, and they on the march this day of spring? Or is it some foreign melodious bird that Sir Valentine is after buying for his delectation? Begor, I'll have the least taste of a squint!" And looking over the privet hedge you would see a very lovely Irish gentlewoman, seated on an old stone bench, her head lifted to the distant mountains, her sweet eyebrows raised, her exquisite hands resting on an antique gold-mounted ebony cane, sending through her lips in notes sweet as the blackbird's some old melody like "The Coolin." But if you wished to hear that you had better not pry, for the song would vanish as all secret lovely things vanish when you pry, like the little shoe-making leprechaun or the young of the otter, or the kingfisher that is the blue bird of poets.

There was magic in her whistling. I have often seen my uncle Valentine when the black mood was on him, standing with his hand thrust into his immense mane of red beard, aloof, terrible. Then my aunt Jenepher would enter the room, and there would begin to float in the air the strains of jig or hornpipe, "The Swallowtail Coat", or "The Green Fields of America", so cogent, so airy, so gay, but you could not help noticing it. She would pay no attention to my uncle Valentine, but go about the room, and sooner or later you would hear the tap-tap of my uncle Valentine's foot upon the floor, and then a rhythmic sound as of a drum beating softly. My uncle Valentine was dancing. But my aunt Jenepher affected never to notice it. She went about her offices and later on out of the room, evidently as unhearing as she was unseeing.

She had the habit of playing the accompaniment to her whistling upon the piano. Nobody had ever heard her at this, I think, but my uncle Valentine and myself and others of the family, until one night we came in with the man, Patrick Herne. Her face flooded with a soft ruddy colour that was like the deeper sort of rose, but she went on playing and whistling.

One day my uncle Valentine and I came into the garden before lunch — Herne had gone off somewhere for the morning, and down near the beehives was my aunt Jenepher. She was whistling but there was no particular set tune to it. It was a clear wild trilling sound like a bird's. Indeed I remember seeing the blackbirds hopping bafflingly near the netted strawberry beds, stopping and putting their heads on one side in critical admiration.

"There you are!" said my uncle Valentine tragically. "That's done it." And he sat down on one of the stone benches.

"What, sir?" said I.

"Did you hear that?" said he.

"I did," said I. "It's only my aunt Jenepher whistling."

"It's only — " he jeered. "It's only — You may be the white-headed boy of the old ducks at Trinity," he told me with great contempt, "but to me, and fundamentally," he said, "you're only an ignorant, mountainy mick!"

V

The re-building, re-furbishing, re-decoration of the Pascoe home bothered my uncle fearfully. "It's deeper than old friendship," he said, "for we have been here since Ireland was first discovered by our great ancestor, the Egyptian Parthelon. The Pascoes have only been here since Oliver

Cromwell's time, and though they were but newcomers, yet our people got used to them. Nearly three hundred years we've been side by side. They were a fine Cornish family.

"I'm cursed if I know what sort are coming here at all," he said. "It was in London the sale was arranged, so the lawyers tell me.

"Myself," he told Patrick Herne, "am a great one for old faces, old ties. Yourself, Mr. Herne, are the first one I've taken to for a long time. I've a great mind," he said, "to go travelling again so as to avoid these new people."

"They mayn't be bad, Sir Valentine," said our butler, James Carabine.

"They'll never be like the Pascoes, a strange roaring race," said my uncle Valentine. And he began to tell the history of the Pascoes. There was great-grandfather Pascoe who had come from India with a fortune, so immense, so fat a man that he had to be assisted up from his chair every time he sat down. He would be served by none but Indian servants, and as the poor devils died off like flies in Ireland he was always sending for more. There was a field near Pascoe Manor called "The Indian Burial Ground." There was also a corner called the "Indian Queen's" where slept two bronze beauties, for great-grandfather Pascoe had not been so respectable as he might have been. There was also "Pirate Pascoe" who had privateered against the French in the Bonaparte wars. He had one mental failing: he believed every vessel on the sea was French, so he stripped and gutted Yankee clippers, honest Hollanders, an occasional British boat, everything that came his way. He was hanged on Tower Hill. They were all a wild race. Digory's father had had a fancy woman from among the gypsies and a child by her before he married Digory's mother.

"She was not his fancy woman, please your Honour, Sir Valentine," said Carabine. "She was his lawful wedded wife."

James Carabine was himself half gypsy and half Irish. He had soldiered with my uncle Valentine in the war against the Boers and earned the Maltese Cross "For Valour" for saving my uncle Valentine's — his officer's — life at Spion Kop. So that James Carabine was more a friend to the house than a servant, and privileged to speak at all times.

"What do you mean, James Carabine?"

"Alick Pascoe, please your Honour, married this woman in the Romany way, across the Romany fire, with Romany witnesses. It was valid in the eyes of the Romany people and valid in the eyes of God."

My uncle Valentine thought for a while.

"What became of her, Carabine?" I asked.

"One day she left, Master Kerry, whether it was on account of ill treatment from Pascoe, or the weight of four walls and a roof, I cannot tell. But she tucked her child under her arm and went down the road with her head high, for she was a princess of Romany. Where she went after, it is beyond me to tell, — to the fertile fields of Alabama, or the lowlands of Holland, or to Grim Tartary, as they call it. Or they may be dead itself. I've heard it denied," said James Carabine, "that gypsies die, but that I know to be untrue, though they die hard."

"That marriage, James Carabine, might be valid in the eyes of God," decided my uncle, "but it would not be valid with the Ulster King-at-Arms."

"Och, him!" said Carabine.

"Nor it wouldn't be valid with me," said my uncle, "who am High Sheriff of the County of Tyrconnell, and a Justice of the King's Peace."

"Then it wouldn't be valid at all," said Carabine.

"You seem to put a great deal of value on birth and breeding," said Patrick Herne.

"I do, sir," said my uncle Valentine, "and so do you, for you're the most sensible man I ever met. Would you take an ordinary horse without any particular blood in him, and run him for the Derby race?"

"I would not," said Herne.

"Would you enter an unbred dog for the Waterloo Cup?"

"I would not."

"There you are," said my uncle Valentine.

"But, Uncle Valentine," I ventured, "from the poorest and most obscure people great men arise. Even in our own day and certainly in all times good and just and powerful men arise from nothing."

"Seemingly, Kerry," said my uncle Valentine, "but these beacons of justice and power are nothing but units of great families lost by marriage on the distaff side, by poverty in which there is nothing ignoble, by this circumstance and that, and when the opportunity arrives, through staying-power and courage, which are the attributes of nobility, these men succeed, proving illustrious blood."

"Uncle Valentine," I laughed, "I suppose you believe that in the Kingdom of Heaven there are nothing but old families."

"Who else could there be, Kerry?" asked my uncle Valentine.

For our own family, my uncle Valentine placed it far above the Plantagenets and Capets, "for we are descended from Par-the-lon," he said, "who was the first invader of Ireland, and who came from Egypt, as the Annals of the Four Masters prove. This Par-the-lon," he continued, "was a younger son of the King of Egypt of his time, as is shown by documentary evidence in the British Museum. And this king was descended from Nimrod, son of Cash, son of Ham, son of Noah. It was from Nimrod," said my uncle Valentine, "that we got our fine seat in the saddle and our taste for the fox.

"The genealogy of Noah you can look up in your Bible, and you'll find him directly descended from Adam and Eve,

so that you might say that we MacFarlanes of Destiny Bay
are personally created by God!"

I wish you could have seen my uncle Valentine as he
pronounced this, his great glossy red beard on his immense
broad chest, his fine head raised. He was like some ancient
ruddy majestic Assyrian king.

"But, Uncle Valentine," I suggested, "every one is personally created by God. Johnny the Gander down in the village, and Mollie McGinty that keeps the hotel, and the
travelling tinkers, and—"

My uncle Valentine brought his vast fist down on the
table so that the plates jumped from their mats, and the por-
traits on the walls rattled and the candles scattered their
wax.

"I will have no atheism talked in this house," thundered
my uncle Valentine.

VI

I never saw a person who loved the country around Destiny Bay more than Patrick Herne did. The heather, the
rowan trees, the little streams, the thunder of the sea's
artillery against the cliffs, its galloping cavalry entranced
him. He had the faculty of silence which is a gift direct
from Heaven.

"I suppose I'll soon have to be going," he said wistfully
to me one day. "Your aunt Jenepher's well now, and—I
have enjoyed myself here."

"Where are you going?" I asked.

"I don't know," he said. "I had a place settled before
I came here, but now it's gone wrong. It's a bad thing to
be this way: to have no occupation and plenty of money,
and no place to go."

"Then why don't you stay with us?" I asked. "Soon
I'll have a wandering fit and my uncle Valentine will get

lonely. And the hunting here is good. Small as it is, there is n't a better pack of foxhounds in Ireland than my uncle Valentine's. We love to have you. My uncle Valentine feels at home with you, and you 're all right."

" I 'm not ' all right '," said Patrick Herne. " I was once a clown in a circus."

He smiled at my astonishment. " Yes," he said, " a clown with a powdered face, and red paint at the tip of his nose."

" Oh, that 's difficult," I said.

" It is," he understood me.

I was afraid of a faint tinge of I won't say contempt but of patronage coming into my uncle Valentine's feeling for Herne. My uncle Valentine comes from a feudal stock, in a place where feudalism existed a hundred years longer than in any other spot in Europe, and where as yet we are but half-civilised. My uncle Valentine was more accustomed to govern people than to philosophise, so one can hardly blame this old-world gentleman for not accepting one who had been a clown with a painted nose as his equal. This is a reprehensible viewpoint in modern days, I know. I will admit freely that the beadle is the equal of the bishop and the foot soldier of the field marshal; but then, I will admit anything, loathing arguments.

" You were n't always a clown?" I asked.

" No," said Herne, digging in his pockets for his pipe. " I was an animal trainer, lions and tigers."

" By God! That 's a man's job."

" It requires some skill," said Herne, " and a great deal of sympathy, and a tremendous faith in the presence of God.

" Oh, I like Destiny Bay," he burst out, " I hate to go. The sea and the bonny mountains and the purple bogs, and the gypsies, coming and going, the Lovells and the Lees and the Hernes — "

" You 're a gypsy, Patrick Herne," I discovered.

"Only half," he said, "the other half —"

"Is Pascoe, by God!" I roared, for now I saw whence the resemblance to Digory came. "You're by Digory Pascoe's father out of the Romany girl, the Romany wife, I mean — I'm sorry, Patrick Herne."

"Wife or girl, does it matter," laughed Herne, "now I'm here?"

I thought I had made enough discoveries for one day, but in the afternoon, talking to my aunt Jenepher in the garden, she broke suddenly into the discussion we were having with this question: —

"Kerry, who is this man you and Valentine have told me was Digory Pascoe?"

There are occasions when lying is of no use.

"How did you know?"

"You might deceive a person with face or hand, Kerry, but you can never deceive with a voice. A voice is the vibrations of a person's being, and, dear Kerry," she put her hand up to where my shoulder was, "Digory Pascoe has been dead these many years."

"And you let us write those letters?"

"It was such a kind sweet thing of you and brother Valentine to do, and I was afraid to tell you I knew. You were both such dears."

"Why aren't you afraid now, Aunt Jenepher?"

But she gave no reason.

"Tell me about this man, Kerry."

"I can't tell you much, Aunt Jenepher. But I like him. I think he is a fine man, a courageous man, and a kind man."

"I know that, Kerry," she said. "I know all that. I can stand beside a person and know him. His virtues and defects, Kerry, they come to me like soft music, or like little jarring sounds. I like this man. I like his silence, Kerry. One would never be afraid while that man is about."

"He's all right," I agreed, "Patrick Herne is."

"It's strange, Kerry," my aunt Jenepher went on, "to get the sense that a person is thinking the same as you're thinking. Often I stand here in the alley of yews when the sun is going down, and the little chill of evening is on the land, and the flowers give their last sigh before closing for the night, and the scent of heather is in the air—I know that God is walking along the cliffs of Destiny, and, Kerry, that man knows it too. Though we say nothing, yet we each know it, and each knows the other knows it."

"Myself," I said lightly, "I have a weakness for the moonlight and a touch of courting," and I kissed her when she blushed.

But I was worried and puzzled, so much that my uncle Valentine noticed it when he came.

"There you are," he said, "with a face on you as long as a fool's funeral! What's wrong with you?"

"I was just thinking."

"You flatter yourself," said my uncle Valentine.

VII

My uncle Valentine was himself worried that night. I could see it in the depth of the wrinkles on his brow; in his lack of attention to the trout Patrick Herne and I had caught that day; in this little detail and that. Sooner or later, I knew, he would acquaint us with what was bothering him, for he was not a man to keep things in long.

"Did you ever," he asked suddenly, "did you ever hear me talk about a horse?"

James Carabine stood still in his tracks, and Patrick Herne smiled. My aunt Jenepher looked up.

"Never, sir," I answered. "Indeed, I might say I never knew the word pass your lips."

"It was Limerick Pride," said my uncle. And then I knew it was serious.

Limerick Pride, by Sarsfield out of Haughty Lady, seventeen years before, was my uncle Valentine's property, and from colt to six-year-old had won everything before it in Ireland. The Leopardstown Gold Cup, the Irish Derby, the Irish Two Thousand Guineas. Indeed, Limerick Pride was so good that for the Baldoyle Vase, he was handicapped at the prohibitive weight of nine stone four pounds. As a hurdler he took everything before him. And then my uncle Valentine had a week of dreadful losses at the Sheridan Club, and sold out his own personal possessions. Limerick Pride went to the States, where he was a complete failure, so much so that he passed from owner to owner and at last came down to work in a cab. Thence some one rescued him, and all trace was lost of him. To part with him all but broke my uncle's heart, and the story of his later misfortunes nearly drove the red baronet crazy. But spend how much money he cared not, he could never find Limerick Pride again.

"The loss of Limerick Pride and the death of your dear father, Kerry, were the two great trials of my life," I've heard my uncle Valentine say. "If it hadn't been a matter of honour, Kerry, I'd have shot the horse with my own hands before parting with him, and letting him into the hands of strangers."

"Do you remember Limerick Pride, James Carabine?"

"Do I remember my mother, your Honour?" answered Carabine.

"Limerick Pride was a horse of mine that I was very attached to," explained my uncle Valentine to Patrick Herne. "He was a great horse with the heart of a lion and some of the best blood in the world. He was by Sarsfield out of Haughty Lady, who was himself by Simple Soldier out of Jessamy Bride, who was by Simplicity out of Simonette, who was by Covenanter out of Quaker Lady —"

"Covenanter," broke in Carabine, "was by Game Cove

out of Aunt Dorothy, and Game Cove was by Irish Game-ster out of Covessa."

"Covessa herself," said my uncle Valentine, "was by Covert Coat out of Dogaressa."

"Best blood in Ireland," muttered Carabine, "and for horses or sportsmen that means the world."

"The last time I saw that horse was fifteen years ago, as a six-year-old, in Vine's auction rooms in Dublin."

We were all silent, knowing how much he took the part-ing to heart.

"Until I saw him to-day," he said, "with two other horses in Pascoe's ten-acre."

"Go to hell!" called Carabine in excitement. "It's a damned lie!"

"'Tis not a lie. James Carabine, would you know that horse?"

"Would I know Limerick Pride, Sir Valentine? Would I know him in the dark! And moreover, hadn't he got the queerest marking I ever saw on a horse? He was pure chestnut but for a white left ear."

"You'll find him in Pascoe's ten-acre," said my uncle. "The fellow that's bought the place from you," he winked violently at Patrick Herne — my aunt Jenepher and I took an immediate interest in our plates — "this man, whoever he is, and you say you don't know, has sent up a collection of cattle would do your heart good to see. Jerseys and Royal Dexters. There are a couple of hunters I like, three harness horses, my old darling Limerick Pride, and a trick mule."

"And a trick mule," shouted my uncle Valentine. I could see Carabine shudder. "What do you think of a fellow would have a trick mule?"

"I have a low opinion," said Carabine.

"I'm going over to London by the midnight train to Dublin," said my uncle Valentine, "and find out from the head lawyers who has bought the place. And I'm going to make him sell me my horse Limerick Pride."

"He might give him to you," suggested Patrick Herne.

"Give away Limerick Pride!" laughed my uncle. "The man would have to be crazy, and moreover, do you think I'd accept a present from the sort of man who would have a trick mule?"

"I don't suppose you would," said Herne.

"But sell him he will," said my uncle Valentine grimly, "for if he doesn't, he might as well settle in Hell as in Destiny Bay."

It was late that night after my uncle Valentine had left that Patrick Herne told me he was going too, the very next day.

"Where to, in God's name?"

"I think I'll put in a while in Africa."

"But why?"

"Oh, I suppose it's the gypsy wandering instinct," he laughed. "By the way, you can bring Limerick Pride across and put him in the paddock. He's a present from me to your uncle."

"Are you—"

"Yes," he said, "I'm the beggar with the trick mule. It's an old pal of mine. We worked together for years."

"But you're not going to leave Pascoe Manor?"

"It's just what I'm going to do, Kerry, my lad. I'll send up a steward from Dublin, and come back now and then. You might use the hunters for me, and if you don't mind keep an eye on Caligula the mule. He's not a bad sort."

"My uncle Valentine will be very put out at your going, Patrick Herne," I said.

"I'm going now so as to avoid arguments. I hate them as much as you do, Kerry."

"There'll be somebody'll be heart-broken at your going,

Patrick Herne. I don't suppose I should tell you, but there it is."

"You don't," said Herne slowly, "mean your aunt Jenepher?"

"I do."

"Are you sure of that? Are you quite sure, Kerry?"

"Utterly sure."

"Then I'll stay," said Patrick Herne.

VIII

I said: "All that's very fine. There's nothing I like better myself than to have a thing out. But why waste these splendid azure days in argument? The sun and the sea will not wait until you have all argued and settled, and had first principles discussed. I know my uncle Valentine. There's nothing he'd like better than to see you and my aunt Jenepher married. But — he'll spend the winter evenings arguing about it. He'll hold up the whole course of Irish politics until he has you knighted. He may even have a private bill introduced into Parliament about the Romany marriage. You don't know my uncle Valentine. This will be meat and drink to him.

"My dear Patrick Herne, go and get a license and be married here. Clear out of the way till he comes back. Take Aunt Jenepher to the Mediterranean with you, and by the time you come back, Pascoe Manor will be ready, and my uncle Valentine will be like a lamb. He'll be ten days in London. He won't stir out of the card room at White's until he's cleaned the place up. There will be old friends at the Service Clubs. Do it now."

So well did I argue and so expeditiously did I put everything through that I had them before the parson in our small Tudor church, before either of them really knew what was happening. Our church is a sweet old church, thick-builded, as it must be near the sea, and grey, and here and there yellow with stonewort. The light comes into it gently and glimmers on the brasses of the MacFarlanes who are dead and gone, and one always feels there is an angel about, a grey-bearded drowsy Georgian angel who takes snuff. The martins and the swallows build their nests in the eaves and the wild bees nest in the graveyard, and my uncle Valentine will not have them ousted, for he is lord of the manor. Without, in the graveyard in spring, are bluebells and primroses, and in summer are woodbine and wild roses. And the huddled mounds do not make you think of Death, but of old folk or children sleeping, so peaceful it is.

"It was ordained," said our padre, "for the mutual society, help and comfort, that the one ought to have of the other, both in prosperity and adversity. Into which holy estate these two persons present—"

I was standing behind so that I could not see my aunt Jenepher's face, but I could her small black hat, her costume of heather tweed, her beautiful small brown shoes, and from her left wrist hung Bishop Berkeley's cane, and in her hand was a great bunch of heather, that Carabine had searched the mountains for the evening before, a royal purple bunch with strands of white heather. And beside her was Herne, big and fine, like some powerful, well-blooded, great-hearted horse, and finer praise than that there is not in this world. I was thinking to myself what a fine recruit we had taken for Clan MacFarlane.

"'Wilt thou have this woman to be thy wedded wife, to live together after God's ordinance—'"

It was nice, a peaceful wedding. Behind us in the body of the church were Carabine, and Duncan the gardener, and the whole household of Destiny Bay, and a swarthy band of gypsies who all loved my aunt Jenepher and who had come to see her married. For best man I had pressed into service my cousin Jenico from Spanish Men's Rest, and as bridesmaid we had Eleanor Pendleton, pretty Nelly Pendleton, with her burning auburn hair. A fine gathering, and a lovely, a peaceful day.

"' . . . Wilt thou obey him in sickness and in health, and forsaking all other, keep thee only unto him, so long as ye both shall live?'" And my aunt Jenepher answered: "I will."

"'Who giveth this woman to be married to this man?'" asked the padre.

I was thinking of the letter I would have to write to my uncle Valentine that afternoon, and picking phrases for it: "My dear uncle Valentine: I know you will be delighted to hear—" when my cousin Jenico brought his heel sharply into my cannon bone.

"'Who giveth this woman to be married to this man?'"

"I give this woman—" I said, and I noticed a look of anxiety in the parson's eyes. Behind us in the church was the heavy thump of feet. I looked over my shoulder, and I saw the big presence, still wrapped in the huge travelling coat, and the immense copper-coloured beard. And then a hand caught me by the shoulder, and sent me spinning down the chancel until I bumped into the baptismal font.

"Stand aside, you pup," I heard, and, "I give this woman to be married to this man," roared my uncle Valentine.

THREE

TALE OF JAMES CARABINE

THREE

Tale of James Carabine

I

If you were to meet him on the roads about Destiny Bay, or in Dublin, whither he goes as body servant sometimes to my aunt Jenepher, with his black clothes, with his erect carriage, with his suspicion of side whiskers, you might take Carabine for a minister of some faith dissenting from the Church of Ireland, by law established. There is something so honest, so clear about his grey eyes. Indeed, you might avoid him, fearing he would pluck you by the sleeve and ask you that most intimate and embarrassing of all questions: Have you found Salvation?

Of course, if you notice his broken nose, his heavy hands, you might say: This man has been a prize fighter in his youth, but there — a Christian missionary might receive these stigmata telling the gentle tale of Bethlehem and Calvary to some emphatic, lusty pagan. We who know the race course and the ring, recognise his craft from the hunched left shoulder, the eye that moves while the head does not. We who know his name recognise him as James Carabine, former champion, the last of the giants of the London Prize Ring, the conqueror of Simon Kennedy, and Diamond, the Black Man; McCoy, the Glasgow Plasterer, and that most terrible of fighters who was called the Bristol Lamb.

I know the modern glove mongers — they are rather a sordid lot. They are not the thugs and monsters the Society of Friends would have us believe — indeed, one wishes often they were, watching a fumbling match of men stalling through a ten-round bout. Nor are they the romantics certain journalists would have us think. Good journeymen athletes with a knack of their hands . . . The Prize Ring bred better, braver men, the men of the bare knuckles and the finish fights — Tom Cribb, who fought and conquered the Negro Molyneux; Tom Sayers, who drew with Heenan, the Benicia Boy, in a battle thought the most terrific of the ring; that Gully, whom the Game Chicken conquered, whose aspiration it was in early life to be champion of England, owner of the Derby winner, and member of Parliament, and who achieved all three; Sir Daniel Donelly, our great Irish Champion, who was knighted by the Prince Regent after his defeat of the gigantic Captain Cooper at the Curragh of Kildare; Bendigo, who gave his name to a great race horse, and to an Australian city; that Gentleman Jackson, winner over Mendoza, who was friend to Byron, and to our own overrated and greatly loved Tom Moore; the Tipton Slasher, that terrific hitter, who succumbed to great Sayers. Great men these, lion-hearted, proud of their craft, —and the last of these was Carabine.

James Carabine is somewhat over sixty years of age. His tale of years he doesn't know exactly, for he can neither read nor write. When he wants to date a matter, he will say it occurred in the spring of the year of So-and-so's Derby, and such a horse's Grand National, or the year that Sullivan beat Paddy Ryan for the championship of America. He has a prodigious memory, and a gift for selecting the outstanding features of comparatives such as we literates, with our science of filing by numbers, can hardly conceive. There is none who knows the moods of the sea better than Carabine, or the approaching changes of the weather. He knows the name of each bird and flower and small animal in our land, and such strength of mind has

Nature given him, such innate kindliness, such broad fearless wisdom, that I have come to think very little of the teaching of books.

James Carabine speaks English, Irish, and the gypsy tongue. His father was Zezil Carabine, a gypsy chief of the tribes that visit us at Destiny Bay, and his mother was a McSorley, an Irish clan that is disappearing but was once great in Northern annals. James Carabine's father was notable for his mastery of horses, his immense kindness to them, and his knowledge of their temperaments and diseases. Also for his strength and agility. He was a smith by trade and once, for a bet of ten pounds with a travelling strong man, he slung his huge sledge hammer, like a golfer's pitch shot, over the spire of Saint Columba's-in-Paganry, and running like a deer around the church caught it before it could touch the ground. A third matter for which Zezil Carabine was noted I have from my uncle Valentine, who had it from my grandfather. The big gypsy blacksmith was a Mason, though of which rite is not evident, and most deeply versed in the craft. I shall say nothing further about this, but that it was most notable. Carabine's mother was a beautiful timid girl, who could not summon up courage to follow the patteran to Persia or Brazil, so the smith left her a roll of English, and French, and Russian notes, and a chamois bag filled with gold coin, and kissed her and the child and went his way — as gypsies must.

I am all for this " kind hearts are more than coronets, and simple faith " and what not. But I am too close a student of race horses and gamecocks, and know too well the chivalry of great-hearted splendidly bred dogs not to believe in blood, and to recognise the strain royal when I see it. And for me there is something in James Carabine of the dignity of forgotten Pharaohs and the stubborn Ulster fighting spirit of that dour old baron who was called the Yellow Sorely — Sorely Boy.

II

Though they have been together now for nearly forty years, yet this close companionship will not explain to my mind the bond there is between James Carabine and my uncle Valentine. It goes deeper than friendship. You would think they were the earth and its moon created from the beginning and to last as long as the Creator wishes. They are both part of a natural order, each in his exact place. Some Eastern or person versed in Eastern beliefs once said of a man we were discussing, a statesman of great mould and high-minded chivalry, but who had no intimates, that he was an old soul who had come back to us, but that none of his friends had come over with him. Now this is going deeper into the maze of religion than I care to follow, but if it is possible, then it is possible that my uncle Valentine and James Carabine are intimates out of a shadow world.

I think James Carabine is wiser in affairs of the head than my uncle Valentine, but in his great heart and fearless soul my uncle is peerless. If my uncle Valentine were to ask Carabine to-morrow as to the possibility of finding Hy Brasil the Gaelic Heaven on the high seas, James Carabine would naturally sum up against it. But if my uncle Valentine were to tell James Carabine that to-morrow morning he was setting out for Hy Brasil in a thirty-foot sloop, James Carabine would collect his own gear naturally and go through my uncle's things for flannel trousers and double-breasted jackets and caps with the insignia of the Royal Ulster Yacht Club.

It was Carabine who pulled my uncle through that famous match of his for a bet of two thousand guineas with Piers Fleming, that in a six-day race he on foot would beat Piers Fleming's beautiful bay mare Lalla Rookh (by The Jackdaw out of Killala Girl), with any jockey Piers wanted up. In those days two thousand guineas was a larger sum than it

is now, and to-day it is no trifle. My uncle Valentine has
told me that had he lost he would have enlisted as a private
soldier under an assumed name, or sought service with the
Turks as Baker Pasha did, for after paying his debt he
would have been a ruined man. James Carabine was at that
time fighting his way to the top, and my uncle told him of
the wager.

"Sure you'll do it on one foot," said James Carabine.

They started off from Donegall Place in Belfast at five on
a June morning, with Captain Head, the lightweight cross-
country rider, up on Lalla Rookh, my uncle Valentine in
shirt and shorts with the green cricket cap upon his head
and James Carabine with him. The mare trotted off and
Carabine and my uncle Valentine started in a long swinging
walk. Though my uncle was fairly fresh at the end of
thirty miles, Carabine would let him go no farther.

"We'll stop here the night," said Carabine.

"But the mare'll be in Dundalk," said my uncle Valentine.

"Let her," said Carabine. And he bundled my uncle
Valentine into a hot bath and pummelled his legs, and after
dinner, saw that he went to bed. When my uncle Valentine rose in the morning Carabine was gone ahead, but
Tubby Sweeny the footballer was by his side.

"I'll be with you the twenty miles to Dundalk," said
Sweeny.

"Have you heard anything of the horse?" asked my
uncle Valentine.

"Devil the word," said Sweeny.

At Dundalk Carabine was waiting. He went over every
inch of my uncle's feet and legs.

"Where's the horse?" said my uncle.

"A bit ahead," said Carabine.

"How far?" asked my uncle.

"A trifle," said Carabine. "About thirty miles."

When they passed through Dublin, Piers Fleming was waiting. He was a thin shifty man.

"Valentine," he said, "give it up and all bets off."

My uncle was going to agree, but Carabine broke in. "Oh, no," said Carabine. "Across my dead body, Mister Valentine."

"Ha," said Fleming. "This isn't for you. This is a matter between gentlemen."

"You may be always a gentleman, Mister Fleming, but Mister Valentine stopped being one in Donegall Place. He is now only a pedestrian or foot-runner and under my charge," said James Carabine.

On the fourth day they passed the game little mare, lame, with Flory Head leading her. They had done one hundred and forty-nine miles in the time. In Waterford Town on the fifth day, they got a message from Fleming, withdrawing his horse and paying forfeit. About all this you can hear in the fairs around Destiny Bay when the penny poets start singing:

> "Come-all-ye Irish sportsmen, 'tis you I call upon,
>   To place Sir Val MacFarlane in the Irish Pantheon —"

and so on to the arrogant boast:

> "Then up spoke bold Sir Valentine: For ten thousand pounds or
>   pence
> There is no horse of any breed I will not run against."

There follows a matter of ten verses giving the breeding of Lalla Rookh and my uncle Valentine respectively, then some thirty describing the itinerary, the inhabitants of the villages through which they passed, a few animadversions on the religion of the Dubliners (for this is the composition of a Belfast bard), a tragic climax in which Piers Fleming cries, "Begod, my horse is bet!" It ends with a flourish:

" All honour to Sir Valentine ! He called Piers Fleming's tune !
He took Piers Fleming's money on the fourteenth day of June !
All honour to James Carabine who stood at his right hand.
He is the powerfullest Christian on the soil of Ireland."

So if you come to Destiny Bay for the hunting or the
shooting or the fishing, and are taken in hand by the huge
dignified butler, you will notice that his ways are strangely
at variance with the customs of butlers you have known.
You will note that during dinner, when he feels like it, he
will mingle casually in the conversation, contradicting often
in a gentle way my uncle Valentine, hovering solicitously
around my aunt Jenepher, or passing a dry comment on a
question of the day that is being discussed. When you return to London or Dublin or New York, I hope you will not
boast that in Destiny Bay you were waited on at dinner by
the last star of the old Prize Ring. We would much rather
you said that you made friends with our friend, James
Carabine.

III

My cousin by marriage, Ann-Dolly, has a little daughter
of three years who is very dear to all of us in Destiny Bay.
She has hair that is butter-coloured and eyes blue as a blue
river. Ann-Dolly herself is very much of a boy with her
boyish hair and her cigarettes, but her small daughter is
very much a woman and a lady, and in her eyes is so much
seriousness that one might think it was for her that Lionel
Johnson wrote his poem :

> " Dear cousin : to be three years old,
> Is to have found the Age of Gold."

There is a picture by a Spanish painter whose name has
escaped me of an Infanta, very serious in the face, very
young, with white skirts hooped out, of which small Jenepher always reminds me, she is so much the lady of qual-

ity. Myself I have taken small Jenepher's education upon myself and she can already lisp phrases in the Gaelic jargon: *Thurrum pogue*, which is: "Have you got a kiss?" And *Will ane woy agul yat?* which is Erse for: "Is there any use going along with you?" A raffish saying. Also *Go Hifren lishan Fapa!* which means: To blazes with a Certain Exalted Ecclesiastical Dignitary, who has got a bad name in Ulster. Small Jenepher likes Destiny Bay more, I think, than her home at Spanish Men's Rest, and Destiny Bay adores her, my uncle Valentine, and her namesake my aunt Jenepher. Me, I flatter myself, she likes, but James Carabine is her hero. To see her walk beside the great fighter, herself like some Little Person of the Hills, her honeysuckle fingers clasping the iron hand that broke the Black Man, Diamond's, jaw, and lifted Simon Kennedy with an uppercut clear out of the ring, — well, to see them coming like that makes me wish I had a harp to express it, if you know what I mean.

Ann-Dolly accuses myself and Carabine of stealing the child away when we get the chance, and swears we will poison it, what with our gifts of apples and dark red strawberries and gooseberries like topazes. But there are few vets can tell me anything about handling a blood horse, and a horse is a delicate feeder, and to see James Carabine nurse a foxhound puppy through distemper is a treat for sore eyes. Also is it likely we'd let anything happen to a child we're both so fond of?

I had taken James Carabine out to the ten-acre field to have a look at an old oak that had been struck by lightning. I hoped something could be done for it, and I wanted Carabine's opinion. Small Jenepher came with us, her arms filled with bluebells and buttercups. And then, under the shadow of the oak tree, she said she was sleepy. It was a drowsy June afternoon when even the bees were quiet. And James Carabine sat down against the bole of the oak tree and took *Shinafor Veg Voy*, small golden Jenepher, in his arms. There was a rugged beauty in the way he made the darling comfortable.

"I know what you're thinking, Mister Kerry," he said.

Everybody does. I have none of your poker faces.

"Oh, sure, what harm?" said James Carabine, seeing me uncomfortable. "And sure wouldn't I be happy with one of my own in my arms. But the days in America," said he, "put that out of the question."

"I never knew you were in America, Carabine," I said.

"There's few knows it," said Carabine, "barring your uncle Sir Valentine. But I was there the better part of a year, and I might be there yet, a corpse, or a broken old beggar, but for him.

"It was this way, Mister Kerry," he said. "It was after the great coursing meeting at Altcar, when Sir Malachi Doyle's dog, the Rapparee, won the Cup, that I fought Shadrach Jones, the Welsh Miner, for two hundred pounds a side and a purse of gold. He was a stout fellow, and a great hitter but he hadn't the wrestling, and the cross-buttock did for him in the latter end. Your uncle Valentine was in Italy that time with your grandmother — God rest her! — and it was one of my fights that he didn't see. But myself and the Swimmer McGeehan, him that swam the crossing between Ireland and Scotland, Larne and Stranraer, were going along the quays of Liverpool, looking for the Belfast packet, when we saw a boat ready to take the sea. She was a sailboat with an engine in the middle of her and two side wheels, and there was a power of Irish on board, and a fiddler fiddling and four people, two men and two girls, dancing a reel on the deck.

"'Is it for Australia you are?' asked McGeehan.

"''Tis not,' they answered, 'but for the town of New York and the green fields of America.'

"'Come on,' said McGeehan; 'we've money in our

pockets and neither chick nor child at home. Let's see the world,' said the swimmer.

"Mister Kerry, as I stood there on the stones of Liverpool and looked at the deck, and thought of all those people going to see new sights, I couldn't resist it. It seemed to me I'd have a wasting sickness if I didn't go. Can you understand that, Mister Kerry?"

"'I was living a most enjoyable life,'" I quoted from Sindbad, "'until one day my mind became possessed with the thought of travelling about the world of men and seeing their cities and islands; and a longing seized me to traffic and to make money by trade.'"

"There was no thought of money in my mind at all," said James Carabine.

"Now, Mister Kerry," said James Carabine, "once we were on the great green sea, the fiddling finished and there was an end to the dancing. And many's a man wished he were back in Ireland, so great is the heaviness of heart under the seasickness. It was a bad spring for crossing, and the waves were tumbling, and sliding, and bumping each other as if the sea were unsteady on its feet. But blow high, blow low, the one man that was never troubled was the Swimmer McGeehan. Now this was the way of the Swimmer: the Swimmer would start drinking and all but drink himself into a madhouse, so that in the end his friends would have to get him locked up. He was one of those Irishmen that don't get drunk but go off their heads. From the day he went aboard the boat he never took a bite of nourishment but drank, drank, drank all the time. And he would come out on the afterdeck and walk up and down it.

"'I'm the Swimmer McGeehan,' he would shout. 'Is there any man here that's the equal of the Swimmer McGeehan in swimming on the water, under the water, diving, floating, or fancy strokes? If such there be, let him put down his money and put off his clothes. I'm the Swimmer McGeehan, the Swan of Ireland, the Marine Marvel, the Aquatic Nonpareil' (for this is the way he was always billed, Mister Kerry, in the circus where he used to perform).

"'Will you keep quiet, Bartley?' I asked him, and I promised myself that when I got him in New York I'd give him a clip on the jaw on a place I know, and lock him up until he was himself again.

"Then he'd lie down on the deck, his face to the heavens and do his great feat. He'd spring from that position with one flirt of his legs, his hands never touching the boards and turning high in the air, he'd dive forward as into water, but save himself with his hands, for he was a good acrobat. This was the Salmon Leap.

"'Beat that,' he'd say, 'and you beat me.'

"And of course nobody could beat that.

"The sea captain was a jolly red-faced fellow with the habit of fooling. He came up to McGeehan on the after-deck. 'McGeehan,' said he, 'I never heard a man boast a lot that was worth a damn.'

"'Didn't I swim between Ireland and Scotland,' said McGeehan, 'over the stormy waters of Moyle?'

"'On a summer's day, maybe,' said the sea captain, 'not on a day like this,' and he points to where the big waves were curling and hissing, 'and maybe,' he smiled, for he was a great joker, 'there was a rope from the boat.'

"'Begod, Captain,' said McGeehan, 'I tell you this: I'm the greatest swimmer of modern or ancient time. Not even the Grecian Hero that swum Hell's Pontoon was equal to me.'

"'So I hear you say,' said the sea captain.

"'We're two days out of New York,' said McGeehan, and there was a queer light in his eye. 'I'll wager a hundred pounds I'll beat you to the landing post.'

"'Done,' said the sea captain, thinking McGeehan was a joker like himself.

"Before I could get to him, he had shied his brown bowler hat into the sea, just as I would pitch my hat into a ring, and 'So long, Shamus!' he called to me, and vaulted over the rail. A great green wave swept him onward. Of course there was hell to pay and boats got out, but there was no sign of Swimmer McGeehan. I saw the last of him, Mister Kerry. The plunge in the water must have sobered him, and the strength of the waves told him where he was. But he didn't throw up his hands or call for help. He just bored in. God be good to the Swimmer McGeehan," said James Carabine; "himself was his only enemy! God be good to the Swimmer McGeehan, he died game!

"The sea captain came up to me later and his face was white. 'That was a madman,' he said.

"'Madman or not,' said I, 'we shared the same bed for a year, and when there was only a crust between us, we shared it. He was my dear friend.'

"'I'm sorry. I'm damned sorry,' said the sea captain. And he went and shut himself up in his cabin and I saw no more of him until we came to Castle Garden. Then I went to him to pay the bet my friend had lost. The big man broke down and cried, and wouldn't touch a penny of the money, so that I had to put it back in my pocket. He was a decent fellow," said James Carabine, "but I wished he hadn't tried his joking on my poor friend."

IV

"So that I came into New York with a cloud in my heart, Mister Kerry," said Carabine, "and what I saw there didn't lift it any. From all I had heard tell of New York, it was a golden city, rich as Jerusalem, and the Irish reigned there. At every corner I expected to see the Irish dancing and fiddling, and jingling the money in their pockets the people had given them just for being Irish, and maybe doing an hour's work now and then, just for the looks of the thing. It is a great city, young and strong, and like everything that is young and strong, cruel, and cruellest of all upon the Irish. The hunger of Famine Days is nothing to the hunger of the unlucky Irish. Many's the decent fellow in Ireland throws down his spade and says: 'I'm off to make my fortune,' and his fortune is this, — to find a spade an inch longer in the blade and when he raises his head from his work there are no mountains to look at or green fields or wide sea, but a bare ugly wall. And he's too proud to go back to where he was happy. And the sickness of the lungs takes a lot of them in America, and the drink takes more. You'll never know how sweet a bird's song is, Mister Kerry, until you listen for it in New York, and it's not there. There's Irish that makes money in America, and they talk loudly and you hear them, but the shoals in Potter's Field, you don't hear them at all.

"The place where you meet the Irish in America, Mister Kerry," said James Carabine, "is in public drinking houses, but they're not like our public drinking houses at all. At home here, when the sun goes down, you can go into a place that is quiet and orderly, order your pot of beer, smoke your pipe, and talk about the weather and the crops, and play a game of five hundred up. But over there you've got to stand against a bar and drink quick and drink often, or they don't want your custom at all. In the latter end I got very tired of it, Mister Kerry, for I'm not by temperament a drinking man. I got weary of being introduced as James Carabine, the great fighter, and 'What'll you have, Mister Carabine?' and the Irish in drink are a noisy tumultuous people. One minute a man will be hanging around your neck, all but kissing you, and trying to prove you're a relation of his, and the next minute, when his heart is height-

ened with liquor, he'll be shouting: 'Are you James Carabine, the fighter? Well, I'm Mick Murphy, the Holy Terror.
Put your dukes up or I'll knock the greasy mush off you.'
So that it takes all the restraint you've learned in your
trade to keep your hands from him. . . . It was drink, drink,
drink, and never a word of getting a fight for me. So that
I decided I'd drop the whole thing and get back to Ulster.
The old ring had nearly gone in America; the glove men,
the tip-and-run fellows were coming along and talking about
scientific fighting. People are always for listening to a
new thing. So I said: 'I'll go back to the old country
where the old things are in honour.'

"I was lodging in New York in Fifteenth Street near
Fourth Avenue with a widow woman, a very decent body,
a Dane. I was all right in the daytime wandering around,
but at night, never having had my letters taught me, I
couldn't read. The other lodgers were shy with me, on
account of my being a fighting man, and the woman of the
house had little English at her, so that for amusement and
passing the time I had to go out at night. There were ten
days to go before I could get a boat for Derry city. It was
then I found the beer hall on Third Avenue, that was known
as Nate's, and the woman with the green eyes."

V

"It was a queer wee place, Mister Kerry. You went
down steps into it, and with every new person that came in,
the people in the beer hall turned and looked at him, looked
at him long, sizing him up. There were never more than
a dozen or twenty people in the place. There were no glar-
ing lights, like in the saloons, but quiet-like. There was a
little platform for concerts, and one fellow at the piano, and
another played the harp and another played the violin. The
man that owned it, Nate, was a tall thin fellow, bald, and

a taker of drugs, Mister Kerry, but decent at heart. If he took a liking to you he was your friend. If he did n't, well, he did n't want you in his place. He was an Italian, he told me, and his name was Grimaldi, Nathan Grimaldi, but Italy he did not remember. They had good beer there, but the waiters were broken-down and slovenly. One waiter instead of a shirt had a piece of white cardboard, with pencil marks for studs. The harpist, Peter, was a wonder, and he would play 'By Killarney's Lakes and Fells' in a way that would make you see home. There were singers there, Mister Kerry, but in the main they were n't good.

"Now, the way of this pub, Mister Kerry, was this. There was a lot behind it. God only knows what happened in the upstairs rooms; maybe it was drugs, maybe it was drink, but whatever it was, was not wholesome. The women who came into that place had a trade that was not pretty, though they let people in the beer hall alone; that was Nate's direction. But there were fellows there would kill a man for a five-dollar fee, or kidnap, or do anything. That was their trade. They were gunmen, and they had a woman or small boy with them to carry their gun. These men did n't drink. Nobody there bothered me on account of Nate's orders, Nate having taken a great fancy to me.

"Everybody there had something wrong with them. They had made a mistake one time or the other. Peter, the harpist, was once a great musician. Nate himself was a clever man. He would sit and talk to me about religion, claiming that Adam and Eve were symbolic for the male and female principle and that the serpent was a symbol for Fate. He told me that Noah's flood was a great period of ice on the earth, and that the old writers had no name for it, but called it a flood. Noah's ark was the preservation of the vital principle. Nate did worse than not believe in God; he did n't believe in the devil, so you can see how far he had gone.

" This man, Mister Kerry, was a wise man. He was not one of those who told me to go to night schools and learn my letters. He knew that for every thousand men who could read books, like himself, there was only one who could read the country and the sea, and the faces of men, like myself. If any one wanted to go to Heaven, though he didn't believe in it, he would give him a hand. If any one wanted to go to Hell, though he didn't believe in that either, he wouldn't put out a finger to stop him. He was a broad-minded man. He was a decent man and would lend you money. He would take care of money for you and give you a strict accounting of it. Also, if any singer or dancer was down on his luck, he could come and perform at Nate's, and be sure of a meal and a dollar or so, until the luck changed. Ordinarily, Mister Kerry, the singers were bad, but occasionally one would come with a voice that would make the birds hush their notes and listen, some one in a streak of bad luck, or that drink had played a trick on.

" I went there one night, Mister Kerry, and I noticed there was little attention paid me. The waiters had no time for a chat, and Nate was busy, and Peter the harpist was hard at his music, so I sat down in a corner and made myself at home, calling for a pint of beer. One singer followed another, poor enough, God knows, and then there was a wait. And after a while a woman came on the platform, and looked around the hall as if everybody were the dirt beneath her feet. She was a tall woman and a fine woman, and no more splendid body have I ever seen, perfect in each degree, and strong, and music to it. But her face was a face to make you stop in the street and wonder. It was a white face, white as a wall, and her hair was black, and sleek as sealskin, and came to a point on her forehead. Her lips were pale and her eyes were green. Her face was like a mask, Mister Kerry, a painter fellow would imagine. And the whole of her was like a drug or some strange foreign drink that would take a grip on you even though you disliked it. There was hatred and contempt in her face.

"She sang a German song, Mister Kerry, which I could n't understand, and at the end of it she turned to the piano player, and very quietly, so that we could hear no word of it, she spoke to him. And the man cringed and cowered like a dog that's being whipped, and turned this way and that way as if he were trying to escape. The poor fellow had made a mistake in the music, I suppose, but nobody stood up for him. Nate went away, and Peter the harpist busied himself with his strings as if he did n't want to be noticed. And all the time she spoke so gently we could n't hear her. Then she sang a lullaby for a small child, and it made me angry, such a sneer was in it. And then another tune came to my ears, a tune that I had often heard, and the woman began the opening verses of 'In Bodenstown Churchyard there is a Green Grave', in the lament for Wolfe Tone.

"Well, Mister Kerry, Wolfe Tone was not of our kind and none of us in this country have sympathy with Tone or Napper Tandy, or those who stood with France against us in the wars, but it's like this. At home here Orangeman and Hibernian are as wide apart as the Poles, but you go a thousand miles away and they draw in together, and you go another thousand, and the two become a blur together, and you go another and they're one. They're Irish. And no matter what your politics, you feel a sorrow for Wolfe Tone, who went by his own hand before the hangman's could touch him. . . . She finished and passed me on her way to the inner rooms.

"'Come hither, girleen,' I said. 'Was it for me you sang that song?'

"She looked at me as if I were something in a showman's case, something curious but cheap and contemptible.

"'And who are you,' she asked; 'and why should I sing a song for you?'

"'I'm Carabine, the Irish fighter,' I told her, 'and every one around here knows me, so I thought Nate had asked you to sing that, by way of compliment.'

"'Compliment? From me?' she laughed at me. 'So you're a fighter. Where are your diamonds? Where is your loud talk? Where are your pals?'

"'I have no diamonds,' I said. 'And as for any kind of talk, I'm not much good at it. And as for my friend—' I told her the story of the Swimmer McGeehan.

"A waiter came up to ask for an order. She turned around and said 'Go away!' and the tone she said it in made the man scuttle off like a rabbit.

"'They seem to be afraid of you,' said I.

"'They are,' said she. 'Aren't you?'

"'And why should I?' I asked her. 'Are you Irish? If you aren't, why do you sing that song?'

"'My father was Irish, a drunken Irish fiddler from Trim. My mother was Italian. Do you see these women around the room? Well, my mother was one of them.'

"It was a facer, Mister Kerry. And the woman was watching me. She had hatred and contempt. If the Great Man Above came down she would look at him in the same way. She was a fearless, bitter woman. But she wasn't a bad woman, Mister Kerry," said James Carabine pleadingly, "even after thirty years I wouldn't say she was a bad woman.

"So I said: 'Well, it's a bad start, but there's many's a horse has won a race after being left at the post.'

"'You're not an Irishman like my father,' said she.

"'I come from the Black North,' said I.

"'My father was a Fenian,' she told me. 'When he was drunk he used to sing that song with the tears running down his cheeks. I liked my father. So I throw that song in the face of the world.'

"There was something fighting and untame in that woman, and what there was in me of the same kind went out to her. And she could see it in my eyes, and she liked it.

"'Are you fighting?' she said.

"'No,' I said. 'I can't get a fight. I'm going back to Ireland. I'm tired of doing nothing in New York.'

"'How do you spend your time?' she asked.

"'Oh,' I said, 'I go on the little boat to Brooklyn and walk in the country, and I look for gypsies and talk to them, for I'm half gypsy and speak their tongue. And I see the sights and marvels,' I said.

"'If you like,' she said, 'you can come around with me.'

"'I'd like to,' said I.

"'You flatter me,' she sneered. 'Well, come and take me out driving to-morrow. Nate will give you my address.'

"'What name is on you, girl?' I asked.

"'Ward,' she told me. 'Lina Ward, the Nightingale of Avenue A.' And she left me.

"I sat there for a while thinking about her, thinking of her as some strange wild thing, some cold furious cat, and one of the waiters came to me.

"'Well, Mister Carabine,' he said, 'you made a hit. It ain't everybody can talk to Marcolina Ward. There's men killed themselves for that woman. And it's not everybody she'll look at, no.' But Nate came along and sent him away.

"'Have nothing,' said Nate in a whisper, 'to do with that woman.'

"'I'm taking her out driving to-morrow, Nate,' said I.

"'I hate to lose you,' said Nate, 'but leave this place and never lay eyes on that woman again. Take my advice.'

"'Och, Nate,' I said, 'have sense. I understand her.'

"'Oh, my God!' said Nate. And he too left me."

VI

"I got a lightish, fast-stepping mare and something that was like a dogcart, but the American name for it I've forgotten, and I went down to look for her the next day. It was the most cutthroat and God-forsaken place you can imagine, on the edge of Manhattan Island, but her house was a pretty little cottage, made of wood, in the American way. You'd have thought a woman would have been afraid to stay in a district where there were so many bad characters, but this woman had no fear in her. When I called she was ready to come out, and she was dressed as if she were a lady of high degree, rich and quiet, but you could see that the quiet of it all only marked the wonder of her face. And she had a dog with her, a bull, and if she was the finest thing I've seen on two legs, he was the finest thing, barring a horse, on four. He was two years old, white, deep in the chest, without much saddle in his back, and forefeet straight as ramrods. The dog and I looked at each other, and I liked him. Then he made a dive for me.

"Said I to myself: 'If we're to be friends, we'd best find out now which is the better man,' and I let him have the loaded end of the whip on the skull, and he rolled over and went to sleep for a while.

"Well, the language that woman used to me, Mister Kerry, would shock the captain of a canal boat. I could understand how the fellow at the piano the night before cowered under it. But I only laughed.

"'Sure, you wouldn't have me let the dog freeze on to me,' I said. 'He's getting all right now. And what you say to me doesn't matter because it isn't true.'

"Sure enough, the dog comes up to me, wagging his stern and we're friends, and when she sees that she laughs. And we all get into the cart, and the dog sits between my feet. I drove her out northwards to where the Hudson River splits and makes New York an island. And she gets out of me about my fights and about Destiny Bay, and the gypsies and the coursing of dogs, and Dublin and the horse racing. And whether there was a woman in my life, which there was n't. In the end I take her back home. And I leave her.

"'I've got some influence in this city,' she said, 'and maybe I can get you some fights.'

"'If you could,' said I, 'I'd be grateful, for it's a long wet way to have come and nothing to show in the latter end for it. I'd be very grateful,' said I.

"'Is that all?' said she.

"'What else?' said I.

"'Come on, Micky,' she said to the dog. But devil a come he'd come. 'You'd better keep him,' said she; 'he's a man's dog, and he's found his master.'

"'Och, I can't take your dog,' I told her.

"'You'll have to,' said she.

"'Well, all I can say is I'm grateful to you.'

"And again she said: 'Is that all?'

"'He's a valuable dog,' says I, and I put my hand in my pocket, but she gives me a look like a knock-down blow, and goes into the house without a word. And I drive back to the stable where I got the mare and cart. The owner is a Carlow man, a decent fellow.

"'I take it very bad of you, Mr. Carabine,' he said, 'that you did n't tell me it was Miss Ward you were going out with and you'd have had the best horse in Manhattan and the best cart too, and silver harness.'

"'It'll do the next time,' said I.

"'By the same token,' said he, 'aren't those the queer clothes for you to be wearing and you going out with the likes of her?'

"'And why?' said I.

"'She's a lady,' said the Carlow man, 'accustomed to ride out in grandeur.'

"'Well,' said I, 'if that's the case we'll have to change. Is there a man in this town can fix me?'

"'There is,' said he. And he gave me the name of a

fellow on Fifth Avenue. For this is the way of that city, Mister Kerry, that the avenues are numbered and go south to north, and the streets are numbered and go east to west, barring a handful in the south or butt end of the town that have names like in a kindly place. The tailor fellow fits me wonderful with an elegant suit and a light-coloured coat and boots with varnish on them, and a silk stock and a top hat, but gloves I would n't have. So the next time I drive up for Marcolina, she looks at me.

"'How 's this?' she says.

"'A man told me I was no credit to you in my country clothes,' I said to her.

"'He was a fool,' she said. 'However, 'twas a nice thought behind it, James Carabine.'

"Well, Mister Kerry, to make a long story short, this woman did all for me that the best friend could do. She took me around and introduced me to sportsmen, to the Tammany Hall fellows whom I did n't care for very much but who controlled the fighting, and to a man that run a paper called the *Policeman's Gazette*, that had very little to do with policemen. It was a queer thing to see this woman come into a room where there was an important man. She would pass office boys and every one, and walk in, even if there were people in the room with the important man. It would be 'Hello, Lina! How 's the kid?' And she 'd say: 'I want to see you a minute.' And he 'd say: 'Sure, kid,' and send the other people out of the room. She was New York born and bred and other New Yorkers understood her and were proud of her. They were all very nice to me. In the end I was fixed up with a fight against a black man, catch weight and gloves.

"In the meantime all over New York there was talk of James Carabine, the Irish champion. And I think the cause of it was Lina Ward. When I drove up Fifth Avenue in the daytime in a fine rig, with the splendid woman at my side, and the white bulldog at my feet, there were always eyes for us. I'm told there were many things in the newspapers, and once I saw a picture a fellow drew of us. All this time Marcolina sang at Nate's and there was always a big crowd there now. And every evening I saw her home and wished her good night.

"'You've been a good friend to me, Marcolina,' I told her. 'You've made me in this city. And I've done a wee bit for you, I think. You don't sneer as much as you did. And your laugh is not bitter. Your heart is getting soft, Marcolina.'

"'I don't know whether to thank you or curse you for that, Carabine,' she wondered.

"'You can thank God, Marcolina,' said I.

"The time came when I went off to train for the fight against the black. I went to Staten Island. I said goodbye.

"'I'll come over and see you,' said she.

"'You will not,' said I.

"'You're not aware of the compliment I'm paying you.'

"'I am indeed, Marcolina,' I told her, 'but I'll take the wish for the act.' So I didn't see her until after the fight.

"The fight itself, Mister Kerry, was not much. The black man was a huge fellow from New Orleans. He was like a statue, so big he was, bigger than the other black man Diamond. He came across the ring at the call of time like a hurricane, and if one of his blows had landed it would have been 'good night, Carabine!' but by the mercy of God I caught him with a straight left as he came in and his own speed more than my hand burst him. His head went back between his shoulder blades. And I got home a left and right in his ribs to take the steam out of him, and banged him hard on the mouth as he straightened up. There was a roar in the club you could have heard a mile away. For two minutes of the round it was like this, the

black man coming like a steam engine, and the left hand
jarring and bursting him. He didn't know how to avoid
it, Mister Kerry; he could neither block it nor duck. He
stood for a second puzzled, and at that instant I saw my
chance and took it. I belted him with the right on the point
of his jaw, and he fell forward with a crash of his face,
and when time was called he was out of it. He was a
powerful man and had a heart of corn, but the straight left
did for him.

"When I climbed out of the ring the first thing I saw was
Marcolina. When I was in the ring, Mister Kerry, I had
no thought but for the man in front of me, and the green
scarf knotted in my corner, so I hadn't seen her. But when
I came out, with my frieze coat around me and the green
scarf around my neck, she was the first to greet me.

"'It didn't take you long, Carabine,' said she, and her
eyes were shining.

"'And what brought you here, Marcolina?'

"'To see you fight, of course,' she told me.

"'This is no place for you, Marcolina.'

"'If this were the worst place I'd ever been in, I'd be
on my way for a saint,' she answered me, 'but there, don't
be angry with me, Carabine.' And when she spoke that way
you couldn't chide.

"I had my supper at Nate's that night, and there was
great talk of the fight. It seems this black fellow had never
been beaten before and the odds were six to one against me.
Marcolina had won a pot of money on me, nearly a thousand
pounds, and Nate had ventured a little and won. Nate was
overjoyed, but Marcolina was quiet.

"'Carabine,' she said suddenly, 'when you were training, I had dinner with an old friend of mine, an old friend
of mine of whom I used to be very fond.'

"'I'm glad of that,' I told her. 'Two old friends meeting, it lifts the heart.'

"'But when he wanted to kiss me good night,' she said, 'I couldn't bear it. I pushed him away. Do you understand that?'

"'I don't,' said I, 'unless you've taken a dislike to this man.'

"'I don't know, Carabine,' she said coldly and bitterly, 'whether you're a damned fool or a very clever man.'

"'Well, I don't think I'm either, Marcolina,' I told her, 'and I don't know why you say it.'

"'Because I'm a dirty cat, Carabine, my big true friend,' she said, and she smiled, and that was all there was said of that.

"I got another fight after that, against a clever fellow from the West, a Californian fellow. He could slip and duck and sidestep like an acrobat, but his punches hadn't much power, so I went after him hammer and tongs. I managed to work him into a corner and against the ropes, and banged him where and as hard as I could. In four rounds the speed was out of him, and I finished him cleanly with a short uppercut. The odds were evens, but Marcolina had doubled her money. She didn't come to this fight because I told her I didn't want her, but she waited for me at Nate's. She was very worried until I turned up. I don't remember any friend of mine ever being so worried.

"All this time I was trying in New York to get a fight according to Prize Ring Rules. The gloves are grand for exercise, but they're not the real measure of a fighting man. Besides, with the gloves there's too much trickery. You can hit harder with the gloves than your bare hands, for there's protection for the hands in gloves. In the prize ring, you've got to think more of your wrestling than hitting. The hitting is more to prevent a man getting into position for a back heel or a cross-buttock or a flying mare. I don't like these three-minute rounds where a crooked timekeeper can shorten or lengthen the round, Mister Kerry, with his watch in his hand. And these draws, and winnings on points, — they are n't good. In my day you went into the ring and you came out either beaten or conqueror. And there was no talk about fouling. And the minute's rest between rounds gave an unlucky fellow a chance to come to. A man may be the better man, and have no luck, and that's not a right thing, Mister Kerry.

"I came at a time, Mister Kerry, when the Prize Ring was setting in glory. The men were n't maybe the equals of Tom Figg, or Sayers, or the Negro Molyneux, though it's hard to say. But they fought like champions. The time when Gentleman Jackson won from Mendoza by holding his hair and hitting him with the other hand, and when a man got his opponent's head in chancery and hammered his face, that time was gone. We fought each other's strength, not infirmities. When I was fighting Simon Kennedy, and slipped on a patch of wet grass, and threw out my hand for the ropes, Simon could have hit me, but he stepped back. And when I twisted my right wrist in a fall against Tom Hill of Bradford, and could n't use my right hand for hitting, Tom would only use his left, too. And they were n't all just bruisers, Mister Kerry; Simon Kennedy was a schoolmaster, and Deaf Wallace was a maker of fine jewellery, and Dan Lane afterward became a great preacher in Sydney.

"They promised me a fight in New York as soon as they could get a man. They said it would be hard on account of it being against the law, but: 'We'll find a man for you,' they said and they smiled.

"All this time Marcolina and I were good friends. Often we'd go down to the sea and look at the water. There's something in a great spread of water that brings your sincerity out. She'd be a while silent, and then she'd say something. Sometimes it would be that she was glad to have me for a friend. It was so hard to have a man friend.

"'I don't see why,' I said.

"'You wouldn't, Carabine,' she told me.

"And then one day, out of nothing, so to speak, she told me something there was no need to tell me at all.

"'Will it make any difference to our friendship, Carabine,' she asked me, and she looked at me, she looked at me square in the eyes, 'if I tell you this, that there have been times when I wasn't what is called a good woman?'

"I thought it over before I answered, and I said to myself: what with this city and a lonely life, you couldn't expect her to be the same, so to speak, as a country girl. And besides, I said to myself, there is great strength in this woman.

"'It will not, Marcolina,' I told her, 'for I understand this: that the lone adventurous person on the road has pitfalls and ambushes where the schooled protected traveller escapes. As long as you know now, Marcolina, sure it's all right. As a fact,' I said, 'and this is a dangerous and maybe wrong thought of mine, but a person has no virtue until they've known and chucked the evil things. I wouldn't like to say I'm sure of that,' I puzzled, 'but this I know,— that the unbeaten person who has never had a fight, there is no credit to him at all.'

"'I used to think nothing about it,' said Marcolina, 'but now I wish it hadn't happened.'

"'Well,' I told her, 'it's over, so think no more about it.'

"'That's easily said, James Carabine.'

"'Marcolina,' I said to her, 'we'll always be true friends.'

"It was a little after this that the fight was arranged for me. They told me I was to fight a Turk. 'Sure, a Turk can't fight,' said I, 'as we know it.' 'If you feel that way about it,' said they, 'you won't win.' I asked Nate's advice, and his advice was this: to train as hard as ever I trained. for the Turk was a wonder. So I said no more.

I settled down to work. There are fine men in every nation.

"The morning of the fight came, and the ring was pitched in Bay Ridge. When I saw the Turk, I said to myself: 'Carabine, you're fighting for your life.' He wasn't finely drawn, Mister Kerry, but there wasn't too much meat on him, and he had arms like a man's thighs. He had a dark moustache, Mister Kerry, and a kind look on his face, and there was no English at him. A German showman had brought him to America as the Turkish Giant, and my heart sank when I saw the sight of him, for big as I am, he'd make two of me, and a bit would be left over. But I chucked my hat into the ring, and jumped the ropes after it, and tied the green scarf to the ring post. I sat down, thinking how I'd fight this fellow, and then they called time.

"He had an awkward spar, Mister Kerry, right hand out, and crouched, but quick as a cat for such a big man. He seemed to want to wrestle more than hit, and for more than a minute not a blow was struck. Then I saw my chance, and 'Here's two for old Ireland,' said I, and I let him have the left and right to the head. He seemed surprised, Mister Kerry, so I punched him around the ring until we closed. The moment he had his arms around me, I knew I was in the grip of a master. Mister Kerry, he wasn't a man; he was a big thing of brass, and it was like machinery his arms going around me. By the mercy of God, I had my right hand free, and I tried my old reliable, putting my hand under his chin, and trying to back heel, but this fellow was as light on his feet as a goat. It was an old story to him. He just lifted me in the air and began squeezing my life out. So I let him have it right in the face, hitting him with my fist as if it were a hammer, and with the pain and shock he dropped me. He turned to the referee, and said something in Turkish, but the referee only clapped his hands as if to say: 'Get on with it!' and then he talked to his German manager, but the German man only smoked his cigar.

So the Turk comes at me with a rush, and he was shouting, Mister Kerry, like a bull. Well, for five minutes I hit him with everything I had. I was like a hare before the hounds. I twisted and turned and then would jump in punching and get away. My hands were sore, and when I hit I grunted, so tired I was, and just as I was on the point of closing with him and going down for the minute's rest, the Turk throws up his arms and says something in a loud voice and walks back to his corner. I stand there for a minute, while the referee goes over to the German man. And then the referee come to the middle of the ring and says: 'Aaron Ahmed,' for that was the Turkish man's name, 'Aaron Ahmed retires.' The round had lasted between eight and nine minutes, and the Turk had n't hit me once.

"A sporting man called Al Mills comes over to me and says: 'Well, Carabine, you finished that fellow.'

"'Mr. Mills,' said I, 'did the Turkish fellow know this was going to be a fight?'

"'Well, he knows it now,' said Mills.

"'That man is a wrestler,' I said; 'he's not a boxing man.'

"'Well,' said Mills, 'what does it matter? You won.'

"'I'm ashamed,' said I. 'I'm ashamed for myself and for that green flag in the corner. You've done the Turkish man an injury but you've done me a worse one,' said I.

"'Oh,' said Mills sharply, 'is that how you feel about it? Maybe I can find a man at your own game will take the crowing out of you.'

"'Find him,' said I. 'I ask nothing better. But this thing is not in my line.' And I went over to the Turk and offers to shake hands with him, but he looks at me coldly. I don't blame him, for he thinks he's been fouled in his match. But I kept talking to him, and in the end he understands me, for fighting men can see into each other, and he shakes hands and smiles. He left the ring, his face cut to pieces — I couldn't help it, Mister Kerry — but his head was high. He was the beaten man but he took more glory out of the ring than I did.

"Marcolina was very nice to me when she knew how hurt I was. 'You're a queer sort, Carabine,' she said. 'You're the first fighter I've ever heard complaining he won.' But she understood why I felt bad. 'I'm the Irish champion,' I said, 'and there's been a long list of them, but I'm the first that's ever been mixed up in a funny fight.'

"'But you didn't know it?' she said.

"'It happened all the same,' said I.

"She was very kind to me over it, and we got closer all the time, so that one day, driving out to Sheepshead Bay, she asked me a question.

"'It's a question,' she said, 'that may ruin this friendship of ours. But I can't keep myself from asking it, Carabine. Apart from being friends, you are fond of me, James Carabine?'

"'I am fond of you, Marcolina,' said I, 'but where's the use? I've little to offer you. A fighter's life and glory is short. And when that's finished, you, that are accustomed to lights and city streets, mightn't like the quiet of the shore and the blue hills of Derry.'

"'Why the hills of Derry, Carabine?' she asked.

"'Because,' I told her, 'a wife will go with her husband to his home.'

"'Are you asking me to marry you, James Carabine?' she said, 'and you know what you know.'

"'That,' said I, 'is over and done with. And we're two big people, you and I.'

"She waited a while, and then she said: 'You wouldn't be content,' she said, 'to be fond of me, and leave marriage be?' I said: 'No.'

"She spent another minute thinking, while I drove on, before she answered.

"'Well then, I'll marry you, James Carabine.'"

VII

All about us were the golden Ulster sky, the breeze of Ulster in the ash trees and the grasses, the bees of Ulster humming their note as of minute organs. All this was remote, in another star, one might say, from the Carabine's scene of the most cruel of cities, of the cursing of the ringside and the shouting, the dark alleys of life where spirits walk for the ruin of souls. Carabine had come through it like steel which had known the furnace, like gold that had been refined. My cousin, small Jenepher, sleeping in his arms, had life before her, and my heart went out suddenly to her butter-coloured hair, her face like warm ivory, her hands like curled rose leaves. God bless you, little gentlewoman, and bring you without too much heartbreak through the intricacy of life, and give you peace in the end among the blue hills of Derry at Destiny Bay.

"It was a change in my life, Mister Kerry," said James Carabine. "I moved from the Danish woman's lodging house, which I was sorry to leave because she was a decent body, to a hotel in Union Square. I was no longer with easy-going comfortable people but with a crowd of politicians and gamblers, and important people who had their names in the papers, for these were all Marcolina's friends, and every day I was dressed up as if it were Sunday, and showed myself. It was a great change of life for me.

"And in the midst of it all I was lonely, Mister Kerry, in spite of Marcolina, for these people were her friends. What I had to talk about outside the ring, were horses and dogs and trees and fishing, and many of these men, though they were heavy betters on horses, knew nothing about them and cared less. And as for the other things, we couldn't talk about them, they knowing nothing. It was as if you and I were together, Mister Kerry, you speaking the French tongue and I the King's English, we could smile at each other, but that would be all.

"I used to think to myself at first Marcolina would like these things I liked, the open country and the hedgerows, and she did her best to like them, but those who are born in cities never get over it. The smoky tang of the street is the same, or more to them, than a field of cowslips. There were things in the American spring I liked to see and hear, things we haven't got in Ireland, the dogwood that comes on the hedges like a fall of snow, and the wee frogs calling at night, whether it is music or unmusic I couldn't tell. And these were wonders and marvels to me. You know how it is with me, Mister Kerry, I can sit for hours whittling out a child's toy with my knife and thinking about the world, thinking of what shape souls are in dogs and horses, and how we will all be and we dead. And thinking about the rights and wrongs of fighting, and how the fighter of to-day should be like the Greek Olympian men, a mirror to the children of his time. The fighting beasts of the forests have weapons, but we have only our brittle hands, as easily snapped as twigs, and a head behind them and a stout heart. We must fight hard and fair, and that teaches us deeper things, for the wild animals have only themselves to fight with, but against us always is the Enemy of the Brethren. And it is from the athletes and fighting men that the citizen has to learn this, that he has to take care of his body, for of all bodies, man's is the chief one to grow coarse and vulgar with age.

"These things to see and these things to think about were enough for me, Mister Kerry, but Marcolina needed more. The lights of the town, the singing and dancing were the breath of life in her nostrils. The balls at Tammany Hall and at this and that place, and houses like Mr. Canfield's gaming house, where there was a straight game, at all these she was welcome and liked. Mister Kerry, I wish you could have seen Marcolina. She was a queen of strange beauty; everywhere she went people used to stop and look at her, and maybe now," said James Carabine, "of all the world I'm the only one to remember her fine carriage and her green eyes.

"Down in her heart she was a strange seeking woman, and the marriage was not all she expected it to be. She turned to me one night and said:

"'Can't you lose yourself, Carabine?' she asked queerly.

"'How?' said I.

"'In your love for me, can't you forget,' said she, 'that there is anything but me in the world?'

"'The world is all about us, Marcolina,' I told her, 'the seen and the unseen world, and we occupy our places in it, big or small. No man or woman is big enough to blot out the rest of the world.'

"'Yes, I know that,' she said, 'but could you forget that?' She stood up, and her eyes were like emeralds against her pointed face. Her arms were like honey. She was altogether beautiful. 'People could get drunk on me, James Carabine. Could you not get drunk on me?'

"'No,' I said, 'Marcolina, I couldn't. The man who would give himself up, give up everything for a woman, no matter how much he loves, is no man, and a woman will despise him.'

"'She'll despise him, yes,' said Marcolina; 'but she'll love him all the more.'

"The way of the country people is this, Mister Kerry, as you know, that a man and woman can be friends and marry and be friends still. The desire of a man for a woman and of a woman for a man is a fever that comes and goes. If the friendship remains when the fever is gone then all is well. Passion, Mister Kerry, is as little to be avoided as death, and maybe it's a little of the same thing," said James Carabine. "for after each there is either true life or no life.

Be that as it may, but a true friendship is worth all the passion in the world. Friendship doubles good fortune and halves disaster. If a friend of yours were dying at a great distance you'd walk all the way to be with him, where if it were a woman you love you'd just mourn. No matter what a friend's faults are you know them and still are friends, but in a woman you love you won't believe there's fault at all. If your friend is wrong you still fight by his side, right or wrong, because he needs you. In love you're like an actor on the stage, talking high. In friendship you are silent. Friendship is the better part.

"This, mind you, Mister Kerry, Marcolina could see, but inside her something kept her from accepting it. In love she was like a poor fellow with the bottle, wanting it all, and certain that he could have his liquor and his health too. It wasn't in the cheap way of the body, Mister Kerry, but some queer twist of the mind.

"Once she said to me: 'I thought myself before you came, James Carabine, some wild thing of the woods, some noble thing, a lioness maybe, but now,' she smiled bitterly, 'but now I know myself for a dirty gutter cat.'

"'Och, Marcolina,' I said, 'have sense!'

"'I am what I am, James Carabine.'

"After this she said nothing more to me, but closed herself up, as if she were locking herself up in a room. She was proud to be married to me, she said, not because I was a prize fighter, but even though I was a prize fighter. In about five months, Mister Kerry, I had three fights with the gloves, and there was nothing of notable in these fights, Mister Kerry. I won them. I took training seriously, and worked hard. Marcolina was singing in a place called Koster and Bials, and then in a place called Tony Pastor's. And often I'd go to a ball with her, but leave her and come back for her. Sometimes she was as nice as a woman could be to me. I once told her I was sorry I couldn't dance.

"'I'm glad, Carabine,' she said. 'You're not a dancing man, thank God! You're a fighting man.'

"But at other times she would be disagreeable. I might come to fetch her and she'd say:

"'There's a man here who's been making love to me.'

"'Well,' I'd tell her, 'what do you want me to do about it?'

"'Aren't you going to hit him?' she'd ask.

"'No,' I said. 'For one thing, Marcolina, it would be like a grown man hitting a child. And another, he couldn't have made love to you if you'd objected, for one twist of your tongue would take the hide from any man, barring myself perhaps.'

"'Well, I let him, then. Aren't you going to hit me?'

"'No, Marcolina,' I told her. 'I'm not going to hit you.'

"'Damn you,' she'd say, 'you think yourself too big to beat me. Damn you, Carabine!' She was just like a naughty child.

"Then after that she'd say: 'I'm sick of myself, Carabine. I'm sick of myself. I wish I'd never been born.' All this I thought was on account of the singing. Singers are queer. One day they'll be high in their hearts and the next they'll be in the depths. And they're forever imagining things, singers are.

"One day she said to me seriously: 'Sometime I'm going to hurt you, Carabine, hurt you so hard that your heart will break.'

"'Why would you do that, Marcolina?' I laughed at her.

"'Because, before you came, Carabine, I was in my own mind big and wild and fine, and now I know I'm not,' said she. 'And that will be your reward for teaching me the truth about myself, Carabine.'

"But I put that down to the tantrums that singers do have."

VIII

"The man, Al Mills, that I was so short to over the fight with the Turk, began making great friends and though I had no liking for him, yet I didn't mind him. He was a short, fat fellow, with a bald head and a cigar in his mouth. And he had a way of looking at you as though he saw through your words into the back of your head. He was a gambling man, and if you saw him in the street, with his flashy clothes, and his deliberate way, you would know him for that. This man always carried a pistol and was very much respected, for people knew that this fellow would draw and kill. He was not one of those loud threatening men, hollow as a drum. This fellow was in everything in which there was money, be it a horse race, a prize fight or a city contract. There was great credit in being seen abroad with this fellow.

"'Carabine,' he told me, 'I've got a man to fight you. A man,' he said, 'that's in the same fix as you are, a London Prize Ring man, and can't get a fight.'

"'I hope it's nothing like the Turkish fellow, for if that's the case I won't touch it.'

"'Oh, he can fight,' he said. 'I don't think he's as good as you are, and frankly that's one of the reasons I'm interested in the fight.'

"'As long as it's a fair ring and no favour,' said I, 'I'll fight anything. I won't say I'll win, but I'll do my best.'

"'Good enough,' said Mills.

"I got to going around a good deal with Mills and his friends, and they were always going into bars. Indeed a lot of their business was done in bars, and they were forever drinking. Myself, I never cared much for drink. I could drink if the need arose as much as the next man. And here there seemed to be need for it. For a man who hangs around bars has little liking for you if you're a blue ribbon.

So I drank with them. It never bothered to the extent of getting drunk, Mister Kerry, or to being unfit the next morning, but I know now that if you take a lot it plays tricks on you. The timing of your punch is not right. You're not so fast as you ought to be, and your head does n't work in a jam the way it would if you were a non-drinking fellow. I'll put it this way, Mister Kerry; it takes the crackle out of your silk. It's good for the old people and they with a chill in their bones and maybe a doubt in their minds, but it's no good for a young or a fighting man. I drunk too much and that's the truth, Mister Kerry, and I wondered how it was the others could keep it up. It was only afterwards I found out that at their favourite houses of call these fellows kept bottles of tea, and when you'd think they were drinking fiery whiskey, they were swallowing weak tea. They were cunning fellows. You would have thought they'd have put me up to this dodge, but maybe they did n't think of it," said James Carabine, " or maybe they thought I liked whiskey better, being Irish.

" At last Mills brought this fellow along he was fixing to fight me. ' Meet Blanco Johnson,' he said, ' the champion of Canada.' And there before me was a fellow you would and you would n't have taken for a fighter. He was tall and broad in the shoulder, Mister Kerry, but very light below for a prize ring man. You would think that the very weight of his shoulders would be too heavy for his legs and that he would have little power when it came to wrestling. I'd have great respect for that fellow in a glove fight, but in the London Ring I was n't worried at all. He had beautiful long muscles, and a small head that would be hard to get the range of, and when he walked he had the nice springy step of a fighter. But there's the funny thing, Mister Kerry, he was the handsomest fellow I ever laid my eyes on. He was fair and he had a face that was symmetrical in each degree, but for one. His hair was wavy

like a woman's. The only thing wrong about him, Mister
Kerry, was that his eyes were too small and a wee bit too
close together. But dress that fellow up, and put him on
at a smoking concert, and you'd never take him for a fighter.
'Beauty' Johnson was his nickname, and there was never
a truer one.

"Well, the match was made, Mister Kerry, for a purse
of two thousand five hundred dollars, which was great
money, and three hundred pounds a side, London Prize
Ring Rules, at a place to be decided later, for this was to
put the police off. We signed our names to the articles,
I making my mark, and he writing like a schoolmaster. He
was a nonpareil.

"Well, Mister Kerry, you'd think I'd done this fellow
the honour of the world in fighting him. It was 'Mr. Carabine' here, and 'Mr. Carabine' there, and 'What is your
opinion of this, Mr. Carabine?' And Al Mills introduced
him to Marcolina, and he kissed Marcolina's hand. He was
a play-acting man. For a week I couldn't get rid of him.
He took Marcolina out to dances at the Five Points Club,
and Tammany Hall, and he was an elegant dancer. There
was nothing this fellow couldn't do, so that I wondered
whether or not he could fight. In a while I cut off to the
country to train, for I don't like being too much friends
with a man before you fight him. There are bad tongues
everywhere, Mister Kerry, and I like to be given the credit
of fighting square.

"'I'll be seeing something of this man while you're
away,' said Marcolina.

"'If it cheers you up, child, see him,' said I.

"'I wish you'd forbid me to see him,' said she.

"But all I did was to laugh. So I went off to West-
chester, that's near New York, with Nick Dolan who trained
me, and a couple of fighters and a black man as cook, and
a fellow who could play the fiddle. Nick was not satisfied
at the way I came along.

"'You're not the man you were four months ago, Shamus,' he said; 'you're slow. Another wouldn't notice it, but I do. I wish to God,' he said, 'you'd done less of this pub crawling in New York.'

"'I was never drunk in my life, Nick,' I said.

"'If you were,' said Nick, 'it would have been better for you, for you'd have known when to quit!'

"It was two weeks before the fight when Marcolina came to see me. I wouldn't have her in the camp but she came for a few minutes.

"'I want to tell you, Carabine,' she said. 'Don't underrate this man. I've seen a good deal of him in New York, and I've been to his camp with Al Mills —'

"'Don't tell me anything about his camp, Marcolina,' said I. 'A man's training secrets are his own.'

"'There's something else I have to tell you, Carabine,' she said. 'This man's in love with me, and I,' she said, 'I'm crazy about him.'

"'Och, is that all?' said I and laughed. 'Run along now, Marcolina. I'll see you after the fight.'

"'Good luck in the fight, and always, Carabine,' said she, and went away.

"When she had gone I laughed again at what she said, for I thought this: that Al Mills and the others had put her up to it, so as to make me fight the harder and finish the quicker. The betting was five to one on me, Mister Kerry, and every one knows that a money on fighting bet is the most dangerous bet in the world. A broken hand, an ignorant swing from your opponent, and the champion of the world goes down before an unheard-of man. 'But aren't they the ignorant crowd,' I thought, 'to consider a mild stratagem a child could see through?'

"The day before the fight Nate came to see me, and he took me aside.

"'I was always your friend, Carabine,' said he.

"'You were. Nate.' said I.

"'I'll give you a friend's advice,' said Nate. 'If anything happens, go right back to Ireland, and forget America and forget all you've seen or anybody you've met here.'

"'You mean if I lose the fight?'

"'If you lose more than the fight.'

"'What do you mean, Nate?' I asked.

"But he would say nothing, and I couldn't understand until I remembered the drugs the poor fellow would be taking. Drink is bad. It wearies and weakens the head, but drugs are the devil's invention. They give false life to you, and the sane clean world becomes a maze like you see in old-time gardens. You wander and wander and think you're going fine, but only by accident or a friend's hand do you come out of it. Drink and women are pitfalls, Mister Kerry, but drugs are chains.

"So I said: 'Of course, Nate.' For I thought I'd humour him. 'Sure if I lost, what would I stay here for?' And I was jolly.

"'You damned fool!' said Nate. 'You'll never understand.'

IX

"The fight was called in New Jersey, across the river from New York, in a clearing in the woods. It was six o'clock of a June morning, and the birds were singing to raise your heart. I never saw a bonnier day. The ring was pitched on fine springy turf and there was a big crowd from New York, Tammany men, gamblers, fellows of society who liked to be known as sportsmen, a big crowd of Irish fellows. When I was in the ring, I noticed Marcolina in the crowd and that annoyed me, for I thought she knew I didn't want her at the fight. She was very white, it seemed to me, and she avoided my eye, and gave me no look at all. Al Mills was there and he smiled at me in what I might call a dirty manner. I thought: 'That isn't the look of a man who has his money on me.' And then it came to me: 'That fellow hasn't his money on you. That fellow has his money on the other man.'

"'What's worrying you, Shamus?' said Nick Dolan.

"'Nothing at all,' said I. But that was wrong, for what with Marcolina's manner and Al Mill's look I wasn't easy at all. The Johnson and I met in the middle of the ring and the referee talked, and Mister Kerry, I've never seen a man in better shape. He shone. He was fit to fight for the world. And his legs that I thought were weak were only light, like a deer's. There was no 'Mr. Carabine' now. He was curt and ugly. And when I held out my hand he looked at it.

"'What's that for?' said he.

"'To shake hands,' said I.

"'To hell with that!' said he, and walked to his corner.

" I felt hurt at that, Mister Kerry. The men I had fought with before hadn't been like that. It was: May the best man win! I tell you there was a queer feel in the air that morning, for all the birds were singing.

"Time was called and we met, Mister Kerry. And he began sparring like a glove lightweight instead of a prize-ring man. One instant he was in front, in the next breaking ground to the right or left, dancing in and out like a ballet master. I had a trick, as most boxers have tricks, of feinting with the left before leading it, and some one must have told this fellow of it, for as my shoulder moved he let fly with his left hand, and Mister Kerry it was like a sling shot or a golf ball going through the air. He got me fair. And before I could answer he was away dancing. Four times he did it in a row. Once I crowded him in a corner, and began to hit, but he rolled to the punch, and when the crowd began to roar, thinking I was doing for him, I wasn't hurting him at all. And when he got out of the corner he began with the left again. He had great tricks, this fellow. When it looked as if I'd corner him, he'd bend like an acrobat and catch me by the ankles. There was nothing in the rules against or for that. So I'd look down at him and wonder what I'd do. And then he'd straighten up and let go with the right. When I'd set myself, as a heavy man will, to let go with a knock-down punch, he'd drop his hands and walk away laughing, so that I felt like a fool. And then I'd do what a fool will do, rush him furiously to be a mark for his left hand. When I'd get close to throw him, he'd go limp and loose and fall with me of his own accord. Take his minute's rest and come up grinning.

"There's no use telling you about that fight, Mister Kerry; there was only one man in it and that wasn't me. First I could hear the crowd roar for me and then be silent, and then begin to roar for the other man. That is always cruel hearing, Mister Kerry. In the fourth round I couldn't see, so that Nick had to open my eyes with a knife to give me a glimpse of the fellow at all. This man fought a great heady fight. He never let up on my eyes, so that in a little while I didn't know that it was day, only for the singing of the birds. They had to lead me to my corner, and once I hung on by hands to the rope to avoid going down. I had a hope he'd close, so that I could take the strength out of him wrestling, but he was too clever.

"And then in my corner I heard the towel go through the air.

"'Are you throwing up, Nick?' I asked.

"'I'm sorry, Shamus,' said he, 'but I can't see a fellow countryman killed.'

"So that was the end of that fight.

"There is no person in the world so lonely as the conquered fighting man. He is like a star that shot across the sky and is lost. The people who were cheering him a month before turn and say: 'Sure, he was no damned good!' The cheering and the hand-shaking are all for the other fellow, while you are in your corner by yourself, and your trainer and your seconds, even they feel uncomfortable, and wish they were with the other man. The crowd that has been waiting for you before the fight now passes you by as if you were a convict. There is no person in the crowd that does n't feel he is a better man than you.

"I went across to New York and to a Turkish bath, to steam the sores out of myself, and to get my face patched up, and my eyes painted. It was afternoon when I got to our hotel. 'Is Mrs. Carabine within?' said I.

"The fellow behind the counter of the hotel gives me a look, and says: 'Mrs. Carabine left here two hours ago, taking all her luggage with her.' Well, Mister Kerry, it was no surprise to me somehow, and I remember saying to myself: 'Well, you might have known it.' But I said to the hotel fellow: 'Yes,' said I, 'we intended moving to-day. Mrs. Carabine 's just gone ahead.' And he said: 'Yes, Mr. Carabine,' and smiled. The fellows behind hotel counters are knowing cynical men, and there is no richness in the hearts of them. Upstairs in our rooms there was nothing but my things, no word for me even, though none was needed. But the white bulldog was there. He barked at me, glad to see me. She must have forgotten him, said I. He 'd have made a grand present for Johnson. 'What are you doing here?' said I. 'Don't you know I 'm a beaten man?' And he barked again. So I said to him: 'You stay with me. You 're one thing they don't get.'

"I spent the rest of the day looking for lodgings where I would n't be known. I did n't want to go back to the Danish woman's, after leaving it to be married in great style. In the end I got a place on the west side of the town, near where the ocean liners dock, and there I shifted my gear and took the dog. When all was settled I thought I 'd go across the town and have a bite to eat at Nate's, for there, thought I, I'll have friends anyway. A tune from Peter the harpist, and a crack with Nate, and it'll take the edge off the hard day. The day itself had turned dreary after the promise of the morning, and I mind walking through the yellow murk across Sixth Avenue and Madison Square and Fourth Avenue across to Third and going along to Nate's. I turned in the door and was going down the stairs when a champagne bottle was opened and the noise of it made me look up. Well, there at a table were the Johnson fellow, with not a scratch on him, Mister Kerry, and Marcolina sitting beside him, and a look on their faces as if there was nothing in the world for one but the other. Well, Mister Kerry, Marcolina had never a closer escape from death, and maybe the Johnson had, neither, but at that moment Nate came up to them and sat down and began drinking with them and chatting, and treating them as if they were his best friends. Well, that was the last straw. Me, that he'd been so friendly with, and professed such friendship to, and to be cheek by jowl with the man that had beaten me and the woman that had left me. Mister Kerry, no blow that day hurt me, or Marcolina's going did n't hurt me as much as that conduct of Nate's did. I had always thought that decency was common in the world, and until that moment I had known no different. I walked back up the stairs without any one seeing me, and as I went through the streets I was glad it was a murky night was in it, so that no one could see my face.

X

"This fellow Johnson was now described as the champion of Canada and Ireland, though how he could be of Ireland I don't know, not being born there, or having anything to do with Ireland. In a way he had a claim to it. So I could n't go back to Ireland again. I could n't face the mountains. I couldn't face the people. So I stayed on in New York, taking my mother's name McSorley, and working on the docks, loading and unloading vessels. Big Jim McSorley they called me. They were decent fellows there.

"Well, now, Mister Kerry, I'll tell you a difficult thing. I took to the drink. It was a cowardly and poor thing to do. But after a hard day's work, the lightsomeness of saloons is welcome, and a man with a load on his mind is not good company for himself. I was never a loud drunk, or a dead drunk, I was just a stupid drunk, but even in a crowd that drunk hard I was notable. Men would say to me: 'God, Jim, you'd better lay off that stuff. It'll kill you.' To myself I'd say: 'What matter if it does?' But to them I'd laugh. In the end they figured it was something on my mind. All the waterfront knew Big Jim McSorley and his white dog. The stuff gave me sleep, Mister Kerry, but it got like this: that I had to have a couple in the morning before I was good for anything. When I look back now, Mister Kerry, I can hardly believe that was me.

"I never met any one I knew in that place, for the way of New York is this: that Seventh Avenue is as far from Fifth as Ireland is from the Lowlands of Holland. People that live in Broadway will not go on another street. The New Yorkers are habitual people. But talk of Johnson came to the saloons, of glove fights he had had, and how there was talk of matching him with Peter Jackson, the black, and Charlie Mitchell, England's champion. There was an occasional word about James Carabine, and the talk was he had gone back to Ireland, and it was said that Johnson's science had beaten Carabine, who had none, but was just an ignorant Irish fighter, good for a street brawl and nothing else. This was queer hearing, Mister Kerry.

"I heard them speak of Marcolina, Mister Kerry, and how she had married Carabine and left him for the better

man. And it was said that she was married before to a
fellow who was a professional killer and now in Sing-Sing.
I asked how could she marry Carabine, if she was married
to another fellow, and they said: Maybe Carabine wasn't
the only one she married. Lina Ward, they said, was a
great favourite with the politicians and what another woman
would get two years for as a crime, Lina would only get
pity for as a mistake.

"I'd say: 'I see. What'll you have, boys?'"

"And they'd say: 'We'll have schooners of beer.'"

"'Schooners of beer all around,' I'd call, 'and just shove
over that decanter of red-eye.'"

"I knew myself that all wasn't well with me, and that
I'd gone a ways from the man I was, for one day near the
boats a man stopped me and he said:

"'Aren't you Mr. James Carabine, the Irish fighter?'"

"'Oh, no,' said I, 'I'm afraid you're mistaken. My
name's McSorley.'"

"'I beg your pardon,' said he. 'Now I see you're not,
when I'm close to you, for you're a fat soft man, and not
the cut of a fighter at all.'"

"I used to think to myself: Well, I'll make a break.
I'll fight a couple of times, and then join a ship on her
way around the Horn, and that way get to Australia. I
got a fight in a little club for a five-pound note under
the name McSorley, but though I won it easily on points,
I should have won it in the first round. The club manager
spoke to me afterwards.

"'You've got a natural style of boxing, McSorley, and
you're a big man, but leave it alone. There's one thing
you haven't got, and that's a fighter's heart.' And to
him I said: 'I haven't.' And to myself I said: 'Not any
more.' And so I let things go. I was like a bird whose
wings had been clipped and was compelled to walk on its
small feeble feet. I was like a fox a man had chained in

a stableyard and made a curiosity of. I was like a man —
the Lord between us and all harm! — on whom some aged
crooked-minded woman had turned the Bad Eye. I was so
far gone as this, Mister Kerry, that I didn't care how I
looked, and what was worse I had let the white bulldog get
dirty, too, and that was meaner than not taking care of
myself.

"If I had been a weak man, I wouldn't have got a job
at all, but with my frame I was always sure of work. But
every night it was the same old tale: the heat and sawdust
of the saloon. I was there one night drinking, and a voice
came through the place that made me drop the glass from
my hands, and turn cold.

"'Aren't you the devil and all for hiding yourself,
James Carabine!'

"I looked up and it was true. There was your uncle
Valentine before me."

XI

"He had no beard in those days, as you know, Mister
Kerry, and he was then like you now, tall and thin. His
head was red as it is now, but more curly, and he had a
merry look in his eyes. There was the smell of Ulster from
his tweed suit, heather and turf smoke, and the ashplant
under his arm, — Mister Kerry, I could tell the coppice
where it was cut. Mister Kerry, it was as if the walls of
that boozing den had fallen apart and shown me the hills of
Derry and the sunlight on Destiny Bay, and the gypsy
women at their caravan doors, weaving their baskets out
of sally rods.

"Your uncle Valentine walked into that saloon as if it
were his own Kildare Street Club with a nod and a smile for
every one as if they were his fellow members.

"'And how is it with you, James Carabine?' And he
took my arm.

"'Mister Valentine,' I said, 'I'm through.'

"And he lets a laugh out of him that was like a church bell bringing you back to security and belief. 'And is that the way to face a run of bad luck? I'm ashamed of you, James Carabine.'

"The people in the pub were silent, and then they turned to him, and one man said:

"'Is that Mister Carabine, the Irish boxer?'

"'And who else?' asked your uncle Valentine.

"'And are you a friend of his?'

"'There's none closer,' answered your uncle Valentine.

"'That's all right,' said they. 'We were getting worried about him. We didn't know who he was, but that he was a good man low in the heart. But now that he has a friend with him, he'll be all right.' You'll find blacker hearts, Mister Kerry, than on the wharves of New York.

"There was once at dinner in Destiny Bay, a soldier, or maybe just some casual, wandering man, who was talking of Constantinople of the Turks, and how there was a great church there from Christian days, and it was not dedicated to any saint, but to a gift of God, and that is Holy Wisdom. Well, if there's one man ever had that healing gift, it's your uncle Valentine. He never spoke to me about the drink, or about my troubles, and he was wise there. I've heard it said that it's best to get a thing off your mind to a friend, but holding a lodge of sorrow only revives the matter, and gives the weakness in you an excuse for keeping up depression. Your uncle Valentine acted as though he'd seen me a month before. I had to come up to his hotel and take a room there, and get decent clothes on, and face New York. As to the drink, your uncle Valentine was always asking every three or four hours, whither I'd like one, and having one with me as if it were just a pleasant thing for both of us, and not for me a loosening of the clutch on my throat. Your uncle was like a small boy. He said he'd come to America to see the Indians on Long Island, and the people murdering each other on the Bowery, but I knew well enough he'd come for me. He took me to Sheepshead Bay to the racing, and if there was ever an Indian let loose in New York, it was your uncle, Mister Kerry, for even I felt sorry for the gamblers when he was through betting. Every day, every hour I was feeling better. We followed the races to Saratoga. In a week I could hardly believe all that had happened to me was true. Only when I was by myself at night I'd see Marcolina's face. And I'd hear the towel whishing into the ring in token of defeat. And then I'd know it was true.

"To get back to good feeling and strength, Mister Kerry, was like throwing off an old suit that you'd worn out and were ashamed of. I noticed myself thinning down and my eye hardening. And one day your uncle Valentine threw his leg across the arm of a sofa and looked straight at me.

"'This fellow calling himself champion of Ireland, it's hard,' said he.

"'It is, Mister Valentine,' I agreed. 'None feels it more than I.'

"'Did he beat you fair?' asked your uncle Valentine.

"'He did,' said I. 'He was too quick for me. His left hand was like a rocket in my face.'

"'Would you take him on again?' said your uncle Valentine.

"'I would,' said I. 'But I don't know if it would be any different. He's too clever for me, and besides, the heart is out of me.'

"'There was never an attack yet that there wasn't a defence for,' said your uncle Valentine. 'As to the heart being out of you, you've no right to say that. If it were your own small fight, for a purse of money or a woman, then you could feel anyway you liked about it, but this is to keep it from being said that the Irish Belt passed to a cheap bully from overseas.'

"'Mister Valentine,' I told him, 'get me that match and I'll fight till I die.'

"'That's better,' said your uncle Valentine.

"Your uncle Valentine took it in hand to get the fight, and it wasn't very difficult, I heard later. There were scores to subscribe to a purse for the satisfaction of seeing us, men who had missed the first one, and had heard afterwards about Marcolina and Johnson and me, and were eager to see a savage dirty fight over a woman. And there was great money to be made in betting over it. So sure were the gamblers of the outcome that they would give six to one against me, and the Irish are fools enough to back their fancy, no matter what odds are against it. Everybody on the other side laughed and said it was easy money. Oh, no, there was no difficulty about the fight.

"It was a queer thing, Mister Kerry, but the fitter I got the more I thought of Marcolina, and for the first time in my life I knew what jealousy was, and it is a disease and sickness. Her face was like something in a sick man's head, always hovering there. The queer sleekness of her hair, and her pointed face, like a fox's, but white, and the green eyes like emeralds. It used to grip me like a sickness. One night it got so bad that I told your uncle Valentine I couldn't go on.

"'Well,' he said, 'we'll let it go for the present, Shamus, and take it up again.' And he left me alone. I rang for a bottle of whiskey and they brought it to me and left it on the table. It just came to me, Mister Kerry, like a truth comes to a man, that if I drank that bottle of whiskey I was done forever. Mister Kerry, there were great battles fought in great fields, but there was never a harder one than that between myself and myself in that little room. I must have prayed, but what words I used, or if any at all, I don't know, but after a while the bottle of whiskey was no more than a bottle to me, and I left it there. I've heard of men throwing it out of the window after a fight like that, but they must have been play-acting with themselves. I just rang for the waiter and told him to take it away.

"'But you wanted it,' said he.

"'Well, I don't want it now,' said I. And I went out to where your uncle Valentine was. Your uncle Valentine must have seen how it was, for there was the moisture of death on my face. But he said nothing.

"So I said: 'Mister Valentine, when do I start training?'

"'Come down to Castle Gardens to-morrow,' he said, 'and meet your trainer. He'll tell you.' But who the trainer was I couldn't get out of him.

"I went down with him, and off the Irish boat there comes an old fellow in a beaver hat, and with a grey shawl around his shoulder, and, Living God! Mister Kerry, it would raise the hair on your scalp, for who was it but Shadrach Kennedy, the Irish fighter who had won the championship of Europe at the age of twenty in the camp of Waterloo. I'd often heard of him, and how he was greater than Daniel Donelly himself. He had killed Gaffer Casey at the Curragh of Kildare, and after that had never fought, but the country people said he had sold his soul to the devil for knowledge of boxing. And looking into his eye you might believe that thing. His body was a man's of near ninety, but his eye was a man's of twenty-five. There was no stroke in the game unknown to him.

"'So you're the young man that lost the championship of Ireland, and have taken me from my deathbed.'

"'I'm sorry, Mister Kennedy,' said I.

"'You'll be sorrier before I'm through with you,' he promised, and he looked me over. 'You've got a fighter's frame. Was it cowardice?' he sneered.

"'He was too quick for me, Mister Kennedy.'

"'Before I'm through with you, you'll beat a hare in full flight.' Your uncle Valentine was for putting him in the carriage, but he turned on him: 'Is it for insulting me you are, Mister Valentine?' he asked. 'I have as good feet as any other.' And to avoid argument he catches the horse a clout over the rump with his stick. I tried to take his carpetbag, but he promised me the same as the horse. He took a look now and then around him as we walked uptown.

"'And what do you think of New York, Mister Kennedy?' said I, so as to make conversation.

"'Belfast is better,' said he. He was a very downright man."

XII

"We had our camp near Stamford in the State of Connecticut, which is a seaport town, but not on the sea, on a sort of lake as it were, Mister Kerry, a great healthy place. Your uncle Valentine chose the boxers and wrestlers. There was a big Pole who couldn't speak English but was a nice fellow, and an American fellow from the Far West, and the boxers were Paddy Moynihan, the Irish-American boxer, and John Rhys, and Cornstalk Bill Ryan, who was looking for a fight. They were the best to be found and if there were better, I'd have had them. They'd all seen men trained in their day, but they themselves had never seen the like of the cruelty of Shadrach Kennedy. Mister Kerry, if I were a poor sinner and he a devil, he couldn't have been worse. He'd sit there with his shawl over his shoulders and his snuffbox in his hand and while I boxed and wrestled, his tongue would cut me like a whip. He would drive out, with me behind the buggy, as they called it, and make me run until I'd nearly drop. It was no trotting. It was swing your legs. And he'd get the Pole to pitch a football at my stomach and ribs, until I could have taken the kick of a mule there. Then he had another trick, which was getting the boys to chuck a bag of sand in the air, and for me to catch it on my jaw and neck. Mister Kerry, at times I could have cried with rage, and killed the old man, and your uncle Valentine would n't stay in the room, he was so sorry for me. But this was n't the worst, Mister Kerry. One day he had my arms tied to my sides with three twists of rope, and made Paddy Moynihan put on riding gloves with welts.

" 'Now cut the face off him,' he told Paddy.

" 'I 'll hit no man that can't put his hands up.'

" Well, Mister Kerry, you 'll hardly believe it, but Shadrach Kennedy laid on to Paddy with a driving whip until the big fighting man was nearly crying. In the end he made Paddy go for me. It was cruel. But after a few days of it, I noticed I could sway and duck and draw away my head in a manner I had n't thought possible. But it was hard.

" 'Mister Kennedy,' I protested, 'I 'm sure you were never trained as hard as this.'

" 'I was not,' he said, 'for two reasons. The one was there was never as good a trainer as myself when I was a boxer. Now, ax me the second,' he said, 'and I 'll give you a good answer.'

" 'Well,' said I, 'Mister Kennedy, what is the second?'

" 'I was never,' said he, 'such a traitorous cowardly third-rate tinker's pup as to lose the championship, and to have to go after it again. Is there anything else you 'd like to hear?'

" 'No, sir,' said I. For I 'd heard enough.

" He was clever, Mister Kerry. He 'd have none of the old slip the left and cross-counter. He 'd make you catch your man's left on your right wrist and counter with the left straight to the face. A dandy blow. He 'd teach you to hit, in a long fight, at the point where a man's left shoulder and arm joins. After a while his left hand is useless. He'd teach you to weave inside a guard instead of breaking it down, and to punish your man with short punches to the body. He taught me to catch my man's left arm, and twisting around pull him over my shoulder in the 'flying mare.' A terrible throw.

"He was good, Mister Kerry. He never pushed me past my strength for all his cruelty. He kept me fresh as new butter. Twice a day he'd work at my hands, fingering the muscles and bones until they were like hard rubber balls with steel inside them.

"He was queer, Mister Kerry. He was a religious man. He believed when he died, he would sleep until midnight of the thirty-first of December, 1999, when an angel would wake him and give him a white robe with gold lettering on it, and a gold crown. He would go to Heaven with a certain number, while all the rest would go to Hell. As to whether he was right or not time will show. But for all his religion, he would play with us at the Irish card game of five thousand up, for a silver shilling a hundred, and cheat like a common vagabond. None of us had courage enough to call him crooked, or even to stop the game. He made great money out of us that way. He would go out fishing with a rug over his knees and a rug over his shoulders, and an umbrella over his head. One day I was putting him in his boat, and noticed he hadn't hooks, but he had worms. I asked him how it was he had forgotten the hooks.

"'I never use them,' said he, 'my purpose in fishing is not to catch fish.'

"I told this to your uncle Valentine, and I said: 'I don't doubt but that man's mad.' And your uncle Valentine thought for a while and smiled, and said: 'Now, I wonder is he?'

"He let up on the training one day, and sent me out for a walk. And that evening he called me into his room. 'I've one more thing to tell you,' he went on, 'don't watch your man's eyes, or his feet, or his hands. Watch the point of his jaw, and when he drops that into his shoulder, jump in and punish.'

"Your uncle Valentine came in and laid his hand on my shoulder. 'We sail over to the Oyster Bay, Jim,' he told me.

"Then I knew I had to fight on the morrow."

XIII

"Your uncle Valentine would not let me out or see anything until the next morning. There was the early note of winter in it, and the trees brown and the black crows in the fields. We left the farmhouse where we were staying after breakfast, and your uncle huddled me up in one of his great frieze coats with a white muffler about my neck.

"'I have a present here,' he told me, 'for you from the gypsy folk of Destiny Bay.' And out of his pocket he pulls a green scarf of silk so delicate you could pull it through a ring. And on it in gold thread was the Irish harp. 'You'll wear it on your way back, Jim.'

"'Please God!' said I.

"The ring was pitched on the shore of the bay, fine springy turf, with the sound of the little waves in your ears. And if there were plenty of people at the New Jersey fight there was a multitude here. You wouldn't have thought it was against the law at all. There were folk of quality, acquaintances of your uncle Valentine, and the scum of the Bowery, horsemen, gamblers, and Irish. There was a sea of faces around the ring, and on the rim of this crowd were carriages of all sorts with people standing on them. I noticed maybe a dozen of our own sort, North of Ireland fellows, very quiet men would knock the head off your shoulders for twopence and I saw your uncle Valentine had taken no chance against the ring being rushed in case of my winning. I was in the ring first and Johnson made me wait a while for him. Your uncle Valentine was talking to Paddy Moynihan about the trotting horse, and I, I'm not ashamed to admit it, Mister Kerry, I was saying a bit prayer. All around the ring the gamblers were shouting: 'I'll lay fives against the Irishman. Here, I'll lay sixes. Six to one against.' One fellow shouted: 'I'll take tens,' said he. No sooner were the words out of his mouth than a big man with a sealskin waistcoat pulls a roll of bills out of his pocket and passes it up. 'A hundred thousand to win ten thousand dollars on Johnson,' he agreed. The man who offered the bet looked green. There was big money at that ringside.

"Your uncle Valentine heard the other man coming through the crowd, and had my coat and muffler off, and pulled the sweater over my head. For an instant I stood stripped. As I looked up and they were throwing the greatcoat around my shoulders I caught sight of Marcolina standing on a dogcart on the edge of the crowd, and she seemed whiter, her face more peaked than ever. She saw me and her eyes widened until I could see the white around the pupil. How long we looked at each other, I don't know, Mister Kerry, but there was a twist to her mouth as if pain were on her, and she turned away.

"'Hy!' said your uncle Valentine, and punched me in the ribs.

"Then I saw my man was in the ring.

"I went forward to hear the referee go over the rules — his name was Kilrain, a fine fellow and a good fighter in his day! — and there I met Johnson, who had a smile on his face, but it left it as I looked at him. He had plaster on his hands.

"'Do you object to this, Carabine?' the referee asked.

"'I object to nothing, Mister Kilrain, not even brass knuckles.'

"As we turned to our corners I held out my hand to Johnson, for a prize ring is no place for private spite, and a championship fight is above personal feeling. He looked at my hand without taking it, and turned away. There was a lot of laughing at the ringside, but there was a good deal of hissing. I went back to my corner, and 'Good luck, Jim!' whispered your uncle Valentine and whipped my coat off, and time was called.

"Mister Kerry, there's nothing in the world as lonely as a man in the ring when his seconds get out of it, and he's left there with the man he's to fight, and the referee like the blinded woman that's the dispenser of justice on the outside of the law courts. Every one who has fought knows the dropping of the heart. The Southern Irish fellow will cross himself and the Jewish fighter touch a praying shawl. I gave a good pull to the ropes to loosen up and walked out to meet my man.

"I don't know what there was about me, Mister Kerry, but I could see Johnson change his mind as he came forward. He closed up, in a way. We fiddled for a few minutes, breaking ground, moving here and there. Around the ring you could have heard a pin fall, as the saying is, with the silence that was in it. Then Johnson jumped at me with his left hand. I didn't try to stop, but pulled my head away, as Shadrach Kennedy had instructed me, and each time he missed. He looked back and looked puzzled. And when he was thinking I rushed him myself, and letting go with the left caught him with a swash in the ribs that made the wind go through his teeth whistling, and bringing it up caught him on the side of the head and sent him staggering across the ring. I followed him, Mister Kerry, but he covered up in the corner, so I had to clout him a couple of right-handers at the back of the neck to straighten him up. He slipped under my guard and got away. We sparred and I noticed his chin going down and I jumped in and hit. It spread him on his back in the middle of the ring, and the first round was over.

"I never heard such a minute's commotion as there was at the ringside then. The crowd was roaring. It stopped as time was called for the second round. One minute it was shouting and the next it was silent as night. I noticed the marks of my blows on Johnson, the red knuckle marks against the white skin. He had taken it too easy, Mister Kerry. It never does to take a man too easy, even though you 've beaten him easily the first shot. He was thinking; he was thinking hard. He feinted at my head and went in for a swing at the ribs, but I got him with right and left as he came in. He was clever, Mister Kerry; he slid behind me to hold and got a full Nelson on. But the Pole had taught me how to beat that. I dropped forward on my knees and threw him over my head. He was quick, so his hands saved him. We were both up on our feet and at it hammer and tongs. He hit hard. He shook me on the neck and jaw. But I got home with an uppercut that finished the round.

"Mister Kerry, in spite of everything, Shadrach Kennedy's instructions nearly did me. He had told me to watch my man's chin and I watched nothing else. In the first fight I had lost to him with my little trick of feinting with my left before leading. The man that beats another to the punch is the man that wins. My feint was a personal trick, but the dropping of the chin to the shoulder is universal. Every one will protect himself before he attacks. I was doing so well beating him to the punch that I paid no attention to anything else. Once he tried a hard left on me, and dropping my head I caught his knuckles on my skull, and that must have hurt his hand, for he switched with his right hand forward quickly.

"'For God's sake, look out!' shouted your uncle Valentine.

"I had only time to set the muscles of my stomach, no time to drop my hands even, before his left with all his body pivoting behind it socked me in the midriff. It was like the blow of a sledge hammer, or a bullet. And the crack of it could be heard all over the ring, so that the people swayed forward, and a big groan came out of them. If I hadn't been in time setting myself for it, it would have been an end of that fight, and maybe of any other fight. And if I hadn't been in condition, I could never have weathered it. Mister Kilrain, the referee, looked at me, and his face was white as a sheet.

"And then some Irish fellow from the ringside shouts: 'Sure, he's laughing at you, Johnson!'

"Well, I wasn't laughing at him, Mister Kerry. My face was just twisted with the grin of pain. Pain does either of two things to you. It makes you senseless or it drives you mad. It drove me crazy and I went for Johnson, hitting him with everything I had, jolt and chop; hooking him, and back-handling him on the return, as we were allowed to do in the Prize Ring. It must have been like hailstones hitting him, until he went down and lay quiet. The ringside was in a roar, men trying to hedge their bets, taking any money offered on Johnson, where before there wasn't a penny to be taken from his supporters except by the ignorant Irish and your uncle Valentine. Your uncle Valentine was the only calm person there. His face was pale and he was whistling 'The Boyne Water,' and he dropped on his knee and began to rub my stomach. Before the minute was up, I was all right. 'I'm fine, Mister Valentine,' I said. 'It's nearly over, Jim,' said he, 'but just keep your eye open.'

"It didn't need any advice from any one to make me pay attention, for the pivot blow was a master tradesman's punch. I went after Johnson in the next round, giving him

the straight left and bringing over the right occasionally.
All he did was to try and push me off with the left hand.
And then after two minutes of fighting he drew his last
trick. He swung his right, high, overhand to my jaw. He
brought it from his right heel and as quick as lightning,
a punch nobody but a fool or a great boxer uses. If it had
caught me on the temple, I'd have been dropped like a
felled ox. If it had caught me on the jaw, I'd have been
through. I took it on the neck and as it was my knees
gave and my hands dropped, and a cloud came before my
eyes. And I could hear the roar of the ringside, and the
cry: 'Carabine's gone!' But the fog cleared away. I
hadn't time to fall, and there was Johnson in front of me,
looking more dazed than myself. He couldn't understand
I wasn't down. I waded in and began to punch at him.
And when I wrestled with him I knew I was strong again.
He gave a look over his shoulder at his corner, and threw
his shoulders up, and then I knew I was only beating a
beaten man.

"He was game, Mister Kerry. There was no black spot
in him. He was a better man losing than he ever was winning. I could feel the vitality pouring out of him with
every punch I landed. Once he slipped from weakness and
fell, and I helped him to his feet. He said: 'Thanks, Jim,'
and he put out his right hand and I took it. It was as fine
an apology as was ever made.

"The ringside was bawling, Mister Kerry, a mad roar.
The men of the North, I noticed, had brass knuckle-dusters
on, and worse than that in their pockets, for they weren't
going to see the ropes cut and me done out of my fight. I
worked Johnson over to his corner, and held him up, he
was so weak, and I called to his seconds: 'Can't you throw
in the sponge? Can't you see your man's done? What's
the use of punishing any further?' But his seconds were
surly and dumb.

"I called to the referee: 'Mister Kilrain,' I said, 'this man's finished. Can't you stop the fight to save him?'

"'It's a championship fight,' said the referee, 'and I've got to give him every chance of keeping his title, if it's only the chance of an earthquake. You've got to knock him out of time,' said Mister Kilrain.

"I appealed to the fellow himself. 'If I land you a light one,' said I, 'will you go down and stay down. There's no disgrace to losing a fight like this. You've given a lot and taken a lot. Will you do that?' said I.

"He shook his head, meaning he wouldn't. And he looked past me, into the crowd, and I knew whom he was looking at, and I understood the appeal in his eyes.

"'Ah, my poor fellow,' said I, 'is that the way with you?'

"There was nothing for it, Mister Kerry, but to finish him, so I pushed him off, and bit my heels into the ground for a stance. He knew the end was coming and he tried to get his hands up, but his arms were tired and numb. I let him have it with both hands, and stood back. And he thumped forward on his face. Then I turned and walked to my corner."

XIV

"I was coming away with the Northern men around me and your uncle Valentine by my side, and around my neck was the green scarf with the gold harp glittering on it. It took courage to face me then in my victory and pride. But she stood in front of me and her face was whiter than I'd ever seen it.

"'I don't suppose you'll believe me, Carabine,' she said, 'but I always knew you were the better man.'

"'Och,' said I, 'I was lucky to-day, Marcolina. Either of those punches might have finished me.'

"We were for a moment quiet, and then she spoke again.

"'I don't know if you understand how much it costs me to say this,' and even her lips were white, 'but I don't suppose you'd have me back.' She must have read my answer in my mind, for she said: 'Well, I don't blame you.'

"'Go back to your friend, Marcolina,' I told her. 'He's a good man, and a game man — I never fought better. And he needs you now.'

"She waited a minute, and her eyes were on the ground. 'I've been a fool,' said she, and she walked back to the ring. And that was the last I ever saw of her."

My small cousin Jenepher was waking up in Carabine's arms, so that he turned his eyes from me to the little lady.

"That's thirty years ago, *sthoreen veg ore*, small golden treasure! And maybe I've been a fool too," said James Carabine.

FOUR

TALE OF THE PIPER

FOUR

Tale of the Piper

I first saw him as I rode from the Irish Village into the gates of Destiny — a burly man with a moustache, a cheap suit of Glasgow reach-me-downs, a cap with a twisted brim, and the most evilly insolent eyes I have ever seen in a human face. At the sight of him Pelican, that wisest and steadiest of horses, reared; and I felt a savage gust of hatred rise in me.

"Now, who are you?" I asked, "and what are you doing here?"

"The same question from me to you." And his eyes were studiedly insulting.

An unaccountable rage made me tremble. I shook out the thong of the hunting crop and edged Pelican toward him.

"I am the Younger of Destiny," I informed him, "and when I pass all folk in Destiny do me the honour of uncovering."

He fumbled with his cap and took it off. His hair was shaggy and matted, like a wild man's.

"I am a piper your uncle Sir Valentine MacFarlane sent from the High Country of Scotland home here to await his coming."

I said no more and rode in. My aunt Jenepher told me of my uncle Valentine's letter which Morag, her Islay maid, had read to her. My uncle Valentine had met the man in an inn in Argyllshire, where he was stalking deer. "None knows anything about him, and he is most reticent about himself, but I am persuaded he is the best piper in the

world. Also, he may help revive the lost art of piping in
Ireland."

"Now if he had only sent me a pair of Ayrshire plough-
men," I grumbled.

At dinner that night the man threw his reeds over his
shoulder and played outside the dining-room window. He
broke into the rollicking country air of the "Palatine's
Daughter." I don't know what he did to it with the knowledge of his art, but out of that tune of frolicsome rural
love-making he produced an atmosphere which made me
uncomfortable as though some cad were telling foul stories.
He swung from that into "*Thorroo a Warralla,*" the "Funeral of the Barrel," a noted drinking song of how a barrel
of porter went dry after a day's flax-pulling. But the picture evoked was not that of country men drinking healthily
at a crossroads, but of a thieves' kitchen where dreadful
blowsy women, as of Hogarth, lay drunk with their rat-
faced cutpurses. . . .

"Stop that man, James Carabine," said my aunt
Jenepher.

He played no more under our window, but in the Irish
Village the next day he piped "The Desperate Battle", that
music that only a great piper can touch, and that night the
only faction fight we had in Destiny for forty years
broke out and raged until the police from the neighbouring
villages were rushed in. He played "The Belles of Perth"
to the men from the fields, and for days afterward I saw
maidservants and young girls in the farmhouses around
with red eyelids. And a young under-gardener flung down
his spade and said out of nothing, to nobody: "I'm sick of
the women in this untoward place." And one morning I
heard him play "*Iss fada may an a walla shuh*" — "I'm a
long time in this one town." And my own feet took an itch
for the road.

I said to my aunt Jenepher at luncheon: "I was thinking

now, with the winter coming, I'll give up hunting for this one season, and go and see Egypt maybe, or go as far as India. A young man ought to see the world a bit."

"Shall we talk about it to-night, Kerry?" said my aunt Jenepher.

She asked me to go with her into the garden after luncheon and sent Carabine for the piper. He arrived with his instrument under his arm.

"You have never played for me yet, piper."

"Your ladyship has never asked me." There was a solid dignity about him.

"I suppose you have many tunes," said my aunt Jenepher.

"What I say now would be immodest in another man, but true in me: no piper has more tunes. I have the lost tunes of McCrimmon. I have tunes that were lost before McCrimmon's day — old, dark tunes. Also tunes of my own making."

"Will you play me the tune of the fishermen, piper, as they raise the brown sails: 'Christ, Who walked on the sea, guard us poor fisher folk!'"

"I am sorry, my lady, but I have not that tune."

"Please play me Bruce's Hymn: 'God of Battles!'"

"That also, my lady, is a tune I have not."

"Then a merry song, piper, which you must know: 'The Marriage Feast which took place in Cana.'"

He was stolid as a rock. "I am afraid I have not that either."

"One of your favourite tunes is: 'I'm a long while in this one town.'"

He bowed with a nobleman's courtesy.

"It is a choice tune," he said slowly, "a darling tune."

"Then play it, piper, then play it," said my aunt Jenepher. "And as you are playing it," she rose up suddenly from the seat and looked at him with her blind eyes, "in God's name, go!"

"I was to wait," said the piper, "until Sir Valentine returned."

Both Carabine and I made a step toward him. My aunt Jenepher must have felt us. "Please, Kerry! Please, James Carabine!"

"Piper, my brother Valentine will not wish you to stay here an instant longer than I would have you stay, and I would not have you stay at all."

"Then I had better go," the piper said. And he swung his reeds to his shoulder; struck the piper's swagger.

"Do you need money for the road?" my aunt Jenepher asked.

"I need nothing."

"But you do, piper," said my aunt Jenepher softly. "I shall pray for you to-night."

He dropped the pipes from his shoulder and turned around. "I thank your ladyship," he said simply, "but I fear it is late for that."

"Nevertheless I shall," said my aunt Jenepher.

He turned and went away from us down the garden path, and what became of him is not known. He did not play his pipes as he went but held them crumpled under his arm, and his walk was more like the rapid amble of an animal than the step of a man. I was convinced that were I to look in the gravel I should find not the footprint of a man, but the slot of an animal. But I did not look. I was afraid.

FIVE

TALE OF MY UNCLE COSIMO AND THE
FAIR GIRL OF WU

FIVE

Tale of my uncle Cosimo and the fair Girl of Wu

I

Myself, who was so accustomed to the splendour of my uncle Valentine, reined in and stood still with admiration. I knew he was practising his pair of harness ponies for the Dublin Horse Show in August. I knew the ponies. I knew the trap. I knew my uncle Valentine. But all these made a picture any horseman would have loved. There were the beautifully matched bay ponies, under fifteen hands each, with the exact melodious movement of ballerinas; there was the trap, its gleaming wood, its polished leather, its shining silver mountings; there was my uncle Valentine, in his clothes that smacked a little of Georgian elegance, — the long brown coat, the brown trousers that ended in a strap under the instep of the varnished boot, the fob with seals, the black satin stock, the brown high hat perched a little to the side of the head, the seamed weather-beaten forehead and aggressive eyes, the immense fan-shaped red beard. One could easily see him in fancy trotting in the enclosure at the horse show, the blue ribbon of the championship of Ireland fluttering from the off-pony's bit, the audience of the most horse-knowledgeable people in the world rising and cheering. There the turnout would be in its element; but to meet it in the lanes of Destiny Bay, heavy with the scent of lupins and wild roses, and none there to see . . .

"I don't drive abroad from emptiness or self-conceit," I heard my uncle Valentine once explain, "but to exhibit to the common people the fallacies of democracy."

My uncle had stopped his trap outside the vicar's house,

beside our lovely old church of Saint Columba's-in-Paganry, and was talking to the new parson. The new parson was a frail, martyr-like man, with an eager ascetic's face and a long cassock. He was a very High Churchman, who had been sent us because he was killing himself in the slums of Derry. His ritual was elaborate and his sermons were short, but he was a very disappointed man. There is no sin to combat in Destiny Bay. There is not a little drinking of sound mellow Irish whiskey, and there is some unconventional love-making, and whole parishes have been known to put off the flax-pulling for a tournament at cards. But there is no sin. None of us cheat in Destiny Bay; and none of us tell lies — we are a big muscular folk and don't have to; and none of us are traitors. God's ocean and God's mountains teach us dignity; and God's birds harmony; and the deep clear mountain streams teach us cleanliness. No, there are no sinners in Destiny Bay. Romany and Irishman and foreigner who have abode with us all regard God as a majestic and infinite Sir Valentine MacFarlane, who will wither the mean man, and see fair play to the good fighter in difficulty, and pass the worthy into His Heaven with a grunt of satisfaction.

I had thought that my uncle Valentine and the parson were passing the time of day with each other, or discussing some trivial parochial affair. But when I rode up I found the parson white with anxiety and looking like some timid thing of the woods, as a deer before the bulk of the lordly elephant or other majestic monster.

"I cannot, Sir Valentine," he cried.

My uncle Valentine's voice was low and gentle. When my uncle Valentine bellows like the great yellow lion, stand your ground, but when my uncle Valentine's voice drops a note and is silky, flee. Flee like blazes!

"You are a stranger here," said my uncle Valentine, "and so I will pardon you for doing what no man has ever done before, for saying he could not do a thing when I have desired it done in Destiny Bay."

"Sir," said the parson, "on this point the Church is most explicit: that the unbaptised and the excommunicate shall not be admitted to the communion of saints. This woman was a woman of strange if any gods, and how shall I admit her into this quiet Christian burial ground, the quiet of which shall not be intruded on. Sir, your saintly brother, the Bishop of Borneo—"

"Blast my saintly brother," said my uncle Valentine quietly, "and blast you! If this service is not taken, pack your duds and get out of Saint Columba's-in-Paganry to-night. And tell your Bishop I chased you, and tell your Bishop, too, to send me no more parsons. I am sick of parsons. In the future the services will be conducted by me, or by my nephew Kerry here, or by my valet, James Carabine—"

"Sir," cried the agonised parson, "you give me no option but to do this unchurchly thing."

"Option!" bristled my uncle Valentine; "do I look as if I gave options?"

"At three then, sir," surrendered the clergyman.

"At three of the clock," said my uncle Valentine.

II

It was by my uncle's command that I went to the funeral that afternoon—that sunny afternoon of Destiny Bay. There was my uncle Valentine, burly, majestic, and grave; there my aunt Jenepher, who has a beautiful, merry face, and looks like some princess of a mellow royalty, leaning on her gold-headed ebony cane; there was my cousin Jenico, from Spanish Men's Rest, with his dark, passionate, puzzled features.

"'Behold, thou hast made my days as it were a span long: and mine age is even as nothing in respect of thee . . .'" The parson proceeded with the words that are like music, and that are not to be said for the unbaptised or excommunicate, so insist the bishops; but my uncle Valentine's insistence was otherwise.

"'For I am a stranger with thee, and a sojourner . . .'"

There also was James Carabine, with his great height and shoulders, his black side whiskers, like a Spanish grandee's, the small gold rings in his battered ears. There was Duncan, our head gardener, who could neither read nor write. And there — God bless him! — was the little Roman priest, with his clerical waistcoat spattered with snuff, his head more concerned with Plotinus than Thomas Aquinas. There they all were, to pay respect to this poor Chinese woman who had spent her days and ended her life among us.

"'There are also celestial bodies, and bodies terrestrial,'" went on the service, "'but the glory of the celestial is one and the glory of the terrestrial another. There is one glory of the sun and another glory of the moon, and another glory of the stars; for one star differeth from another star in glory. So also is the resurrection of the dead.'"

The brown bees droned, and the wild roses nodded, and everywhere was the rich blue of lupins, and foxgloves tall and dainty, like ladies of the Stuart times. Near us chimed the sea, green and white, apple-green and silver-white, and around us was the glory of the mountains, the mountains purple with heather. Everywhere was peace, but nowhere more peace than in the graveyard of Saint Columba's-in-Paganry. The parson might intone the words that argue townsfolk into the belief that being dead, we live. For us of the mountains and the sea there is no need of argument; we know. Around the little lichened church was a sense of welcome. The communion of saints, much as the parson feared, did not refuse hospitality to the alien sister. For the dead, with few exceptions, are a nice and kindly folk, else where is the profit in being dead?

I knew suddenly we would miss this woman from the countryside. We have a strange transient population in Destiny Bay, going to or coming from the lowlands of Ireland: gypsies in their caravans, Lovells, and Hernes, and Petulengros; mad Highlanders from Scotland, leaving rocky Argyll for fertile Fermanagh and Tyrone; Donegal men going to America, some who have never had a shoe on their foot or a word of English in their mouth. But the hard-faced, bitter, black-eyed, black-haired Chinese woman stood above their strange unharmony like a tower. I can always, and always will, remember her in her little cottage, a mile up the road from the great house, a figure in blue trousers and tunic digging in her garden, or sitting by the rose-covered porch smoking a long churchwarden pipe, with her unwinking jet eyes. Whence she came I had not known. I always thought she was something brought by gypsies and left there, but her upkeep and cottage and all were a charge on our family.

Against all of our house, except possibly against my uncle Valentine and against James Carabine, she had a black hatred. Whenever I rode past, she stood and cursed me in her singsong speech. When my aunt Jenepher went by, the Chinese woman writhed in an agony of anger against that lovely lady who was so helpless that all the world must feel warm toward her, as to a child, and so beautiful that all the world must love her. At one time, too, she loathed my uncle Valentine. He will carry to his grave the marks of her teeth in his left hand. Very quietly but very efficiently he throttled her until she was black in the face. She let go and she didn't try it again. In a measure they became friends, as much friends as a great Irish baronet and a poor Chinese woman can be, neither of whom understands a word of the other's language. Now, my uncle's friend-

ship is potent as strong wine, and just as dangerous when
taken in excess.　My uncle Valentine, reading somewhere
that the Chinese of both sexes are addicted to opium much
as we smoke cigarettes, procured a large quantity for her,
which she probably thought was medicine. . . . At any rate
it took the local doctor and a specialist from Dublin a week
to bring her to.

My uncle Valentine heard somewhere that the Chinese
are fond of fireworks, so he had come to the house a worker
in pyrotechnics to display his art.　All around her cottage
withes and frameworks were set up, and that night such an
orgy took place as brought out the police, the coastguards,
and the local militia under the impression that the French
had landed.　The poor Chinese woman was found cowering
in a corner of the house, white and trembling with terror.

My uncle Valentine, coming once from Dublin, brought
her two little orange trees in pots, at the sight of which, for
the first time since we had known her, she burst into such a
paroxysm of tears that she shook from head to foot.　She
passed her hands over the glossy leaves as over the head of
a child, and hugged the red pots to her breast.　Such grief I
had never seen before, nor, I hope and pray, may I ever see
again.　What recollection it stirred I do not know.　But my
uncle Valentine, when he returned to our drawing-room, blew
his nose, like a trumpet of Joshua, loudly and severally, and:

"God damn my soul!" he said.　"God damn my soul!"

"If you ask as fervently as that, brother," said my aunt
Jenepher tartly, "He probably will."

But then my aunt Jenepher could not see my uncle Valentine's eyes.

III

"There is only one thing I could have wished, Kerry, my
boy," said my uncle Valentine, "and that is, that your saintly

uncle, the Bishop of Borneo, had taken that service this afternoon."

It was after dinner, and over his full formal dress, and under his immense red beard, my uncle Valentine was adjusting the broad sash of the Orange Order. To-night he would drive to Williamstown, that was seven miles away, to make arrangements in our old lodge for the celebration of the Twelfth of July of glorious memory. Outside, Jimmy the Whistler was in the dogcart with the beautiful bay mare, Kilkenny Belle.

"But why, sir?"

"Because it would have served your saintly uncle, the Bishop of Borneo, damned well right!"

Carabine was helping him into his great frieze coat, adjusting the silk muffler, standing back now and then like a modiste before a mannequin.

"Where's my speech?"

"'Tis in your Honour's right-hand overcoat pocket, Sir Valentine. The newspaper fellow from Derry is after finishing writing it in the kitchen."

"Is it a good speech, Carabine?"

"'Tis a bit on the mild side, your Honour, but 'twill do."

"'Tis a mild year," said my uncle Valentine.

"But why should the Bishop of Borneo take over the burial service for the heathen woman?"

"Carabine will tell you," answered my uncle Valentine.

IV

"Well?" I asked.

We had gone into the gunroom, and James Carabine was making flies for my uncle's and my fishing. He sat by the table under the lamp with his tray of feathers, plovers' and moorhens' and woodcocks', and some eagles' feathers the Raghery fishermen had got for him; sheep's wool, pure white, and wool that was dyed red and brown and black; the small dainty hooks, the shining catgut; his broken hands were adroit as a fiddler's at his work. James Carabine's flies would make a fish's mouth water.

"You know your uncle Cosimo's picture?"

"I do." There is a famous picture of my uncle Cosimo in cassock and surplice, holding his Episcopal crozier, his fierce aquiline face like a sentry's of Christendom against the powers of darkness. My uncle Valentine is like a great two-handed Crusader's sword, but my uncle Cosimo is like a deadly Latin rapier. My uncle Valentine is generous in victory, but my uncle Cosimo is merciless at all times. There is something of Torquemada in his face. One can easily understand his meteoric rise in the Church. One can also understand why the Most Reverend His Grace the Lord Archbishop of Canterbury had him translated to the see of Borneo. Nobody of sense would leave an archiepiscopal mitre and seat in the House of Lords lying around anywhere my uncle Cosimo was.

"You see him now, Mister Kerry," said Carabine, "with his eagle's face and the look in his eyes as if he were riding the heathen on the curb, but twenty years ago he was looking older than he is now, and there was no surplice on him or crozier in his hand, but an old shooting coat on him, and a gun under his oxter, and a stubble of grey beard on his chin, and always drink in his eyes."

"I can hardly think, James Carabine, that any of our family dishonoured themselves by drink, hard drinkers though they are."

"A MacFarlane cannot dishonour himself save by treachery or cowardice," said Carabine, "which none ever did. Your uncle Cosimo did not dishonour himself through drink. I would put it this way: he over-honoured the drink by constant consumption of it.

"Your uncle Cosimo was the wildest of them all, aye, and

maybe the most gifted. At school he couldn't be kept. So your grandfather put him in the Navy. And right away he was sent to China to help fight the river pirates. For there's pirates still in China, it being an old conservative country," said James Carabine. "But after three years of it he was ordered back, and in a while he came back to Destiny Bay."

"With the Chinese woman?" said I.

"With none but himself," said James Carabine. "But he was through with the Navy for good. In London he went to see the Lords of the Admiralty, for your uncle Cosimo could go anywhere on account of his connections. And he asked them was there to be any more fights like Camperdown or Trafalgar Bay.

"'We survey Europe from East to West,' said the Lords of the Admiralty, 'likewise America, North and South, and we see no great fights in the future.'

"'Then you don't want fighting, tearing Ulstermen,' said your uncle Cosimo; 'you want tactful, sea-going police.'

"'True for you,' said the Lords of the Admiralty.

"'I'm no damned peeler,' said your uncle Cosimo, and he came home.

"Well, for ten long years your uncle Cosimo did nothing but drink steadily and read and enjoy the sport of the country. He was always in this village shebeen or that, barring when he was out shooting or hunting or fishing, and then always he had a silver flask, which would hold nearly a quart of whiskey, in his pocket. He could ride better drunk than he could sober, and fish better, but he couldn't shoot as well. And everybody about the countryside would say what a great pity it was about him, that he was the greatest genius in Ireland, and could rise to anything, as he has proved since, if it weren't for the drink. He was never obnoxious drunk, if you know what I mean, Mister Kerry, but always steady on his feet, though crazy in the eye. With women he had the courtliness of a king.

"Though he could discourse on any subject under the sun with ease, though maybe not with accuracy," said James Carabine, "his favourite topic was China. He considered them to be the most civilised people in the world. He would speak about their poetry and customs, and he would tell how if two Chinese gentlemen met each other, they wouldn't talk about ignorant subjects like the weather and the crops, but sit down and discuss the movements of the stars and the shapes of trees.

"He would tell Duncan the gardener that his sea of roses was an agglomeration of vulgarity. The only virtue he could find in Destiny Bay was the hanging together of the family, which he said was a great virtue and much practised by the Chinese.

"At times he would take it into his head to go and live in China, and he would go and ask your uncle Valentine to lend me to him to pack his bags, and off he would go to say good-bye while I was packing them. But when he would come back he had forgotten all about it. 'What have you been doing to my things?' he would shout. 'Is it trying to get rid of me you are? Unpack those traps and don't touch them again.' He was a terrible heartscald in those days, was your uncle Cosimo," said James Carabine, and he bit off a piece of catgut with his strong gypsy teeth; "but maybe he was loved better then than now, bishop and all as he is," added James Carabine.

V

"There was an old fellow living near Toberdine, and he had a young wife," said James Carabine, "and this old fellow was mad. He was a black-hearted man, would lose all control of himself in anger, so that he'd come roaring at you. There was a Romany man, a cousin of my mother's, Anselo Loveridge by name, and he was sweet on this fellow's wife, and she on him. How far into it this pair had gone devil a one of me knows, Mister Kerry. But no matter how far, I'm not for blaming them. She was a copper-haired, apple-like young woman, and her husband was a mad old man, with spittle-covered grey beard. And this Anselo was a tall, fine-looking fellow. He was a breaker of horses by trade. He was a tall fellow, dressed in corduroy trousers, bound at the knee with horseman's straps, and a grey shirt, with a velveteen waistcoat. He wore a Romany diklo, the red gypsy handkerchief around his neck, and a hat I never saw on him. He was as brown as a coffee berry and his hair and eyes were like black ink. He was a grand upstanding fellow.

"This fellow was a horse-breaker by trade, as I told you, Mister Kerry. But poaching was his hobby. Many's the moonlight night he would go out with his gun barrels chalked, for though your uncle Valentine didn't mind a little poaching, he insisted it should be done discreetly. If a hog or greedy fellow went too far, your uncle Valentine wouldn't put him in gaol, but he'd ride down with a hunting lash and take the skin off his back. And everybody would say: 'Serve him right!' There is great appreciation for your uncle Valentine in the countryside.

"One fine morning they found the old fellow, him that had the young wife, dead on the roadside with a charge of shot in his head. So knowing the liking Anselo had for the girl and knowing he had a gun, the sergeant of police comes around.

"'We want you,' said the sergeant of police.

"'What do you want with me?' said Anselo.

"The sergeant of police made a motion to put a halter around his neck, and 'k-k-k-k-k!' says he, like a man choking, and he winked, for he was a great wit. 'Just to draw your trapple,' said the sergeant of police.

"Your uncle Cosimo at this time was bad, taking a little

more than even he could hold, so that he was imagining
things to be there that were n't there at all, horses with
horns and peacocks with human faces, so your uncle Valentine persuaded him to take a trip on the sea. Myself I think
the sea bad for a drinking man, for the salt water induces
drouth, but 'twould seem otherwise. The morning your
uncle Cosimo left for a voyage to Greece they took Anselo.
And the morning he came back the jury had retired to consider his case. It was assizes at Londonderry, and a cousin
of the house was Lord Justice. Your uncle Cosimo read the
newspapers and went straight into Derry.

"When he got into the court there was the jury, glum
and white, for 'tis no easy thing to find a man guilty of
murder. And there was the Crown Prosecutor pleased as
Punch himself. And there was Anselo hanging on to the
dock rail with both hands, but saying nothing, for he was
a brave fellow. And there was your uncle Cosimo's cousin,
Lord Justice Grant, putting the black cap on his head, and
blue in the jowl, for for weeks after you sentence a man to
death there is no sleep for you, nor much taste to your food.

"'Take that thing off your head, Cousin Grant,' said your
uncle Cosimo, 'for the gypsy did n't kill the old man at all.'

"'Order! Order!' called the Clerk of the Court.

"'Aye!' said your uncle Cosimo, 'the like of you prefers
order to justice any day in the week.'

"'Well, if the gypsy did n't, who did?' asked the Lord
Justice.

"'I did,' said your uncle Cosimo.

"Instead of cheering up, the whole court looked sadder
than ever, for bad as it is to hang a man, a gypsy is only a
gypsy, but a MacFarlane of Destiny Bay is a jewel in the
nation's crown.

"'The man was crazy and came at me with a scythe,'
explained your uncle Cosimo, 'so there was nothing for me
to do but let him have it with a gun.'

" ' Oh, that 's different,' said the Lord Justice, ' but there was no scythe there.'

" ' Do you think I 'd leave a scythe in the road for people to hurt themselves on, maybe children itself ? No, I chucked it in the ditch alongside, where you 'll find it if you look.'

" ' But you never said anything about it ? ' said the Lord Justice.

" Your uncle Cosimo up and gives a cool hard look around the Court. ' It passed out of my mind,' said your uncle Cosimo. And nobody said anything, for they knew what had happened. Your uncle Cosimo had drunk that night to such an extent that he forgot.

" Well, the upshot of it was that your uncle's story was found to be true, and the gypsy was set free."

" I suppose he married the copper-haired girl, Carabine."

" He did not, Mister Kerry. What with the spilt blood and the shadow of the rope, and all the trouble, their love was killed. No, she married the sergeant of police that was such a witty fellow."

VI

" Mister Kerry, my dear son," said James Carabine, " I 've taught you a lot about life. I 've told you that a clear conscience, a kindly heart, and a punch in both hands will land you in the Kingdom of Heaven. Add this to your store of knowledge. You can put money in the Bank of England, you can buy a green field in America, but for a really good investment you can't beat a kindness done to a gypsy or a Jew. It 's got to be a real kindness out of the heart, and not studied, for that would defeat itself.

" You wouldn't call what your uncle Cosimo did a kindness, for it was but justice, and you, or your uncle Valentine, or any Irish gentleman would have done it. The Romanies are more accustomed to French or Spanish or Hungarian gentries — and a foreign gentleman would n't rise from his rubber of whist, or courting his lady, if you were to hang all the gypsies in the world, for to him the wandering people are only bloody ruffians and great rogues. Not that foreigners have n't their good points — we must n't be narrow, Mister Kerry! — but what they are I can't remember," said James Carabine.

"Well, all the gypsies of the countryside and the new arriving gypsies treated your uncle Cosimo as if he were King of Egypt. This fellow Anselo became a sort of bodyguard to him. In winter they were with him on the bogs, helping him to bring down the jacksnipe and the wild duck. In summer they were always finding out for him where the fattest, cunningest old trout lay. They would never let him be alone, for wherever he went, a young gypsy man followed on moorland or by bog or river, though the gypsy might n't be visible, for these people are like ghosts or like the hare in the grass when they want to be. They all knew, Mister Kerry, that with his tremendous gifts of brain and personality, he had this little fondness for the silver flask. And they were n't going to have a false step by the river or a slip into a boghole deprive them of their friend. Also, at nights in the public houses there would always be Anselo or some caravan-brother of his standing by to see that your uncle Cosimo got home safe.

"It's a funny thing, Mister Kerry," said James Carabine, "but if you treat a gypsy like a rogue, he will be a rogue. It's his way of getting back at you. But if you treat him like a gentleman there is n't a greater gentleman alive."

Carabine was sewing his flies now. He had needle and fine thread in one hand, and thimble on finger, and out of the tails of his long butler's coat he had fished a pair of steel-rimmed spectacles, and what with these on his nose and his black side whiskers, and the gold rings in his ears, he looked incongruous and amiable and very wise, and dignified too, I would have you know. But it was hard to see in that strange old man the great fighter who had gone fifty rounds by London Prize Ring Rules, with the Limehouse Bob Taylor for a gold belt and a purse of one hundred guineas in gold, and had smitten Diamond, the Jamaica black man, so hard between the eyes that as he lay on the ground blood gushed from his mouth and nostrils. "They are a very ancient folk, Mister Kerry, and tracing them back they come from the snowy mountains in the North of India and their tongue is like the Indian speech. But India may have been only a stopping place on their way from the heart of the world. The Romany gentleman, Mister Kerry, may have a genealogy as long and as fine as your own. And they are a wise folk, not with the wisdom of books, which is second-hand wisdom, and which is like second-hand clothes — it may be shoddy or it may n't fit or suit the buyer at all. They know these things: by the moon they know what weather will be in it, and how soon after the rising of the west wind the rain will come; the diseases and fancies of the horse, and the playing of music; they know if a man is true, and a woman is virtuous and other valuable things to know. They understand freedom. They are not prisoners of the pocket or of the market place. Oftentimes you 'll pass a caravan and see an old man smoking in front of the open-air fire, and you 'll figure he 's thinking of the hare that 's grilling before him, or the trout stretched on a stick. But the old man may be admiring God's mercy or have his mind on the jagged edges of the stars.

"The common man, Mister Kerry, will treat the Romany as a rogue, and the Romany in his wisdom and contempt will be a rogue and catch the common man in his own snare. But your uncle Cosimo was a wise man and a gentleman, and he treated Anselo Loveridge as a gentleman, and never did a man have truer, loyaller friend.

"Your uncle Cosimo's mind was like this, Mister Kerry, in respect to the drink. You've seen the sun going down and some high green hill catching the last light of it. All about the foot of the hill is darkness. And the darkness creeps up the hill, little by little, while the top gets more brilliant and brilliant, and the higher the darkness creeps, the more shining and grand is the peak. Your uncle's mind was like that. He had many discourses. He would talk for hours on the state of the country, arguing from the times of the Normans to Charles Stuart Parnell. Also he would talk about the inhabitants of England being the lost tribes of Israel, and bringing out pieces of the Bible, prophecies and the like, would set your mind working like a mill wheel in the stream. He would talk about the future of America, a most instructive discourse. As the drink rose in him, it would be like the darkness on a green hill. But the most brilliant discourse of all was on China. China was the peak of the hill, where the sun was shining. It was, Mister Kerry, as if every part of his brain were dead but that which spoke of China. That was the last part of his brain to die, when the sun went down on the lush green hill. He would talk about the immense intricacy of Chinese card games, and of the great wall of China, and of the man that builded it, Ta-Wak, a Master Mason. He would talk about Chinese religion, of something called 'The Way', and of Confucius, that was heavy with wisdom — and both religions were sensible, but intricate and very Chinese. He would talk about Chinese poets — a lad called Li Po, the chief song-maker of his time, and a heavy drinking man, and Tu Fu, an ascetic hard worker whose love poems were better than whiskey for chills, and whose philosophy was a grand cure for fever. As a matter of fact, Mister Kerry, it was an eyeopener to know, after the way the parsons do be talking of the heathen, that at the other end of the world, there was such a highly civilised bunch of men."

James Carabine threaded another needle.

"Your uncle Cosimo told Anselo Loveridge something that he had never told your uncle Valentine, nor your father, nor your aunt Jenepher, no, nor me. He told him there was a woman in China, whom he had seen about three times, and to whom he had never spoken (for for all his love of China your uncle Cosimo had not the Chinese tongue), and that his mind was with her. 'You might think, and not unnaturally, Anselo Loveridge, that my heart was in this body of death standing beside you, but my heart has transformed itself into a small melodious bird, and it abides among the almond trees in this lady's father's garden. The little bird is dumb there, Anselo Loveridge, until she comes into the garden, and then it flutters its throat with song.' And mind you, Mister Kerry, he had only seen her three times in his life and never once spoken to her! Can you understand that?"

"'There is a lady sweet and kind,'"

I quoted for James Carabine;

> "'Was never face so pleased to mind;
> I did but see her passing by,
> And yet I love her till I die.'"

"And yet," said James Carabine, "neither your uncle Valentine, nor you, nor your uncle Cosimo would touch horse or dog until you had gone over it from muzzle to rump, and had the stud-book certificate and the vet's papers, and even then you wouldn't be satisfied until you'd tried it out.

"Well, your uncle Cosimo," said James Carabine, "once he had broken the ice, would talk of nothing but the wonder and beauty of this woman. 'Twas like in a play, begod!— your uncle, the fine young naval lieutenant wandering in the Chinese garden, talking to the old Chinese merchant, drinking tea and eating ginger, all for a look at this woman.

You'd think all Irish women were vulgar mares to hear him speak, and that Venus herself was a blowsy German woman, fit only for a drinking den of sailors, compared to the delicacy and mystery and beauty of this Chinese girl. She had blue-painted eyebrows, and wore shoes of red brocade, and the song she sang was called 'Downy Grasses.'

"You know your uncle's hymns?" asked Carabine.

I did. They were cold ascetic things. "Lord, on this black Satanic strand!" composed on his entry to Borneo, and the prayer to be said on going asleep: "If in the interests of God." They are too foreign to the warmth of life and to sportsmanship to be pleasing. But James Carabine was fumbling in the tails of his coat. A red bandana handkerchief appeared, a huge clasp knife, a small form book of Irish racing, and several pieces of yellowish paper. I opened the sheets, and before my eyes appeared, straggling but undeniable, the writing of my saintly uncle, the Bishop of Borneo.

"I rescued these in his room," said James Carabine. "There were hundreds of others, but he burned them all before he went away. These he must have forgot."

"For the Fair Maid of Wu" I found written:

"I have not turned my steps to the East Country these forty separate seasons.
So that I wonder how many times the plum and peach trees have blossomed.
Two white clouds in the green sky meet and part.
Is she still there in the house that views the setting of the young moon?"

"The Moon of Lushang Mountain", another was called:

"The autumn moon is half round above the Lushang Mountain,
Its golden light falls in, and flows with the shadowy river.
To-night I leave the Yellow Crane House for the towers of Nanking,
And I glide down the Peach Tree Valley thinking of you whom I cannot see."

The third was another poem to " The Fair Girl of Wu ":

" She is the flowering branch of the almond tree,
    Heavy with honey dew.
She is the purple fish swimming daintily
    In the Peach Tree Lake.
She is the Flying Swallow, newly dressed,
    In the Rainbow Skirt and Feather Jacket dance.

" Northern water . . . Clear northern moon . . .
    In the moonlight the wild swans are trumpeting. . . .
But, hush! I can hear her gathering the water chestnuts,
    And singing the song called Falling Plum Flowers, though half a
      world away.

" I pass along the white road from the tavern.
So close are the stars I could pluck them with my hand.
I dare not speak aloud in the moonlight,
Lest I disturb the sleeping folk of Heaven.

" I enter my companionless room,
With me is only the chill friendship of the moonlight.
Without there is a little frost upon the ground.
I lift my head and look out on the mountain moon,
And know that lacking you, Fair Girl of Wu,
I am the Green Lotus Man,
Who will never attain crimson leaf, or troubling fragrance."

" Well?" said James Carabine.

" Damned if I know, Carabine," I answered. " They are cold, and there is a great lonesomeness to them, and they have no rhyme or metre."

" Rhyme and metre," I heard your uncle Cosimo say, " are vulgar and an appeal to the jingly mind of the common people."

" Now if I were writing a poem to a girl," said I, " my moonlight would be warmer, and the hay would be freshly cut, and there would be a dry and snug quality to it, and there would be courting and kissing in that poem. But my mind is not such, James Carabine, that I 'll end up a bishop."

" By damn, but you won't!" said James Carabine, with conviction.

"Well, Mister Kerry, these are only three of what were hundreds. How often have I seen your uncle Cosimo, down at the Widow McGinty's hotel, in the private bar, read them, battering a queer time with one hand, and holding a glass in the other, to Anselo Loveridge. And Anselo would sit there as if he understood every line of them, which maybe he did, for the Romany is a queer understanding man.

"'Mister Cosimo,' he asked one night, 'what name was on this woman?'

"''Tis Pin-Yong,' said your uncle. And Anselo Loveridge thought a long time, remembering it.

"'And what name was on her father?'

"'His name was Li-Chin.'

"'And what business was at her father?' asked the gypsy.

"'Oh, a various business,' said your uncle Cosimo. 'He used to export fine tea in bricks to the Russians, and he breeds and trains nightingales for lords' gardens, and he has a fine smith's business, making golden tortoises for ornaments, and ivory elephants and jade bees.'

"'At where?' says Anselo Loveridge.

"'At Peng-tse, in the province of Wu,' answered your uncle.

"'At Peng-tse, in the province of Wu,' repeated the gypsy. 'Tell me,' he said, 'Mister Cosimo, brother, if you and the pretty girl of Wu had come to be married, brother, you would not be wasting time and health?' He meant the drink.

"'Of course I wouldn't, you damned fool!' said your uncle Cosimo.

"'I thought not, brother,' said the gypsy, and that was all there was to it. But the next day, when your uncle went to look for him, Anselo Loveridge wasn't there. 'He's gone to Derry for the day,' said your uncle Cosimo. But he didn't come back for weeks. ''Tis to Waterford he's gone, to meet the horse-dealing people,' he thought. But for six years your uncle Cosimo never saw him. 'You make a friend of a man,' he grumbled, 'and he goes off without good-bye, good luck, or to hell with you!' And then he would get sad in himself, and say: 'He's a Romany and the open road a greater temptation to him than the open bottle to me. Sure he's young, and has sap in him, and why should he stay here with me that's no more than an old root in the soil with the life and pride and grace gone from it?'

"There were other gypsies looking after him now, but there was none the like of Anselo Loveridge, cunning and all as they were in finding the otter's hiding place, or the pool where the heavy trout lay. Of them he would be always asking news, but they could give him none. 'Is it Anselo Loveridge, Mister Cosimo, your Honour? Sure who would know where that wild bold lad might be?'"

VII

Anselo Loveridge took the two colts he owned, and throwing a bag over one's back and riding it and leading the other, he set off for Dublin by the light of the moon. In Dublin city he sold them, maybe for a bit more than they were worth, but that's neither here nor there. And with the money in his belt he started for England. Not that Anselo Loveridge or his kind cared for money one way or another, but to cross deep water you must have it. With a piece of rabbit wire in his pocket, and a flint and steel, he could walk to the end of the world. When he wanted a clean shirt and handkerchief, he would find a deep stream and wash them and put them on a bush to dry while he lay there motionless as a stone, tickling for trout. He had a great gift for a horse and was a good man with the cards, so that a day on a race course would set him up for a

month. Also, if he was taken short and needed a meal, he
would go up to a door and ask for it nicely. And if there
was e'er a woman in the place he would get it. He would
pay for it, even though there was no payment asked, by
gypsy trade, such as making a couple of brooms or carving
a horse or cow out of a piece of wood with a jackknife for
the little treasures of the house. Also he was not a bad
hand with the gloves and had a knack of wrestling. A fellow like that, Mister Kerry, can go through the world more
comfortable than kings.

"All through England he was with his own people, the
gypsy tribes, the Petulengros, the Lovells, the Hernes. At
the end of a day's walking, he would come to a crossroad,
and where the ordinary man would see nothing, he would
look around until he found what he wanted, a peeled willow
rod, or three twigs of an elm tree, or a bunch of heather
laid so, or a handful of ferns in the crotch of a shrub.
That's the patteran, and tells you where there's a camp.
So he would stroll up to where the caravan was, and '*Sa
shan, mi puri-dai!*' 'Good evening, granny!' he would call.
And the *jukels*, the gypsy dogs, would wag their tails for
him, and the *Romany raklis*, the gypsy girls, would shake
their ears with the gold coins in them. And he would sit
down to take the dinner of *zimen* and *kanengro*, and *levina*,
which is broth and hare and beer, and sit around the blazing
yog and smoke *tuvalo* in his *swegler*.

"And then he would ask them about China, but none of
the English Gypsies he met had been to China. They had
been to Australia and India, and they gave him good tips
about these countries. At Dover he said good luck to
them — '*Kushto bok, pals!*' — and went off to France. In
France for a while he was well off. There were country
fairs with heavy wrestling fellows there, and he made a bit
throwing them or staying the limit. At Marseilles he ran
into a hard bit of luck. He found a little girl-child wan-

dering on the road, half-starved, and being fond of children, he fed her and kept her by his camp fire that night, and to-morrow he was going to bring her to the police. But before he got to the police, the police came to him.

"'Aha,' they bristled up, 'you kidnap l'ongfong!'

"'I found l'ongfong on the route,' says Anselo Loveridge.

"'You are a *sale* Bohemian,' they screamed. 'You must go to gaol. All *sale* Bohemians go to gaol.'

"So they put him in gaol and kept him there six months, making post-bags and mending roads. And when he came out he was no longer a fine man. He was a thin skeleton of a fellow with a bad cough. And this all for showing kindness to a child. But when he got out he picked up the gypsy patteran and soon got to his people, and they nursed him and got him back to health, journeying through France to the far edge of Italy. At Trieste they let him out. 'For from here,' they said, 'we go into the Magyar country, and the land of Bohemia. If you want to come, you're welcome. If you don't, *kushto bok*, good luck!'

"'I thank you kindly,'" said Anselo Loveridge.

"There was a girl with this caravan, and a finer, wilder girl you never saw. She had eyes like black diamonds, and her hands were soft, like the tips of ferns, and she was like the red deer on foot for grace and beauty. And Anselo Loveridge liked her well. But he said nothing.

"'Since you like me,' she came up to him, 'and I like you, and since you won't speak, I'll speak. Will you marry me?'

"'I won't,' said Anselo Loveridge.

"'Why won't you?' asked the girl.

"'Because I'm on my way from the Irish country to the end of the world to do a kindness for a friend who once saved my life for me.'

"'Well, then,' she said, 'you can't. You've got to go.

But I'll tell you this, Irish gypsy, that having seen you, I'll never marry with another man. God knows where I'll be in the coming years, but the name that is on me is Telaitha Solivaino, and the patteran of our camp is a twig of elm and a twig of gorse, with a fern laid crossways.'

"'I sha'n't forget,' said Anselo Loveridge.

"'I don't think you will,' said the girl. And they exchanged their neckerchiefs, and held hands, and kissed, and 'Kushto bok, pal' and 'Kushto bok, pen,' 'Good luck, brother' and 'Good luck, sister.' And that was that. And Anselo Loveridge sat on the pier at Trieste, far from camp and country, and he felt very poor in himself.

"There was a boat there was loading for Egypt, and a foxy-haired fellow with an ash plant and a big fur coat comes along with three horses, race horses by the looks of them. The first was a grey gelding, fifteen hands high.

"'I know that horse,' says Anselo Loveridge.

"'By God, you don't,' says the foxy fellow, and the English that was at him was the English of the County of Meath.

"'I do,' says Angelo. 'He's Gambler's Fancy, by Gambler out of Fancy Woman, by Game Cock out of Rambler's Joy, by Hazard out of Minorca, by Hell's Bells out of Purity, by—'

"'Will you hold your whisht?' says the foxy fellow.

"'It won the Steward's Cup at Leopardstown, the Yeoman's Plate at Baldoyle, the Erin-go-bragh stakes at Dundalk, and the Duke of Connaught's Trophy at Limerick Junction.'

"'I'm a ruined man,' says the foxy fellow. 'For if you know him,' he says, 'there's hundreds at Cairo will know him, Irish officers and soldiers, and the black men will weight him to the ground. And I thought I'd clean up,' he said, 'as I've been doing in France, and Austria. Where are you off to?' says the foxy man.

"'I'm off to China,' he said, 'to do an errand for an Irish friend.'

"'I've often heard tell,' said the foxy one, 'that a gypsy could make a horse look like a hippopotamus. Can you put strangeness on him?'

"'I can alter his looks,' said Anselo Loveridge, 'so that his own dam wouldn't know him.'

"'Come with me to Egypt and stop over a bit, and help me with the racing. Sure, China's so far away, a month or so won't matter.'

"'I'll do that thing,' said Anselo Loveridge.

"So he went to Egypt and became known and respected as a trainer of horses. The Khedive of Egypt sent for him and asked him to stay and train his, but Anselo had money in his pocket again, so he thanked the Khedive for the compliment, but said he had a job of work to do in China, and off he sails to India and lands at Bombay.

"'Am I near China?' he asks.

"'You're next door,' they tell him. 'You're only about five thousand miles off.'

"Anselo Loveridge only laughs, for he could take a joke as well as the next one. So he figures it's up to him to sit down and make a good deal of money so as to get to China quick. He takes a job with a wealthy woman who bred polo ponies. After a while this woman comes to him and says: 'Will you marry me?'

"This woman was a big hard woman, and she was no better than she ought to be. This woman had married an Indian rajah, but as an Indian rajah has dozens of wives, it was no distinction. But he left her money in his will, and she was by way of being a great woman and rich. This woman was a bad woman. She would take men and throw them over. But she took so great a fancy to Anselo Loveridge that she was for marrying him.

"'I can't. ma'am.' said he.

"'And why not?' says she.

"'There's a girl in the gypsy trail,' said Anselo, 'and her I'll marry, or none.'

"'You'll forget her in a month,' says the blondy woman, 'with me.'

"'I'll not forget her till I die,' said Anselo. 'And there's another matter. I've got to go to China. My honour's in it.'

"'Honour!' laughs she. 'It's not worth that,' and she snaps her fingers. 'If I'd thought about honour, I wouldn't be Begum of this province, with more money than I could count. I'd have been polishing dishes in a pantry.'

"'It might have been better for you, ma'am,' says Anselo Loveridge.

"Instead of getting mad, she just wants him the more for saying that, for it shows her he's a proper man.

"'Well,' she says, 'marry me now, or marry me later. You'll never see China. You can't leave this place without my permission.'

"Anselo Loveridge knew that was right, but said nothing. He set himself to making money, and he soon had a score of ponies of his own would delight your eye. He thought of the riots of buyers at Bombay when he would lead them in. But the blondy woman comes to him.

"'Loveridge,' she says, 'you marry me to-morrow.'

"'And if I don't?' says he.

"'Were you ever in gaol?'

"'Twice,' says he; 'once in Ireland, and once in France.'

"'Did you like it?'

"'I did not,' said he. For in both places he sickened for the open road and the wind.

"'You'll like it less here,' said she.

"'And why should I go to gaol, ma'am?' he asks respectfully.

"'Oh, any excuse'll do,' says the blondy woman. 'The head of police is a friend of mine, and has a great hatred of gypsies, on account of a gypsy once cheating him over a horse. Take your pick,' she laughs.

"'I'll have the marriage,' says Anselo.

"He figured he'd cut his stick that night, and leave the ponies, but the woman kept a watch on him so he couldn't get away. In the morning she comes to him. 'The carriage is ready,' she says.

"'You take the carriage,' he says, 'I'll ride.'

"'Do,' says she, 'for if there's one thing I like, it's a fine man on a fine horse.'

"So he rode by her side in state with the church bells ringing. And suddenly he fetches the horse a belt with the whip, and jams the spurs into its ribs.

"'Hold him,' orders the blondy woman. And the bullets came humming at him, but he took no hurt, barring one that cut a ridge in his hair. And that ridge," said James Carabine, "if you ever meet him, you'll see to this day.

"Anselo Loveridge never stopped until he came to the quay at Bombay. There was a boat pulling out, and on the back platform of it is the captain in blue and gold.

"'Where are you off to?' asks the gypsy.

"'T' Australia,' says the captain.

"'Is it on the road to China?'

"''Tis,' says the captain.

"'Back the boat to the ditch, Captain,' says Anselo, 'till I come with you.'

"'Is it murder you're running from?' says the captain, hard.

"''Tis worse,' said Anselo; ''tis a woman is set on marrying me.'

"The captain gives a laugh and says: 'Throw a rope over, and give a leap, you,' he tells Loveridge, 'and we'll have you aboard.' This captain was a decent fellow, not like another captain I'll tell you of, and when he heard the story Anselo had at him he wouldn't take a penny passage money from him, but was good friends with him, and landed him at the Australian goldfields.

"'I'm sorry I'm not able to give a lift any further,' said the captain, 'but good-bye and good luck.'

"Anselo Loveridge didn't go for the mining, for the gypsies are not a digging or a sea-going people, but he went in for fighting in the goldfields. He was never a first-class man with his hands, but he was willing and would take any punishment, so that fight after fight came his way. The gold miners were easy with their money in the matter of purses, so that he was well heeled after six months of it. The fighting was prize-ring rules, bare knuckles and close and throw, and a minute's rest between rounds. He lost only two fights, one to Joe Tate, the Sydney Cornstalker, and the other to Williams, a black man, but in six months he took bad punishment, so that his nose was broken in two places, and his left ear crumpled the like of a dwarf potato, and there was the least droop to his left eyelid from six stitches that had to be taken in lid and brow, where the black man hit him the terrible knock-out blow. The miners were very sorry to see him go. Wherever Anselo Loveridge had stayed a little, the folk were sorry to see him go.

"He found a boat going to Macao, which is Portuguese China, and the boat was a Portuguee boat with a Portuguee captain and a Portuguee crew. They weren't far out to sea when the Portuguee captain came to Anselo.

"'Have you any money?' says he.

"'I have,' says Anselo, for he had all the prizefighting money with him.

"'Do you play cards?' says the Portuguee captain.

"'I do,' says Anselo.

" ' Then we'll play cards,' said the Portuguee captain.

" They weren't long playing cards until Anselo Loveridge found the Portuguee captain was cheating right, left, and centre. Now the way of Anselo Loveridge was this, if you played cards straight with him, he'd play straight with you, but if he caught you cheating, he'd say nothing, but the devil himself would be ashamed of the way Anselo Loveridge would cheat back. So that when they came into Macao, Anselo had won all the Portuguee captain's money, which he said he didn't have on him but kept in the bank, and the captain's ship, and the captain's uniform, and the captain's home and farm outside of Lisbon, Portugal.

" ' Wait here on board the ship,' said the captain, ' till I send to the bank for the money, and to the town for a lawyer to draw up the transfer of the ship and farm, and for a tailor will make me new clothes on tick.'

" ' Oh, you can keep the clothes,' said Anselo.

" But instead of a lawyer and a bank messenger there came aboard nine policemen and an officer that the captain had sent for. ' Take him and gaol him,' says the captain, ' for an inveterate rogue and a common gambler. He has three hundred English sovereigns of mine in a belt about his middle.' It took the nine policemen with fixed bayonets and the officer with a drawn sword to protect the captain ; but that only made the case look blacker against Anselo, so that they gave him nine months in the black hole, and took the money he had earned in desperate battles and handed it over with their compliments to the Portuguee captain.

" When the nine months were up they kicked out the wreck that Anselo Loveridge was. ' And if we ever find you again in Macao,' says they, ' we'll crucify you.'

" ' If you ever find me again near anything Portuguee,' says Anselo Loveridge, ' you'll be welcome to, for I'll deserve it.'

"So he sets out on foot through China with one copper coin in his pocket, looking for the province of Wu. Now a gypsy can support life anywhere but in China, for the people there are starving themselves, forbye hard on foreigners, and he could not get near any of the great lords to trade his knowledge of horses for money, because of the soldiers. There was nothing to eat, for even the rats were eaten by the starving Chinese people, and there was no place to rest, and he was weak, and after nine months of darkness his eyes were blinded by the sun. And then one day, when all strength and courage was gone, he stood in the high road when the sun was setting and he spread out his arms.

"'God,' he cried, 'that gives the small fowl of the air wings to carry them from Arctic cold to summer weather, and that after making the immense smithy of the sun remembered to give the field mouse its dun colour, and that after composing your masterpiece the swift horse, did not forget that the lowly porcupine needed protection, let me not perish among this silent, devilish people, for the sake of Caspar Magus, the Gypsy King, who came with offerings to the Little Lord, when He, too, like the gypsy folk, had no fixed habitation, but lay in a manger in Bethlehem.'

"And he lets his hands fall by his sides, and bows his head, and waits until there comes to him the message: I hear.

"And then he takes the copper coin from his pocket, and he says: 'I'll toss it in the air, and if it comes down heads I'll go east, and if it comes down tails I'll go west. Whichever way I go I'll find help, for God is good.' And he pitches it high in the air and waits for it to fall, and when he goes forward he finds it beside two twigs of a plum tree, making an angle, and that he knew for the gypsy trail, and he follows it until he comes into the heart of a wood, and he was all trembling, for God had spoken to him. And there was a caravan there.   A dark, pleasant-looking woman was carrying water from a well, and she gazed hard at him.

"'*Romanitshel?*' she asks.   'Are you a gypsy?'

"'*Ava, pen.*   Yes, sister,' says Anselo Loveridge.

"'Where are you from?'

"'From Ireland,' says Anselo.

"'I never heard of it,' says the woman, 'but it may be a good place for all that.   Where are you for?'

"'For the Province of Wu,' answers Anselo.

"'We're going there ourselves,' says the gypsy woman. And she comes closer to him, and she sees the weakness and bad way of him, and she notices the ulcers on his wrists where the irons of Macao gaol had worn into him. '*Dabla!*' she calls.   'My God!   This gypsy boy is ill and without luck.'   And they all came running up to him, and put him on a bed of bracken beside the fire, and fed him, and the mothers of the tribe get out herbs for his sores, and suddenly Anselo Loveridge, the strong man, the horse-breaker, and prizefighter, puts up his hands to his face and cries like a child.

"'It's all right, brother,' they say.   'It's all over now. You're with brothers and sisters.   We'll take care of you, and bring you to Wu.'

"Through all the voyage to Wu, Anselo Loveridge learned hard these Chinese phrases: 'Are you the Lady Pin-Yong?' and 'Are you the daughter of Li-Chin, the great nightingale-fancier and maker of gold ornaments?' The other Romanies laughed at him, thinking it was some kind of riddle, and with the laughter and the fresh air and sunshine he came back to himself.   He looked different to the way he was in Ireland, what with the parting in his hair that the Bombay bullet had made, and the broken nose and crumpled ear, and the scars on his wrists.   But he was always thinking of the little girl he had left at Trieste and the patteran of her tribe, a twig of elm with a twig of gorse and a fern laid crossways, and that thinking brought a friendly light in his face, like the light of the moon.

"At Peng-tse he told the caravan he'd leave them for a while. 'You'll be going down the river, brothers, and I'll follow you.' 'Very good, brother,' they said. And with a gay diklo, and a whip for horses and dogs, he left them, and found the house of the Chinese merchant. He didn't go into the house, but hung around as an army scout would, and at last the Lady Pin-Yong came into the garden.

"She was just the same as Mister Cosimo said she'd be, with glossy hair, and blue-painted eyebrows, and shoes of red brocade. She was not of the number of Chinese small-footed women, but proud and free in her bearing, and she was always tending the plants and flowers in the garden by the river. But where Anselo Loveridge expected a slip of a girl, soft as a newly hatched blackbird, here was a woman with disappointment and iron in her eyes, and though she was not old, she was not a young woman. And Anselo Loveridge said to himself: 'I wonder now if Mister Cosimo could have had a drop taken and he looking at her, for she's like the bare edge of a knife, that woman!' And he thinks: 'Ah, well, the way of the *gawjo rai*, the gentile noble, is not the way of the Romany. And maybe a harsh woman will keep Mister Cosimo straight. However, he wants her and he'll have her.'

"He began casting about how he'd get off with her, and he found there was a rich Chinese poetic man lived a bit down the river. He had a fine horse and a fine boat, but the night Anselo tried for the boat he found it bound with locks and chains. The way of the poetic man was this: In the morning he'd ride abroad on the horse, in the afternoon he'd sit and drink and write poetry, and at night if there was a moon in it, he'd have himself rowed on the river, mad with verses and wine and moonlight. The horse was a white ten-year-old with a good trot and a nice canter. Anselo Loveridge makes a few purchases in the town with the money the chief of the caravan had lent him, and one night he whistles the horse out of the field.

"There was hell to do in the Chinese town over the loss of the poet's horse, but it was never seen or traced, at that time. A few days later Anselo Loveridge came in from the country, with a black docked hack, that had a white star on its forehead, and one white stocking, and he finds him an interpreting man, and he goes to the Chinese poet's.

"'I hear you want a horse,' he says.

"'I want a horse bad,' says the Chinese poet, 'for what with the great fatness of me, 'tis hard for me to go abroad on my feet. But it is n't every horse 'd suit me,' says the Chinese poet.

"'This one will,' said Anselo Loveridge. 'You 'll never notice the difference between it and the other horse.'

"''Tis a better horse than the other one,' said the Chinese, 'but I think it 'll suit. How much do you want for it?'

"'I 'll swap it,' says Anselo Loveridge, 'for your boat.'

"'That would be robbery,' says the poet, 'for the boat is n't worth as much as the old horse, much less this grand animal.' The Chinese are an honest people.

"'I 'll have the boat or nothing,' says Anselo Loveridge. 'I look at it this way. Poets should get things easier than any one else, on account of their great simplicity. The cunning of the merchants would overtop the world, if it were n't for the simplicity of the poets like yourself.' And Anselo Loveridge never even smiles.

"'If you put it that way,' says the Chinese fellow. 'Will you have a drop of refreshment?'

"'Thank you all the same,' says Angelo Loveridge, 'but I 'm a teetotaler.'

"So he takes the boat and rows upstream and waits about till it's dark and then he goes into the garden of the merchant's house. And after a while the girl of Wu that Mister Cosimo was mad about comes out.

"'Are you the Lady Pin-Yong?' says Anselo Loveridge in his best Chinese.

"'I am,' she said, and she looks at him. He has a bag under his arm.

"'Are you the daughter of the rich merchant, Li-Chin, the great nightingale fancier.'

"'I am,' said she. And then she understands that there is kidnapping in the air, and she opens her mouth to screech. But Anselo Loveridge has her gagged with his handkerchief before she can let the yell out of her, and tips her into the bag with a kick on the ankle, neat as be-damned. He ties her up and puts her in the boat. 'Now for Ireland,' says Anselo Loveridge.

"When he comes near the gypsy camp, he makes a mooring, and takes the bagful of woman ashore, and then he overturns the boat and sets it adrift, so that people may think they were drowned, the pair of them. The gypsies crowd around asking if it is a fat pig he has in the bag, but when he opens it they become afraid.

"'Oh, brother, brother,' they wail, 'you have brought disgrace and danger on us, all for the sake of a *gawjo* woman, and we thought you were a true Romany.'

"'There is a man in Ireland, and he saved me from the hangman's noose'—and he tells them about your uncle Cosimo and the great love that was in him for this woman. 'And could I do anything else, brothers?'

"'No, brother,' they tell him.

"So he sets on his way home across land, for it would have been very dangerous to go on sea with the Chinese woman. She would lay information against him, and this time it wouldn't be gaol, but the naked Chinese executioner with his vast sword. He lets her out all the time, except when they are near towns, when he gags and binds her. 'You'll have to be that way, my lady,' he says, 'until we get somewhere where none speak the Chinese tongue.' And she looks hatred at him. But after a while she sees he means no harm to her, and she sees a kindness in his face. She becomes reconciled, for now she is dizzy with wandering, but she never becomes what you might call affable.

"And all this time there is great luck with Anselo in the trading of horses, so there is always money at him. When they come to Rangoon, he takes ship to England. All the time on his travels, whether there is money at him or not at him, he manages to take the height of care of the Chinese woman. And every time Anselo meets the gypsy caravan, he asks if ever on their wanderings they have seen a patteran of a twig of elm and a twig of gorse with a fern laid crossways. But none has ever seen it until he comes across a caravan at Naples in Italy, where the boat stops, and he sees the gypsy fires, and goes on shore to speak to the gypsy people.

"'That will be the patteran of the Solivainos. I've seen it, but I'll never see it any more.'

"'And why not?' says Anselo Loveridge.

"'Because the Solivainos were crossing on a ferry on the Kattegat, and a big wind came, and the boat turned turtle, and the Romany people went deep in the water, and the life went from out of them.'

"'Did it go from out of the girl Talaitha?' asked Anselo.

"'It went from out of her the first, brother.'

"He said nothing, but stood there, looking lost, so that the man who told him said, '*wafro dok, pal,*' 'bad luck, brother.' And all the gypsies whispered, '*wafro dok, pal,*' 'bad luck, brother.' Anselo Loveridge nodded and went off by himself, and where he was and what he thought that night is past knowing. But the grey hours of the morning he took the neckerchief the gypsy girl had given him, and after the manner of gypsy people he burned it. For the gypsies burn what belongs to the dead, for fear that keepsakes will hinder the dead folk and chain them to the world, out of pity for the sorrow of those behind. They are a deep, knowledgeable people, the Romanies. And from that day on Anselo Loveridge was a changed man. He was a kindly, gentle, well-mannered, quiet man. A woman would say: 'There is great friendship in that man, but there is no love in him.'

"All this," said James Carabine, "I got from Anselo Loveridge's sister Morjiana, when I saw her at Liverpool, the year that Empress, the five-year-old mare won the Grand National. . . . The rest of the story I can tell you with my own knowledge.

"I came down to the stables one May afternoon, and standing in the stableyard with a key in his hand was the gypsy lad. 'Is it yourself is in it, Anselo Loveridge?' I asked. 'It is, Mister Carabine,' he said. 'I misdoubted you a minute,' I said, 'for your hair is grey.' 'There's more nor my hair grey,' says Anselo Loveridge, and he touches his chest. 'What's in here is grey, Mister Carabine. Once it was green and springy like a live turf, and then it was warm and comforting like a peat on the fire, and now it's grey and cold and ash, like a burnt peat. This is the key of the little stable,' he says. 'Will you give it to Mister Cosimo? There's something there I've brought him.'

"'Won't you stay and see him yourself?' I asks.

"'Ah, I won't,' Anselo answered me. 'There'd be questions and he'd be pressing me to stay. And just now I'm not for facing people. I've had a loss,' he said, 'and the moving foot is best for the heavy mind. You understand, Mister Carabine.'

"'I think I do,' I said.

"'Tell Mister Cosimo I'm always thinking of him, and

tell him I hope he 'll have great happiness, and tell him it was no trouble at all.' And he went down the road and we never saw Anselo Loveridge any more.

"Your uncle Cosimo came out of the house, with his fishing rod under his arm, and his right-hand pocket bulging with the big flask, and though it was n't late in the day, he was, well, he was happy. You could see it in his eyes.

"'Anselo Loveridge has been here, Mister Cosimo, and he 's left something in the little stable for you,' and I gave him the key.

"'Where is he?' asks your uncle Cosimo.

"'There was a weight on him, Mister Cosimo, and he 's walking it off in the four corners of the world. 'Tis how it is with the badly hurt ones that they can't bear to talk. So he would n't stay.'

"'I 'm sorry for that,' says your uncle Cosimo. 'There 's no one I rate higher than Anselo Loveridge.' He goes over to the stable door and he 's not quite steady on his feet.

"''Tis a horse,' he says; ''tis a horse in the stable.'

"'What else would be in it?' says I.

"'Or a foal he 's brought me, a yearling foal.'

"'Aye, maybe a foal!'

"Then your uncle Cosimo opens the door.

"We see the woman inside it with the coat and Chinese trousers, and her face is white and there 's terror in it.

"'My God in Heaven!' says your Uncle Cosimo.

"And his eyes clear of the drink all at once, and his face grows whiter than the Chinese woman's, and from brow to chin it 's shining with sweat. 'My God in Heaven!' he says again. And he closes and locks the door.

"'Give that key to Sir Valentine when he comes back this afternoon,' he tells me, and his voice is changed. 'I 'll leave a letter for him.' And he walks into the house. I stand there destroyed with astonishment, and in a little while your uncle Cosimo comes out. He has changed his suit and has an ash plant in his hand and a deerstalker hat on his head. There is no stagger in the feet of him or flask in his pocket. And he walks past me without a word, and he walks down the drive and he walks down the road, and we never see sign or light of him again.

"When your uncle Valentine came home, he read the letter and I gave him the key, and he did all he could, but that wasn't much, God knows. So he put her in the cottage and provided for her, and there she dwelt, a lone, bitter woman. Soon afterwards we hear your uncle Cosimo is working in the slums of London, reclaiming the drunken, tragic people; and then, after that, he's a clerk in holy orders, and soon he's preaching before the Queen; and then there's the devil's own row with his Archbishop, so they send him off to Borneo."

James Carabine removed his spectacles and put them back in the case; took off his thimble, pushed the needle in the red bandana handkerchief, and stowed all in his capacious tail pocket.

"So that's how your uncle became Bishop of Borneo, Mister Kerry," said James Carabine, "and the Chinese woman came to Destiny Bay."

VIII

I could now understand the cold contempt of my uncle Valentine for my saintly other uncle, the Bishop of Borneo. His Episcopal crozier and throne — bah! His slow martyrdom — bah! Anselo Loveridge I knew, as we country and mountain people know, was all right — was all right in this world or the next. He would grow in strength and kindliness, that Romany. And he was not one to suffer sympathy. But the picture of the lone little foreign woman will never leave me. She could never have understood.

And month after month and year after year she had gone through exile and imprisonment, far from friends and home and garden.

"Weep not for the dead, neither bemoan him," writes Jeremiah, "but weep sore for him that goeth away, for he shall return no more, nor see his native country." And so to the Chinese their formal gardens, their ridiculous houses, their soft plum and pear blossoms are as dear as are to us of Destiny Bay the sweet bogland of snipe and bittern, the purple mountains and the peacock sea, which are around us and are deep in our hearts.

"Why didn't you find out about her? Why didn't you send her back? Why didn't you do something?"

My uncle Valentine had returned from his lodge meeting and had come into the gunroom. There he stood, the six feet four of him, the immense red beard of him! Out of that brown lined majestic face wisdom should speak with the tongue of men and angels.

"And how could we?" answered my uncle Valentine with his vast simplicity. "And how the hell could we? And not a word of her language at us!"

SIX

TALE OF GOLFER GILLIGAN

SIX

Tale of the Golfer Gilligan

"There comes that damned nuisance!" said my uncle Valentine.

We were sitting in the gun-room in the morning, going over a list of things to be ordered from Dublin, when up the little path to it came a small wizened figure whose right hand was bound up in bandages. Duncan and an under gardener were protesting at the intrusion. The small figure was Golfer Gilligan, a professional player who was acknowledged fifteen years before to be a genius, but whom liquor had ruined. Twice he had been in a lunatic asylum, and now he played no more in tournaments, for he could find no partners in medal play, so unsure were they whether he would turn up dead drunk or not turn up at all. Gilligan and some friends had laid out a golf course in the dunes of Destiny, whither outside professionals were lured to play him for vast stakes. His hitting powers were marvellous and his putting uncanny. He was one of the thousand tragedies buried in Irish villages.

"What the blazes do you want?" roared my uncle Valentine.

"Och! Sir Valentine and Mister Kerry, there are dirty men in this country."

"No dirtier than in any other," said my uncle Valentine.

"In God's wide world," said Gilligan, "there are no dirtier men than in this country."

"What's wrong with you then? And what's wrong with your hand?"

"You know the Spoiled Doctor?" Gilligan gulped.

We did — a rogue struck off the medical register for malpractice, who lived in the surrounding villages by gambling, smuggling, and by worse.

"The Spoiled Doctor got up a match for me against Bartley Hughes for a hundred guineas a side over Destiny. He thought he had easy money and was backing Hughes. The landlord of the Williamite Arms put up my money. I beat him easy yesterday. I went around that wild country in fours. The Spoiled Doctor was furious.

"We had a drop of drink after the match, one drop after another. The Spoiled Doctor said nothing. Only when I said: 'I'll better fours over that yet,' did he speak. 'You never will,' said he.

"And I never will, for when I was dead with liquor he cut off my right hand."

"You're dreaming, Gilligan; you've got the horrors. You cut your hand. That's all."

"No, he cut off my right hand."

"Let's see it," said my uncle Valentine, and he nodded to the bandages.

Gilligan put his left hand in his left pocket. "There it is!" he said, and he flung the severed right hand on the papers before us.

SEVEN

TALE OF THE GYPSY HORSE

SEVEN

Tale of the Gypsy Horse

I

I thought first of the old lady's face, in the candlelight of the dinner table at Destiny Bay, as some fine precious coin, a spade guinea perhaps, well and truly minted. How old she was I could not venture to guess, but I knew well that when she was young men's heads must have turned as she passed. Age had boldened the features much, the proud nose and definite chin. Her hair was grey, vitally grey, like a grey wave curling in to crash on the sands of Destiny. And I knew that in another woman that hair would be white as scutched flax. When she spoke, the thought of the spade guinea came to me again, so rich and golden was her voice.

"Lady Clontarf," said my uncle Valentine, "this is Kerry, Hector's boy."

"May I call you Kerry? I am so old a woman and you are so much a boy. Also I knew your father. He was of that great line of soldiers who read their Bibles in their tents, and go into battle with a prayer in their hearts. I always seem to have known," she said, "that he would fondle no grey beard."

"Madame," I said, "what should I be but Kerry to my father's friends!"

It seemed to me that I must know her because of her proud high face, and her eyes of a great lady, but the title of Clontarf made little impress on my brain. Our Irish titles have become so hawked and shopworn that the most hallowed names in Ireland may be borne by a porter brewer or former soap boiler. O'Conor Don and MacCarthy More mean so much more to us than the Duke of This or the Marquis of There, now the politics have so muddled chivalry. We may resent the presentation of this title or that to a foreigner, but what can you do? The loyalty of the Northern Irishman to the Crown is a loyalty of head and not of heart. Out of our Northern country came the United Men, if you remember. But for whom should our hearts beat faster? The Stuarts were never fond of us, and the Prince of Orange came over to us, talked a deal about liberty, was with us at a few battles, and went off to grow asparagus in England. It is so long since O'Neill and O'Donnell sailed for Spain!

Who Lady Clontarf was I did not know. My uncle Valentine is so offhand in his presentations. Were you to come on him closeted with a heavenly visitant he would just say: "Kerry, the Angel Gabriel." Though as to what his Angelicness was doing with my uncle Valentine, you would be left to surmise. My uncle Valentine will tell you just as much as he feels you ought to know and no more — a quality that stood my uncle in good stead in the days when he raced and bred horses for racing. I did know one thing: Lady Clontarf was not Irish. There is a feeling of kindness between all us Irish that we recognise without speaking. One felt courtesy, gravity, dignity in her, but not that quality that makes your troubles another Irish person's troubles, if only for the instant. Nor was she English. One felt her spiritual roots went too deep for that. Nor had she that brilliant armour of the Latin. Her speech was the ordinary speech of a gentlewoman, unaccented. Yet that remark about knowing my father would never fondle a grey beard!

Who she was and all about her I knew I would find out later from my dear aunt Jenepher. But about the old drawing-room of Destiny there was a strange air of formality. My uncle Valentine is most courteous, but to-night he was courtly. He was like some Hungarian or Russian noble welcoming an empress. There was an air of deference about my dear aunt Jenepher that informed me that Lady Clontarf was very great indeed. Whom my aunt Jenepher likes is lovable, and whom she respects is clean and great. But the most extraordinary part of the setting was our butler James Carabine. He looked as if royalty were present, and I began to say to myself: "By damn, but royalty is! Lady Clontarf is only a racing name. I know that there's a queen or princess in Germany who's held by the Jacobites to be Queen of England. Can it be herself that's in it? It sounds impossible, but sure there's nothing impossible where my uncle Valentine's concerned."

II

At dinner the talk turned on racing, and my uncle Valentine inveighed bitterly against the new innovations on the track; the starting gate, and the new seat introduced by certain American jockeys, the crouch now recognised as orthodox in flat-racing. As to the value of the starting gate my uncle was open to conviction. He recognised how unfairly the apprentice was treated by the crack jockey with the old method of the flag, but he dilated on his favourite theme: that machinery was the curse of man. All these innovations —

"But it isn't an innovation, sir. The Romans used it."

"You're a liar!" said my uncle Valentine.

My uncle Valentine, or any other Irishman for the matter of that, only means that he doesn't believe you. There is a wide difference.

"I think I'm right, sir. The Romans used it for their chariot races. They dropped the barrier instead of raising it." A tag of my classics came back to me, as tags will. "*Repagula submittuntur*, Pausanias writes."

"Pausanias, begob!" My uncle Valentine was visibly impressed.

But as to the new seat he was adamant. I told him competent judges had placed it about seven pounds' advantage to the horse.

"There is only one place on a horse's back for a saddle," said my uncle Valentine. "The shorter your leathers, Kerry, the less you know about your mount. You are only aware whether or not he is winning. With the ordinary seat, you know whether he is lazy, and can make proper use of your spur. You can stick to his head and help him."

"Races are won with that seat, sir."

"Be damned to that!" said my uncle Valentine. "If the horse is good enough, he'll win with the rider facing his tail."

"But we are boring you, Madame," I said, "with our country talk of horses."

"There are three things that are never boring to see: a swift swimmer swimming, a young girl dancing, and a young horse running. And three things that are never tiring to speak of: God, and love, and the racing of horses."

"A *kushto jukel* is also *rinkeno, mi pen*," suddenly spoke our butler, James Carabine.

"*Dabla*, James Carabine, you *roker* like a *didakai*. A *jukel* to catch *kanangre!*" And Lady Clontarf laughed. "What in all the *tem* is as *dinkeno* as a *kushti-dikin grai?*"

"A *tatsheno jukel, mi pen*, like Rory Bosville's," James Carabine evidently stood his ground, "that *noshered* the Waterloo Cup through *wafro bok!*"

"*Avali!* You are right, James Carabine." And then she must have seen my astonished face, for she laughed, that small golden laughter that was like the ringing of an acolyte's bell. "Are you surprised to hear me speak the *tawlo tshib*, the black language, Kerry? I am a gypsy woman."

"Lady Clontarf, Mister Kerry," said James Carabine, "is saying there is nothing in the world like a fine horse. I told her a fine greyhound is a good thing too. Like Rory Bosville's, that should have won the Waterloo Cup in Princess Dagmar's year."

"Lady Clontarf wants to talk to you about a horse, Kerry," said my uncle Valentine. "So if you would like us to go into the gunroom, Jenepher, instead of the withdrawing room while you play —"

"May I not hear about the horse too?" asked my aunt Jenepher.

"My very, very dear," said the gypsy lady to my blind aunt Jenepher, "I would wish you to, for where you are sitting, there a blessing will be."

III

My uncle Valentine had given up race horses for as long as I can remember. Except with Limerick Pride, he had never had any luck, and so he had quitted racing as an owner, and gone in for harness ponies, of which, it is admitted, he bred and showed the finest of their class. My own two chasers, while winning many good Irish races, were not quite up to Aintree form, but in the last year I happened to buy, for a couple of hundred guineas, a handicap horse that had failed signally as a three-year-old in classic races, and of which a fashionable stable wanted to get rid. It was Ducks and Drakes, by Drake's Drum out of Little Duck, a beautifully shaped, dark grey horse, rather short in the neck, but the English stable was convinced he was a hack. However, as often happens, with a change of trainers and jockeys, Ducks and Drakes became a different horse and won five good races, giving me so much in hand that I was able to purchase for a matter of nine hundred guineas a colt I was optimistic about, a son of Saint Simon's.

Both horses were in training with Robinson at the Curragh. And now it occurred to me that the gypsy lady wanted to buy one or the other of them. I decided beforehand that it would be across my dead body.

"Would you be surprised," asked my uncle Valentine, "to hear that Lady Clontarf has a horse she expects to win the Derby with?"

"I should be delighted, sir, if she did," I answered warily. There were a hundred people who had hopes of their nominations in the greatest of races.

"Kerry," the gypsy lady said quietly, "I think I will win." She had a way of clearing the air with her voice, with her eyes. What was a vague hope now became an issue.

"What is the horse, Madame?"

"It is as yet unnamed, and has never run as a two-year-old. It is a son of Irlandais, who has sired many winners on the Continent, and who broke down sixteen years ago in preparation for the Derby and was sold to one of the Festetics. Its dam is Iseult III, who won the Prix de Diane four years ago."

"I know so little about Continental horses," I explained.

"The strain is great-hearted, and with the dam, strong as an oak tree. I am a gypsy woman, and I know a horse, and I am an old, studious woman," she said, and she looked at her beautiful, unringed golden hands, as if she were embarrassed, speaking of something we, not Romanies, could hardly understand, "and I think I know propitious hours and days."

"Where is he now, Madame?"

"He is at Dax, in the Basse-Pyrénées, with Romany folk."

"Here's the whole thing in a nutshell, Kerry: Lady Clontarf wants her colt trained in Ireland. Do you think the old stables of your grandfather are still good?"

"The best in Ireland, sir, but sure there't no horse been trained there for forty years, barring jumpers."

"Are the gallops good?"

"Sure, you know yourself, sir, how good they are. But you couldn't train without a trainer, and stable boys —"

"We'll come to that," said my uncle Valentine. "Tell me, what odds will you get against an unknown, untried horse in the winter books?"

I thought for an instant. It had been an exceptionally good year for two-year-olds, the big English breeders' stakes having been bitterly contested. Lord Shere had a good horse; Mr. Paris a dangerous colt. I should say there were fifteen good colts, if they wintered well, two with outstanding chances.

"I should say you could really write your own ticket. The ring will be only too glad to get money. There's so much up on Sir James and Toison d'Or."

"To win a quarter-million pounds?" asked my uncle Valentine.

"It would have to be done very carefully, sir, here and there, in ponies and fifties and hundreds, but I think between four and five thousand pounds would do it."

"Now if this horse of Lady Clontarf's wins the Two Thousand and the Derby, and the Saint Leger —"

Something in my face must have shown a lively distaste for the company of lunatics, for James Carabine spoke quietly from the door by which he was standing.

"Will your young Honour be easy, and listen to your uncle and my lady."

My uncle Valentine is most grandiose, and though he has lived in epic times, a giant among giants, his schemes are too big for practical business days. And I was beginning to think that the gypsy lady, for all her beauty and dignity, was but an old woman crazed by gambling and tarot cards, but James Carabine is so wise, so beautifully sane, facing all events, spiritual and material, foursquare to the wind.

"— 'what would he command in stud fees?' continued quietly my uncle Valentine.

"If he did this tremendous triple thing, sir, five hundred guineas would not be exorbitant."

"I am not asking you out of idle curiosity, Kerry, or for information," said my uncle Valentine. "I merely wish to know if the ordinary brain arrives at these conclusions of mine; if they are, to use a word of Mr. Thackeray's, apparent."

"I quite understand, sir," I said politely.

"And now," said my uncle Valentine, "whom would you suggest to come to Destiny Bay as trainer?"

"None of the big trainers will leave their stables to come here, sir. And the small ones I don't know sufficiently. If Sir Arthur Pollexfen were still training, and not so old—"

"Sir Arthur Pollexfen is not old," said my uncle Valentine. "He cannot be more than seventy-two or seventy-three."

"But at that age you cannot expect a man to turn out at five in the morning and oversee gallops."

"How little you know Mayo men," said my uncle Valentine. "And Sir Arthur with all his triumphs never won a Derby. He will come."

"Even at that, sir, how are you going to get a crack jockey? Most big owners have first or second call on them. And the great free lances, you cannot engage one of those and ensure secrecy."

"That," said my uncle Valentine, "is already arranged. Lady Clontarf has a Gitano, or Spanish gypsy in whom her confidence is boundless. And now," said my uncle Valentine, "we come to the really diplomatic part of the proceeding. Trial horses are needed, so that I am commissioned to approach you with delicacy and ask you if you will bring up your two excellent horses Ducks and Drakes and the Saint Simon colt and help train Lady Clontarf's horse. I don't see why you should object."

To bring up the two darlings of my heart, and put them under the care of a trainer who had won the Gold Cup at Ascot fifty years before, and hadn't run a horse for twelve years, and have them ridden by this Gitano or Spanish gypsy, as my uncle called him; to have them used as trial horses to this colt which might not be good enough for a starter's hack. Ah, no! Not damned likely. I hardened my heart against the pleading gaze of James Carabine.

"Will you or won't you?" roared my uncle diplomatically.

My aunt Jenepher laid down the lace she was making, and reaching across, her fingers caught my sleeve and ran down to my hand, and her hand caught mine.

"Kerry will," she said.

So that was decided.

IV

"Kerry," said my uncle Valentine, "will you see Lady Clontarf home?"

I was rather surprised. I had thought she was staying with us. And I was a bit bothered, for it is not hospitality to allow the visitor to Destiny to put up at the local pub. But James Carabine whispered: "'Tis on the downs she's staying, Master Kerry, in her own great van with four horses." It was difficult to believe that the tall graceful lady in the golden and red Spanish shawl, with the quiet speech of our own people, was a roaming gypsy, with the whole world as her home.

"Good night, Jenepher. Good night, Valentine. *Boshto dok*, good luck, James Carabine!"

"*Boshto dok, mi pen.* Good luck, sister."

We went out into the October night of the full moon — the hunter's moon — and away from the great fire of turf and bogwood in our drawing-room the night was vital with an electric cold. One could sense the film of ice in the bogs, and the drumming of snipes' wings, disturbed by some roving dog, came to our ears. So bright was the moon that each whitewashed apple tree stood out clear in the orchard, and as we took the road toward Grey River, we could see a barkentine offshore, with sails of polished silver — some boat from Bilbao probably, making for the Clyde, in the daytime a scrubby ore carrier but to-night a ship out of some old sea story, as of Magellan, or our own Saint Brendan:

"*Feach air muir lionadh gealach buidhe mar ór*," she quoted in Gaelic; "See on the filling sea the full moon yellow as gold. . . . It is full moon and full tide, Kerry; if you make a wish, it will come true."

"I wish you success in the Derby, Madame."

Ahead of us down the road moved a little group to the sound of fiddle and mouth organ. It was the Romany body-guard ready to protect their chieftainess on her way home.

"You mean that, I know, but you dislike the idea. Why?"

"Madame," I said, "if you can read my thoughts as easily as that, it's no more impertinent to speak than think. I have heard a lot about a great colt to-night, and of his chance for the greatest race in the world, and that warms my heart. But I have heard more about money, and that chills me."

"I am so old, Kerry, that the glory of winning the Derby means little to me. Do you know how old I am? I am six years short of an hundred old."

"Then the less — " I began, and stopped short, and could have chucked myself over the cliff for my unpardonable discourtesy.

"Then the less reason for my wanting money," the old lady said. "Is not that so?"

"Exactly, Madame."

"Kerry," she said, "does my name mean anything to you?"

"It has bothered me all evening. Lady Clontarf, I am so sorry my father's son should appear to you so rude and ignorant a lout."

"Mifanwy, Countess Clontarf and Kincora."

I gaped like an idiot. "The line of great Brian Boru. But I thought—"

"Did you really ever think of it, Kerry?"

"Not really, Madame," I said. "It's so long ago, so wonderful. It's like that old city they speak of in the country tales, under Ownaglass, the grey river, with its spires and great squares. It seems to me to have vanished like that, in rolling clouds of thunder."

"The last O'Neill has vanished, and the last Plantagenet. But great Brian's strain remains. When I married my lord," she said quietly, "it was in a troubled time. Our ears had not forgotten the musketry of Waterloo, and England was still shaken by fear of the Emperor, and poor Ireland was hurt and wounded. As you know, Kerry, no peer of the older faith sat in College Green. It is no new thing to ennoble, and steal an ancient name. Pitt and Napoleon passed their leisure hours at it. So that of O'Briens, Kerry, sirred and lorded, there are a score, but my lord was Earl of Clontarf and Kincora since before the English came.

"If my lord was of the great blood of Kincora, myself was not lacking in blood. We Romanies are old, Kerry, so old that no man knows our beginning, but that we came from the uplands of India centuries before history. We are a strong, vital race, and we remain with our language, our own customs, our own laws until this day. And to certain families of us, the Romanies all over the world do reverence, as to our own, the old Lovells. There are three Lovells, Kerry, the *dinelo* or foolish Lovells, the *gozvero* or cunning Lovells, and the *puro* Lovells, the old Lovells. I am of the old Lovells. My father was the great Mairik Lovell. So you see I am of great stock too."

"Dear Madame, one has only to see you to know that."

"My lord had a small place left him near the Village of Swords, and it was near there I met him. He wished to buy a horse from my father Mairik, a stallion my father had brought all the way from the Nejd in Arabia. My lord could not buy that horse. But when I married my lord, it was part of my dowry, that and two handfuls of uncut Russian emeralds, and a chest of gold coins, Russian and Indian and Turkish coins, all gold. So I did not come empty-handed to my lord."

"Madame, do you wish to tell me this?"

"I wish to tell it to you, Kerry, because I want you for a friend to my little people, the sons of my son's son. You must know everything about friends to understand them.

"My lord was rich only in himself and in his ancestry. But with the great Arab stallion and the emeralds and the gold coins we were well. We did a foolish thing, Kerry; we went to London. My lord wished it, and his wishes were my wishes, although something told me we should not have gone. In London I made my lord sell the great Arab. He did not wish to, because it came with me, nor did I wish to, because my father had loved it so, but I made him sell it. All the Selim horses of to-day are descended from him, Sheykh Selim.

"My lord loved horses, Kerry. He knew horses, but he had no luck. Newmarket Heath is a bad spot for those out of luck. And my lord grew worried. When one is worried, Kerry, the heart contracts a little, — is it not so? Or don't you know yet? Also another thing bothered my lord. He was with English people, and English people have their codes and ordinances. They are good people, Kerry, very honest. They go to churches, and like sad songs, but whether they believe in God, or whether they have hearts or have no hearts, I do not know. Each thing they do by rote and custom, and they are curious in this: they will make excuses for a man who has done a great crime, but no excuses for a man who neglects a trivial thing. An eccentricity of dress is not forgiven. An eccentric is an outsider. So that English are not good for Irish folk.

"My own people," she said proudly, "are simple people, kindly and loyal as your family know. A marriage to them is a deep thing, not the selfish love of one person for another, but involving many factors. A man will say: Mifanwy Lovell's father saved my honour once. What can I do for Mifanwy Lovell and Mifanwy Lovell's man? And the Lovells said when we were married: Brothers, the *gawjo rai*, the foreign gentleman, may not understand the gypsy way, that our sorrows are his sorrows, and our joys his, but we understand that his fights are our fights, and his interests the interests of the Lovell Clan.

"My people were always about my lord, and my lord hated it. In our London house in the morning, there were always gypsies waiting to tell my lord of a great fight coming off quietly on Epsom Downs, which it might interest him to see, or of a good horse to be bought cheaply, or some news of a dog soon to run in a coursing match for a great stake, and of the dog's excellences or his defects. They wanted no money. They only wished to do him a kindness. But my lord was embarrassed, until he began to loathe the sight of a gypsy neckerchief. Also, in the race courses, in the betting ring where my lord would be, a gypsy would pay hard-earned entrance money to tell my lord quietly of something they had noticed that morning in the gallops, or horses to be avoided in betting, or of neglected horses which would win. All kindnesses to my lord. But my lord was with fashionable English folk, who do not understand one's having a strange friend. Their uplifted eyebrows made my lord ashamed of the poor Romanies. These things are things you might laugh at, with laughter like sunshine, but there would be clouds in your heart.

"The end came at Ascot, Kerry, where the young queen was, and the Belgian king, and the great nobles of the court. Into the paddock came one of the greatest of gypsies, Tyso Herne, who had gone before my marriage with a great draft of Norman trotting horses to Mexico, and came back with a squadron of ponies, suitable for polo. Tyso was a vast man, a *pawni Romany,* a fair gypsy. His hair was red, and his moustache was long and curling, like a Hungarian pandour's. He had a flaunting *diklo* of fine yellow silk about his neck, and the buttons on his coat were gold Indian mohurs, and on his bell-shaped trousers were braids of silver bells, and the spurs on his Wellingtons were fine silver, and his hands were covered with rings, Kerry, with stones in them such as even the young queen did not have. It was not vulgar ostentation. It was just that Tyso felt rich and merry, and no stone on his hand was as fine as his heart.

"When he saw me he let a roar out of him that was like the roar of the ring when the horses are coming in to the stretch.

"'Before God,' he shouted, 'it's Mifanwy Lovell.' And, though I am not a small woman, Kerry, he tossed me in the air, and caught me in the air. And he laughed and kissed me, and I laughed and kissed him, so happy was I to see great Tyso once more, safe from over the sea.

"'Go get your *rom, mi tshai,* your husband, my lass, and we'll go to the *kitshima* and have a jeraboam of Champagne wine.'"

"But I saw my lord walk off with thunder in his face, and all the English folk staring and some women laughing. So I said: 'I will go with you alone, Tyso.' For Tyso Herne had been my father's best friend and my mother's cousin, and had held me as a baby, and no matter how he looked, or who laughed, he was well come for me.

"Of what my lord said, and of what I said in rebuttal, we will not speak. One says foolish things in anger, but, foolish or not, they leave scars. For out of the mouth come things forgotten, things one thinks dead. But before the end of the meeting, I went to Tyso Herne's van. He was braiding a whip with fingers light as a woman's, and when he saw me he spoke quietly.

"'Is all well with thee, Mifanwy?'

"'Nothing is well with me, father's friend.'

"And so I went back to my people, and I never saw my lord any more."

We had gone along until in the distance I could see the gypsy fire, and turning the headland we saw the light on Farewell Point. A white flash; a second's rest; a red flash; three seconds occultation; then white and red again. There is something heartening and brave in Farewell Light. Ireland keeps watch over her share of the Atlantic sea.

"When I left my lord, I was with child, and when I was delivered of him, and the child weaned and strong, I sent him to my lord, for every man wants his man child, and every family its heir. But when he was four and twenty he came back to me, for the roving gypsy blood and the fighting Irish blood were too much for him. He was never Earl of Clontarf. He died while my lord still lived. He married a Herne, a grandchild of Tyso, a brave golden girl. And he got killed charging in the Balkan Wars.

"Niall's wife—my son's name was Niall—understood, and when young Niall was old enough, we sent him to my lord. My lord was old at this time, older than his years, and very poor. But of my share of money he would have nothing. My lord died when Niall's Niall was at school, so the little lad became Earl of Clontarf and Kincora. I saw to it he had sufficient money, but he married no rich woman,

He married a poor Irish girl, and by her had two children, Niall and Alick. He was interested in horses, and rode well, my English friends tell me. But mounted on a brute in the Punchestown races, he made a mistake at the stone wall. He did not know the horse very well. So he let it have its head at the stone wall. It threw its head up, took the jump by the roots, and so Niall's Niall was killed. His wife, the little Irish girl, turned her face away from life and died.

"The boys are fifteen and thirteen now, and soon they will go into the world. I want them to have a fair chance, and it is for this reason I wish them to have money. I have been rich and then poor, and then very rich and again poor, and rich again and now poor. But if this venture succeeds, the boys will be all right."

"Ye-s," I said.

"You don't seem very enthusiastic, Kerry."

"We have a saying," I told her, "that money won from a bookmaker is only lent."

"If you were down on a race meeting and on the last race of the last day you won a little, what would you say?"

"I'd say I only got a little of my own back."

"Then we only get a little of our own back over the losses of a thousand years."

We had come now to the encampment. Around the great fire were tall swarthy men with coloured neckerchiefs, who seemed more reserved, cleaner than the English gypsy. They rose quietly as the gypsy lady came. The great spotted Dalmatian dogs rose too. In the half light the picketed horses could be seen, quiet as trees.

"This is the Younger of Destiny Bay," said the old lady, "who is kind enough to be our friend."

"*Sa shan, rai!*" they spoke with quiet courtesy. "How are you, sir?"

Lady Clontarf's maid hurried forward with a wrap, scolding, and speaking English with beautiful courtesy. "You are dreadful, sister. You go walking the roads at night like a courting girl in spring. Gentleman, you are wrong to keep the *rawnee* out, and she an old woman and not well."

"Supplistia," Lady Clontarf chided, "you have no more manners than a growling dog."

"I am the *rawnee's* watchdog," the girl answered.

"Madame, your maid is right. I will go now."

"Kerry," she stopped me, "will you be friends with my little people?"

"I will be their true friend," I promised, and I kissed her hand.

"God bless you!" she said. And "*kushto bok, rai!*" the gypsies wished me. "Good luck, sir!" And I left the camp for my people's house. The hunter's moon was dropping toward the edge of the world, and the light on Farewell Point flashed seaward its white and red, and as I walked along, I noticed that a wind from Ireland had sprung up, and the Bilbao boat was bowling along nor'east on the starboard tack. It seemed to me an augury.

V

In those days, before my aunt Jenepher's marriage to Patrick Herne, the work of Destiny Bay was divided in this manner: my dear aunt Jenepher was, as was right, supreme in the house. My uncle Valentine planned and superintended the breeding of the harness ponies, and sheep, and black Dexter cattle which made Destiny Bay so feared at the Dublin Horse Show and at the Bath and West. My own work was the farms. To me fell the task of preparing the stables and training grounds for Lady Clontarf's and my own horses. It was a relief and an adventure to give up thinking of turnips, wheat, barley, and seeds, and to examine the downs for training ground. In my great grandfather's time, in pre-Union days, many a winner at the Curragh had been bred and trained at Destiny Bay. The soil of the downs is chalky, and the matted roots of the woven herbage have a certain give in them in the driest of weather. I found out my great-grandfather's mile and a half, and two miles and a half with a turn and shorter gallops of various gradients. My grandfather had used them as a young man, but mainly for hunters, horses which he sold for the great Spanish and Austrian regiments. But to my delight the stables were as good as ever. Covered with reed thatch, they required few repairs. The floors were of chalk, and the boxes beautifully ventilated. There were also great tanks for rainwater, which is of all water the best for horses in training. There were also a few stalls for restless horses. I was worried a little about lighting, but my uncle Valentine told me that Sir Arthur Pollexfen allowed no artificial lights where he trained. Horses went to bed with the fowls and got up at cockcrow.

My own horses I got from Robinson without hurting his feelings. "It's this way, Robinson," I told him. "We're trying to do a crazy thing at Destiny, and I'm not bringing them to another trainer. I'm bringing another trainer there. I can tell you no more."

"Not another word, Mr. Kerry. Bring them back when you want to. I'm sorry to say good-bye to the wee colt. But I wish you luck."

We bought three more horses, and a horse for Ann-Dolly. So that with the six we had a rattling good little stable. When I saw Sir Arthur Pollexfen, my heart sank a little, for he seemed so much out of a former century. Small, ruddy-cheeked, with the white hair of a bishop, and a bishop's courtesy, I never thought he could run a stable. I thought, perhaps, he had grown too old and had been thinking for a long time now of the Place whither he was going, and that we had brought him back from his thoughts and he had left his vitality behind. His own servant came with him to Destiny Bay, and though we wished to have him in the house with us, yet he preferred to stay in a cottage by the stables. I don't know what there was about his clothes, but they were all of an antique though a beautiful cut. He never wore riding breeches but trousers of a bluish cloth and strapped beneath his varnished boots. A flowered waistcoat with a satin stock, a short covert coat, a grey bowler hat and gloves. Always there was a freshly cut flower in his buttonhole, which his servant got every evening from the greenhouses at Destiny Bay, and kept overnight in a glass of water into which the least drop of whiskey had been poured. I mention this as extraordinary, as most racing men will not wear flowers. They believe flowers bring bad luck, though how the superstition arose I cannot tell. His evening trousers also buckled under his shoes, or rather half Wellingtons, such as army men wear, and though there was never a crease in them there was never a wrinkle. He would never drink port after dinner when the ladies had left, but a little whiskey punch which James Carabine would compose for him. Compared to the hard shrewd-eyed trainers I knew, this bland, soft-spoken old gentleman filled me with misgiving.

I got a different idea of the old man the first morning I went out to the gallops. The sun had hardly risen when the old gentleman appeared, as beautifully turned out as though he were entering the Show Ring at Ballsbridge. His servant held his horse, a big grey, while he swung into the saddle as light as a boy. His hack was feeling good that morning, and he and I went off toward the training ground at a swinging canter, the old gentleman half standing in his stirrups, with a light firm grip of his knees, riding as Cossacks do, his red terrier galloping behind him. When we settled down to walk he told me the pedigree of his horse, descended through Matchem and Whalebone from Oliver Cromwell's great charger The White Turk, or

Place's White Turk, as it was called from the Lord Pro-
tector's stud manager. To hear him follow the intricacies
of breeding was a revelation. Then I understood what a
great horseman he was. On the training ground he was
like a marshal commanding an army, such respect did every
one accord him. The lads perched on the horses' withers,
his head man, the grooms, all watched the apple-ruddy face,
while he said little or nothing. He must have had eyes in
the back of his head, though. For when a colt we had
brought from Mr. Gubbins, a son of Galtee More's, started
lashing out and the lad up seemed like taking a toss, the
old man's voice came low and sharp: "Don't fall off, boy."
And the boy did not fall off. The red terrier watched the
trials with a keen eye, and I believe honestly that he knew
as much about horses as any one of us and certainly more
than any of us about his owner. When my lovely Ducks
and Drakes went out at the lad's call to beat the field by
two lengths over five furlongs, the dog looked up at Sir
Arthur and Sir Arthur looked back at the dog, and what
they thought toward each other, God knoweth.

I expected when we rode away that the old gentleman
would have some word to say about my horses, but coming
home, his remarks were of the country. "Your Derry is
a beautiful country, young Mister Kerry," he said, "though
it would be treason to say that in my own country of
Mayo." Of my horses not a syllable.

He could be the most silent man I have ever known,
though giving the illusion of keeping up a conversation.
You could talk to him, and he would smile, and nod at the
proper times, as though he were devouring every word
you said. In the end you thought you had a very interesting conversation. But as to whether he had even heard
you, you were never sure. On the other hand when he
wished to speak, he spoke to the point and beautifully. Our
bishop, on one of his pastoral visitations, if that be the

term, stayed at Destiny Bay, and because my uncle Cosimo is a bishop too, and because he felt he ought to do something for our souls he remonstrated with us for starting our stable. My uncle Valentine was livid, but said nothing for no guest must be contradicted in Destiny Bay.

"For surely, Sir Valentine, no man of breeding can mingle with the rogues, cutpurses and their womenfolk who infest race courses, drunkards, bawds and common gamblers, without lowering himself to some extent to their level," his Lordship purred. "Yourself, one of the wardens of Irish chivalry, must give an example to the common people."

"Your Lordship," broke in old Sir Arthur Pollexfen, "is egregiously misinformed. In all periods of the world's history, eminent personages have concerned themselves with the racing of horses. We read of Philip of Macedon, that while campaigning in Asia Minor, a courier brought him news of two events, of the birth of his son Alexander and of the winning, by his favourite horse, of the chief race at Athens, and we may reasonably infer that his joy over the winning of the race was equal to if not greater than that over the birth of Alexander. In the life of Charles the Second, the traits which do most credit to that careless monarch are his notable and gentlemanly death and his affection for his great race horse Old Rowley. Your Lordship is, I am sure," said Sir Arthur, more blandly than any ecclesiastic could, "too sound a Greek scholar not to remember the epigrams of Maecius and Philodemus, which show what interest these antique poets took in the racing of horses. And coming to present times, your Lordship must have heard that his Majesty (whom God preserve!) has won two Derbies, once with the leased horse Minoru, and again with his own great Persimmon. The premier peer of Scotland, the Duke of Hamilton, Duke of Chastellerault in France, Duke of Brandon in England, hereditary prince of Baden, is prouder of his fine mare Eau de Vie than of all his titles. As to the Irish families, the Persses of Galway, the Dawsons of Dublin, and my own, the Pollexfens of Mayo, have always been interested in the breeding and racing of horses. And none of these — my punch, if you please, James Carabine! — are, as your Lordship puts it, drunkards, bawds, and common gamblers. I fear your Lordship has been reading — " and he cocked his eye, bright as a wren's, at the bishop, " religious publications of the sensational and morbid type."

It was all I could do to keep from leaping on the table and giving three loud cheers for the County of Mayo.

VI

Now, on those occasions, none too rare, when my uncle Valentine and I differed on questions of agricultural economy, or of national polity, or of mere faith and morals, he poured torrents of invective over my head, which mattered little. But when he was really aroused to bitterness he called me " modern." And by modern my uncle Valentine meant the quality inherent in brown buttoned boots, in white waistcoats worn with dinner jackets, in nasty little motor cars — in fine, those things before which the angels of God recoil in horror. While I am not modern in that sense, I am modern in this, that I like to see folk getting on with things. Of Lady Clontarf and of Irlandais colt, I heard no more. On the morning after seeing her home I called over to the caravan but it was no longer there. There was hardly a trace of it. I found a broken fern and a slip of oaktree, the gypsy patteran. But what it betokened or whither it pointed I could not tell. I had gone to no end of trouble in getting the stables and training grounds ready, and Sir Arthur Pollexfen had been brought out of his retirement in the County of Mayo. But still no word of the horse. I could see my uncle Valentine and Sir Arthur taking their disappointment bravely, if it never arrived, and murmuring some courteous platitude, out of the reign of good Queen Victoria, that it was a lady's privilege to change her mind. That might console them in their philosophy, but it would only make me hot with rage. For to me there is no sex in people of standards. They do not let one another down.

Then one evening the horse arrived.

It arrived at sundown in a large van drawn by four horses, a van belonging evidently to some circus. It was yellow and covered with paintings of nymphs being wooed by swains, in clothes hardly fitted to agricultural pursuits: of lions of terrifying aspect being put through their paces by a trainer of an aspect still more terrifying: of an Indian gentleman with a vast turban and a small loincloth playing a penny whistle to a snake that would have put the heart crosswise in Saint Patrick himself; of a most adipose lady in tights swinging from a ring while the husband and seven sons hung on to her like bees in a swarm. Floridly painted over the van was "Arsène Bombaudiac, Prop., Bayonne." The whole added no dignity to Destiny Bay, and if some sorceress had disclosed to Mr. Bombaudiac of Bayonne that he was about to lose a van by fire at low tide on the beach of Destiny in Ireland within forty-eight hours— The driver was a burly gypsy, while two of the most utter scoundrels I have ever laid eyes on sat beside him on the wide seat.

"Do you speak English?" I asked the driver.

"Yes, sir," he answered, "I am a Petulengro."

"Which of these two beauties beside you is the jockey?"

"Neither, sir. These two are just gypsy fighting men. The jockey is inside with the horse."

My uncle Valentine came down stroking his great red beard. He seemed fascinated by the pictures on the van.

"What your poor aunt Jenepher, Kerry," he said, "misses by being blind!"

"What she is spared, sir! Boy," I called one of the servants, "go get Sir Arthur Pollexfen. Where do you come from?" I asked the driver.

"From Dax, sir, in the South of France."

"You're a liar," I said. "Your horses are half-bred Clydesdale. There's no team like that in the South of France."

"We came to Dieppe with an *attelage basque*, six yoked oxen. But I was told they would not be allowed in England, so I telegraphed our chief, Piramus Petulengro, to have a team at Newhaven. So I am not a liar, sir."

"I am sorry."

"Sir, that is all right."

Sir Arthur Pollexfen came down from where he had been speaking to my aunt Jenepher. I could see he was tremendously excited, because he walked more slowly than was usual, spoke with more deliberation. He winced a little as he saw the van. But he was of the old heroic school. He said nothing.

"I think, Sir Valentine," he said, "we might have the horse out."

"Ay, we might as well know the worst," said my uncle Valentine.

A man jumped from the box, and swung the crossbar up. The door opened and into the road stepped a small man in dark clothes. Never on this green earth of God's have I seen such dignity. He was dressed in dark clothes with a wide dark hat, and his face was brown as soil. White starched cuffs covered half of his hands. He took off his hat and bowed first to my uncle Valentine, then to Sir Arthur, and to myself last. His hair was plastered down on his forehead, and the impression you got was of an ugly rugged face, with piercing black eyes. He seemed to say:

"Laugh, if you dare!" But laughter was the furthest thing from us, such tremendous masculinity did the small man have. He looked at us searchingly, and I had the feeling that if he did n't like us, for two pins he would have the bar across the van door again and be off with the horse. Then he turned and spoke gutturally to some one inside.

A boy as rugged as himself, in a Basque cap and with a Basque sash, led first a small donkey round as a barrel out of the outrageous van. One of the gypsies took it, and the next moment the boy led out the Irlandais colt.

He came out confidently, quietly, approaching gentlemen as a gentleman, a beautiful brown horse, small, standing perfectly. I had just one glance at the sound strong legs and the firm ribs, before his head caught my eye. The graceful neck, the beautiful small muzzle, the gallant eyes. In every inch of him you could see breeding. While Sir Arthur was examining his hocks, and my uncle Valentine was standing weightily considering strength of lungs and heart, my own heart went out to the lovely eyes that seemed to ask: "Are these folk friends?"

Now I think you could parade the Queen of Sheba in the show ring before me without extracting more than an off-hand compliment out of me, but there is something about a gallant thoroughbred that makes me sing. I can quite understand the trainer who, pointing to Manifesto, said that if he ever found a woman with a shape like that, he'd marry her. So out of my heart through my lips came the cry: "*Och, asthore!*" which is, in our Gaelic, "Oh, my dear!"

The Spanish jockey, whose brown face was rugged and impassive as a Pyrenee, looked at me, and broke into a wide, understanding smile.

"*Sì, sì, Señor,*" he uttered, "*sì, sì!*"

VII

Never did a winter pass so merrily, so advantageously at Destiny Bay. Usually there is fun enough with the hunting, but with a racing stable in winter there is always anxiety. Is there a suspicion of a cough in the stables? Is the ground too hard for gallops? Will snow come and hold the gallops up for a week? Fortunately we are right on the edge of the great Atlantic drift, and you can catch at times the mild amazing atmosphere of the Caribbean. While Scotland sleeps beneath its coverlet of snow, and England shivers in its ghastly fog, we on the northeast seaboard of Ireland go through a winter that is short as a midsummer night in Lofoden. The trees have hardly put off their gold and brown until we perceive their cheeping green. And one soft day we say: " Soon on that bank will be the fairy gold of the primrose." And behold, while you are looking the primrose is there!

Each morning at sun-up, the first string of horses were out. Quietly as a general officer reviewing a parade old Sir Arthur sat on his grey horse, his red dog beside him, while Geraghty, his head man, galloped about with his instructions. Hares bolted from their forms in the grass. The sun rolled away the mists from the blue mountains of Donegal. At the starting gate, which Sir Arthur had set up, the red-faced Irish boys steered their mounts from a walk toward the tapes. A pull at the lever and they were off. The old man seemed to notice everything. " Go easy, boy, don't force that horse!" His low voice would carry across the downs. "Don't lag there, Murphy, ride him!" And when the gallop was done, he would trot across to the horses, his red dog trotting beside him, asking how Sarsfield went. Did Ducks and Drakes seem interested? Did Rustum go up to his bit? Then they were off at a slow walk toward their sand bath, where they rolled like dogs.

Then the sponging and the rubbing, and the fresh hay in the mangers kept as clean as a hospital. At eleven the second string came out. At half-past three the lads were called to their horses, and a quarter of an hour's light walking was given to them. At four, Sir Arthur made his "stables", questioning the lads in each detail as to how the horses had fed, running his hand over their legs to feel for any heat in the joints that might betoken trouble.

Small as our stable was, I doubt if there was one in Great Britain and Ireland to compare with it in each fitting and necessity for training a race horse. Sir Arthur pinned his faith to old black tartar oats, of about forty-two pounds to the bushel, bran mashes with a little linseed, and sweet old meadow hay.

The Irlandais colt went beautifully. The Spanish jockey's small brother, Joselito, usually rode it, while the jockey's self, whose name we were told was Frasco, Frasco Moreno — usually called, he told us, Don Frasco — looked on. He constituted himself a sort of sub-trainer for the colt, allowing none else to attend to its feeding. The small donkey was its invariable stable companion, and had to be led out to exercise with it. The donkey belonged to Joselito. Don Frasco rode many trials on the other horses. He might appear small standing, but on horseback he seemed a large man, so straight did he sit in the saddle. The little boys rode with a fairly short stirrup, but the gitano scorned anything but the traditional seat. He never seemed to move on a horse. Yet he could do what he liked with it.

The Irlandais colt was at last named Romany Baw, or "gypsy friend" in English, as James Carabine explained to us, and Lady Clontarf's colours registered, quartered red and gold. When the winter lists came out, we saw the horse quoted at a hundred to one, and later at the call over of the Victoria Club, saw that price offered but not taken. My uncle Valentine made a journey to Dublin, to arrange for Lady Clontarf's commission being placed, putting it in the hands of a Derry man who had become big in the affairs of Tattersall's. What he himself and Sir Arthur Pollexfen and the jockey had on I do not know, but he arranged to place an hundred pounds of mine, and fifty of Ann-Dolly's. As the months went by, the odds crept down gradually to thirty-three to one, stood there for a while and went out to fifty. Meanwhile Sir James became a sensational favourite at fives, and Toison d'Or varied between tens and one hundred to eight. Some news of a great trial of Lord Shire's horse had leaked out which accounted for the ridiculously short price. But no word did or could get out about Lady Clontarf's colt. The two gypsy fighters from Dax patrolled Destiny Bay, and God help any poor tipster or wretched newspaper tout who tried to plumb the mysteries of training. I honestly believe a bar of iron and a bog hole would have been his end.

The most fascinating figure in this crazy world was the gypsy jockey. To see him talk to Sir Arthur Pollexfen was a phenomenon. Sir Arthur would speak in English and the gypsy answer in Spanish, neither knowing a word of the other's language, yet each perfectly understanding the other. I must say that this only referred to how a horse ran, or how Romany Baw was feeding and feeling. As to more complicated problems, Ann-Dolly was called in, to translate his Spanish.

"Ask him," said Sir Arthur, "has he ever ridden in France?"

"*Oiga, Frasco*," and Ann-Dolly would burst into a torrent of gutturals.

"*Si, si, Doña Anna.*"

"Ask him has he got his clearance from the Jockey Club of France?"

"*Seguro, Don Arturo!*" And out of his capacious pocket he extracted the French Jockey Club's "character."

They made a picture I will never forget, the old horseman ageing so gently, the vivid boyish beauty of Ann-Dolly, and the overpowering dignity and manliness of the jockey. Always, except when he was riding or working at his anvil, — for he was our smith too — he wore the dark clothes, which evidently some village tailor of the Pyrenees made for him — the very short coat, the trousers tubed like cigarettes, his stiff shirt with the vast cuffs. He never wore a collar, nor a neckerchief. Always his back was flat as the side of a house.

When he worked at the anvil, with his young ruffian of a brother at the bellows, he sang. He had shakes and grace notes enough to make a thrush quit. Ann-Dolly translated one of his songs for us.

> *No tengo padre ni madre . . .*
> *Que desgraciado soy yo!*
> *Soy como el arbol solo*
> *Que echas frutas y no echa flor . . .*

" He sings he has no father or mother. How out of luck he is ! He is like a lonely tree, which bears the fruit and not the flower."

" God bless my soul, Kerry," my uncle was shocked. " The little man is homesick."

" No, no! " Ann-Dolly protested. " He is very happy. That is why he sings a sad song."

One of the reasons of the little man's happiness was the discovery of our national game of handball. He strolled over to the Irish Village and discovered the court back of the Inniskillen Dragoon, that most notable of rural pubs. He was tremendously excited, and getting some gypsy to translate for him, challenged the local champion for the stake of a barrel of porter. He made the local champion look like a carthorse in the Grand National. When it was told to me I couldn't believe it. Ann-Dolly explained to me that the great game of Basque country was *pelota*.

"But don't they play *pelota* with a basket?"

"Real *pelota* is *à mains nues*, 'with the hands naked.'"

"You mean Irish handball," I told her.

I regret that the population of Destiny made rather a good thing out of Don Frasco's prowess on the court, going from village to village, and betting on a certain win. The end was a match between Mick Tierney, the Portrush Jarvey and the jockey. The match was billed for the champion of Ulster, and Don Frasco was put down on the card, to explain his lack of English, as Danny Frask, the Glenties Miracle, the Glenties being a district of Donegal where Erse is the native speech. The match was poor, the Portrush Jarvey, after the first game, standing and watching the ball hiss past him with his eyes on his cheek bones. All Donegal seemed to have turned out for the fray. When the contest was over, a big Glenties man pushed his way toward the jockey.

"Dublin and London and New York are prime cities," he chanted, "but Glenties is truly magnificent. *Kir do lauv anshin, a railt na hooee*, 'Put your hand there, Star of the North.'"

"*No entiendo, señor*," said Don Frasco. And with that the fight began.

James Carabine was quick enough to get the jockey out of the court before he was lynched. But Destiny Bay men, gypsies, fishers, citizens of Derry, bookmakers and their clerks and the fighting tribes of Donegal went to it with a vengeance. Indeed, according to experts, nothing like it, for spirit or results, had been seen since or before the Prentice Boys had chased King James (to whom God give his deserts!) from Derry Walls. The removal of the stunned and wounded from the courts drew the attention of the police, for the fight was continued in grim silence. But on the entrance of half a dozen peelers commanded by a huge sergeant, Joselito, the jockey's young brother, covered himself with glory. Leaping on the reserved seats, he brought his right hand over hard and true to the sergeant's jaw, and the sergeant was out for half an hour. Joselito was arrested, but the case was laughed out of court. The idea of a minuscule jockey who could ride at ninety pounds knocking out six foot three of Royal Irish Constabulary was too much. Nothing was found on him but his bare hands, a packet of cigarettes and thirty sovereigns he had won over the match. But I knew better. I decided to prove him with hard questions.

"Ask him in Romany, James Carabine, what he had wrapped around that horseshoe he threw away."

"He says: 'Tow, Mister Kerry.'"

"Get me my riding crop," I said; "I'll take him behind the stables." And the training camp lost its best lightweight jockey for ten days, the saddle suddenly becoming repulsive to him. I believe he slept on his face.

But the one who was really wild about the affair was Ann-Dolly. She came across from Spanish Men's Rest flaming with anger.

"Because a Spanish wins, there is fighting, there is anger. If an Irish wins, there is joy, there is drinking. Oh, shame of sportsmanship!"

"Oh, shut your gab, Ann-Dolly," I told her. "They didn't know he was a Spanish, as you call it."

"What did they think he was if not a Spanish? Tell me. I demand it of you."

"They thought he was Welsh."

"Oh, in that case . . ." said Ann-Dolly, completely mollified. *Ipsa hibernis hiberniora!*

VIII

I wouldn't have you think that all was beer and skittles, as the English say, in training Romany Baw for the Derby.

As spring came closer, the face of the old trainer showed signs of strain. The Lincoln Handicap was run and the Grand National passed, and suddenly flat-racing was on us. And now not the Kohinoor was watched more carefully than the Derby horse. We had a spanking trial on a course as nearly approaching the Two Thousand Guineas route as Destiny Downs would allow, and when Romany Baw flew past us, beating Ducks and Drakes who had picked him up at the mile for the uphill dash, and Sir Arthur clicked his watch, I saw his tense face relax.

"He ran well," said the old man.

"He'll walk it," said my uncle Valentine.

My uncle Valentine and Jenico and Ann-Dolly were going across to Newmarket Heath for the big race, but the spring of the year is the time that the farmer must stay by his land, and nurse it like a child. All farewells, even for a week, are sad, and I was loath to see the horses go into the races. Romany Baw had a regular summer bloom on him and his companion, the donkey, was corpulent as an alderman. Ducks and Drakes looked rough and backward, but that didn't matter.

"You've got the best-looking horse in the United Kingdom," I told Sir Arthur.

"Thank you, Kerry," the old man was pleased. "And as to Ducks and Drakes, looks aren't everything."

"Sure, I know that," I told him.

"I wouldn't be rash," he told me, "but I'd have a little on both. That is, if they go to the post fit and well."

I put in the days as well as I could, getting ready for the Spring Show at Dublin. But my heart and my thoughts were with my people and the horses at Newmarket. I could see my uncle Valentine's deep bow with his hat in his hand as they passed the Roman ditch at Newmarket, giving that squat wall the reverence that racing men have accorded it since races were run there, though why, none know. A letter from Ann-Dolly apprised me that the horses had made a good crossing and that Romany Baw was well— "and you must n't think, my dear, that your colt is not as much and more to us than the Derby horse, no, Kerry, not for one moment. Lady Clontarf is here, in her caravan, and oh, Kerry, she looks ill. Only her burning spirit keeps her frail body alive. Jenico and I are going down to Eastbourne to see the little Earl and his brother . . . You will get this letter, cousin, on the morning of the race. . . . "

At noon that day I could stand it no longer so I had James Carabine put the trotter in the dogcart. "There are some things I want in Derry," I told myself, "and I may as well get them to-day as to-morrow." And we went spinning toward Derry Walls. Ducks and Drakes' race was the two-thirty. And after lunch I looked at reapers I might be wanting in July until the time of the race. I went along to the club, and had hardly entered it when I saw the boy putting up the telegram on the notice board.

1, *Ducks and Drakes,* an hundred to eight; 2, Geneva, four to six; 3, *Ally Sloper,* three to one. "That 's that!" I said. Another telegram gave the betting for the Two Thousand: Threes, *Sir James;* seven to two, *Toison d'Or;* eights, *Ca' Canny, Greek Singer, Germanicus;* tens, six or seven horses; twenty to one any other. No word in the betting of the gypsy horse, and I wondered had anything happened. Surely a horse looking as well as he did must have attracted backers' attention. And as I was worrying the result came in, *Romany Baw,* first; *Sir James,* second, *Toison d'Or,* third.

"Kerry," somebody called.

"I have n't a minute," I shouted. Neither I had, for James Carabine was outside, waiting to hear the result. When I told him he said: "There 's a lot due to you, Mister Kerry, in laying out those gallops." "Be damned to that!" I said, but I was pleased all the same.

I was on tenterhooks until I got the papers describing the race. Ducks and Drakes' win was dismissed summarily, as that of an Irish outsider, and the jockey, Flory Cantillon (Frasco could not manage the weight), was credited with a clever win of two lengths. But the account of Romany Baw's race filled me with indignation. According to it, the winner got away well, but the favourites were hampered at the start and either could have beaten the Irish trained horse, only that they just did n't. The race was won by half a length, a head separating second and third, and most of the account was given to how the favourites chased the lucky outsider, and in a few more strides would have caught him. There were a few dirty backhanders given at Romany's jockey, who, they said, would be more at home in a circus than on a modern race track. He sat like a rider of a century back, they described it, more like an exponent of the old manège than a modern jockey, and even while the others were thundering at his horse's hindquarters he never moved his seat or used his whip. The experts' judgment of the race was that the Irish colt was forward in a backward field, and that Romany would be lost on Epsom Downs, especially with its "postillion rider."

But the newspaper criticisms of the jockey and his mount did not seem to bother my uncle Valentine or the trainer or the jockey's self. They came back elated; even the round white donkey had a humorous happy look in his full Latin eye.

"Did he go well?" I asked.

"He trotted it," said my uncle Valentine.

"But the accounts read, sir," I protested, "that the favourites would have caught him in another couple of strides."

"Of course they would," said my uncle Valentine, "at the pace he was going," he added.

"I see." said I.

"You see nothing," said my uncle Valentine. "But if you had seen the race you might talk. The horse is a picture. It goes so sweetly that you wouldn't think it was going at all. And as for the gypsy jockey—"

"The papers say he's antiquated."

"He's seven pounds better than Flory Cantillon," said my uncle Valentine.

I whistled. Cantillon is our best Irish jockey, and his retaining fees are enormous, and justified. "They said he was nearly caught napping—"

"Napping be damned!" exploded my uncle Valentine. "This Spanish gypsy is the finest judge of pace I ever saw. He knew he had the race won, and he never bothered."

"If the horse is as good as that, and you have as high an opinion of the rider, well, sir, I won a hatful over the Newmarket meeting, and as the price hasn't gone below twenties for the Derby, I'm going after the Ring. There's many a bookmaker will wish he'd stuck to his father's old-clothes business."

"I wouldn't, Kerry," said my uncle Valentine. "I'm not sure I wouldn't hedge a bit of what I have on, if I were you."

I was still with amazement.

"I saw Mifanwy Clontarf," said my uncle Valentine, "and only God and herself and myself and now you, know how ill that woman is."

"But ill or not ill, she won't scratch the horse."

"She won't," said my uncle Valentine, and his emphasis on 'she' chilled me to the heart. "You're forgetting, Kerry," he said very quietly, "the Derby Rule."

IX

Of the Derby itself on Epsom Downs, everybody knows. It is supposed to be the greatest test of a three-year-old in

the world, though old William Day used to hold it was easy.
The course may have been easy for Lord George Bentinck's
famous and unbeaten mare Crucifix, when she won the
Oaks in 1840, but most winners over the full course jus-
tify their victory in other races. The course starts up a
heartbreaking hill, and swinging around the top, comes
down again toward Tattenham Corner. If a horse waits
to steady itself coming down it is beaten. The famous Fred
Archer (whose tortured soul God rest!) used to take Tattenham Corner with one leg over the rails. The straight is
uphill. A mile and a half of the trickiest, most heartbreaking ground in the world. Such is Epsom. Its turf has
been consecrated by the hoofs of great horses since James I
established there a race for the Silver Bell: by Cromwell's
great Coffin Mare; by the Arabs, Godolphin and Darby;
by the great bay, Malton; by the prodigious Eclipse; by
Diomed, son of Florizel, who went to America. . . .

Over the Derby what sums are wagered no man knows.
On it is won the Calcutta Sweepstake, a prize of which
makes a man rich for life, and the Stock Exchange sweep,
and other sweeps innumerable. Some one has ventured the
belief that on it annually are five million of pounds sterling,
and whether he is millions short, or millions over none
knows. Because betting is illegal.

There are curious customs in regard to it, as this: that
when the result is sent over the ticker to clubs, in case of
a dead heat, the word "dead heat" must come first, because within recent years a trusted lawyer, wagering trust
funds on a certain horse, was waiting by the tape to read
the result, and seeing another horse's name come up, went
away forthwith and blew his brains out. Had he been less
volatile he would have seen his own fancy's name follow
that, with "dead heat" after it and been to this day rich
and respected. So now, for the protection of such, "dead
heat" comes first. A dead heat in the Derby is as rare a

thing as there is in the world, but still you can't be too cautious. But the quaintest rule of the Derby is this: that if the nominator of a horse for the Derby Stakes dies, his horse is automatically scratched. There is a legend to the effect that an heir-at-law purposed to kill the owner of an entry, and to run a prime favourite crookedly, and that on hearing this the Stewards of the Jockey Club made the rule. Perhaps it has a more prosaic reason. The Jockey Club may have considered that when a man died, in the trouble of fixing his estates, forfeits would not be paid, and that it was best for all concerned to have the entry scratched. How it came about does not matter, it exists. Whether it is good in law is not certain. Racing folk will quarrel with His Majesty's Lord Justices of Appeal, with the Privy Council, but they will not quarrel with the Jockey Club. Whether it is good in fact is indisputable, for certain owners can tell stories of narrow escapes from racing gangs, in those old days before the Turf was cleaner than the Church, when attempts were made to nobble favourites, when jockeys had not the wings of angels under their silken jackets, when harsh words were spoken about trainers — very, very long ago. There it is, good or bad, the Derby Rule!

X

As to our bets on the race, they did n't matter. It was just bad luck. But to see the old lady's quarter million of pounds and more go down the pike was a tragedy. We had seen so much of shabby great names that I trembled for young Clontarf and his brother. Armenian and Greek families of doubtful antecedents were always on the lookout for a title for their daughters, and crooked businesses always needed directors of title to catch gulls, so much in the United Kingdom do the poor trust their peers. The boys would not be exactly poor, because the horse, whether or not it ran in the Derby, would be worth a good round sum. If it were as good as my uncle Valentine said, it would win the Leger and the Gold Cup at Ascot. But even with these triumphs it wouldn't be a Derby winner. And the Derby means so much. There are so many people in England who remember dates by the Derby winners' names, as "I was married in *Bend Or's* year", or "the *Achilles* was lost in the China seas, let me see when,—that was in *Sainfoin's* year." Also I wasn't sure that the Spanish gypsy would stay to ride him at Doncaster, or return for Ascot. I found him one day standing on the cliffs of Destiny and looking long at the sea, and I knew what that meant. And perhaps Romany Baw would not run for another jockey as he ran for him.

I could not think that Death could be so cruel as to come between us and triumph. In Destiny we have a friendliness for the Change which most folk dread. One of our songs says:

"When Mother Death in her warm arms shall embrace me,
   Low lull me to sleep with sweet Erin-go-bragh—"

We look upon it as a kind friend who comes when one is tired and twisted with pain, and says: "Listen, *avourneen*, soon the dawn will come, and the tide is on the ebb. We must be going." And we trust him to take us, by a short road or a long road to a place of birds and bees, of which even lovely Destiny is but a clumsy seeming. He could not be such a poor sportsman as to come before the aged gallant lady had won her last gamble. And poor Sir Arthur, who had come out of his old age in Mayo to win a Derby! It would break his heart. And the great horse, it would be so hard on him. Nothing will convince me that a thorough-bred does not know a great race when he runs one. The streaming competitors, the crackle of silk, the roar as they come into the straight, and the sense of the jockey calling on the great heart that the writer of Job knew so well. "The glory of his nostril is terrible," says the greatest of poets. "He pauseth in the valley and rejoiceth in his strength: he goeth on to meet the armed men." Your intellectual will claim that the thoroughbred is an artificial brainless animal evolved by men for their amusement. Your intellectual, here again, is a liar.

Spring came in blue and gold. Blue of sea and fields and trees; gold of sun and sand and buttercup. Blue of wild hyacinth and bluebell; gold of primrose and laburnum tree. The old gypsy lady was with her caravan near Bordeaux, and from the occasional letter my uncle Valentine got, and from the few words he dropped to me, she was just holding her own. May drowsed by with the cheeping of the little life in the hedgerows. The laburnum floated in a cloud of gold and each day Romany Baw grew stronger. When his blankets were stripped from him he looked a mass of fighting muscle under a covering of satin, and his eye showed that his heart was fighting too. Old Sir Arthur looked at him a few days before we were to go to England, and he turned to me.

"Kerry," he said, very quietly.

"Yes, Sir Arthur."

"All my life I have been breeding and training horses, and it just goes to show," he told me, "that goodness of God that he let me handle this great horse before I died."

The morning before we left my uncle Valentine received a letter which I could see moved him. He swore a little as he does when moved and stroked his vast red beard and looked fiercely at nothing at all.

"Is it bad news, sir?" I asked.

He didn't answer me directly. "Lady Clontarf is coming to the Derby," he told me.

Then it was my turn to swear a little. It seemed to me to

be but little short of maniacal to risk a Channel crossing and the treacherous English climate in her stage of health. If she should die on the way or on the downs, then all her planning and our work was for nothing. Why could she not have remained in the soft French air, husbanding her share of life until the event was past!

"She comes of ancient, violent blood," thundered my uncle Valentine, "and where should she be but present when her people or her horses go forth to battle?"

"You are right, sir," I said.

XI

The epithet of "flaming" which the English apply to their June was in this year of grace well deserved. The rhododendrons were bursting into great fountains of scarlet, and near the swans the cygnets paddled, unbelievably small. The larks fluttered in the air above the downs, singing so gallantly that when you heard the trill of the nightingale in the thicket giving his noontime song, you felt inclined to say: "Be damned to that Italian bird; my money's on the wee fellow!" All through Surrey the green walls of spring rose high and thick, and then suddenly coming, as we came, through Leatherhead and topping the hill, in the distance the black colony of the downs showed like a thundercloud. At a quarter mile away, the clamour came to you, like the vibration when great bells have been struck.

The stands and enclosure were packed so thickly that one wondered how movement was possible, how people could enjoy themselves, close as herrings. My uncle Valentine had brought his beautiful harness ponies across from Ireland, "to encourage English interest in the Irish horse" he explained it, but with his beautifully cut clothes, his grey high hat, it seemed to me that more people looked at him as we spun along the road than looked at the horses. Behind us sat James Carabine, with his face brown as autumn and the gold rings in his thickened ears. We got out near the paddock and Carabine took the ribbons. My uncle Valentine said quietly to him: "Find out how things are, James Carabine." And I knew he was referring to the gypsy lady. Her caravan was somewhere on the Downs guarded by her gypsies, but my uncle had been there the first day of the meeting, and on Monday night, at the National Sporting, some of the gypsies had waited for him coming out and given him news. I asked him how she was, but all his answer was: "It's in the Hands of God."

Along the track toward the grand stand we made our way. On the railings across the track the bookmakers were proclaiming their market: "I'll give fives the field. I'll give nine to one bar two. I'll give twenty to one bar five. Outsiders! Outsiders! Fives *Sir James*. Seven to one *Toison d'Or*. Nines *Honey Bee*. Nines *Welsh Melody*. Ten to one the gypsy horse."

"It runs all right," said my uncle Valentine, "up to now."

"Twenty to one *Maureen Roe!* Twenties *Asclepiades!* Twenty-five *Rifle Ranger*. Here thirty-three to one *Rifle Ranger, Monk of Sussex,* or *Presumptuous —* "

"Gentlemen, I am here to plead with you not to back the favourite. In this small envelope you will find the number of the winner. For the contemptible sum of two shillings or half a dollar, you may amass a fortune. Who gave the winner of last year's Derby?" a tipster was calling. "Who gave the winner of the Oaks? Who gave the winner of the Steward's Cup?"

"All right, guv'nor, I'll bite. 'Oo the 'ell did?"

Opposite the grand stand the band of the Salvation Army was blaring the music of "Work, for the Night is Coming." Gypsy girls were going around *dukkering* or telling fortune. "Ah, gentleman, you've a lucky face. Cross the poor gypsy's hand with silver —"

"You better cut along and see your horse saddled," said my uncle Valentine. Ducks and Drakes was in the Ranmore Plate and with the penalty he received after Newmarket, Frasco could ride him. As I went toward the paddock I saw the numbers go up, and I saw we were drawn third, which I think is best of all on the tricky Epsom five-furlong dash. I got there in time to see the gypsy swing into the saddle in the green silk jacket and orange cap, and Sir Arthur giving him his orders. "Keep back of the Fusilier," he pointed to the horse, "and then come out. Hit him once if you have to, and no more."

"*Si, si, Don Arturo!*" And he grinned at me.

"Kerry, read this," said the old trainer, and he gave me a newspaper, "and tell me before the race," his voice was trembling a little, "if there's truth in it."

I pushed the paper into my pocket and went back to the box where my uncle Valentine and Jenico and Ann-Dolly were. "What price my horse," I asked in Tattersall's. "Sixes, Mister MacFarlane." "I'll take six hundred to an hundred twice." As I moved away there was a rush to back it. It tumbled in five minutes to five to two.

"And I thought I'd get tens," I said to my uncle Valentine, "with the Fusilier and Bonny Hortense in the race. I wonder who's been backing it."

"I have," said Ann-Dolly. "I got twelves."

"You might have the decency to wait until the owner gets on," I said bitterly. And as I watched the tapes went up. It was a beautiful start. Everything except those on the outside seemed to have a chance as they raced for the rails. I could distinguish the green jacket but vaguely until they came to Tattenham Corner, when I could see Fusilier pull out, and Bonny Hortense follow. But back of Fusilier, racing quietly beside the filly, was the jacket green.

"I wish he'd go up," I said.

"The favourite wins," they were shouting. And a

woman in the box next us began to clap her hands calling: "Fusilier's won. Fusilier wins it!"

"You're a damn fool, woman," said Ann-Dolly. "Ducks and Drakes has it." And as she spoke, I could see Frasco hunch forward slightly and dust his mount's neck with his whip. He crept past the hard-pressed Fusilier to win by half a length.

In my joy I nearly forgot the newspaper, and I glanced at it rapidly. My heart sank. "Gypsy Owner Dying as Horse runs in Derby," I read, and reading down it I felt furious. Where the man got his information from I don't know, but he drew a picturesque account of the old gypsy lady on her deathbed on the downs as Romany Baw was waiting in his stall. The account was written the evening before, and "it is improbable she will last the night," it ended. I gave it to my uncle Valentine, who had been strangely silent over my win.

"What shall I say to Sir Arthur Pollexfen?"

"Say she's ill, but it's all rot she's dying."

I noticed as I went to the paddock a murmur among the racegoers. The attention of all had been drawn to the gypsy horse by its jockey having won the Ranmore Plate. Everywhere I heard questions being asked as to whether she were dead. Sir James had hardened to fours. And on the heath I heard a woman proffer a sovereign to a bookmaker on Romany Baw, and he said: "That horse don't run, lady." I forgot my own little triumph in the tragedy of the scratching of the great horse.

In the paddock Sir Arthur was standing watching the lads leading the horses around. Twenty-seven entries, glossy as silk, muscled like athletes of old Greece, ready to run for the Derby stakes. The jockeys, with their hard wizened faces, stood talking to trainers and owners, saying nothing about the race, all already having been said, but just putting in the time until the order came to go to the gate. I moved

across to the old Irish trainer and the gypsy jockey. Sir
Arthur was saying nothing, but his hand trembled as he
took a pinch of snuff from his old-fashioned silver horn.
The gypsy jockey stood erect, with his overcoat over his
silk. It was a heart-rending five minutes standing there beside them, waiting for the message that they were not to go.

My uncle Valentine was standing with a couple of the
Stewards. A small race official was explaining something
to them. They nodded him away. There was another
minute's conversation and my uncle came toward us. The
old trainer was fumbling pitifully with his silver snuff horn,
trying to find the pocket in which to put it.

" It's queer," said my uncle Valentine, " but nobody seems
to know where Lady Clontarf is. She's not in her caravan."

" So — " questioned the old trainer.

" So you run," said my uncle Valentine. " The horse
comes under starter's orders. You may have an objection,
Arthur, but you run."

The old man put on youth and grandeur before my eyes.
He stood erect. With an eye like an eagle's he looked
around the paddock.

" Leg up, boy ! " he snapped at Frasco.

" Here, give me your coat." I helped throw the golden-
and-red shirted figure into the saddle. Then the head lad
led the horse out.

We moved down the track and into the stand, and the
parade began. Lord Shire's great horse, and the French
hope Toison d'Or; the brown colt owned by the richest
merchant in the world, and the little horse owned by the
Leicester butcher, who served in his own shop; the horse
owned by the peer of last year's making; and the bay filly
owned by the first baroness in England. They went down
past the stand, and turning breezed off at a gallop back, to
cross the downs toward the starting gate, and as they went
with each went some one's heart. All eyes seemed turned

on the gypsy horse, with his rider erect as a Life Guards-man. As Frasco raised his whip to his cap in the direc-tion of our box, I heard in one of the neighbouring boxes a man say: "But that horse's owner is dead!"

"Is that so, Uncle Valentine?" asked Ann-Dolly. There were tears in her eyes. "Is that true?"

"Nothing is true until you see it yourself," parried my uncle Valentine. And as she seemed to be about to cry openly, — "Don't you see the horse running?" he said. "Don't you know the rule?" But his eyes were riveted through his glasses on the starting gate. I could see deep furrows of anxiety on his bronze brow. In the distance, over the crowd's heads, over the bookmaker's banners, over the tents, we could see the dancing horses at the tape, the gay colours of the riders moving here and there in an in-tricate pattern, the massed hundreds of black figures at the start. Near us, across the rails, some religious zealots let fly little balloons carrying banners reminding us that doom was waiting. Their band broke into a lugubrious hymn, while nasal voices took it up. In the silence of the crowded downs, breathless for the start, the religious demonstration seemed startlingly trivial. The line of horses, formed for the gate, broke, and wheeled. My uncle snapped his fingers in vexation.

"Why can't the fool get them away?"

Then out of a seeming inextricable maze, the line formed suddenly and advanced on the tapes. And the heavy silence exploded into a low roar like growling thunder. Each man shouted: "They're off!" The Derby had started.

It seemed like a river of satin, with iridescent foam, pouring, against all nature, uphill. And for one instant you could distinguish nothing. You looked to see if your horse had got away well, had not been kicked or cut into at the start, and as you were disentangling them, the banks of gorse shut them from your view, and when you saw them again they were racing for the turn of the hill. The erect figure of the jockey caught my eye before his colours did.

"He's lying fifth," I told my uncle Valentine.

"He's running well," my uncle remarked quietly.

They swung around the top of the hill, appearing above the rails and gorse, like something tremendously artificial, like some theatrical illusion, as of a boat going across the stage. There were three horses grouped together, then a black horse — Esterhazy's fine colt — then Romany Baw, then after that a stretching line of horses. Something came out of the pack at the top of the hill, and passed the gypsy horse and the fourth.

"Toison d'Or is going up," Jenico told me.

But the gallant French colt's bolt was flown. He fell back, and now one of the leaders dropped back. And Romany was fourth as they started downhill for Tattenham Corner. "How slow they go!" I thought.

"What a pace!" said Jenico, his watch in his hand.

At Tattenham Corner the butcher's lovely little horse was beaten, and a sort of moan came from the rails where the poor people stood. Above the religious band's outrageous nasal tones, the ring began roaring: "Sir James! Sir James has it. Twenty to one bar Sir James!"

As they came flying up the stretch I could see the favourite going along, like some bird flying low, his jockey hunched like an ape on his withers. Beside him raced an outsider, a French-bred horse owned by Kazoutlian, an Armenian banker. Close to his heels came the gypsy horse on the inside, Frasco sitting as though the horse were standing still. Before him raced the favourite and the rank outsider.

"It's all over," I said. "He can't get through. And he can't pull around. Luck of the game!"

And then the rider on the Armenian's horse tried his last effort. He brought his whip high in the air. My uncle Valentine thundered a great oath.

"Look, Kerry!" His fingers gripped my shoulder.

I knew, when I saw the French horse throw his head up, that he was going to swerve at the whip, but I never expected Frasco's mad rush. He seemed to jump the opening, and land the horse past Sir James.

"The favourite's beat!" went up the cry of dismay.

Romany Baw, with Frasco forward on his neck, passed the winning post first by a clear length.

Then a sort of stunned silence fell on the Derby crowd. Nobody knew what would happen. If, as the rumour went around, the owner was dead, then the second automatically won. All eyes were on the horse as the trainer led him into the paddock, followed by second and third. All eyes turned from the horse toward the notice board as the numbers went up: 17, 1, 26. All folk were waiting for the red objection signal. The owner of the second led his horse in, the burly Yorkshire peer. An old gnarled man, with a face like a walnut, Kazoutlian's self, led in the third.

"I say, Kerry," Jenico called quietly, "something's up near the paddock."

I turned and noticed a milling mob down the course on our right. The mounted policemen set off at a trot toward the commotion. Then cheering went into the air like a peal of bells.

Down the course came all the gypsies, all the gypsies in the world, it seemed to me. Big-striding, black men with gold earrings and coloured neckerchiefs, and staves in their hands. And gypsy women, a-jingle with coins, dancing. Their tambourines jangled, as they danced forward in a strange East Indian rhythm. There was a loud order barked by the police officer, and the men stood by to let them pass. And the stolid English police began cheering too. It seemed to me that even the little trees of the downs were cheering, and in an instant I cheered too.

For back of an escort of mounted gypsies, big foreign

men with moustaches, saddleless on their shaggy mounts, came a gypsy cart with its cover down, drawn by four prancing horses. A wild-looking gypsy man was holding the reins. On the cart, for all to see, seated in a great arm-chair, propped up by cushions, was Lady Clontarf. Her head was laid back on a pillow, and her eyes were closed, as if the strain of appearing had been too much for her. Her little maid was crouched at her feet.

For an instant we saw her, and noticed the aged beauty of her face, noticed the peace like twilight on it. There was an order from a big Roumanian gypsy and the Romany people made a lane. The driver stood up on his perch and manœuvring his long snakelike whip in the air, made it crack like a musket. The horses broke into a gallop, and the gypsy cart went over the turfed course toward Tatten-ham Corner, passed it, and went up the hill and disappeared over the Surrey downs. All the world was cheering.

XII

"Come in here," said my uncle Valentine, and he took me into the cool beauty of our little church of Saint Col-umba's-in-Paganry. "Now what do you think of that?" And he pointed out a brass tablet on the wall.

"In Memory of Mifanwy, Countess of Clontarf and Kin-cora," I read. Then came the dates of her birth and death, "and who is buried after the Romany manner, no man knows where." And then came the strange text, "In death she was not divided."

"But surely," I objected, "the quotation is: ' In death they were not divided.'"

"It may be," said my uncle Valentine, "or it may not be. But as the living of Saint Columba's-in-Paganry is in my gift, surely to God!" he broke out, "a man can have a text the way he wants it in his own Church."

This was arguable, but something more serious caught my eye.

"See, sir," I said, "the date of her death is wrong. She died on the evening of Derby Day, June the second. And here it is given as June the first."

"She did not die on the evening of Derby Day. She died on the First."

"Then," I said, "when she rode down the course on her gypsy cart," and a little chill came over me, "she was —"

"As a herring, Kerry, as a gutted herring," my uncle Valentine said.

"Then the rule was really infringed, and the horse should not have won."

"Wasn't he the best horse there?"

"Undoubtedly, sir, but as to the betting."

"The bookmakers lost less than they would have lost on the favourite."

"But the backers of the favourite."

"The small backer in the silver ring is paid on the first past the post, so they'd have lost, anyway. At any rate, they all should have lost. They backed their opinion as to which was the best horse, and it wasn't."

"But damn it all, sir! and God forgive me for swearing in this holy place — there's the Derby Rule."

"'The letter killeth,' Kerry," quoted my uncle gravely, even piously. "'The letter killeth.'"

EIGHT

TALE OF KERRY

EIGHT

Tale of Kerry

I

There is in Destiny Bay, near the Irish Village, a little graveyard called Dunfandle, that I have never been able to pass without going in for a minute's visit and a cigarette. Our own folk rest in Saint Columba's-in-Paganry, and there, in Saint Columba's, is great peace and dignity. But in Dunfandle is merriment. It is as though the population there had left for the wide spaces in careless adventure, without taking the precautions of urban people: travel tickets, spiritual insurance and baggage, what not. The old church, of Queen Anne's time, is a ruin, and there is no parson to preach there, nor any congregation to preach to, if you except the sleepers, who are past theology. But in Dunfandle church the foolish rook is happy, and the darting swallow. And around the field is a bulwark of white hawthorn, thick as the walls of a walled town. And in spring there is munificence of daffodils and violets and primroses. And in autumn there are no more bursting varnished blackberries than there.

I had turned in to sit on the slate stone that covers what was mortal of Sir Jonathan Bingham and his lady, and to smoke, and to let the universe hum by for some minutes, when I was aware there was another person inside the gates. Never in Dunfandle had I met any but children, blackberrying at Michaelmas or making garlands of posies on May Eve, but there before the grave of Florence O'Grady, the country poet, was the spare erect figure of an old man. His hair was white and his face was weather-beaten and lined. He wore a sort of loose morning coat of black broad-cloth, and across his waistcoat was a heavy gold chain. In his hand was a silk hat, oldish, but good. He might have been a tenement landlord or some old-fashioned small merchant, but for this fact, that instead of a collar and tie he wore a silk handkerchief tied about his throat in what sailors call a square knot. For an instant I asked myself: "Is this some old-time ghost?"

And then I remembered him.

He was Kevin Plunkett, the last living of the old Irish school of poets, or itinerant bards more properly, who was now a sort of exhibit for the enthusiasts of the Erse revival. Englishwomen with money, artistic instincts, and nothing to do kept the old man on visits or dragged him from meeting to meeting of esthetes, where he would recite his verse. A rather sorry ending to a devil-may-care career, but in their old age even poets must eat.

He was standing before his brother-poet's grave, his silk hat in his hand, leaning on his stout blackthorn stick, and his voice came to me heavy with sorrow:

"I remember O'Grady — no lady, or village queen
But wished on a May-day, or play-day, his choice to have been;
To a barrel of liquor, none quicker to run was seen;
Nor at fairs had a stick or club thicker, or brogues more clean;
Like a ha'penny candle, he'd handle his sapling green,
Now, alas! in Dunfandle, a bramble his grave doth screen!"

There was a shake in the old man's voice, and tears in his washed-out blue eyes. So I went up to him.

"I'll have the brambles cleared away, Kevin," I told him. "I'll send a couple of gardeners up this afternoon."

"Ah, is it you, Mister Kerry? It's Sir Garrett now, is n't it—"

"It's Kerry always, in Destiny Bay."

"He was a great man, Sir Valentine!"

I nodded. I did n't want to talk about it.

"That fellow," said old Kevin, "that fellow lying there was a fine poet and a good friend. We walked together from Rome to Hamburg, with a loaf of bread and a flute between us, after fighting against Garibaldi, and getting beaten, and it's many's the muddy road we tramped through and the hard ground we slept on, and the hungry day we saw, but he was never anything but a true friend. And he was a great poet, Mister Kerry."

"I know The Thirty-Two Counties," I said.

"*Nach truagh libh, a chairde.*"

"Sure, that's nothing," said Kevin; "did you ever hear the poem in praise of Mary Hines?"

"I don't think I did," said I.

"You wouldn't," said the old poet; "it's an intricate and mystic piece of work.

> "*Is fear gan cheill a rachfadh a' dreim leis an
> chloidh bheidh ard —*

"Sure 'tis only a man without sense would go jumping against the wall that is high
And a ditch by his side that's no more than the heighth of his hand
The blackberry and the raspberry are the fruit that's easy to pluck,
But my two eyes are on the cluster at the top of the rowan tree."

"What he meant was this, Sir Kerry, that Mary Hines was utterly out of his reach, but that once having her in his heart, the pleasant women he could have were nothing to him. He never married with a woman, though a hundred thought they had him when the drink was in him, but sure the next morning he was gone from them in heart, and maybe in body too. They called him the *Spalpeen Sugach,* the Merry Rover, but there was never a man less merry, and there was reason on him to rove."

"But who was Mary Hines?" I asked.

"Ah, sure you're young, Sir Kerry, or you'd never ask that. Thirty years ago there was never a Hunt Ball in all Ireland was a success if Mary Hines weren't there. They lived near Distiny, in the old house on Flynn's Mountain, that General Kennedy has now for a shooting box."

"I remember," said I, "but vaguely."

"They were an old Irish family, Sir Kerry, so old that no man knows their beginning, and only old men like myself remember their end. They were a great-hearted big-giving people, but luck had a grudge against them. They never picked the winner in a war or a horse race or out of a pack of cards. Only for their courage they'd have vanished centuries before. They'd limp home after each defeat, and sit down for a while, and come out again, smiling and clean and poor and courageous. I mind the grandfather. He was out with the United men. I mind the father and mother. They died within thirty-six hours of each other — it was like in the Bible, Sir Kerry, 'in death they were not divided.' Then there were three of them left, Colin and Patrick and Mary Hines. If you looked at them you'd say there were never three could make finer marriages in the world than those three. Patrick was grave and had great courtesy, and was a dark handsome man, and Colin was merry and favourite and no finer amateur rider ever sat on a horse — didn't he take the Grand National and the Grand Military in the same year! He was a fair fellow with blue eyes. And Mary Hines, sometimes she would be grave, and sometimes she would be merry. She could be so grave and quiet that you got the impression she was a bigger woman than she was, and she could be so merry that you would think she was a smaller one. She was slim and a trifle over nine stone in the saddle. She had an Irish face, Sir Kerry, merry as a child's and all eyes. Her hair was the colour of an old red guinea, and her eyebrows were black, and her eyes were brown. The old doctor at Indian Queen's, him that they used to say could raise the dead, used seriously to send people when they were sick and mournful to look at Mary Hines, or often he'd ask Mary Hines to come and see them. When they'd see Mary Hines they'd feel that God was good, and when a sick man or woman feels that God is good, he's got a grip on himself.

"Now, Sir Kerry," said old Kevin, "wouldn't you say that out of those three would come a family would blind the world?"

I said nothing, for I could feel ill luck in the tale.

"Patrick took to coughing," said the old man, "and he died." If you notice we never mention consumption in Ireland. "Well, it was the will of God! But Colin, that had lifted horses over the highest jumps in the world, let his mount stumble in the hunting field over a ditch a cow would take. When they picked him up he was alive, but he would never move again. A month or so after that by some miracle Colin Hines dragged himself in the early hours of the morning, when every one was asleep, to where his sporting guns were, and put an end to himself. You see, Sir Kerry, Colin loved two things, horses and his sister. He could never ride a horse again, and he knew that while he lived, his sister would never leave him to marry. He was such a clean sportsman, such a big unselfish fellow, that we needn't ask God to be good to him, need we, Sir Kerry?"

"Not the God of Destiny Bay, at any rate," said I.

"Well, Mary Hines felt the same way about it. There was no man in the country but wanted to marry her, but with the cloud of her two brothers' going, there was no thought in her mind of another man's house, and another man's children. It took years for it to lift, brave and all as she was. It made her more beautiful, Sir Kerry. It made her terribly understanding.

"Well, sir, to make a long story short, one summer Mary Hines threw her head up and looked life in the eye, and began to take an interest in events and horses. At the Dublin Horse Show she met an Italian officer, a marquis no less, that fell head over heels in love with her. He saw her at the Viceroy's Court and he saw her in the paddock at the Leopardstown races, and he met her and was polite to her and adoring to her, as Italians are. Don't I know them, Sir Kerry! Didn't I fight with and against them! By damn, but I know those lads.

" This Italian was a penniless rogue and a crooked fellow, for all he was an officer and a marquis. He thought, seeing her surrounded by wealth and power, that she was a rich woman, for he couldn't understand that in Ireland people can be rich in friendship and honour and have hardly a brown penny to put on a horse. If I come out in the open, says he, then the Irish will damned well see to it that I don't marry their darling. So he played cunning, and he persuaded Mary Hines to run off with him and be married to him in Italy. In Italy, when they were drawing up the contracts, he found out she was a poor woman, so he wouldn't marry her at all.

" It was only about six months later Ireland heard of this thing. Not from Mary Hines, but through some of the Irish priests that are always on their way to pay their homage to the Holy Father. Well, Sir Kerry, nobody said a word, but immediately every one began to take an interest in the antiquities of Italy. Old Lord Clanduncan left immedately to visit the Coliseum, and your uncle Valentine went hotfoot off to see Vesuvius, and Sir Mick McCartney got a great longing on him to see Venice, and Colonel Hugh O'Hara, he couldn't wait for his baggage to be packed he was so eager to see the leaning tower of Pisa. There were others too, Sir Kerry, and even a couple of the Destiny Bay gypsies that sharpened their knives to go excavating around Pompeii. They all met in Florence, where this fellow came from. But a fortnight before they arrived there this fellow had been shot over a game of cards. So they were saved dirtying their hands on him. But there was no trace of Mary Hines."

"There was never any word of her since?" said I.

"There was," said old Kevin, "but myself, and the Merry Rover here, that's finished his roving, and your uncle Valentine, God rest him! were the only ones to know. Do you mind Shamus Hogan, the free trade sea captain?"

"The one the Spaniards shot in Cuba for gun-running?"

"The same bold hero! Well, Shamus was in Savannah in America. 'Tis a seaport, Sir Kerry, either in Ohio or Illinois, I disremember which."

"'Tis in neither," I corrected. "'Tis in Florida!"

"Begad, so it is! Well, Shamus was carrying out his craft as sea captain, and exercising his principles of free trade. In fine he was landing a cargo of choice French brandy in Savannah, and he was sitting talking to a fellow on a hotel verandah, when who goes past but the lass herself, in a carriage the king himself hasn't the like of, drawn by two horses Joe Widger of Waterford would give his eyes for. And there were two Negro Black men on the driver's seat. So Shamus lets a shout out of him.

"'Lord God and the blue sky above! It's Miss Mary Hines!'

"She stops the carriage and looks at him. 'Is it Captain Shamus Hogan is in it,' said she, 'from Destiny Bay?'

"'And who else?' said Shamus.

"'Get in beside me,' said she.

"'I can't,' said Shamus. 'I have a matter of diplomacy I can't leave for a minute.' For Shamus at that time was bargaining to pick up a fellow out of a South American country, and the treasury of the country with him.

"'Will you come up and see me?' she said, 'and give me news of Destiny Bay?' And she gives him a piece of stiff paper with her name printed on it, as the quality use. 'You won't fail me, Shamus?' said she.

"But he did fail her. He was going out on the next morning's tide, so he went up that evening. Shamus was a cautious fellow. When he was on business, he never walked a road when he could take the fields, or went into the front door of a house, where there was a side one. So he skirted around the shrubbery, and it happened that he got a look in the dining room. And there was a crowd of gentry, Sir Kerry, and Mary Hines in the mistress' seat, and at the head of the table a fine noble-looking fellow, that would be twenty years older than her, but a stout admirable man. And everywhere were Negro black men as servants.

" So Shamus says to himself: ' Maybe I'd shame her before all her friends,' he said. ' Maybe the American people wouldn't understand,' he thought, ' the queer tie there is between Irish, gentle and simple. I'll go back to my ship,' said he, ' and God bless the ground you walk on, Mary Hines! '

" And that's all we know, Sir Kerry."

" It's queer," said I, " that I never heard of all this."

" The young people forget," said Kevin Plunkett, " and the old folk die, and what they know dies with them, and those that live, Sir Kerry, get kindly and wise with age, and say little of peoples' mistakes."

" But my uncle Valentine," said I, " surely he might have told me, or my aunt Jenepher, or James Carabine."

" I told you, Sir Kerry," said the old poet, " that there were hundreds in the country had a great fancy for Mary Hines, but none had a greater fancy for her than Sir Valentine. So that you would hear nothing about her from him, God rest him! nor your aunt Jenepher, God bless her! And as to your uncle's affairs," said Kevin Plunkett, " you'd more easily get a word out of that stone slab you're sitting on, than out of the mouth of the same James Carabine."

II

I never knew a Dublin Horse Show so gay, and so deserted for me, as in that year of grace Patrick Herne and my aunt Jenepher were cruising in their yacht off Norway and my cousin Jenico and Ann-Dolly were in Switzerland. But what I missed more than anything else was that great red-bearded uncle of mine. It seemed to me strange that there should be a Dublin Horse Show and he not there; and I felt bitter. . . . I showed his beautifully matched bay ponies and took the blue ribbon amidst a volley of hand-clapping. I was lucky myself, Pelican taking first in the heavyweight hunter class, more by his own wise fencing than my riding, so that I should have been happy. But there you are. I had always considered the Dublin Horse Show as a background for my uncle Valentine, rather than the national function it is.

There it rolled on without him, as though he had never been. The Viceroy and the Vicereine attended in state. Thither came the prettiest women in Ireland. Thither came the ugliest, though undoubtedly the best-hearted women in the world, the hard bitten hunting women. Thither came the riffraff of the racing world, looking like Guards' officers out of a book of Ouida. Thither came dragoon officers from the Curragh of Kildare, looking like farmers. Thither came Irish peers poorer than their smallest tenant. Thither came Irish farmers with greasy rolls of banknotes that would have made the peers drop dead with envy. Thither came remount officers of European nations to buy horses for cavalry — very stolid Germans, beautifully uniformed Italians, keen Belgians, and the French, sad-looking, a little sloppy, but beautiful horsemen, and excellent judges of cattle. Thither came the winsome *corps de ballet*, which George Edwardes, the impresario, had imported into Dublin for our delectation during Horse Show Week. Thither came a handful of pretty ladies from Deauville and Trouville, though what for, God knoweth! Never was there keener racing at Leopardstown. Never was a lovelier, a more flaming August, and the hills that hover over Dublin, the Sugar Loaves and Three Rock Mountains, and the Scalp, were so blue, light as clouds. And my uncle Valentine was not there!

I was going across to the cattle exhibit to buy a beautiful Friesian bull I could nowise afford, for it is wisdom when you are weighed down with an abstract desolation to get something large and concrete to worry about, when I was stopped by three people. There was a venerable looking kindly old man whose nationality I could not fix, a girl or young woman whom I would have sworn to be Irish, and a large, evil-looking, gentlemanly foreigner who was either Spanish or Italian.

"I beg your pardon," said the old gentleman, with a peculiar soft slurring accent I had never heard before, " but is your name not MacFarlane? And do you not come from Destiny Bay?"

"My name is Garrett MacFarlane, usually called Kerry MacFarlane, and I come from Destiny Bay."

"Are you any relation to Sir Valentine MacFarlane?"

"Sir Valentine was my uncle."

"Was?" the old gentleman asked.

I nodded.

"I am very sorry," he said. "I had been looking forward to meeting your uncle, but that," he continued, "will have to be put off for a little while."

I looked at the old gentleman with a little curiosity. We of the North are abrupt to rudeness, and believe it, God help us! to be a virtue. My uncle Valentine had a vast and terrible courtesy, but he used that as a weapon and an armour. This old gentleman's courtesy came from his heart.

"My name is Sheridan," the old gentleman told me; "generations back I am Irish too, and not unproud of it, but I have a closer tie, young sir, with your country, than my name or ancestry, and with your own part of the country, also, for my dear wife," and the old gentleman's voice shook, "came from Destiny Bay. Her name was Mary Hines."

Apart from the surprise of that, I was surprised at two other things. The young girl was looking at me in a white-faced, strained way. And the foreign, evil-looking gentleman, either Italian or Spanish, had his eyes levelled at me, as I have seen big gamblers watch one another, when the stakes were great and the game critical — granite-like features, all the life fled into the eyes.

"Sir," I told him, "it was my misfortune to have been too young to have ever seen Mary Hines, but in Destiny Bay her name is fragrant for beauty and gallant courage. My uncle Valentine, who should have welcomed you, is gone, and I am now the Master of Destiny Bay." I shook hands with him. "*Faltha!*" said I, giving him the Irish word of welcome.

The old gentleman said nothing, but I think he was moved. "This is my daughter, Allegra," he said, "the daughter of Mary Hines. Allie," said he, "this is one of your dear mother's countrymen."

She gave me a nervous hand, and said nervously, "I have heard so much from my mother of Destiny Bay and the men of Destiny Bay."

"And this," went on the old gentleman, "is the Principe di Monterosso, who is to be married to my daughter Allegra at Christmas. And now," said he, "shall we go somewhere and talk about Destiny Bay?"

"If you'll give me a minute, sir —" for I had to go and leave some instructions about the horses. I was coming back from the stalls when I ran into Mooney, the crack jaunting-car driver of Dublin, flushed with wine, so to speak, and the triumph of having won the Jarvies' Marathon.

"Does your Honour know," asked Mooney, "who that old one is?"

" He 's a Mister Sheridan," said I.

" He 's a Colonel Sheridan," said Mooney triumphantly. " Can your Honour keep a secret ? " he asked me.

" I 'll try," I told him.

" That one owns cotton fields in the South of America. Cotton fields ! " impressed Mooney.

" Well, let him."

" Here 's the point of it, your Honour. Did you ever hear of John D. Rockefeller ? "

" Never," I admitted.

" Well," said Mooney wearily, " he 's one of the richest men in the world, and that one is richer than him. Here, I 'll make it plain to your Honour. That one is richer than Martin Murphy of Rathmines."

III

They had asked me to dine with them that night at their hotel, and first because I had nothing else to do, and secondly because I felt it was my duty, and thirdly because I very much wanted to, I went. I walked up from the club through the soft peace of Dublin that is like a dream, some youth's or girl's soft dream, and turned in to Stephen's Green. In August, in our Ireland, there is light until nearly ten. And in the Green, the birds were a-twitter, and a sea gull floated overhead like a blown feather, and the mountains were drawing themselves off, to sleep. I turned and watched before going into the hotel, and I felt a hand on my arm, and heard a voice.

" Sir Garrett, my father and Ercole will not be down for twenty minutes yet. Will you bring me into and show me Saint Stephen's Green ? "

" To be sure I will."

Her face was not white and strained now, but calm, and there was an air of confidence and friendship about her.

Perhaps the bare head and soft frock and Spanish shawl had a little to do with it, for a woman with her hat on is something like a helmeted Crusader. We crossed the street and entered the soft alleys of the Green.

"Well," said I, "this is Stephen's Green. Those are the Dublin Mountains. Over there is the house that Buck Whaley owned and lived in, the lad that bet ten thousand pounds he would play handball against the walls of Solomon's temple and did it. Over there is the famous execution place, the Irish Tyburn. But sure you know all that," said I, " for I believe that the main topic of conversation in America is the beauties and sorrows of Ireland."

She said nothing, so we walked on to the stone bridge that spans the little lake, and watched the drakes, gaudy as kingfishers, guide their complement of wives homeward to the sedge, and a swan, stately as a galleon of Old Spain, move through the lake and the twilight, as Dido, Queen of Carthage, must have moved, in white grace and majesty.

"I wouldn't look at it too long," I said. "Dublin is a bad place for people from foreign parts. They go Irish all of a sudden and shout for a green flag and a pike, and go out on the hills to fight the British Army, and if the British Army won't fight they want to fight the rest of Ireland, so — "

But she wasn't listening to me. She turned around suddenly and there was decision on her face.

"Sir Garrett," she said, "first I want to tell you something about my mother, Mary Hines, and then to ask you a question, and then to ask you to do something for me."

"Very well," said I.

"My mother," she told me, "was more to me than a mother, she was a goddess. And I was more to her than a child; I was her friend, her true and loyal friend."

"I think I understand."

"Everything of her life, of her brothers, of Destiny Bay

she told me. My father, Colonel Sheridan, was very much in love with her, and is more so now that she is dead. I am not saying it because I am his daughter, for I am more the daughter of Mary Hines than of him, but no kindlier, nobler gentleman walks the earth. Because he is kindly and so noble, my mother kept part of her life from him, lest he should be hurt. Do you understand me, Sir Garrett?"

"Are you speaking of Italy?" I asked; "and a marriage that did n't take place?"

"Yes," she said bravely. "I am speaking of that. One day when he is dead, and past hurting, Mary Hines will tell, and all will be well. But I am terrified of his hearing now. It would kill him, Sir Garrett, and embitter his last days."

"Then he sha'n't hear in Ireland," said I. "Does any but you know?"

"None," she said hesitatingly, "who will ever tell him. Sir Garrett—"

Said I: "If your mother were alive, or your uncles Colin and Patrick, I would be Kerry to them, as I am to all kith of Destiny Bay. And you are Irish, though born away from us, and we of Destiny Bay claim you."

"Thank you, Kerry," she said without embarrassment. "Now, another thing. I don't want my father to go to Destiny Bay. I am afraid of Destiny Bay."

"Sure, in God's name," said I, "there's nobody in Destiny Bay would ever say a word."

"Still I am afraid of Destiny Bay."

"Then he sha'n't go to Destiny Bay," I promised her.

We went back to the hotel through the twilight, and she took my arm, and I felt somehow we were like two friends who had met after a long space of years, to each of whom God had been kind, so that each had a good story to tell, and each was glad for the other. And I felt that Dublin, that can be so sweet, so benign, in the summer twilight, was glad too.

At dinner, the old Colonel was charming, and from Allegra as I must call her, all the nervousness, all the tension had gone, and she was so merry, so quietly merry, that it was as though birds were singing. But the heavy, saturnine Italian glowered at me. His Latin courtesy made me feel a boor, as perhaps I am, but it was conveyed to me that the chap didn't like me. When Allegra called me Kerry, he gave me a glance that told me: "I'll see you later." And I said under my breath in my courteous Irish way: "Any time you like, you fat foreign slob!"

The old gentleman broached the subject of Destiny Bay. It had been the dream of his life to go there, "but my daughter is against it, Kerry, if I may call you so, and so is Ercole here."

"I'm afraid your daughter's right, sir. It's a lonely savage country," said I, "and what with Rapparees and Fenians, and the rainy season just now and the potato famine, I'd rather you didn't myself. I'd hate to see you disillusioned, sir, I would indeed."

Well, God forgive me! There hasn't been a Rapparee in Ireland since 1641 or thereabouts, or a Fenian since sixty years, and as for famine and wet seasons, ah! the purple cloak of heather around Destiny Bay and the yellow sunshine, and the green sea. But Allie had said he wasn't to go to Destiny Bay, and he wasn't going. The Italian, who had been watching me out of his gambler's eyes, seemed relieved.

"Poor Ireland!" said the Colonel. "When will her troubles ever cease?"

"Ah, sure, God knows!" said I, with a great show of emotion. "But I'll be in Dublin all the time you are here, sir, and anything I can do to show you around—"

"I should like," said the Colonel, "to see an Irish race meeting, Kerry, for I have heard so much of it and we Southerns love horses and the racing of horses."

"There's a meeting at Leopardstown to-morrow, and I'm glad I'm going with you. For though the Irish nation is the most honest in the world, and Irish racing the straightest, yet hay and feed bills and trainers' fees have to be paid, and sometimes a horse doesn't run for the benefit of the public. Yes," I thought, "I'd better be along."

Going home that night to my rooms in the club, I was not lonely any more.

IV

It was the next day at Leopardstown that Ercole and I had our first little encounter. I had introduced them all to everybody I knew, but an Italian prince, worthy fellow though he be, is not quite the Emperor Charlemagne around Dublin. When an Italian prince, duke, marquis, baron, or count marries, all his male childern are dukes, marquises, princes, barons and counts, and the female children, or girls, bear the feminine counterpart of these titles, so we believe in Ireland. Also, from superficial observation, Italian families are numerically magnificent. So that one wonders how ordinary citizens are raised in Italy. Are they bribed to be citizens? This is a mystery.

Ercole was not a mad success and was chagrined at it. He somehow connected me with the lack of cheering. So that when he went to the paddock to look at the runners for the three-thirty, and he picked a beauty of a two-year-old as winner, and I told him honestly that the weedy-looking filly, Silver Chime (by Nugget out of Bells of Shandon) would walk the five furlongs, he grew offensive.

"I will bet you," he said, "a thousand pounds level that the horse I picked will beat the filly."

"But sure that's ridiculous," I told him. "I know these horses. You don't. If you want to bet that much you can get three to one against from the bookmakers."

"I don't want to bet with bookmakers; I want to bet with you."

By this time a few people had gathered who were looking at the Italian in that detached way you look at a man who's making a nuisance of himself. The old Colonel was frowning, and Allie looked red and uncomfortable.

I said: "In the first place I don't want your money and in the second I don't bet as high as that —"

"Aha," he laughed, "I thought so —"

"But," said I, "seeing as you're asking for it, I'll take you. A thousand pounds level that Silver Chimes beats Chimney Sweep, one of them to win the race or no bet."

I walked over to the rails, thinking a bit, for to my mind, who knew the horses, there was only one horse in the race. Still and all, no bet is a good bet till well hedged. I singled out Micky Swain.

"What price Chimney Sweep?" I asked him.

"Threes to you, Sir Garrett."

"Will you lay three monkeys to one?" I asked him. A monkey is the old Anglo-Saxon word for five hundred pounds.

"Go away, Sir Garrett, you're drunk. And so early in the day, too!"

"I mean it," said I.

"Well," said Micky. "I'll lay it. A fool and his money —"

"'Tisn't my money," I said.

"Aw, begob!" said Micky Swain, "why did I doubt you, heart o' corn!"

Chimney Sweep ran a good race, I'll say that for him. The filly beat him only by a length and a half. With a great flourish the Italian paid me ten crinkling one-hundred-pound notes.

"Sir Garrett," he said, "you are a sportsman and a gambler. A thousand pounds loss would have meant a lot to you, while to me — "

I put his money away safely. "Barring an earthquake or the Last Day, I stood to gain five hundred pounds whichever won," I told him and explained to him about the hedging. And Allie and her father laughed. Ercole got red as a cut beet.

"So!" he said quietly. And "So!" he said a second time. And he repeated "So!" And from the way he said it I could see that he and I were not going to be pals at all. Not anyhow.

They stayed in Dublin a week before going on to Paris, and I did all I could to show the daughter of Mary Hines all of Ireland she could see there. Myself, I am a Northern man. The blue hills of Derry and the little town of Derry and the islands of the north mean more to me than did the rivers of Damascus to antique Naaman, but our crowning city of the North — fair and famed Belfast, well, I have never known anybody die of homesickness for Ballymac-arett or Donegall Place. There is a touching memorial to Prince Albert, spouse and consort of Queen Victoria, in Belfast, but outside that, God forgive me, I can remember nothing of interest. And oh, yes, we have trams.

But there is something about Dublin, whether you are Northern or Southern or foreigner, that pulls at your heart. There is no stone of Dublin that is not hallowed by tra-dition. The surly, the savage Castle; the ancient college of the Holy Trinity; the stout bank that was once the Par-liament House where Grattan thundered. Green Street, where men were tried and hanged for treason — patriots or traitors, have it as you will, but they fought, they died, and now God rest them! And there are pikes in hidden rooms, and smoke and blood-stained green banners, standards that shake your loyalty to the core, and every fifty years or so, folk wake from the sleep of prosperity into a day of violence, and there is shooting then and tragedy, and once more they fall asleep, and the pikes and standards are hidden. But that they will see the light again is certain. Nothing is more certain than that they will see the light again.

I showed Allie and her father and Ercole, Dublin as I know it, the peaceful Liffey, the canals that come from the Shannon, bearing on their bosoms the barges laden with peat, the sites of the little rivers of Dublin city that rustle under the ground toward their mother. Three Rock Mountain of the Hell Fire Club. And Allie dreamed, and her father stood and looked with his hat off his dear old cardinal's head, and Ercole was most magnificent, in varnished pointed boots, and a vast Malacca cane, and most violent yellow gloves. All the day there was sunshine, and at night the August moon put out a veil of magic on the dreaming land. Not only I, but Ireland, was welcoming the daughter and the husband of Mary Hines.

I introduced them to such people as were in Dublin at the time, and I presented James Carabine. Allegra went to him at once, and put out her hand, and he enveloped her small hand in that great bear's paw of his.

"I have heard of you, James Carabine, from my mother, Mary Hines. The greatest Irish fighter of his time," she told Ercole. "My mother spoke so often of you, James Carabine. You were one of the heroes of her youth."

"She was one of my princesses, and I in my prime," said James Carabine.

He spoke to Colonel Sheridan of his brothers-in-law — Patrick Hines, in whom my people saw the makings of a great statesman, and of Colin, in whom horses had such confidence that when he was on their backs they feared no jump, stone wall, water or Irish bank. I don't think Ercole liked being introduced to a valet, but he manfully put out his hand. Carabine forestalled him by bowing. If Ercole didn't like Carabine, Carabine wasted no love on Ercole.

I really think Ercole tried to be decent that week, in spite
of our little incident on the race course, but it wasn't quite
in his temperament to be reserved and quiet. He took me
by the arm and walked me into Stephen's Green at the heel
of an afternoon we had all spent at Lucan.

"I don't know if you quite understand, MacFarlane," he
purred, "but Miss Sheridan and I are to be married."

"So I heard," said I. "You are a very lucky man."

"Yes, yes, indeed," he said, "but I am very old-fashioned. I do not think it quite correct that a stranger should
take up so much of her interest and time."

"I am not a stranger," I told him. "I am Irish and she
is Irish too. And I am only doing what any other Irishman would do for the daughter of Mary Hines, — showing
her her mother's country."

"Quite, quite!" said Ercole; "but I am old-fashioned,
as I said. I think for any young girl the man she is to
marry is of more interest than any country." And out of
his fat malevolent face he gave me a look of hatred.

I said: "If you wish to quarrel with me, which I rather
think you do, let us leave the lady's name out of it, and
quarrel about the relative merits of Irish and Italian scenery.
On that score I can promise you an interesting quarrel."

"But I shouldn't dream of quarreling with you," said
Ercole. And he added: "In Ireland."

Now in those two words there was the making of a most
splendid row, if he meant what I thought he meant. He
watched me with his malevolent eyes, waiting for my next
move or word. But the old Colonel came out and joined
us and we became as turtle doves or gambolling lambs —
the sort of lambs that gambol with dignity.

But that week came to an end, as all time sooner or later
does, and they went away, as all people sooner or later do.
The Irish mail sped over the Irish sea and when I returned
to Dublin, I noticed that something had gone wrong with

it, for the houses were only old grey houses, and the blue beckoning mountains were only mountains after all, and the moon — well, sure, the moon shines everywhere. I said to Carabine: "Pack up, James Carabine; we leave for Derry on the midnight train."

"I have everything of your Honour's packed," said Carabine, "for I thought that in the end your Honour would sicken of this town."

We bowled along through O'Connell Street in the soft night, and Carabine leaned across from his side of the jaunting car.

"'Tis a great pity," he said, "that the Big Man," and he meant my uncle Valentine, "didn't wait awhile before going to his rest."

"How so?"

"He'd never have let that wee one out of the country," said Carabine. "We'd have had a woman of the house in Destiny Bay."

"Are you daft, James Carabine?" I asked. "Sure my uncle Valentine was never the man to be marrying in his winter a girl in her May."

"Sure, Sir Valentine wasn't the only man in the house," insinuated James Carabine. And I was glad of the dusk of the night that was in it, for I felt my face flame.

"You're forgetting," said I, "the Italian Prince she's engaged to."

"Devil a forget," said James Carabine. "Sure to the Big Man that fellow would be no more than a fly left over into winter and it buzzing on the window pane."

V

Summer and autumn we worked at the harvest in Destiny Bay. Flax pulled and stooked, and the swish of the scythes going through golden corn and barley. The turf cutters laid their rectangular peats out for drying on the hillside, so that they would burn with their fierce red flame against the winter. And I thought to myself : If Allie were here, how much she would enjoy, would understand all this. The golden corn, the dark peat, the song of the sky-lark, the hiss of the catgut through the drowsy summer air to tempt the trout at the bottom of the Grey River. The purple heather and the hare in it, and the small field mouse sitting on its haunches in the hedgerows, and regarding the vast world with its small shiny eye, and the whistling of the otter in the night time, and the repose of wise dogs. All this would be kin to her. But Italy, the vine with its grapes, the silver olive, and the purple fig, they were things to wonder at, not to feed one with. All the nightingales of Italy would not bring to her ears, I knew, I felt, the melody of the larks and blackbirds of Destiny Bay.

I used to wander by the river fishing and try to remember her face, and what there was about her gave her such grace and charm. Her black hair and the shape of her head were beautiful and so were her grey eyes. She was not hand-some and she was not pretty. But from inside there burned a goodness and a flame that made her beautiful. Helen of Troy, I am convinced, was neither pretty nor handsome. Neither is Artemis, who comes with the dusk. But all loved women, all greatly loved women, derive their beauty from their inner fire. Venuses are for the middle classes, who say, when they have eaten their midday Sunday dinner : " Now we will investigate beauty."

You might see her anywhere in any capital city and say : " Here is a young woman, a beautiful woman " and pay her the tribute of a smile. But to see herself, the inmost her, you would have to see as I remembered her in my mind, listening to some ballad singer striving to put his native feeling in an alien tongue and rhythm, and achieving the most grotesque of results:

"I will now declare my fancy for pretty Rose O'Shiel.
  Oh, her eyes are like the violets and her carriage is genteel—"

Or to some blind piper, who had wandered into Dublin
out of Galway or Clare, and was sitting in an archway
playing his beautiful elbow pipes, "Hunting the Fox,"
until you could hear the song of the pack and the rhythm
of the galloping hunt, until you forgot you were in Dublin
streets and thought you were in the saddle going hard for
a stone wall— Steady, girl, steady! Hup! Ah, sweetly
taken!—and then swinging into the magic of a reel, "The
Birds among the Trees" or "The Swallow-Tail Coat." And
to see Allie's small troubled feet was a joy, and her embarrassed shy smile. And then she would go up to the
piper and hand him his handsel. Not the largeness of the
gift but the intuition that blindness and music breed in a
man made the old piper cry out: "*Ah, cree beg gaelagh!*
Little Irish heart!"

And to see her at Leopardstown, when the silken horses
and the silk-jacketed jockeys crept, as in the distance they
seem to creep, up the five-furlong course to the post. Her
eyes flashing, the colour in her cheeks, her clasped hands.
Ah, Irish as the Irish moss, as the Irish heather.

I said to myself: "There must be more in this fellow
Ercole than I see." And I said again: "This is finished
and done with. You will now mind your own damned
business, Kerry!"

November of the cub hunting came, and for the first time
in my life I professed secretly a treason it would in Ireland
be death to own openly. I said: "As far as I'm concerned
the fox can sit on his hunkers outside the hall door. I'm
sick of amusing the beggar by hunting him." But you
can understand I kept that to myself.

The truth is, I suppose, I was lonely. I was lonely for
the silent companionship of my cousin Jenico; for the merry
ways of Ann-Dolly, his wife; for the quiet wisdom, the

wisdom deep and quiet as a deep river, of Patrick Herne, my aunt Jenepher's husband, and for my aunt Jenepher, who is so beautiful that we all worship her, myself most of all. So when I got a letter from Patrick Herne, saying their yacht was at Cannes and would stay there over the New Year, and that Jenico and Ann-Dolly were coming up from Madrid to be with them, I called for Carabine.

"By God! James Carabine," I told him, "I eat no Christmas dinner by my lee lone. You'd better pack up. We're for foreign parts."

"Do we hit the hard road, your Honour, or do we loll at our ease?"

"We loll at our ease," said I. "We go to Cannes, in the nation of France."

VI

This Cannes, if you do know it, is a place that carries no conviction with it. There is the blue Mediterranean at your feet; there are the Maritime Alps behind you, more hills than mountains. There are two islands, on one of which the Mysterious Man in the Iron Mask sojourned for seventeen years. There are the cork forests of the Esterel, behind which the sun sets. But this small town, these hills, this sea seem more like a stage setting than a part of the habitable globe. You are never sure that a robust tenor will not trot down to the foreshore, followed by a bevy of village maidens, and burst into "Pretty, pretty Provencale!" or the like. And the setting of the sun is like an effect in a melodrama, very vulgar to our Northern eyes.

But on board Patrick Herne's yacht there were peace and beauty. There was my aunt Jenepher, more lovely than ever; behind her James Carabine who had seemingly deserted me for her; Patrick Herne, bronzed and wise. Jenico, poring over maps of the Yemen, which he was set on exploring, and Ann-Dolly, smoking furiously and studying form for the jumping season, so utterly Irish had that young woman become. In the daytime we drove about to Nice, to Monte Carlo, to Grasse, to Vence, and then came back on board ship and played bridge with my aunt Jenepher. My aunt Jenepher's bridge cards are things of beauty, with their raised surfaces which she touches with her finger tips. Playing with my aunt Jenepher as partner is like having money left to you in a will.

But at night this town of Cannes undergoes a strange transformation. It is no longer a sleepy stage setting, but a spot of real and tense drama. The Casino opens its doors and in the baccarat rooms the real gamblers, those who consider roulette a childish game, sit down to cut one another's throats. The *chemin-de-fer* box slides around the table, and you have always nines and eights which makes a lot of enemies for you, or there are nines and eights against you, which makes you feel like climbing the hillside and singing sad songs.

I had a great deal of luck that second night. Six naturals in a row. And I was very successfully making a large Bulgarian, with a greasy black beard and huge emerald rings, lose his temper and year's income. The other players at the table loved me and I could read in the benevolent croupier's eye: "If it pleases God to grant me male issue, let him resemble this gallant Irish gentleman!" I was about to deal for the seventh time when I felt a soft hand on my shoulder. In all the world I would know that hand.

And then I heard her soft voice: "Is it you, Kerry?"

"Myself, Kerry." And I stood up and faced her.

I forgot the indignant Bulgarian and the astounded croupier. I let them clamour while I looked at Allegra. I consented calmly to the passing of the bank, and cared nothing for the croupier's lost illusions. I gathered up my

winnings in two pockets and went off with her, while the
Bulgarian said bitter things in his native tongue, which I
am certain voiced his belief that I was born out of wedlock
but which moved me not. We went out to the balcony of
the Casino, into the soft Mediterranean night. And Allegra turned to me. She was as strained, as nervous, as the
first time I had seen her.

"Why are you here, Kerry? Of all the places in the
world, why are you here?"

"I'm here," said I, "because my aunt Jenepher's here,
and Patrick Herne, and my cousin Jenico, and his wife
Ann-Dolly. That's why."

"Oh," she said. And was silent for a little space. "And
where have you been since August? Have you been at
home? Tell me about home — about Destiny Bay."

"Do you call it home too, Allie?" I asked. "Sure, that's
funny. I always think of it as your home." And I told
her all about the blue hills of Destiny, the golden harvest
and the drowsy river, and of how I'd thought about her enjoying this and that there. "Sure, one day you must see
it," and the word slipped out of my mouth, "*mochree*."

"What does *mochree* mean, Kerry?"

"'Tis just a word used among friends in Ireland," I
said. "It is, in English, 'my heart.'"

"Don't, please, Kerry."

There was an awkward little silence, and then I asked
her, "How's your father, and how's dear old Ercole?"

"My father is not well, Kerry. He is as you remember
him, gentle and fine and uncomplaining, but there is little
strength in him. To-morrow you will see him. As for
Ercole, he is at home here. In the afternoons he goes to
Monte. At night he plays baccarat. You might have seen
him at the big gambling table with the Greeks. We are
to be married after Christmas, Kerry."

I didn't know very well what to say to that, so there

was another awkward pause and before it was ended, a striking-looking subtle foreign woman had borne down on us. Allegra presented me and informed me the lady was by way of a chaperon to her, and a relative of Ercole's. I could see the evening ended there and then.

"Will you and your father lunch with us to-morrow, Allie," I asked, "and Ercole too? My aunt Jenepher will call at your hotel in the morning."

"My father and I would love to," she said, "but, Kerry, Ercole has a sort of prejudice against Ireland and Irish folk, so I shouldn't ask him. So — good night, Kerry," she said.

"Good night, Allie. Good night, *Marchesa*," I bowed. And I was alone on the terrace.

I knew I would be foolish to go back and pick up the luck where I had left it. Luck resents your turning your back on her, even for the daughter of Mary Hines. Jenico and Ann-Dolly were dancing in the Casino, but I didn't feel like breaking in on their merriment. I went down to the quay and blew the whistle for the yacht's pinnace. When I came on board my aunt Jenepher was seated at her piano.

"Well, Kerry?" she said, playing on.

"Where is Pat?" I asked.

"I chased him ashore," she said. "I sent him to dance with Ann-Dolly, but he's probably sitting in a corner philosophizing."

"Aunt Jenepher, will you do something for me?"

"We'll go out on deck, Kerry, and you'll tell me about it."

We went out on deck and sat under the stars.

"When I was at the Dublin Horse Show I met two of our own people," said I, and I went on and told her about the Colonel and Allie. I told her all I could remember about Allie.

"I remember Mary Hines, Kerry," my aunt Jenepher said. "I remember her hand, before Patrick and Colin died. The life that came from it then was a merry singing life. And when they died I held her again and the life in her was sleeping. And later, before she disappeared from us, out of her finger tips came a gallant courage. There was nothing but goodness and beauty in Mary Hines."

"You'll like her daughter," I said.

"Do you like her, Kerry?"

"Aye," I took refuge in Ulster speech. "I like her fine."

"Kerry," said my aunt Jenepher, "I often blame myself for being a dissatisfied woman, me, who have so much in life —" oh, my dear aunt Jenepher! —"Pat and you, and all there is in the world. But, Kerry," she said softly, "in Pat's house the nursery is empty and I fear will always be empty, so if I'm to take an interest in children, Kerry — Kerry, you don't mind my speaking, do you?"

"No, my dear."

"Well, Kerry, I'm afraid. You're the last MacFarlane outside Cozzie the Bish —" that is my uncle Cosimo, the Right Reverend the Bishop of Borneo —"and he'll never marry. Kerry, I distrust men whose interest is in horses. There's something about the beauty of a horse that comes between their eyes and the beauty of women, so that they grow into bachelors, like Valentine. Do you understand me, Kerry?"

"I do," said I, and I rose and walked to the rail, "and as soon as I return to Dublin, I'll begin having a look around. I'm very sorry, Aunt Jenepher, for having been so stupid, but I forgot to tell you that the Sheridans have Allie's fiancé with them. I don't think he likes Irish folk, but I think you'd better invite him to lunch too. Do you mind?"

My aunt Jenepher said nothing for an instant, and then she rose. "Indeed I will, Kerry," she agreed. "Now don't let's be serious any more. Let's have Carabine make tea for us, and I'll play you the reels and hornpipes you love —'The Green Fields of America' and 'The Little Stook of Barley' and 'The Birds Among the Trees.'"

VII

We had all risen from the luncheon table. "I don't know what the rest of you are doing," I said, "but there's a golf links at Mandelieu, and I'm off for a feast of agricultural clouting."

"Who's playing with you, Kerry?" Allegra asked.

"Nobody," I said. "I'm just going to spy out the lie of the land. I expect to make a few million francs out of the natives at this game."

"May I come with you, Kerry?" Allegra asked.

"If you come alone," I agreed, "and don't give away stable secrets, and don't ask me to look at the pretty little birdie while I'm driving, you may."

Given the sporting-minded and somewhat weak-minded native, the place was going to be a gold mine. It was made for the Irish school of golf, whose only canon is: Keep your hands low and hit like hell! It was not pretty now, as it would be in a month when the groves of mimosa would be like vast golden gongs. There was a swift river over which we had to be rowed. And always in your ears was the soft chiming of the Mediterranean, correcting your timing as you swung the club. In the hills were the little towns of Provence: Grasse, like a bird's nest on the mountain side, and the others whose names I have forgotten or perhaps never knew. The golf links of Mandelieu are like golf links set in a king's park.

"Are there golf links in Ireland, Kerry?" Allegra asked.

"Good God! Woman!" I dropped the pitcher I was taking out of the bag. "Have you never heard of Portrush and Portmarnock and Newcastle, County Down? Is there anything in the world we lack in Ireland?"

And I was off like one of those fellows who put puffs in the journals for *prime donne,* talking of Irish golf and Irish football; Irish hunting of the fox and coursing of the hare; and the superiority above all other dogs of the blue Irish terrier in drawing the badger "in native den." I spoke of the esoteric conclaves in which cockfights were held, and of my own most excellent fowl, Destiny Bay King Billy, victor of mains innumerable. Yea, I spoke exceedingly.

And she said: "Kerry, a year after I am married, do you think I could come to Ireland, and perhaps buy back our old house?"

"I doubt it frankly, Allie. If you don't mind my telling you, Ercole is undoubtedly the Derby winner in Italy and on the Riviera, but in Ireland, *asthore,* he wouldn't get backing in a selling race. Not that we have anything against him. But—well, he isn't a pal, dear old Ercole."

"But I wouldn't have Ercole with me."

"I don't understand, Allie. Aren't you going to marry Ercole?"

"Yes, but, Kerry, marriages on the continent and marriages in Ireland are very different. I know that within a year, Ercole will be glad to get rid of me. He will be very polite, and kiss my hand when we meet, but—"

"Look here, Allie," I asked, "why are you marrying Ercole?"

"Ercole, Kerry, is very much in love with me."

"Is that a reason, Allie?" I questioned her. And I know I was white and my voice shook. "Amn't—aren't others in love with you as well as Ercole? Allie, what is your reason? Surely it isn't to become Principessa di Monterosso! You are a woman of Destiny Bay, and your father is a gentleman. It isn't that?"

"I have given my word, Kerry." And she was white as I was, and her voice shook as much as mine.

"But why did you give your word?" I insisted with cold brutality.

"Oh, Kerry," she said, "I should n't tell but I've got to make myself right with you. If I tell you," she pleaded piteously, "will you promise that you will not quarrel with Ercole?"

I thought for a minute. "Very well, tell me."

"Kerry, do you believe in God?"

"I do," I said.

"Swear by God that you will not quarrel with Ercole!"

I never thought any one could be so earnest, so agonised. So I bowed.

"Well," she told me, "I promised to marry him because—because of what he knows about my mother, and because my father is an old, dreaming man; do you see, Kerry?"

I must have gone mad for a minute on the fairway of the pretty golf links, walking around in circles and cursing dreadfully in English and Irish, and pleading with God to strike Ercole dead, demanding it of Him, being insane.

"But this is impossible," I said. "How could he know?"

"His family are friends of the family of Salamone Regale, whom my mother was going to marry. He was in Washington at the Embassy for a while, Kerry, and there he met my father, and my father—you know, Kerry, how he is always talking of Mary Hines—" she buried her face in her hands.

"Ercole is very poor," she said, "and Continentals have a different code of honour from ours. They are meticulous about details we think nothing of, and in other things, well— At first he was only after money, Kerry, but then later, he got to caring for me. He never said a word,

Kerry, but I could see in his eye that he was desperate. He saw I knew, and he saw that I knew he knew, Kerry. And when he asked me to marry him, I said yes."

We walked back to the golf house and got into the car.

"Kerry," she said. "Don't be so tragic. Surely I have less to go through than my mother had."

"But, Allie," said I, "surely there is a way out of this. May I tell my aunt Jenepher, who understands everything, and Patrick Herne, who is so very wise—"

"Kerry, you may n't!" she said decisively.

"Listen, Kerry," she asked anxiously, "you will not forget your oath not to quarrel with Ercole?"

"No," said I bitterly, "I won't forget that."

"And, Kerry," she asked, "promise me this: though I get married, you will not take your friendship from me— No, listen, Kerry. I have nobody but my father and he is an old man. The girls I was at school with are married and scattered. And all my life, from my mother's stories, I have been hearing of home, of Destiny Bay. You have made it real, Kerry, the rock whence I am hewn. It is something to cling to. Don't take it away. Please, Kerry, remain my friend."

"Allie," I told her, "not only myself, but all the folk of Destiny Bay, and—this is a certain thing—all the men of Ireland are your friends for ever."

"Thanks, Kerry," she said, and went quickly, before there could be another word between us.

I wandered through the town of Cannes, wondering what to do—whether it wouldn't be a good idea to catch the next train, and go—oh, anywhere. I sat down at a table of a café on the shore and was hailed loudly, Irishly. And there bore down on me the red face and fifteen stone of Tom Chevenix-Boyd.

He is great in the annals of archæology, is Tom, for drawing, as he puts it in the native sporting phrase, "the Egyptian

king in native den." He is known in Ireland as the man
with the copper intestines. His hobby is the consumption
of alcohol. He arrives on the Riviera from Ireland on his
way to Egypt, and from Egypt on his way to Ireland and
the open season for wine of the country is officially begun.
At every town from Mentone to Marseilles his arrival is
heralded by a telegram, and in the hotel lobby the head
waiter stands with a brandy and soda and the band plays
" The Wearing of the Green " as a French band will play it,
with gusto — particularly the " hanging men and women "
part.

Under the influence of friendship and the demon rum
you will remonstrate with Tom Boyd and point out that he
must have delirium tremens within the month. He will bet
you a hundred he won't have it within two. Now friendship is friendship, but betting is betting, so you scurry
around the town, looking up head waiters and studying
Tom's form, and you ask a doctor. And the thing seems
a certainty. So you take the bet but you always lose. A
great scientist, a great alcoholist, and the staunchest of
friends, one day a native Plutarch will write a Book of
Irish Worthies, and lo! Tom Boyd's name will lead all the
rest, beating Buck Whaley and Tiger Roche with a stone
in hand.

" What's wrong, Kerry? " he asked. " You look like a
ghost."

" Devil a thing, Tom," said I. " You're just tight."

" Not yet. Here, have a drink. You need it."

But before the waiter came, I heard a voice at my elbow,
very silky, very polite, but somehow threatening: " May I
have a word with you, Sir Garrett, in private? "

And there was Ercole. He was spick and span as ever.
His voice was gentle, but his eyes were bloodshot, and his
sallow large face was grim. His face was threatening as
a gray cloud.

"Hullo, Monterosso," said Tom.

"Signore!"

"Sorry, Tom, just a moment," I said as I rose. Tom laid a hand on my arm, and all the superficial Irish gaiety went out of his eyes, and they were clear and hard, as the eyes of our people are when we are alone, or working, when we have no audience to play boy to, to laugh at us — and for us to laugh at.

"Steady, Kerry!" he said, very quietly.

"Eh?"

"Take care, boy. Take care."

"Sure, I'll take care. What are you talking about?" And I rose and followed Ercole.

He led me a little aside from the café tables, and I noticed for the first time that accompanying him but not exactly with him were two compatriots, one a small dapper chap, and the other a thin hungry-looking man, with the eye of a bad dog.

"Sir Garrett," said Ercole, "once I told you I disapproved of your taking up so much of my fiancée's time —"

"'Twas in Dublin you said that," said I, resolved to change the conversation. "Tell me," I asked, "did you like Dublin?"

"It is a peculiar city. Do you remember, Sir Garrett, I said I would not quarrel with you — in Ireland?"

"Devil the word!" I told him. "Sure there was never a hard word between us."

"You are pleased, or perhaps it fits you, to forget." I must say I flushed a little. "The Irish," he went on, "are a great race of fighters — for a price. And in a city where an assassin can be hired as cheaply as a washerwoman —"

Well, that finished it. He might have gone ahead insulting me and I wouldn't have quarrelled with him. But when he started at my country —

"You filthy swine!" I shouted at him, and I let go with

the right. He must have been on his toes, for he spun and lurched through the tables like a wobbling top, hitting this and that, and collapsed with a crash against the window. In an instant Tom Boyd was beside me.

"You thick Mick," he said; "now you've done it for fair."

"Stand aside, Tom," I ordered, "I'm going to tender up this oily organ-grinder if I swing for it." And I stood waiting for Ercole's rush. But Ercole didn't rush. He did something more terrifying. He got up slowly, and he smiled. And Ercole's smile was like the smile you can imagine on the mask of a cat when it has got a mouse in a corner. If Ercole smiled, Tom Boyd roared with laughter.

"By God, Monterosso, but you've picked the wrong one this time. I always said you'd go one too many in the long run. By this time to-morrow," he went on cheerfully, "you'll be dead and damned."

A little of the smile went off Ercole's face, but he bowed.

"That may be," he said, "but Sir Garrett cannot insult an Italian gentleman with impunity. I see two friends of mine —"

"Get out, Kerry," Tom Boyd said to me. "Jump in a car and go off to Nice. Leave all this to me. We'll meet at Monnet's café at eight. Go on. Get out!"

I got out and drove to Nice. I was more than a little worried and quite a bit frightened, if you'll have the truth. But luckily there were a couple of English bookmakers on a holiday in the Casino, and we fought out every race in the last flat season, and the prospects of the coming season over the sticks. It's extraordinary how fast the time passes when you're talking horses. Between that and a few shoes at *chemmy,* it was eight o'clock before I noticed it. I went across to Monnet's café and as I was sitting to wait, Tom and my uncle by marriage Patrick Herne drove up.

"Kerry," said Patrick Herne, "you're an awful lad.

You're hardly ten days in the country before you start raising blazes." But for all his cheerfulness I could see he was worried. Tom paid no attention to us until he found the head waiter who was evidently a lodge brother. "A brandy and soda, Pat? Another, Kerry? Good! Five brandies and sodas, and," he produced a hundred-franc note, "the band will cease playing that muck and start 'The Wearing of the Green'!"

"*Bien, milord!*"

"Well, Kerry," he vouchsafed, "I've bluffed at poker, I've bluffed Arabs, but I never bluffed as hard as I did this afternoon. I've saved your life."

"Is it off?" I asked.

"Off be damned! Listen, I got those fellows to believe you're the best shot in Ireland. I told them you had the record for jacksnipe."

"But I haven't," said I. "Nor anywhere near it. Sure I'm no good of a shot at all."

"Don't I know that! So I got them to agree to swords."

"But I never had one in my hand even. Tom, you've done me, I'm afraid. I'd have had some chance with a pistol."

"Kerry, at the word 'fire!' before you crooked your finger around the trigger, that fellow would have drilled you. And killed you, Kerry! I know all the gamblers and bullies and wrong 'uns on the Riviera and he's the worst," said Tom Boyd. "Now this way, if you keep on your toes, and use your feet as you do in a boxing ring, you'll get off with a wound in the arm that'll be of no more consequence than the pulling of a tooth."

"And I'm to be a mark for this fellow, without a chance of a return? It's not fair! Look," said I, "is a swine like this swine always to go ahead, sinning and winning and killing, always in safety, and nothing to stop him?"

"Devil a thing!" answered Tom Boyd.

"You're forgetting, Tom," said my kinsman, Patrick Herne, in his grave forceful way, "you're forgetting just one element: the ultimate vast justice of God."

VIII

It seemed like a thing you'd dream, and you after reading a picaresque book. Of all the places in the world to fight a duel on, a golf course seemed fantastic. But here was privacy. Here the pine trees made their angle toward the putting green. The rime was on the stiff scant grass, and not an hundred yards off the Mediterranean made its gentle murmur. All the countryside seemed sleeping, and in the East, above Monte Carlo, the sun lumbered up the mountains and looked over them, like some god surly from his sleep.

And I remember thinking to myself, as I looked at the mountains: "Will I ever see that sun again?" And then the red flag of the putting green, twenty-five yards away, caught my eye, and I'd say: "I wonder what the devil's making me hook my putts? Is it my right hand that's too much under the shaft?"

I stood there in my tennis flannels, wrapped up in my big frieze coat, and Carabine, who wouldn't stay behind under any circumstances, talking to me. There were Patrick Herne and Tom Boyd speaking to the tall saturnine Italian, while on the ground between them lay a long case. It was open and the rising sun struck flashes from the blades in it. I call to mind a little chill. There was the French surgeon in morning clothes, looking excessively clean, excessively healthy. A little farther off stood Ercole, in his big-waisted driving coat, a soft hat jauntily on his head, and I'm damned if he wasn't wearing yellow gloves!

"Keep on your toes, Sir Kerry, my dotey boy," Carabine was pleading. "Remember. Go for him as if you were a lightweight attacking a heavyweight, and his sword were his right hand. You may tire him out. Keep him turning all the time — "

Pat Herne came up.

"He won't apologise, Kerry, so — "

I slipped off my coat and left it in Carabine's hands.—

The thing I will remember, probably, longest in my life, is the shock of surprise I got when Ercole stood in front of me, sword in hand. He was in black, — black dress trousers and a black silk shirt. He no longer gave the impression of being a fat ridiculous foreigner. He was like some huge complicated machine, all power and concentration, behind the pretty graceful blade. He dropped into a crouch, and in it he seemed like a toad, some baleful earth-thing. But out of that crouch, I knew, he would come like a shell from a trench mortar. His big jowl had power in it; his black eyes, half closed, glittered. His mouth was firm and cruel. His hair was neatly parted, beautifully smoothed.

My heart sank a little, for I knew that no matter how I stepped in and out, it was no go. He had me. He smiled as he saw me handle the rapier. He smiled again as he saw my tactics. He shuffled toward me as I turned, in a way that was grotesque, but powerful, terrifying, like some vast animal shuffling.

He straightened up, and I felt as if somebody had stuck a big needle in my right side. I knew somehow it was only a scrape, and I jumped back and lowered my blade, saying: "Well, thank God! that's over!"

Then Tom Boyd shouted: "Look out, Kerry. Oh, you bloody swine!"

Before Tom's voice had reached me even, the swift change in Ercole's face had warned me. The flushed insane red of it, the eyes open now, blazing. And as he rushed at me, I had the luck to knock his blade down with mine. I side-stepped and left him with my left fist between the eyes, and bringing my right hand up for the hook, forgetting the blade in it, I felt it stopped somehow, and a great weight on it, and the weight gave way, and the blade broke with a light musical twinkle. And there lay Ercole!

And I said stupidly: "What's happened? Is he foxing?"

It was Carabine who removed the broken sword from my hand and shoved me into my frieze coat. There was a silence all around as the surgeon knelt down. He knelt only for as long a space as it takes to count a boxer out, yet it seemed to me he was there for a century. When he stood up he made no gesture, said no word.

Then I knew that Ercole was dead.

"I suppose I'd better go to the police," I ventured.

"Police be damned!" Tom returned. "They'd only be jealous of you for doing their job. There'll be no trouble, Kerry. I've seen to that already. Still and all," he said, "it's considered tactful, after an incident like this, to disappear for a while. Both the police and the relatives appreciate it." And he looked keenly at Patrick Herne.

"Papers in order," said Pat, "steam up and anchor's aweigh. We'll be out of sight of land in an hour."

"Good-bye, Kerry," said Tom. "Don't worry about this. There'll be many a widow woman and fatherless child will bless you to-night, and many a decent man will sleep easy in his bed."

"So long, Tom!"

We were passing through the pine wood toward the car when I noticed an ominous bulge in Carabine's right-hand pocket. I reached forward with my left hand and yanked out a vicious-looking revolver.

I said: "James Carabine, what was that for?"

"Oh," he answered easily, "I had it in my mind that that one was for doing your Honour in, and if he had —" and Carabine only smiled.

"But Carabine," said I, shocked, "you couldn't have done that evil thing. A duel's an agreement between gentlemen —"

"Your Honour's forgetting that I'm not a gentleman," interrupted James Carabine.

IX

So winter passed in Destiny Bay, and spring came. Daffodils and shy primroses, white of pear tree and pink of apple and the brown rabbit scuttling through the golden whins. The jumping season had gone, and already the great flat classics were passing into turf history, the Lincolnshire and Queen's Prize, the Great Metropolitan Stakes and the City and Suburban. And in steel sky when the sun went down, the evening star flashed out like a mariner's beacon. And the eels found their way back to Grey River from the depths of the occult Sargasso, and in the waters off the coast you would see occasionally the sleek head and shoulders of the gentle seal.

Had it all been but a year ago, it would have been so happy, so peaceful, with my aunt Jenepher and Patrick Herne ever in and out of the house, and Jenico, who had such luck with the salmon that spring, and Ann-Dolly who was so happy, so alive. She was the only one who ventured a word as to the Riviera and the people I had known there.

"I wish I could talk to that damned woman for ten minutes!" she exploded.

"I don't know whom you're talking about, Ann-Dolly. Also I wish you wouldn't be coarse."

"Oh, high and haughty," she sneered; "the MacFarlane of Destiny Bay. You mooning idiot!" And she flounced out.

Of course there was no apology, but she sent her daughter, small Jenepher, across to Destiny Bay for myself and James Carabine to spoil for the afternoon.

And Carabine was always around now. He would come in and make suggestions.

"It's a terrible thing to have an old fellow like myself around, Sir Kerry, but a great longing has come on me to see America, the trotting horses, and the American boxers knocking hell out of each other, begging your Honour's pardon, in the fierce American style. Would your Honour think of going at all, and taking me along with you?"

"'Tis an idea, Carabine."

Or he would come with a new inspiration.

"I've been thinking, your Honour, if you don't mind my saying, that 'tis a great pity your Honour and your uncle Cosimo never met. Would you ever think of the pair of us going out there for a span of time? A long sea voyage is most instructive."

"I'll think that over, Carabine," I promised.

So it came and it went, said I, as perhaps in every man's life it comes and it goes. And every wise man closes his heart and locks it, I thought, and goes about his affairs and responsibilities. My uncle Valentine knew the hard and lonely road after Mary Hines, and so did the Merry Rover; gentle and simple it came to them both, and to many an one. But there was harder for me. The grey house at Destiny Bay urged me dumbly, and all the knolls, the cliffs, the murmuring trees. There had always been a MacFarlane in Destiny Bay. Had the old Irish chroniclers not written: *Nomen mansurum in tota saecula mundi,* a name that shall remain in all the ages of the world! From Par-the-lon, the adventurous Egyptian or perhaps Sidonian rover to myself, the name and stock had descended, if Irish tradition were true, through old fathers who had gone across to fight with Boadicea against Caesar; and who had limped home, licking their wounds, and had hired out to the Red Rose of Lancaster, and had contended at Benburb against the Younger Hugh O'Neill, and had mingled their blood with the Boyne Water. *Nomen mansurum in tota saecula mundi.*

" No," I said, " I won't let it down."

I had gone out to Dunfandle, where O'Grady sleeps, and was looking across the merry spring grass to where his resting place is, and the beginning of his poem in praise of Mary Hines came into my head:

"Sure 'tis only a man without sense would go jumping against the wall that is high
And a ditch by his side that's no more than the heighth of his hand —"

I said: "I'll take that part of your poem as gospel and let the rest go." And I said to myself: "If I marry a girl I'll have to tell her right out that it's for Clan Mac-Farlane I'm doing it. Thank God there are women in Ireland who love Ireland and Irish tradition enough to understand."

And as I stood there thinking, that little part that's like a watchdog signalled to me: "Kerry, there's a car coming up the road, and going to pass." And I answered: "All right, let it pass and be damned to it!"

But the car stopped behind me, and I could hear the driver call: "Woh! Girl, woh!" and then came "Kerry!"

"It isn't the drink," I pondered. "It's just that you've gone crazy like that foreign fellow Hamlet in the play." And as I turned around she had slipped down from the side-car, and stood in front of me.

"Oh, Kerry," she said, "how thin and white you are!"

"'Tis just," said I, stupidly as usual, "the spring that's in it." I kept looking at her. "Why didn't you write me?" I asked.

"I was afraid you mightn't want ever to hear from me, after — after Cannes. Oh, Kerry, aren't you glad to see me?"

"'Tis a poor word the same 'glad.' Where's your father?"

"My father, Kerry," she hesitated. "I think all is well with him."

"He was a good man and a fine gentleman, Allie. God rest him!" And I said: "You've come to see us at last."

"No, Kerry," she said. "Not quite that. You see, when my father went, America seemed empty, and I thought of my mother's country, and of my uncles who are resting here—"

"Did you think of me?" I asked abruptly.

"And of you, Kerry. And so—and so— Oh, Kerry, stop making it hard for me!"

"And so you came home," said I. And taking her right hand in mine, and putting my left arm about her shoulders, I welcomed her home.

NINE

TALE TOLD IN DESTINY BAY

NINE

Tale Told in Destiny Bay

Now when the High Hat Magician saw himself settled for the night in the turf cutter's cabin, a wave of kindliness came over him, and he decided he'd show the turf cutter some of the marvels of his art. So he chucks a handful of powder on the fire, and a great wave of blue smoke fills the little house. And in the heart of the blue cloud, you could see as it were Dublin city: coaches rolling up to the Houses of Parliament; merchants on Cork Hill counting spade guineas taken in the easiness of trade; bucks ruffling it down Bachelors' Walk; three-card-trick men at every corner; Dean Swift with his two wives; ladies of quality with Negro pages; King Billy on a white horse.

"What place might that be?" asks the turf cutter.

"'Tis Dublin," says the High Hat Magician, "the grandest capital on any sod."

"Now is that a true picture of Dublin?" says the turf cutter.

"It is," says the High Hat Magician. "'Tis a picture made up out of old memories and natural genius."

The turf cutter gives a kick to his wife, drowsy on the pile of heather. "Up, woman, and put the ass in the cart, for we're off to Dublin!"

"Are we off now, strong darling?"

"This very minute," says the turf cutter.

"For God's sake," says the High Hat Magician, "what

about the supper you promised me? My two grilled trout, my soda bread with butter, my India tea, and the slug of whiskey to open the throttle, and the slug of whiskey to close it."

"Oh," says the turf cutter, "use your natural genius."

COOLMAIN CASTLE, 1927